Acclaim for Wendy Wasserstein's

Elements of Style

"A bright social comedy. . . . Sleek, entertaining."
— *The New York Times Book Review*

"With her usual keen ear, Wasserstein pins [her characters] in the pages like gilded butterflies, brilliantly contrasting a society committed to status and surface glitter with the fragility and impermanence of life. . . . [A] wry, clear-sighted book—a final gift this generous, funny woman has left us." — *The Plain Dealer*

"Wasserstein peppers her dishy humor with piquant and poignant insights. . . . You would expect no less from such a sharp and generous spirit." — *USA Today*

"Wasserstein's posthumous debut novel showcases all her comic gifts, and unforgettable *Elements of Style*." — *Vanity Fair*

"A tart satire. . . . Once again, Wasserstein, who will always be remembered as a woman's woman and a New Yorker's New Yorker, proves that humor is the best refuge from life's sorrows." — *Vogue*

"At the heart of Wasserstein's social critique lies the same intriguing paradox Henry James explored: those with old money, sophistication, and polish are attracted to the raw energy (the vulgarity even) of society's nakedly aspiring climbers."   —*The Atlantic Monthly*

"Wasserstein's book has a wit and a heart."
                                                    —*Rocky Mountain News*

"Quintessential Wendy."   —*Entertainment Weekly*

WENDY WASSERSTEIN

Elements of Style

Wendy Wasserstein is the author of the plays *Uncommon Women and Others*, *Isn't It Romantic*, *The Sisters Rosensweig*, *An American Daughter*, and *The Heidi Chronicles*, for which she received a Tony Award and the Pulitzer Prize, and of the books *Bachelor Girls* and *Shiksa Goddess*. She was admired both for the warmth and the satirical cool of her writing; each of her plays and books captures an essence of the time, makes us laugh, and leaves us wiser. Wendy Wasserstein was born in 1950 in Brooklyn and died at the age of fifty-five. Her daughter, Lucy Jane, lives in New York.

Elements of Style

A NOVEL

WENDY WASSERSTEIN

VINTAGE BOOKS

A Division of Random House, Inc.

New York

FIRST VINTAGE BOOKS EDITION, MAY 2007

Copyright © 2006 by The Estate of Wendy Wasserstein

All rights reserved. Published in the United States by Vintage Books, a division
of Random House, Inc., New York, and in Canada by Random House of Canada
Limited, Toronto. Originally published in hardcover in the United States by
Alfred A. Knopf, a division of Random House, Inc., New York, in 2006.

Vintage and colophon are registered trademarks of Random House, Inc.

The Library of Congress has cataloged the Knopf edition as follows:
Wasserstein, Wendy.
Elements of style: a novel / Wendy Wasserstein—1st ed.
p. cm.
1. Upper East Side (New York, N.Y.)—Fiction. 2. Women pediatricians—Fiction.
3. Female friendship—Fiction. I. Title.
PS3573.A798E44 2006
813'.54—dc22
2005044962

Vintage ISBN: 978-1-4000-7687-1

Book design by Robert C. Olsson

www.vintagebooks.com

Printed in the United States of America
10 9 8 7 6 5 4 3 2 1

For Gerald Gutierrez
—*more than a director*

Acknowledgments

I first mentioned the idea for this novel to my agent, Lynn Nesbit, over drinks after I delivered a lecture about *Sloth* at the New York Public Library. I remain grateful to her for preventing me from adhering to my own wisdom. Her insights have been incisive, and her knowledge of New York social mores is encyclopedic.

Throughout this process, my editor, Victoria Wilson, has been a source of wisdom, unsentimental guidance, and real friendship. Her support has been constant and invaluable.

Finally, even the daunting task of a playwright finishing a novel is worth it when at the end of the road there are drinks and a Bruce Willis movie with Sonny Mehta.

Jeremy Strong is a young talented actor. Michael Barakiva is a young talented director. They are both voracious readers of novels, and I am grateful to them for being able to read my handwriting and type this one.

My father, Morris Wasserstein, arrived at Ellis Island at age seven in 1928. He lived the next seventy-five years of his life in New York City. I am grateful for his belief in the promise of New York and its people.

I am eternally grateful to my five-year-old daughter, Lucy Jane, for her love, foresight, and courage in taking me, as a mother, to the offices of the best pediatricians in New York.

Elements of Style

CHAPTER ONE

Frankie

Frankie Weissman pushed open the door to her new offices with two double-sized Penny Whistle Toys shopping bags. After spending the morning on her hospital rounds, she had gone into the store just to look. Soon she fell under the spell of a motorized "furr real" pink poodle and Smart Cindy, a foot-tall scholarly doll equipped with 16,000 megabytes of intelligence. Frankie was certain that within an hour she would be hearing her patients' parents warning them, "Be careful. You don't know where Smart Cindy's been," or "Don't play with the poodle. You could get anthrax." But at least Frankie knew she was making a fresh start.

"Dr. Weissman, Dr. Steele is on line one for you." Rosita the receptionist looked up from the desk as Frankie walked into the waiting room.

Frankie's jaw tightened. The part of her that was both a Princeton College and Harvard Medical School graduate secretly believed that people who insisted on calling themselves "doctor" generally had credentials like "director, International Hair Club for Men."

"Tell him I'll call him back." Frankie lowered her head. She had learned over the years never to make eye contact when walking into a waiting room.

As she furtively glanced around for obvious catastrophes, she was simultaneously pleased and a little anxious that the office was packed. After almost fifteen years of experience, Frankie viewed general pediatrics as twenty percent emergency and the rest an oddly seasonal practice—early September school checkups, Presidents' Day pneumonia, spring break sprains, and Fourth of July poison ivy. But this September the World Trade Center disaster had altered all familiar routine. Only now, in October, were the prominent city mothers putting their tumbling tots' medical permission slips in order.

Frankie had known most of her patients since infancy. She was happy to spot six-year-old Brooke Santorini coloring on the floor in her three-hundred-dollar Bonpoint cashmere painter's overalls and matching sweater. Her mother, Clarice, in autumn white size 4 jeans and matching twin set, was chatting avidly about the new Spence Lower School building with her decorator, Pippa Rose. Mrs. Rose was bobbing her head up and down in concerned agreement worthy of a Middle East peace treaty negotiator. Her own son, Alex, who was notorious at age six for being rejected by every ongoing school in Manhattan, Riverdale, and Brooklyn, was coughing directly into the watercooler. Slumped against a wall was Jessica Rodman, only ten but already filling out a Dolce & Gabbana red leather halter. Jessica was wailing something to herself about being "jilted one more time." Frankie wasn't sure if it was a pop song or Jessica's real-life experience.

On the periphery of the room sat the caregivers, the current evolved term for nanny. Only a few of the caregivers were from the traditional nanny breeding grounds of Great Britain and Ireland. The rest were a diverse group of East Indian, Dominican, and Filipino. Frankie had deduced that the newer the money the older the nanny source. Thus Mrs. Adrienne Strong-Rodman, Jessica's mother, had a nanny who claimed to have weaned Prince William and Prince Harry, heirs to the throne of England.

"Dr. Weissman! Dr. Weissman!" A large African-American woman exploded into the room with a small child and a baby. "Dr. Weissman, I see you over there! This is an emergency!"

Frankie turned around as the woman charged toward her.

"I need to leave my kids here with you. I've got to get my mother to the hospital in Brooklyn and I have nobody else to stay with them."

"Mrs. Caesar, what happened to the day care center I arranged for you?" Frankie asked. All the other mothers and caregivers stopped their conversations to listen.

"They don't want to go there. They're still scared from the Trade Center."

"I told you she won't take us." The older child, who was around eight, held her baby brother Clayton in her arms.

Frankie opened her shopping bags and pulled out the pink poodle. "Venette, I have some great new toys." She pulled out the poodle and the dog began to bark to the tune of "La Marseillaise." The girl gave Frankie the baby and took the poodle's leash.

"Thank you, Dr. Weissman." Mrs. Caesar raced out the door.

As Frankie passed the baby to a nurse she was blocked by Mrs. Adrienne Strong-Rodman, whose fringed Balenciaga leather jacket was now vibrating. Frankie's receptionist had once made the mistake of simply calling her Mrs. Rodman and was immediately rebuked. "Please make a point of using all three of my names and both of my degrees, if possible, when referring to me." Adrienne Strong-Rodman, J.D., Ph.D., claimed to be both a lawyer and a child psychologist. Somehow after a brief stint as a Hollywood publicist she reemerged as a high-powered entertainment lawyer with an expertise in children's advocacy rights. Her career profile changed again once she landed the multibillionaire Paul Rodman.

No longer able to contain her fury, Adrienne Strong-Rodman turned to Frankie. "Listen. No one did more to raise money for social welfare in this town last year than I did. Just ask Lunch for Children,

Women for Women, or Bottomless Closet. I work my ass off for diversity! But we've been waiting here for over twenty minutes and that's unacceptable."

Frankie looked down at Mrs. Rodman's $1,950 rust crocodile Manolo Blahnik mules. She wondered if she had been equally irritated waiting for them. Then Frankie corrected herself. Adrienne Strong-Rodman would have the Manolos delivered to her home for perusal. That way she could get upstairs to her yoga hut, which she had just installed on the roof of her twin town houses, without wasting valuable time. In between working her ass off, Adrienne was in deep pursuit of inner stillness and calm.

"Just sign this." Adrienne pulled a piece of paper and a pen from her white ostrich Hermès Birkin bag and put it in front of Frankie. "Jessica needs a note for skydiving class."

"But Jessica's only ten." Frankie signed her name.

"Her father wants her to be fearless. And these days you need to be prepared. Have a nice day."

She grabbed Jessica, the royal nanny, turned on her crocodile slide, and walked out.

Pippa Rose was already on her cell phone with the fast-breaking story. "Adrienne Strong-Rodman just lost it in Dr. Francesca Weissman's office. I guess all that yoga isn't working. Personally, I don't think she was entirely out of line. I love Frankie Weissman, but she should never have moved her practice."

Frankie knew the move had been a gamble. She had made her reputation at Park Avenue Pediatrics, a well-heeled practice with a chic neighborhood clientele. But when she turned forty, Frankie began teaching preventive medicine at a series of day care centers and elementary schools in East Harlem. Moving her own practice to 102nd Street and Fifth Avenue was her attempt to accommodate both ends of her Upper East Side patient spectrum.

But the truth was Frankie had a long history of ambivalence

toward the entire privileged New York landscape. She had moved to the Upper East Side from Queens when she was twelve. Frankie's father, Abraham, was a manufacturer of women's hosiery who sent her to the Spence School simply because it was up the block. Abraham had few social pretensions, and he passed that trait on to his daughter. Frankie could not have found an office address more reflective of her personality than 102nd Street and Fifth Avenue. She knew that if she had a world, the Fifth Avenue one was it, but she was most comfortable on its fringes.

"Mrs. Santorini, I'll be with you and Brooke in a minute." Frankie smiled at them and walked back into her office.

As soon as she sat down the phone rang. "Dr. Weissman, Mrs. Schultz is on the phone. She says it's an emergency."

She picked up the phone. "Hello, Frankie Weissman here."

Mrs. Schultz's voice was quavering. "Dr. Weissman, Taylor has swollen glands and she's sweating. I think there's a rash on her hand, and Zitomer pharmacy has run out of Cipro!"

"She doesn't necessarily need Cipro," Frankie said calmly. "It sounds like it could be all sorts of things."

"Should I rush her to an emergency room?"

"I would bring her here first. Tell Rosita to make an appointment for today."

Ever since the first anthrax case was reported in New York Frankie got at least two hundred calls a day for Cipro. Mothers like Mrs. Schultz were constantly on the brink of biological warfare.

"Brooke, this way please. You're in room three." Irina, the Russian nurse, escorted Brooke and her mother into the examining room. When Frankie walked in to join them Brooke had picked up the book *Go Away, Big Green Monster!* which was lying on the windowsill.

"We have this book at my school. Dr. Weissman, I can make all the green monsters go away and never come back again."

"Good girl! I'm glad to hear that!" Frankie imagined a roomful of kindergarten girls defending themselves against big green monsters. She also wondered if any of their parents were still missing among the Trade Center rubble.

Frankie asked Brooke to breathe deeply and put her stethoscope on the child's toe. "Is this your heart, Brooke?"

The girl giggled. "No!"

Frankie put her stethoscope on Brooke's elbow. "Is this your heart?"

The child began shaking her head no and laughing. "You're silly, Dr. Weissman!" Finally, Frankie put the stethoscope on her chest.

"Stop, Dr. Weissman! Stop! This is my heart!"

"Thank you, Brooke. Thank you. I would have never guessed."

Brooke grinned triumphantly as Frankie continued the examination.

Frankie was only running an hour late when Brooke left and by seven o'clock she had caught up with herself.

"Have you seen this, Dr. Weissman?" Rosita came into her office waving the latest issue of *Manhattan* magazine, the established doyenne of urban magazines.

"Is someone we know in it?" Frankie took a wry pleasure in the social escapades of her patients' mothers.

"It's not about a patient. It's about you. This is their postponed back-to-school issue and they named you the best pediatrician in Manhattan. Here, look!" She pushed the magazine in front of Frankie's face.

"God, that's an awful picture!" Frankie recoiled.

"I don't think you look so bad." Rosita peeked her head over Frankie's shoulder. "You look like someone people could count on."

"As my stepmother Helen would say, 'Looking like someone you can count on never found anyone a husband.' And furthermore they

didn't say I was 'the best.' Just 'the best on the Upper East Side.'"
Frankie put the magazine down. "Do we have any tuna fish?"

"Aren't you going home for dinner?" Rosita asked.

"No, I think I'll catch up on some things here." It was an answer
Frankie used at least twice a week to savor the calm of being alone in
her office.

The staff kitchen was a small closet to the left of exam room five.
There was only enough space for a counter, a microwave, and an
avocado plant that managed to grow without sunlight or water.
Gulping a diet iced tea, Frankie reread her mention in *Manhattan*
magazine. She was angry at herself for being a little too pleased about
it. But she was even angrier at herself for still secretly coveting Mrs.
Rodman's Hermès Birkin bag.

Her stepmother referred to her patients who lugged the $8,000
Hermès tote as "Birkin babes." One year for Christmas, Helen even
gave her a thirty-dollar plastic Birkin imitation with a note that said,
"God willing, one day your husband will give you the real one."

There was something almost detoxifying for Frankie about leafing
through *Manhattan* magazine that night. It was the first issue since
September 11 in which the magazine returned to business as usual
with "Quality Goods" shopping hints and "Buzz-Worthy" local
celebrity gossip. But she was caught off guard when she turned the
page and saw a picture of a woman posing as a 1930s movie star, in a
retro Balmain gown, feeding a seal in the Central Park Zoo. When
Frankie looked up to read the headline, "The Fashionable Mrs. Acton,"
she immediately recognized Samantha Acton from her seventh-grade
class at Spence. As children they hardly knew each other. Even at that
age, Samantha was the girl everyone else wanted to be. Samantha was
beautiful then and she was obviously beautiful now. Frankie opened
another diet iced tea and began to read.

"Samantha Acton, in the style-blazing tradition of Mrs. Astor or
Babe Paley, defines the social order. Friends say that her secret is 'she

manages to make perfection effortless.' Unlike the current flock of sunflower-seed socialites, Samantha has a zany lust for life. In a time when things seem haphazard, Samantha, great-granddaughter of New York legends August Van Rensselaer and Virginia Carnegie, is a true thoroughbred. And on top of that, she knows everything there is to know about modern art, music, and dance. She also single-handedly spearheaded the restoration of the seal fountain in the zoo in Central Park. After 9/11, Samantha made certain that the daily public seal feeding was back on schedule for the children of the city."

Frankie wondered what the seals thought of Samantha's ballgown. She continued to read.

"Her entertaining is like her guest list—her mix of friends from young downtown artists to social heavyweights and corporate players is irresistible. She is credited by everyone with having the foresight to abandon vertically stacked sashimi and reintroduce roast beef and Yorkshire pudding. Finally, the signature of a truly A-list New York party is having Samantha Acton singing barefoot before the last guest departs."

" 'She has a very sexy easygoing style,' says society pal art dealer Jil Taillou. 'But the truth is every move, every smile, every table setting is calculated with the precision of a four-star general. Her classic, carefree appearance requires remarkable dedication and discipline. Plus, it doesn't hurt that she's unbelievably smart.' "

Frankie put down her diet iced tea and leaned back in her chair. She liked the idea of a four-star general in charge of table settings. She imagined Norman Schwarzkopf organizing a frontal attack with roast beef carts. Samantha's joie de vivre seemed so untimely now, so much even of the previous century, that Frankie found it anachronistically comforting.

· CHAPTER TWO ·

Judy

Judy Tremont came to the Frédéric Fekkai Salon twice a week for maintenance. She accepted this schedule as part of her social contract. But between her grooming, running and redecorating her two homes, her four children, and her husband, Albert, Judy was stretched to the max. Even with a personal assistant, a calligrapher, a dog walker, two housekeepers, a driver, and a cook, she still honestly felt she couldn't get everything done. Or, more important, she couldn't get anything done *right*.

In a concerted effort to multitask, Judy usually had a mani-pedi while her individual hair strands were highlighting, or just a manicure during a blow-dry. Judy maintained her thick black hair in a chic geometric blunt cut and prided herself on a strand never being out of place. Although Judy also knew most fashionable women maintained shorter nails, she was consistent in sticking with a square-shaped longer look with deep red Chanel or Dior polish. This way her hands always appeared long and lean just like her figure. Unfortunately today her favorite Thai manicurist, Kim, was off duty, and she certainly wasn't going to take a chance on one of the Russians. Making the best of a bad situation, she ordered in a Cobb salad: hold the bacon, hold the dairy, dressing on the side.

Having already devoured *Harper's Bazaar, Town & Country,* and *W* at the facialist's, Judy picked up *Manhattan* magazine from the nearby salon stash. As soon as she noticed "The Fashionable Mrs. Acton" in the table of contents she reached into her purse for an Ativan antianxiety tablet to place beneath her tongue. Her internist had first prescribed the drugs the week after 9/11 just to take the edge off. But they seemed to come in handy for other unexpectedly stressful occasions like this one. It wasn't that Judy didn't like Samantha Acton. Samantha was, in fact, her idol. But she was also her competition. And what angered Judy most was that she didn't even really know Samantha. They weren't in the same league.

Judy allowed the tablet to dissolve, felt her pulse slow, and began reading.

"Samantha Acton, in the style-blazing tradition of Mrs. Astor or Babe Paley, defines the social order." Judy skimmed ahead. Her eye landed on "If there's still a Mrs. Astor's 400, then Samantha Acton is number one."

Judy was truly agitated. Unlike other aspirational Upper East Siders she could name, Judy Tremont didn't need to define the social order. But she certainly deserved an honorable mention. No one cared more about New York society than Judy. It had become, in a real way, her life's work.

Judy's mother had worked in a jewelry and novelty shop in Modesto and her father was a cop. They lived in a white two-bedroom ranch home in a postwar development. Judy's mother subscribed to *Good Housekeeping, Ladies' Home Journal,* and, for her business, *Town & Country.* By age eight Judy had zeroed in on *Town & Country* and neglected the others. More than the ballgowns and the jewels, Judy coveted the lives of the women photographed at charity balls or opening-night galas. In Judy's eyes these magical women glided into rooms and never took public transportation. Their skin glowed from facials and never from the perspiration of a ridiculous summer job.

By senior year of high school Judy knew the names of every woman at the Metropolitan Museum Costume Institute Benefit Gala. By the time she graduated Fresno City College, she had memorized the history of New York's four hundred richest families.

When Judy first came to New York, she began a successful career as an editor at *Mademoiselle*. But she had no intention of maintaining a five-figure editorial career. Her destiny was in the lifestyle she had long ago imagined for herself. As soon as the new accessories editor mentioned in passing that she was Albert Tremont's best friend from Deerfield, Judy became her best friend too. Within a month, all three were having dinner together, and exactly a year later Judy was debating between bridesmaid dresses at Bergdorf Goodman and Vera Wang.

"Judy, I can take you now." William, the hair colorist, came to retrieve her.

As Judy got up she saw one of the Piel sisters walk into the salon. Although Judy was forty-one and this Piel sister was twenty-six, Judy took some pride that their bodies were in surprisingly similar shape, both probably around five foot eight and a size 4. This affirmation that her daily Pilates class was clearly the right way to go, plus the aftereffects of the Ativan, put Judy in a far more tolerant mood.

She decided she'd get Frédéric to cut her hair and keep her mind off Samantha Acton and anything else remotely distressing. Ever since 9/11 Judy was making a real effort to channel positive energy. Today she was even picking her daughter Charlotte up from her flu shot at Dr. Weissman's. It would be easier for the nanny to bring her home but Judy was, honest to God, trying.

Judy's car was waiting at the Fifty-seventh Street entrance. If it had been up to her, Judy would have preferred a Mercedes sedan, but her husband, Albert, insisted that with the kids it made much more sense to have the Mercedes G500 SUV. Albert didn't seem to care that when Judy got out of that car, onlookers were disappointed she wasn't the rapper Jay-Z.

"Let me help you, Mrs. Tremont." Bill, her driver, took her alligator Birkin and almost lifted her onto the two-foot step into the car.

"I'm fine, Bill." She smiled at him. Bill never quite got that because Judy spent sixty minutes on a StairMaster four times a week at level ten that the incline into the Mercedes SUV was a piece of cake. "I'm going to 102nd Street and Fifth Avenue. We're picking up Charlotte at the doctor's office."

From Judy's point of view, shortly after 9/11 everyone and their mother felt a need to come and visit New York. But the worst traffic days were the ones when the president decided to come to town. As she sat stalled on Park Avenue and Eighty-sixth Street, Judy's positive energy began collapsing. She didn't know who she resented more— the president for showing up, the terrorists for executing their hideous plan, or Dr. Francesca Weissman for moving her goddamn office.

"Could you take Madison, please!" Judy lowered the glass divider. "Bill, Madison Avenue please!" She was a little more irritable than she meant to be, and she decided to finally blame it all on Frankie Weissman. Adrienne Strong-Rodman had warned Judy about the waiting room with the welfare mothers and the germ-ridden toys, and Judy was not about to sacrifice her daughter's health for some liberal doctor's political agenda.

"Sorry, Mrs. Tremont. I'm doing the best I can." Bill smiled into the mirror.

"Bill, it's not your fault," Judy sighed. She often wished the rest of the world could be as courtly as Bill.

Right then Judy resolved that after this appointment she'd ask Arnie Berkowitz for the name of a new pediatrician. Arnie had a joint degree in pediatrics and psychiatry with a specialty in adolescent medicine. He was everyone's answer to medical anxiety, and he did wonders with Ritalin. Surely he could recommend someone who was a little more convenient and a little less strange.

When Judy's car finally pulled up to the building on 102nd and Fifth she was thirty minutes late.

"Bill, I'll be right out." Judy smiled at him. She had no idea how people could get anywhere without a car. Seeing several off-duty yellow cabs pass by, Judy once again felt centered. She'd go into the office, pick up her daughter and the nanny, and never come back to this hellhole again.

"Your daughter will be right out." Rosita looked up at Judy. "She's inside getting her flu shot. You can join her back there if you like."

A small Puerto Rican child began coughing on a toy car while a grungy pink poodle barked at Judy's shoes.

"I'll just wait here." Judy had no desire to encounter the germs that must be alighting in the examining room. She picked up a copy of *Manhattan* magazine from the side table. Deliberately she flipped past the 1930s glamour photo of Samantha and stopped at the bright headline of a new page. "The Best Pediatricians in New York."

Some days things just work out, Judy thought to herself. She'd pick out a new doctor on Park Avenue from this list and check them out with Arnie. Positive energy really paid off.

Judy ran her finger down to the Upper East Side entry and emboldened in black letters with four stars was Dr. Francesca Weissman—listed as "an Upper East Side must. The choice of today's A-list."

Judy was miserable again. If Francesca Weissman was really the best, Judy was stuck with her.

CHAPTER THREE

Albert

With his two older sons off at Deerfield, Albert Tremont read to his nine-year-old twin daughters every night. Even if Judy had booked him for drinks and into another dinner, Albert was unwavering in his routine and his commitment.

"But Daddy, I'm not interested in *Great Expectations*," Charlotte whined to him. Her sister Jane was hanging on every word. Jane had started the lower-school poetry journal and had gotten a verse poem published in *The New Yorker* in second grade. Charlotte would have preferred to e-mail her friends about the Collegiate boy who was the first to tongue-kiss Taylor Schultz, the fastest girl in sixth grade.

"Charlotte, when you grow up you'll remember that I read to you every night. Something my father never did at all."

Albert tried to do everything his father never did. But despite all of Albert's rigor, his father still informed every nuance of his life. Ten years ago, at the time of his father's death, Albert openly predicted that the great man's specter would finally diminish. Now Albert just never mentioned to his wife or his therapist that he continued to see his father as both his social calling card and the source of his underlying insecurity.

William Blanchard Tremont had been the founding partner of

W. B. Tremont, the venerable Wall Street investment banking boutique. Although William Tremont was a Boston Brahmin, he was quick to recognize the energy of C. W. Cahn, the German Jewish financier, and initiated a formidable partnership. Tremont Cahn became an international investment bank on a par with Lazard Frères and Crédit Suisse. Before he died, William Tremont sold the company to the Singapore Bank and walked off with a major fortune and a Wall Street legacy. He also left one son, Albert.

Albert was a graduate of Deerfield Academy, Amherst College, and Stanford Law School. Throughout his academic career he excelled in the classics, and by the time he graduated Amherst he was able to read ancient Greek, Latin, Aramaic, and Old Norse. He also mastered junior varsity croquet. Not that Albert really cared about hitting wooden balls with a mallet, but he liked the link to Lewis Carroll.

For someone who had spent so much time struggling to find his own niche, Albert had very little fire under him. His sophomore year at Amherst he sold drugs in the surrounding Connecticut River Valley, but it was a limited period of entrepreneurship. Albert took PCP, rhinoceros tranquilizers, on the beach in St. Barths over a Christmas vacation and offered them to a member of the French Foreign Legion. He ended up in a Gustavia jail until his father arrived to post bail. From that time on Albert did what he was told—first by his father, then by his wife.

When Albert got out of law school he worked as an associate at Sullivan & Cromwell for five years. Although he was on a partner track, Albert saw no reason for the law to overwhelm his life and left to join the family banking business. Even during his stint at Tremont Cahn, Albert's idea of banking was closer to a nineteenth-century gentleman's model than to the aggressive dealmakers of the late twentieth century. He preferred to go home to dinner at 6 p.m. and then on to the Philharmonic. Albert was relieved when his father sold the bank, and he happily retired at age thirty-five.

Although Albert called himself a "private investor," he mostly hired people to do that for him. He had an office on East Fifty-eighth Street where he went sporadically to manage the family money. "Managing" was, in Albert's linguistic mind, a euphemism for exchanging pleasantries with assorted accountants, bankers, and notaries. Happily, Albert often said, it all seemed to run on its own.

Walking down the steps of his Park Avenue triplex to join Judy and the guests in the library, Albert caught a glimpse of himself in the mirror. He still had a full head of thick black hair and the shining green eyes of his Irish mother. Albert had always been a very good looking man, and unlike the sartorial fastidiousness of his father, it all came very naturally to him. He knew the outside world was ominously unstable, but he loved the predictable routine of his own life. He enjoyed his biweekly trips to his office and serving on the boards of the American Academy in Rome, the New York Society Library, and his daughters' all-girls school. The fact that one daughter was a nine-year-old intellectual and the other on probation for purchasing a Prada bag on eBay and charging it to a Spence fourth-grade teacher was something Albert tried not to think about. Anyway, it couldn't compare with Jessica Rodman e-mailing a nude photo of herself to the entire eighth-grade class of St. Bernard's School for boys.

Besides, Albert took a secret delight in his difficult daughter's acquisitiveness. Charlotte wanted Prada and Juicy Couture with a passion that he had for very little, except maybe single malt scotch. The girls with private planes in Charlotte's class had fathers whose materialistic ambitions Albert admired. At least they weren't what he most loathed in himself, "Old-Boy Ineffectual."

"Did Charlotte listen?" Judy asked Albert as he walked into the chocolate-colored library. For the past four years, Judy had been devoted to dark walls and multiple brocade window treatments. If you asked her period, she'd simply say, "Empire."

"She said she wasn't listening but I think she did." Albert turned to their two guests. "Mr. and Mrs. Rose, I presume. How do you do?" Albert often resorted to false formality as a family joke. He then embraced Pippa and shook her husband Joe's hand. All he really knew was she was the new decorator, and this was the first time they had come to dinner.

"Judy was telling us you read Dickens every night."

"Not only Dickens." He smiled. "I read them Cicero, Herodotus, Sappho, and the Kama Sutra."

Judy chirped. "Oh Albert, stop it!"

"Sir, what are we drinking tonight?" Albert gave Joe a gentle pat on the back.

"I had Henry make up some cosmopolitans." Judy quickly answered. Even though she never touched anything but a sip of champagne, she had cocktail management completely under her belt.

"I was just telling Judy what an extraordinary collection of books you have here." Pippa smiled at Albert.

"Albert won't tell you this but he won a prize for best personal library when he was an undergraduate at Amherst." Judy offered all the guests tiny thimbles of smoked salmon wrapped with an Earl Grey tea leaf.

"How marvelous!" Pippa nodded.

"Is that a Braque?" Joe asked, examining the one painting that wasn't clearly a small Degas or Pissarro.

"Joe, you are kidding!" Pippa bit her cheeks. "Does that look like a Braque to you?"

"That's all right, Joe." Judy made a mental note never to sit him next to anyone important at a dinner party. "It's a Brice Marden. Albert and I have begun to seriously collect contemporary art. I mean, I love all our Impressionists, but really getting to know the artist is so exciting. That's one of the reasons I'm having Pippa redecorate. I want a fresh start with the art."

"Honey, there's nothing wrong with Braque." Albert helped himself to another salmon thimble.

"Albert refuses to acknowledge any art past 1918. But I just adore it."

Albert felt another tinge of contentment. He believed if not for Judy, he could retreat into his own isolated world of Old Norse and Latin poetry. But Judy was an unending source of life-affirming energy. She was also devoid of cynicism. It was, however, far more soothing for Albert to placate Judy than engage her. He preferred, for instance, not to tangle with her decorating whims or dinner party scenarios. But recently she had begun demanding that Albert make a substantial donation to the Museum of Modern Art. Although most spouses did not base their philanthropy on their wives' current interests and social aspirations, Albert decided to go along with it. He would draw the line, however, at video installations in the living room. That would be worth fighting for, even with Judy.

"This is scrummy! I could eat it every night!" Pippa took a bite of her beef medallion.

"I know. Albert and I got so tired of going to dinner, and there's nothing to eat!" Judy pushed her medallion around her plate. The chef was always told in advance to give Judy around a third of everyone else's portion.

"I think real food is coming back. We need comfort right now, and when you're anxious it's no time for sprouts!" Pippa smiled at Albert.

"Absolutely. I keep telling Judy we should ask Henry to prepare mac and cheese and chicken à la king." Albert twinkled and sipped his Lafite Rothschild '89.

"Oh Albert, stop it!" Judy swatted his arm.

"You know Albert's not so way off. We were at Samantha Acton's house the other night, and she really did serve chicken à la king and then snowball sundaes. I was in heaven!"

"You know Samantha Acton?" Judy almost choked. She had more important things to do now than pretend to be interested in her food.

"Because of Jennifer, my oldest daughter, I'm very involved in the School of American Ballet, and Samantha is too. She went there as a child, and I'm hoping she'll help me get my youngest into Spence. After my disaster with Alex and the ongoing schools, I'm not taking any chances." Pippa spoke quickly, "Judy, I just assumed you knew her."

Judy covered for herself. "Well I do, of course. Did you see the piece in *Manhattan* magazine? So flattering! And I had another friend in that issue too, Francesca Weissman. Best Pediatrician."

"She's ours. We love her." Pippa smiled.

"Adrienne Strong-Rodman says she's more interested in the welfare kids than ours."

"Honey!" Albert preferred that Judy stay off the topic of politics or social equality.

"We swear by Frankie Weissman," Joe piped in. "When our daughter Jennifer couldn't dance because of strange pains in her leg, Dr. Weissman was the only one who really diagnosed it."

Pippa shook her head. "She's definitely worth the wait, the schlep uptown, and I happen to approve of her politics. I think she's a friend of Samantha's too, or at least when I mentioned her to Samantha she knew her."

Judy was stumped. "But Samantha doesn't even have children."

"They were at Spence together."

"Of course"—she was quick to cover—"I knew that."

Judy was excited. Finally, she saw a way to get Samantha to her table. Albert would make a respectable donation to the ballet school in honor of Pippa Rose plus put in a good word for her at Spence. Pippa Rose would be forever grateful, and reciprocate by inviting them to an A-list dinner including Samantha Acton. Judy would make contact with her and in no time Samantha would be singing barefoot in the Tremonts' living room after dinner.

Albert had a habit of saying good night to Judy after the guests had gone and coming downstairs to read. It was the time of day Albert most looked forward to because the stillness made it finally possible to concentrate. Immediately after the World Trade Center disaster Judy decided they should begin building a house in Aspen as a security alternative. But Albert had never felt more entrenched. New York was their home. It was the city where his father had made his fortune. And he, more than ever, wanted it to be the city where his children would be raised. In fact, after 9/11 Albert decided he wouldn't send his daughters to Deerfield like his sons. The challenge would be not to run away but to persevere. Life presented Albert with very few external obstacles, so he was determined to look this one in the face.

Albert poured himself a glass of port before going to bed. Recently he had begun reading the teachings of the Dalai Lama, which he had first encountered in his postdrug phase at Amherst. He pushed the Dalai Lama aside and wrote a $20,000 check in order to buy a $10,000 table at the New York City Ballet *Nutcracker* plus make another $10,000 donation. Judy told him to be sure to enclose a note that he was doing it to honor his new friend Mrs. Joseph Rose and her talented daughter. Judy had taught Albert that in this way his money could work in his favor. Looking back, he wished he had known this as a child. It could have saved him a great deal of pain and psychoanalysis.

CHAPTER FOUR

Abraham

Abraham Weissman had a system. Five years ago he began writing down his daughter Frankie's name in his vest pocket diary every time he'd see her. He wrote down all the names he was most frightened of forgetting.

Frankie took her father to a museum—The Frick, the Whitney, the Metropolitan—almost weekly. She looked forward to being alone with him but her stepmother for the past twenty years, Helen, wouldn't let him out of her sight. Abraham Weissman was eighty-two years old and Helen Ginsburg was still convinced that a Birkin babe in leather pants with plenty of Botox would snatch him away.

"Is that Gypsy Rose Lee?" Abraham asked Frankie as they walked past a statue of Venus in the Frick garden.

"No, Dad." Frankie took her father's arm. "But it could be. Want to see the girl with the bow? C'mon, you like that one. She's very intelligent."

When Frankie was a child it took a while for her to understand that when her father said a girl was "intelligent" it did not mean she scored double 800s on her SATs. This first dawned on her when they were in the Versailles Room at Miami's Fontainebleau Hotel and her father pronounced that the Lido showgirls who opened for the Supremes were "Einsteins."

Frankie began walking slowly with her father toward the *Diana* by Houdon. Even in his seventies her father had been a spry dancer. Now he walked carefully as if to be certain he was still doing it correctly.

"You go ahead. I'll just rest." Abraham stopped at a bench.

"Don't let him sit down." Helen rushed over from Bellini's *St. Francis of Assisi,* her bouffant red hair bouncing as she moved. She still had a slight trace of an accent from her childhood in Argentina over half a century ago. "He sits and he sits and he sits. That's all he does all day! He'll turn into an old man if you let him sit."

"Yes, dear." Abraham beamed at her. After twenty years of marriage he had an almost Pavlovian response to her.

"How about some lunch? I'm really hungry," Frankie deliberately suggested. She never wanted to eat when she saw him but she always pretended she did. Eating out was one way to allow Abraham to rest without watching television. Over the summer he had begun talking back to the television and accusing suspects on *Law & Order* of breaking into his apartment and taking his things. On September 11 Abraham was very concerned that Tom Brokaw knew he was all right. "I'm here! I'm here!" He had knocked on the television. "Tell them Abraham Weissman is here!"

When Helen told Frankie this story all she could think was thank God he wasn't still taking the subway. Helen thought Abraham taking the subway proved he was still vital and in the world like Mike Wallace, or some other kryptonite octogenarian.

"He doesn't need to eat. He forgets when he eats," Helen corrected Frankie.

"Who forgets?" Abraham asked.

"No one, Dad." Frankie kissed her father. "I just want some pasta. I have to see patients tonight."

"I'll have salade Niçoise, chopped, no potatoes, only two anchovies, and ranch dressing tossed in, not just floating on top." Helen always recited her litany to the waiter.

"Just coffee." Abraham smiled. "And fish. Any kind you got."

"Okay, I'll see what I can do."

"Nothing fancy. I don't like fancy."

"Okay, I've got my orders." The waiter perfunctorily wrote down the order.

"I'll just have coffee," Frankie added.

"I thought you were seeing patients tonight and wanted some pasta?" Helen never missed a beat.

"I don't see patients on Sunday nights unless there's an emergency."

"But you said . . ." Helen corrected her.

"I forgot what I said." Frankie was tired of defending herself.

"Like father, like daughter." Helen sighed.

"I don't forget. I can say the entire alphabet. A-B-C-D-E-F-G-H-I . . ."

"That's great, Dad!" Frankie forced herself to smile. She had, in fact, heard this at least a hundred times before.

"J-K-L-M-N-O . . ."

"That's enough, Abe, that's enough!" Helen gave him another maternal pat.

"P-Q-R-S . . ."

"Abe, I said, enough!" Helen was now his fourth-grade teacher.

Abraham sat silently until the waiter came with bread and butter. Abraham turned to him.

"I can say the alphabet. Want to hear? A-B-C-D-E-F-G-H-I-J . . ."

"That's terrific." The waiter began walking away.

Abraham continued. "K-L-M . . . Goddammit. What the hell comes after M? Goddammit!" He hit the table. "I knew this yesterday! I know I knew this yesterday!"

Walking home up Madison Avenue, Frankie took her father's arm and Helen charged at least a block ahead of them. She would not let Abraham's lethargic stride put a damper on her pace. Abraham began to sing, "New York, New York, it's a wonderful town."

Frankie pulled herself closer to her father.

"New York, New York, it's a helluva town." He repeated it again. "Is that the whole song, honey?"

"Yes, Daddy." Frankie rubbed her fingers down his hand. "That's the whole song." He began to sing it again.

Frankie walked Abraham and Helen home to Eighty-ninth and Madison. It was the same building Frankie had gone to high school in, a forty-story modern red brick high-rise and the first on the Upper East Side not to be in the popular post-1950s wedding-cake style. When they arrived at their lobby Abraham put his hand in his pocket.

"Let me give you some money so you can take a taxi home."

"Thanks, Daddy. I'm okay." She held his hand anticipating what would come next.

"Where is my wallet?" He became increasingly flustered. "The goddamn bastards came in last night and took my wallet. Sons of bitches!"

All his life Abraham seldom swore. In fact, for a man who spent his life in the garment business he was uncommonly gentle and courteous. But then the bastards started coming in to take his wallet, his sweaters, and even his oatmeal.

"I have the wallet. Dear, I have the wallet!" Helen pulled a billfold from her purse.

"That's not fair." Abraham tried to snatch it from her.

"You always think they come in and take things. This way at least you know I have it." She put it back in her purse.

Abraham reached for Helen's hand and turned to Frankie. "Isn't she beautiful? My bride is so beautiful."

Helen looked directly at Frankie. "This should be the happiest time of my life. I should be traveling, I should be entertaining."

"Then travel," Frankie snapped at her.

"You just don't know what it's like to be part of a couple." Helen's purple fingernails gripped Abraham's arm. "I'm not like you, Frankie. I don't feel comfortable alone. Maybe you like it that way, but I don't."

"Isn't she beautiful?" Abraham continued to squeeze Helen's hand.

"Let's go upstairs, Abraham."

Frankie watched as Helen walked her father to the elevator bank.

When Frankie got home to Columbus Avenue, she fed the cat and put her feet up on the kitchen table. Because the kitchen in her father's apartment was virtually a closet, Frankie had always wanted a large "eat-in" one when she grew up. Frankie never cooked but she spent hours in her kitchen staring at the Planetarium. It was the only room in her apartment with a saleable view.

Gilda, her fifteen-year-old calico cat, jumped on her lap. Ever since Frankie met Helen her senior year, she had a habit of dissecting her stepmother's every criticism like a high school anatomy student. As she stroked the cat Frankie thought Helen was once again probably right. Maybe she was perfectly comfortable living alone. By now maybe she couldn't imagine living any other way. Except she always thought things would have turned out differently.

When Frankie was thirty and in the third year of her residency at Columbia Presbyterian she began dating Dr. Jack Stanley, an immunologist with a Ph.D. in public health. Frankie had just assumed that when the right man came along she would fall in love. That's what she remembered her mother telling her when she was young. Unfortunately, however, Frankie's mother died when she was twelve, so she never got to meet Jack or any of the young men Frankie brought home.

Frankie and Jack moved in together to an affordable apartment in Washington Heights. Jack, who was five years older than she, had an idea to research and write a book about the new viruses. Believing in both his abilities and their permanent partnership, Frankie offered to support Jack while he wrote. After completing her residency, she turned down a fellowship at Einstein Hospital in the Bronx to study Tay-Sachs disease and took a more lucrative position at Park Avenue Pediatrics instead.

It took Jack five years to write his book. Although Frankie's mind would wander to her biological clock, she accepted his proposal that they postpone marriage and starting a family until this literal chapter of their lives was completed. Every time Helen would comment, "I know what you're doing for him, so what's he doing for you?" Frankie dismissed it.

The New Viruses made the cover of *Time* magazine and became an instant best seller. Jack was on television almost daily talking up the new plagues with Katie, Oprah, and Charlie Rose. Practically overnight, the obscure doctor and public health advocate became a hot dinner guest at all the best tables. When Frankie had to work late, it amused her to hear that Jack had met Hillary Clinton, Steven Spielberg, and Luciano Pavarotti at a casual "potluck" supper at Adrienne Strong-Rodman's house.

"I'm surprised Tony Blair wasn't there," Frankie quipped when Jack came home.

"You're right. I think Adrienne is very good friends with Tony," he replied without a whiff of irony.

At a *Vanity Fair* dinner to celebrate the 100 Most Creative Minds in America, Jack sat next to Lizzie Gomez, a twenty-six-year-old sugar heiress from Palm Beach. As far as Frankie could make out, Lizzie's family owned most of Hawaii and the Dominican Republic, and had sold a good portion of Puerto Rico for a fortune. Lizzie shocked her mother when after just five weeks of courtship, she announced she planned to marry a forty-three-year-old Jewish doctor. The wedding was in Santo Domingo, and on the invitation he sent to Frankie, Jack scrawled "Dearest F—I hope we will always be friends—Love, Jack."

Getting over Jack would have been easier if he hadn't carved out a multimedia monopoly on germ warfare. His wife, after the birth of their twins, began a children's clothing line. She hired the best designer from Bonpoint and had her monograms emblazoned on her entire line of cashmere play clothes. LG quickly became the Louis Vuitton of the toddler set and was omnipresent on the status diaper bags in Frankie's waiting room.

On the days she visited Abraham, Frankie was usually overcome by exhaustion. At eight-thirty she got up from the kitchen to begin her bedtime ritual. But when she finally turned off the lights and got under her covers, her mind wandered till dawn, from her father's alphabet scavenger hunt, to Mrs. Caesar having no place to leave her children, to the man on the fourth floor of her building who had died in the Trade Center. Finally, she fixed on her ossifying loneliness.

CHAPTER FIVE

Clarice

Clarice Santorini bought a $10,000 table for the *Nutcracker* family benefit every year. When she was growing up in the suburbs of Philadelphia, she had been a Candy Cane in a local production, and now her older daughter, Venice, was playing an angel in the New York City Ballet production of the Christmas classic.

"Fuck! I can't get there this year!" Clarice's husband, Barry, spit out his morning coffee when she reminded him that the benefit was that weekend.

"We'll miss you," she said softly.

"Why does that goddamn benefit always have to come out a week before the Golden Globe nominations and I have to be in Hollywood rat-fucking the foreign press. Shit!" Barry was getting himself worked up and began perspiring through his signature black sweatshirt.

"There's always next year, dear. I'm sure they'll be doing *The Nutcracker* again." Clarice bit into her whole-wheat toast with jelly.

"But the *Nutcracker* benefit is at least the kind of rat-fuck I like."

Clarice was horrified and secretly very excited every time Barry called it that.

"I'm serious! What's not to like? You get the Sugar Plum Fairy and all that tutu shit! Music that's stayed in the top 100 for at least a hundred years and that tree that grows before your eyes without the help of fucking Pixar or some other CGI crap! Plus the most important people in New York and their children come to see it. Why the hell wouldn't I rather be there than have my head up the ass of the Hong Kong stringer for *Variety*?"

Barry put his hand on Clarice's rear and kissed her cheek. He loved that she was wearing the Mikimoto choker pearls he had given her for Christmas with a powder blue Ralph Lauren sweater set. Only an Italian supermarket heiress would work so hard at pulling off the look of a WASP princess. Barry Santorini considered himself a man with an eye for talent, and Clarice's gift was class.

Clarice's father, Dan D'Annato, started with a vegetable stand in South Philadelphia and now owned over fifty supermarkets in the tristate area. When she was six years old, Clarice's family moved to the suburbs and bought their first Cadillac Seville. Clarice was always a good girl; she did well in school, didn't fight with her parents, and was always pulled together. She graduated cum laude from Notre Dame with a degree in Italian. Even though her father would say, "We left that country for a reason and now I'm paying for you to study it," he was proud that his daughter could walk into the best restaurant and order like a young contessa.

Until she met Barry, Clarice worked as a media rep for Giorgio Armani in Manhattan. Barry, who grew up in South Philly upstairs from his father's shoe repair store, often bragged to interviewers that he was man enough to marry a classy woman and she was woman enough to give up her career for him.

Clarice happily accepted devoting her life to her family. Other Spence mothers talked about getting back to work when their children got to middle school, but Clarice believed being a good mother was a full-time job. She personally took her children to Italian classes, ballet, and Suzuki violin class. Clarice knew she was running in fancy New York circles, but in her heart she was a good suburban mom. She also knew Barry felt secure flying around the world because her first priority was their family. Just in case, however, he had her carry a beeper.

The two organizations Clarice openly gave her time to were her children's school and the ballet. She left politics and anything remotely to do with entertainment to Barry. After all, she wouldn't want to cochair a dinner saluting the Weinstein brothers if Barry had just rat-fucked them or vice versa.

"I think I might be going to Deauville tonight, but call the office." Barry got up from the table. "And tell Venice next year I'll definitely be at her show."

"She knows that, honey," Clarice reassured him.

"I just can't let the shit that happened with the Oscars last year happen to me again."

"It won't." She tried to maintain his equilibrium.

Barry was still furious his movie didn't win Best Picture, and he still blamed it on the Golden Globes. Those goddamn awards are the New Hampshire of the awards season. As the Globes went, so did the Oscars. He'd honestly rather be at the ballet with Clarice and their daughter, but they knew he was a terrific family man and they'd want him to get the goddamn Oscar.

"Babe, I'll call you tonight either from Deauville or L.A. Fuck! I should quit and stay home and write goddamn cookbooks."

As Barry walked out of the kitchen, Clarice's teacup began shaking. For a very thin man with an overactive thyroid, Barry always upset the balance of the area around him when he walked.

Clarice thought the soloists at the *Nutcracker* benefit performance brought a little more spunk than usual to both the Sugar Plum Fairy and her Cavalier. She was delighted when ballet seemed like an activity that girls who preferred soccer could appreciate. For Clarice high culture was most valid when it had accessible educational components.

"Venice was just wonderful!" Pippa Rose waved to Clarice after the curtain call.

"The whole thing was terrific." Clarice beamed in her red Chanel holiday suit. "And your daughter was outstanding. I don't think I've ever seen a better young dancer than Jennifer."

Pippa gestured to meet her when they finished getting out of their rows. Every time Pippa came to the New York State Theater, she thought if she had been the decorator for this building, she would never have let Philip Johnson get away with the no-center-aisle decision.

Hands were waving, kisses were blowing, and eyes were winking as those audience members destined for the benefit luncheon headed up the staircase to the Grande Promenade. Pippa happily took Clarice's arm.

"There's something about that Christmas tree growing that always makes me weep," she confided.

"Oh Barry cries, too," Clarice added.

"Well if Barry cries then I feel like less of a sap."

"He loves this benefit but he had to be away."

"Joe isn't here either," Pippa consoled her without realizing she didn't need any consolation. "He doesn't really approve of Jennifer wanting to be a dancer. He says it's good for poise, but frankly, she'd have a better life going to Wharton and becoming a patron. At least she'd know she'll eat."

"Dancers don't really need to eat," Clarice added.

"Yes, I guess that's true." Pippa laughed.

When the women arrived at the top of the stairs, they were delighted to see that the white marble promenade had been transformed into a holiday party wonderland. Everywhere you looked were round tables draped in crushed red satin and, in the center of each, giant nutcrackers surrounded by white and red amaryllis. Throughout the hall at least a thousand votive candles were shimmering.

The student Candy Canes, Angels, and Harlequins had already begun milling among their parents. Four-year-old girls in smocked velvet dresses squealed with joy as they touched the Sugar Plum Fairy's tiara and scepter. Clarice thought to herself, Barry was right, this is the kind of rat-fuck he'd really like. Other cities could have their annual *Nutcracker* benefits, but not with some of the world's best dancers and children from some of the world's most accomplished families. And the children had the most remarkable names— Sea Bernstein, Triumph Trump, Persimmon McCarthy, Savoy Navez, Dutch Barakiva, Yale Franklin, and Clarice's favorite four-year-old, Real Chen.

Judy Tremont was eyeing Clarice Santorini's center table with envy when Samantha Acton swept into the room, gaily chatting with Jock Soto, the debonair principal dancer. Unlike Clarice in her traditional holiday suit, Samantha wore Lucky blue jeans with a bleached-down front, four-inch-heel red leather boots, and a skintight green paisley Dolce & Gabbana velvet jacket. Her formal nod to the holidays were two Christmas tree chandelier earrings bobbing around her shoulder-length auburn hair.

As Samantha strode across the floor, Judy became momentarily dispirited. She realized that no matter how much she spent on exercising, skin care, or even plastic surgery, it would be impossible to purchase the effect Samantha had on a room. It was as if Samantha were perpetually surrounded by a soft light, so if you could manage to be in her radius, you'd be part of the most flattering kind of picture. Judy wished she could pinpoint if it was Samantha's gait, or her body, or her face, that made every head turn. If you scrutinized each factor individually, they were lovely, but not astonishing. But some-how the cumulative effect was dazzling.

Samantha pecked Jock Soto on the cheek, crossed to the bar, and ordered a beer. Judy felt her face getting hot. She couldn't believe Samantha Acton had the audacity to drink that many carbs, espe-cially in the late afternoon. She was even more horrified because if Samantha Acton was drinking beer, it may well have been making a comeback.

"My God! Samantha looks fantastic," Pippa gasped to Clarice at their table. "Only she could pull that off."

"Yes, she has great flair." Clarice nodded. "I admire her for it. I'm so boring. I always stick to basics."

"Are you kidding? You are absolutely exquisite and everyone says that, especially Barry." Pippa wanted to move on to more fast-breaking news. "Do you know if Samantha's bringing Charlie today?"

"I've never really met either of them," Clarice admitted, "except I hear he's a fabulous doctor."

"Oh, I love Charlie," Pippa chimed in. "He's been my dermatolo-gist for years. He was on that list with our own Dr. Frankie here." Pippa tapped Frankie's shoulder. Clarice had invited Frankie to fill out her table. She enjoyed her company and she knew all her guests would appreciate an informal chat with a respected pediatrician. Frankie was flanked by Tina Schultz and Antonia Chen, who were grilling her about which preschool had the best emergency medical plans.

"Frankie, do you know Charlie Acton?" Pippa interrupted them.

"Not really." Frankie looked up, grateful to be pulled away from nursery school evacuations.

"Oh, well you should. Why don't I introduce you to his gorgeous wife." Pippa waved and happily Samantha caught her eye.

"I'm so glad you found me. Your daughter was just breathtaking." Still holding her beer, Samantha stopped by to give Pippa two kisses on the cheek.

"Thank you so much." Pippa graciously took the compliment and introduced Samantha to Clarice and Frankie.

"It's a pleasure to meet you. I love your husband's films." Samantha shook Clarice's hand, then embraced Frankie. "Of course, we've known each other for a thousand years, from school!"

"It's good to see you again." Frankie was caught off guard.

"You must come over and have dinner sometime soon. I'd love to catch up. I've really lost touch with most of the girls in our class and we were just in the same ridiculous magazine. Who the heck were they talking about, right?" Samantha flashed a smile.

"Oh yes, definitely." Frankie assumed Samantha said "You must come over and have dinner" in the same nonbinding way that many of her patients' mothers almost reflexively suggested "Let's do lunch."

From across the room, Judy watched Samantha kissing and joie de vivring Frankie Weissman. Her anticipation and awe now literally forced her out of her seat. "Just sit here," she told her daughters. "Don't move!"

Judy leapt across the Grande Promenade, setting what must have been a table-hopping world record. "Pippa, hello! And hello, Dr. Weissman. What a great treat to see you too!" She beamed.

"Hello, Judy. Do you know Samantha Acton?" Frankie introduced her ex-classmate, still standing beside her.

"No. But I am so happy to meet you." Judy was now firmly rooted holding hands with Frankie and Samantha with no intention of letting go of either. Bingo!

Clarice vaguely recognized Judy. She knew Judy was married to Albert Tremont, who was on the board with her at Spence. When Clarice had mentioned to Barry what a nice man Albert seemed to be, Barry had dismissed him as a "soft trust-fund kid with too-good fucking manners."

"Hello, Judy. Clarice Santorini." She extended her hand. "Would you care to join us?"

"If you have room." Judy immediately pulled over an available chair.

"Judy, where are your children?" Pippa asked.

"Oh, they're over there. They're fine." Judy shrugged, then covered for herself. "Charlotte is an enormous ballet fan but *The Nutcracker* is not her favorite. She prefers *Giselle*."

Clarice saw Tina Schultz catch the eye of Antonia Chen at the mention of Judy's daughter. The eBay Prada purchase had become infamous. "Yes, well so many of us prefer *Giselle*." Clarice smiled. "But wasn't Pippa's daughter wonderful today?"

"Wasn't Clarice's daughter Venice wonderful today?" Pippa immediately responded.

"Hear, hear." Samantha lifted her glass. "To all your wonderful daughters."

"Hear, hear!" all the women toasted. "To our daughters."

Clarice was grateful to Samantha for the generous toast. Despite Samantha's almost uncanny sophistication, she seemed like a lovely person. Watching Samantha take a small sip of her beer, Clarice thought how grateful she was to Barry for giving her this wonderful life in New York.

CHAPTER SIX

Frankie

Frankie completely forgot Samantha ever said she would call. But on a Thursday night while she was dressing for an exercise class the phone rang. Frankie decided to let the machine pick it up and concentrate instead on getting to the gym. If it was her office or something important, it would have been on her pager or the other line.

"Hi, this is Samantha Acton. Great to see you at the ballet." Frankie stared at her phone machine as if it were malfunctioning. "Will you come to dinner next Thursday? I mentioned to my husband, Charlie, that I saw you and he said he'd love for us to get together."

Frankie uncharacteristically lunged for the phone with her exercise tights still around her knees.

"Oh, hi, Samantha."

"Oh, you're there. Screening, are you?"

"I win a lot of free trips to Orlando. And then there's my father's wife, Helen."

"Oh, I remember her. She wore leopard while all our mothers were in tweeds."

"I'm amazed you remember her!" Frankie was truly impressed.

"She was sexy, and you know, there wasn't a whole lot of that back then. So will you come?"

"Sure. I think so."

"Great. We live at East Sixty-sixth and Fifth, number 4. Say eight o'clock. Can't wait. Charlie will be so pleased."

Frankie took her tights off her legs and sat down on the couch. She knew there was no way she would still be exercising tonight. Somewhere, she felt enough sense of accomplishment that after thirty years she was finally invited to the cool girls' table.

"I'm going upstairs to Acton." Frankie stopped at the white-gloved Fifth Avenue doorman.

"Elevator to your right."

As Frankie entered the formal lobby she wondered why Samantha didn't live somewhere hipper or less imposing. Then again, Christmas tree earrings in a room full of painters and filmmakers is a yawn. But in a room full of investment bankers and inherited wealth it's practically performance art.

The elevator door opened to a spare gallery of beige walls and Rothkos. A butler opened the door and a waiter appeared with a tray of caipirinhas.

"Can I take your coat?" the butler asked.

"Oh sure."

Frankie gave him her coat and, for some reason she didn't understand, her purse.

"Would you like to take your shoes off?"

Frankie actually didn't want to. They were suede boots which took her forever to get on. But she was too good a guest not to do what she was told. She sat down in the vestibule to remove them.

The multiple shades of beige continued into the living room. Even Frankie, who had virtually no sense of décor, couldn't miss the deliberately understated eggshell and dusted cocoa linen couches, the bleached floors, the faded Gustave Lefèvre and Eugene Atget photographs on the walls, and the contemporary Cindy Shermans and Clifford Rosses in the corner. She decided that a speck of dust would never have the chutzpah to rear its head here.

Samantha walked into the room arm in arm with an elegant older-looking man. As far as Frankie could make out, Samantha was wearing Prada, or maybe it was Gucci, sheer silver-spangled bell-bottom pants and a sleeveless silver lamé tank top. Her shoes were at least four-inch-high Manolo, or maybe Jimmy Choo, silver sandals, with lace ties around the ankle. For a moment, Frankie was flummoxed why Samantha and her friend were permitted to wear shoes and she wasn't. As she turned her head to acknowledge her host, Frankie noticed a small Giacometti sculpture inconspicuously placed on the bookshelf.

"Welcome. I'm so happy you're here." Samantha leaned down and kissed both of Frankie's cheeks. "Do you know my dear friend Jil Taillou?"

"No, I don't think so," Frankie replied.

"Jil worked for years at Sotheby's, and I was just showing him our renovations."

"It's a wonderful apartment. So calm. And I love the view," Frankie said, looking out at the Sixty-sixth Street transverse and the lights of Central Park South. "Did Pippa Rose design it?"

Jil put down his Grey Goose on the rocks. "Pippa Rose! You must be joking!" he said with a slight European accent. "She couldn't do anything as elegant as this. She's a chintzaholic!"

Samantha and Jil shared a laugh and sat down. Frankie followed them while silently sizing up her fellow guest. She hated herself for so easily categorizing people, but she was after all a scientist, and methodology had to start somewhere. As Jil Taillou reached for an olive, Frankie decided he was definitely gay, on the board of City Opera, well read, and actually from Brooklyn. Nobody's real name is

Jil Taillou, especially if they worked at Sotheby's. Plus anyone with that kind of untraceable Middle European accent most likely studied French at Midwood High in Brooklyn.

At this point in her life, Frankie wished all her hosts would stop inviting an extra man to dinner for her. She frankly would prefer not having the illusion of an escort. Besides, these men were always decidedly unavailable but full of opinions, gossip, and connections. But every hostess she knew insisted on an even number of boy-girl seating. Frankie looked forward to a time when she'd be too old for anyone to bother.

"So there I was in Rome with Beatrice." Jil made the point of using the Italian pronunciation. "And we are supposed to fly to Beirut the next day for Amir's engagement party. And you know Mrs. Ouiss had organized the most fabulous party. But we can't go because the entire country is on strike."

"Oh, the Italians are always on strike." Samantha lit a cigarette.

"No, but here's the best part. We had the party in the Vatican instead."

"No!" Samantha seemed riveted.

"Really?" Frankie attempted to dive in.

"Beatrice is related somehow to the captain of the guards who gives private tours to Barbra Streisand and Sting in the pope's closet."

Samantha grinned. "I love this!"

"So they had the engagement party in the pope's closet. *Dona nobis pacem,* darling. If you think your Gucci pants are a great brocade, you haven't seen the pontiff's evening wear!"

Samantha was now convulsively laughing with her hand in Jil's lap as he continued. "Oh my God! Of course I had to try something on! His Holiness is a little shorter than I am but I look a lot nicer in a high collar. And this is the best! I told them anytime they want to have a Vatican sale, I'd do the auction."

"Whose auction?" a middle-aged man in black corduroys and a dark blue shirt asked as he walked into the room. "You guys are having entirely too much fun in here."

Frankie recognized him immediately. Charlie Acton, Omaha, Nebraska. He was a year behind her at Princeton. Nice Guy. A little straight. Army ROTC. He was someone Frankie said "hey" to while walking across campus. She didn't really know him except for a zoology class they had together, and she hadn't thought about him in at least twenty years. Charlie kissed Samantha and sat down beside her.

"Sorry I'm late, sweetheart, I got caught up with that interview."

"Well, we're having a wonderful time. Jil's telling us about Amir's engagement party at the Vatican."

"Wow! Sorry I missed it. Great to see you, Jil." He embraced Jil in the way that Frankie recently noticed straight men pointedly do.

"Francesca Weissman." He took her hand. "I haven't seen you since sophomore-year zoology. I was so happy when Samantha told me she had run into you."

"Were you two college buddies?" Jil asked.

"I always wished we were. Just very nice acquaintances," Charlie answered, and helped himself to a caipirinha. *"Deixa bebida!"* He raised his glass and tossed off the toast in effortless Portuguese.

"What does that mean?" Frankie put down her glass.

Charlie laughed. "It gets you drunk."

While Jil repeated the pope's closet story for Charlie during dinner, Frankie remembered talking to Charlie once after class. It was the day he was rejected from the Ivy Club. Frankie had very deliberately never tried to belong to any eating clubs. Instead, she spent her time outside of class stage-managing for the Triangle Club, the illustrious collegiate theatrical group. But Charlie decidedly wanted the validation. Charlie was a bit awkward as an undergraduate. He listened to James Taylor and Simon & Garfunkel when everyone else had moved on. Frankie remembered that for weeks he carried around a copy of *This Side of Paradise* in his back pocket. Charlie was the kind of kid who wore a denim jacket because that's what he grew up wearing in Omaha. Frankie also remembered he always called her Francesca. He said it was what F. Scott would have done.

When the dessert bowls came Jil exclaimed, "I love these bowls. Très moderne classique."

"It's Alvar Aalto." Charlie casually mentioned the name.

"The Finn?" Jil asked only to underscore that, of course, he knew the origins of modern design.

"Yes. We're collecting him now. After dinner I'll take you into the library to see the most terrific chair. In my mind Aalto makes Mies look like Ethan Allen." Charlie smiled wryly at his insider put-down.

"Ever since I burnt all of Charlie's old home furnishings all hell has broken loose." Samantha laughed heartily.

A waiter appeared with a dessert tray of sliced bananas, nuts, ice cream logs shaped like miniature bananas, hot fudge, and whipped cream in silver pitchers.

"Ooh-la-la! Are these the hot fudge sundaes we all read about in *Manhattan* magazine?" Jil twinkled.

"Francesca." Charlie turned away from his wife. "You're a Princeton graduate. Explain to our guest what bananas, hot fudge, and ice cream generally add up to."

Frankie felt she had no choice but to answer. "A banana split!"

"Correct! That's Princeton for one hundred points! Go Tigers!" Charlie slapped Frankie on the back. Suddenly, Frankie remembered that Charlie's father was a veterinarian in Omaha and Charlie had spent his freshman summer with his dad containing an outbreak of sheep parasites on a Navajo reservation.

"Anyone want a cookie?" Samantha offered a plate of Florentine lace goodies to the table.

"I have to say, ever since 9/11 I've been eating up a storm. Mashed potatoes, peanut butter and jelly, and any cookie or cake I can get my hands on. Charlie, I bet your office is booming with people breaking out from eating too much junk." Jil then bit into his second cookie.

"Oh Jil darling, Charlie's clients don't eat junk." Samantha took a sip of dessert wine. "They just make sure to nibble enough rabbit food so they can put a little butt fat in his refrigerator."

"Excuse me?" Frankie had had enough wine to admit she was lost.

"Francesca, my refrigerator is the most exclusive club for butt fat in the country," Charlie nonchalantly explained.

Samantha put her arm on Charlie. "My husband invented the natural alternative to Botox. I can't believe you haven't read *You Can Stay Forever Young*. Charlie was the first dermatologist guru."

"Francesca, please don't read it. I just inject a patient's own fat cells back into wrinkles and crevices instead of questionable foreign substances." Charlie elaborated further. "I'm even doing it now with some of the burn victims from the Trade Center."

"Did you go down there?" Frankie asked.

"Right away. I'm still working with a woman who severed her hand."

"Oh God, life will never be the same." Jil reached out for another cookie.

"Honestly, Charlie's just legitimizing keeping Adrienne Strong-Rodman's butt fat in his refrigerator because he has a social conscience." Samantha lit another cigarette.

Charlie pulled his wife over toward him. "Honey, as long as your butt is in my house and not in my refrigerator, I'm a happy man."

Jil smiled. "I tell you, the best tonic these days, even better than mashed potatoes or great art, is being with two people who are really in love. Isn't that right, Dr. Weissman?"

"Oh yes. Absolutely," Frankie said while her mind drifted to reading Samantha's first marriage announcement in the *Times*: "Samantha

Bagley to marry Pearson Stimson Phillips." Samantha was getting her M.F.A. in art history from NYU, and Pearson was a graduate of Exeter and Harvard, and currently working in the Training Division of J. P. Morgan. He also had a brief stint on the United States Olympic water polo team. Two years later, Frankie got a call from a high school friend asking if she'd heard that Pearson went off to live in San Francisco with Rick Feldstein, his lover and former roommate from Exeter. Samantha left the country for Paris for two years, ostensibly to do research for her master's. Watching Samantha and Charlie cuddle now, Frankie wondered if she married him because there would be no surprises. If she was his ideal, perhaps he was her semblance of order.

After dinner while Samantha was occupied helping Jil with his coat, Charlie put his arm around Frankie and walked her to the door.

"I'm sorry I didn't know until now that you and my wife were in the same class at Spence or we would have gotten together sooner." Charlie's almost boyish charm combined with his newfound love of Finnish modernists made him an irresistible balance of Omaha and urbane. "I remember I spoke to you the day I was rejected from the Ivy. I didn't want to tell any of my friends who were already admitted that I was devastated. But you were the ideal sympathetic stranger. I've always been grateful to you."

Frankie looked into Charlie's eyes. They were a clear and intelligent light blue. Suddenly everything fell into place. The clean but classic décor, the fifteen rooms on the Park, the marriage to Samantha, the Atgets in the living room. Charlie was a romantic like Gatsby. Only the green light across the sound wasn't Daisy Buchanan, but this life with Samantha. Frankie altered her earlier diagnosis. Perhaps it was a more equitable relationship. They were probably each other's Pygmalion and Galatea, mutually filling out the crevices of each other's lives.

· · ·

"How much would you say that apartment is worth?" Frankie asked Jil as they shared a cab to the West Side. She was appalled that she actually said it, but then again he had worked at Sotheby's.

"Let's put it this way." He smiled. "If you have to ask, you can't afford it."

Francesca laughed.

"At least that's what my daughter says!" Jil continued.

Francesca looked up at him. He had a daughter? What man named Jil has a daughter? Maybe her name was Bruce.

"My daughter's at the architecture school at Harvard. Lousy profession right now. I begged Richard Meier and Charlie Gwathmey to tell her not to do it."

Okay, he's a well-connected former heterosexual now-everybody's-favorite-extra-man-at-a-party, Francesca concluded as the taxi pulled up in front of her apartment house.

"I'd like to see you again." He looked at her warmly. "Maybe we could go to the opera sometime. And if it's dreadful, we'll leave after the first act and go to the Lincoln Center Starbucks for a venti mochaccino. That's one of my favorite things to do in life."

Frankie kissed his cheek and got out of the cab. She wished he had said "movie" and not "opera." That was usually a dead giveaway. The last thing she needed was to get involved with an unavailable man. "Great, I'd love to," she said casually and walked inside her building.

"Good evening, Dr. Weissman." Her doorman nodded his head.

"Good evening, George." She chuckled.

Frankie noticed Jil waving good-bye from the taxi window.

CHAPTER SEVEN

Judy

Judy knew that Christmas this year would be a hell of a lot easier with a private plane. Under ordinary circumstances the thought of changing flights in Puerto Rico for Anguilla or Nevis was unbearable. But 9/11 made commercial travel close to impossible, even in first class. Of course she knew she could fly directly to Jamaica or St. Martin, but why on earth would she want to go there? Judy was well aware of exclusive pockets in Jamaica, like the gated communities of Round Hill and Tyrell, but the truth was the crowd was too staid. Judy wanted to be where the fun money was, especially this year when everything had been so dreary.

"Why don't we go to Palm Beach this year?" Albert said one night after Trina, the night housekeeper, had cleared away dinner.

Judy couldn't believe what she was hearing. Rich Jewish girls from Great Neck who moved to Manhattan and sent their children to Temple Emanuel Nursery School went to Palm Beach.

"That's where Serena Bernstein goes. That's where Natalia Zeckendorf goes. We can't do that!" Judy gasped.

"But it makes a lot of sense, dear. Just think about it. Palm Beach is the new Southampton. And it's not the right year to leave the country." Albert looked at his wife.

After a minute Judy revised her thinking. Actually Palm Beach was coming back. Anyone with serious money and a private plane had at least four homes now—city, country, summer, and winter. The winter choice for the A-list snowbirds was between sandy beaches in the south or powdery slopes in the west. Since their house in Aspen wouldn't be ready for at least another year, Albert was right. Given the world, Palm Beach made sense this year.

"Absolutely. Palm Beach. We can stay at The Breakers. And if we have to fly commercial, it's just two and a half hours." She took his hand.

"I think we can hitch a ride with Paul Rodman on their plane." Albert looked up for his wife's approval.

Judy was not overwhelmingly sexual but she felt a tingling in her toes. "I love you," she said as she kissed him on the cheek. A private plane made dealing with the entire entourage—children, nannies, suitcases—plus her security anxiety just so much easier.

Since 9/11 Judy had made a few obvious changes in her life. First of all she never let her nannies take her children in taxis anymore. Any turbaned driver talking on a cell phone could be a terrorist. She kept a supply of iodine pills in her home plus gas masks for the entire family and their pets. Every day she carried a Fendi emergency kit in her purse neatly packed with Cipro and folding flat shoes. In Judy's personal safe she kept $50,000 in cash just in case they had to make a quick getaway. And perhaps the biggest change was she always wore her good jewelry in the event she'd have to trade it for easy passage off Manhattan.

"The Rodmans' plane. I can't believe I didn't think of that. Albert, you are a genius!" She kissed him again.

"I'm so glad you agree, honey." He patted her knee and got up to go to his study.

. . .

On her first day at The Breakers Judy made an appointment for an hour-and-a-half European facial followed by a full-body wrap. Her sons had gone to Miami ostensibly to play tennis and Albert had taken the girls to the croquet court. He could happily spend hours demonstrating for them and other guests his idiosyncratic sport.

Walking through the lobby with its ornate gold vaulted ceiling reminiscent of a Medici villa, Judy had a sense of well-being she had missed all fall. As she stopped to study a pair of pink ostrich sandals in the window of Giorgio's lobby shop, Judy felt the tension literally slipping out of her body. She whistled along to the *Magic Flute* Muzak as she walked through the corridor to the spa.

"I'm Judy Tremont. I have a ten o'clock," she announced to the well-groomed spa attendant.

"Of course, Mrs. Tremont." The young woman smiled graciously. "Here is your locker key. Make yourself comfortable and your technician will meet you in the waiting room." Judy appreciated that the attendant had the gift all well-trained service people did of making you think everything was tailor-made just for you. She wished her own staff would work a little harder to acquire the same skill.

While Judy changed into her robe and slippers she carefully examined the other women in the locker room. When it came to female bodies, Judy had the eye of a forensic detective. No liposuction, implant, or peel passed her thorough inspection. She dismissed the chubby women in golf skirts as midwestern CEO wives. Judy knew people lived in major homes in Winnetka and Grosse Point, but she just didn't feel the need to pay any attention to them. Standing in the center of the room in La Perla bikini briefs were two shiny-haired brunettes with French manicures and Cartier diamond tennis bracelets who Judy catalogued as the expected Temple Emanuel Nursery School mothers. She assumed their noses had been done by Dr. Austin but wouldn't swear to it.

Her eye finally settled on a woman with terrific cheekbones and taut skin from the C. Z. Guest school who was advising her daughter about her upcoming wedding. Judy envied the ease between the mother and daughter in their matching white terry robes but she envied their arms even more. Judy knew that she had one trouble spot left on her body and it was the eighth inch of dangling flesh below her triceps. She took great pride these days that her tummy issue had been completely solved by a combination of Pilates and a rigorous sit-up regimen. But despite her daily power yoga and weight-lifting routine, she could not get to that eighth of an inch of upper-arm flesh. She considered liposuction, but Judy had contempt for those Third Avenue dentists' wives who solved all their body issues surgically. She was much more disciplined than that.

When the C. Z. Guest mother erupted in laughter at something her daughter said, Judy decided she would offer to bring her own mother here. Except she would never come. The Christmas Judy bought her mother a leather Coach bag she sent it back because it was too extravagant. Now every year Judy had her assistant send her mother a Tower of Treats from Harry and David's Fruit-of-the-Month Club.

As Judy slipped into her complimentary slippers, she momentarily flashed on the only family vacation her parents had ever taken her on. It was to Disneyland, and she loathed it. She loathed staying five miles away from the park in an Anaheim motel. She loathed waiting on line for hours to see Mickey Mouse while the special people with special escorts were escorted inside. She loathed that before every ride her father said, "This will bankrupt me," and then her mother nagged him, "Just do it once for the child." And most of all, she loathed that she knew from magazines that far away from Anaheim there were grand hotels like The Breakers where beautiful women lounged in ostrich sandals by the pool.

A month after that vacation her father was shot during a Modesto fast-food robbery. He was discharged from the force with honor and spent the rest of his life racing model cars in the basement and drinking Smirnoff every night. He died ten years later.

Judy was not so much embarrassed by her parents as flabbergasted that they never figured out that life could be controlled if you only had the right resources. Ever since that childhood holiday, Judy firmly believed that with the right amount of cash no one could afford to get to Mickey Mouse before you did. Even better, Mickey'd be all spiffed up and waiting for you.

When Judy walked into the treatment waiting room she was stunned to see Samantha Acton, unplugged, reclining in just a towel. Obviously, 9/11 had changed more than just Judy's travel plans. Studiously, Judy turned her eyes on Samantha's body. As Pippa Rose would say, "She was just scrummy!" Not an ounce of anything unnecessary, and what was there was tight.

"Hello!" Judy walked directly in front of her. Samantha had plainly no recollection of who the stranger before her was.

"We met through Dr. Frankie."

For a moment Samantha didn't know who that was either.

"We met at the Nutcracker benefit. Francesca Weissman is my daughter's doctor and she's a very good friend of mine, too."

Samantha sat up slightly. She had just had an hour and a half of reflexology and was looking forward to not moving at all before another hour was over.

"Oh, Francesca Weissman. We went to school together," she said softly.

"That's right." Judy's dad had taught her that in any investigation the crucial thing is to get your fish to first bite. "Frankie is also good friends with my decorator, Pippa Rose."

"Uh-huh." Samantha was hoping the chattering would stop now that she had been pleasant enough.

"You were at Clarice Santorini's table. I adore her, and her husband, Barry. I went to a screening of *Tristram Shandy* that he just produced. Oh my God! I think it was the best thing I've ever seen!"

"Oh." Samantha felt the benefits of her reflexology going straight to hell.

"My husband, Albert, and I would love to get together for drinks with you and Charlie tonight. I think you and Albert would have a lot in common. He's from an old New York family and likes snowball sundaes, too."

"Uh-huh." Samantha considered swatting her.

"Great! So we'll meet you tonight in the lounge at six."

Samantha tried to muster the energy to say that she was busy, but she decided it was easier to put a "Do Not Disturb" on her phone and simply be unreachable.

"You know I didn't think I wanted to come to this hotel but there's something about the grand Floridian style that really is so fun! See you later! Just relax. Don't get up." Judy practically skipped out of the room.

More than anything at that moment Samantha wished she wasn't staying at that goddamned hotel, but on the other hand she couldn't bear to stay at her mother's house either. She associated Palm Beach with her mother's deadly fund-raisers—women in pink and green Lilly Pulitzer dresses with clunky white alligator Lana Marks bags. Samantha's mother, Dorothy, known to the world as Doddie, was an avid social do-gooder ever since her graduation from Mount Holyoke. In fact, Samantha's mother's roommate from college became a Christian missionary, and if Dorothy hadn't fallen in love with Clifford Bagley at a Williams College mixer, Samantha thought her mother could have been a missionary, too. But Dorothy remained true to her lineage. She had inherited a fortune second only to the Rockefellers', and both her husband and family would never let her drift away to volunteerism in China. Samantha's mother became a pillar of Palm Beach society and her father a stalwart of the Republican Party.

When Samantha was a sophomore she transferred from Spence to Emma Willard, a girls' prep school in Troy, New York. Although she referred to the school as "my mother's nunnery," she snuck out regularly to frat parties at the nearby Rensselaer Polytechnic Institute, which she never mentioned had the same surname as her grandfather. Samantha had her first affair with a college senior that year. His name was Raymond Verrazano, like the bridge, and he drove a red Mustang. Samantha couldn't remember much about him now except that he had very large hands. He also was obsessed with her feet, which she subsequently learned to use to give him great pleasure.

By the time she was nineteen, Samantha had great confidence that her life would be very different from her mother's. She dropped out of Vassar College after one year to become a cabaret singer. She had a few gigs in Palm Beach and one night at The Blue Note in New York. But after eight months of a bohemian lifestyle, Samantha realized she had the yearning of an artist without much of the talent. She could attract a crowd more successfully by standing still than by actually performing.

Samantha returned to Poughkeepsie the next year, and graduated magna cum laude with a major in art history. Twenty years later, she was entrenched on the boards of the Whitney Museum and the Central Park Conservancy. As she approached her fortieth birthday, Samantha feared that her life was merging into a version of her mother's. But while Doddie took it all very seriously, Samantha's secret was holding her life at a distance with a touch of stylish disdain.

Since Judy, monsoonlike, had destroyed her tranquillity, Samantha decided to go back upstairs to her room. As she entered the elevator, she immediately felt the eyes of every man on her. She certainly wasn't interested in attracting some other woman's dreary husband, but all the attention put her back into a fairly relaxed frame of mind.

Samantha needed to know that she excelled in something, and if it was that she had the elusive key to men's sexuality, she would hold on to that A+ status.

"Getting out please." She flashed a grin at the gentleman by the front of the elevator.

"My pleasure." He immediately stepped aside.

"Someone named Judy Tremont called here and said we're having drinks with her tonight." Charlie looked up from the Faulkner he was reading when she walked into the room.

"Oh God!" Samantha threw herself in a chair. "I meant to take the phone off before she could reach us."

"Well, we're not going."

"She accosted me. She has the persistence of a rabid terrier. She's a friend of your friend, what's-her-name." Samantha was getting irritated with herself.

"That's not helpful, darling."

"She's a friend of Frankie Weissman's," she said quickly.

"She couldn't be," he said, sloughing her off.

"What does that mean?" Samantha found Charlie's social analysis was based on ridiculous things like comparative SAT scores.

"What would Francesca Weissman want with Judy Tremont? She's a flibbertigibbet."

"You know her?" Samantha didn't expect that, and it annoyed her even more when she couldn't predict Charlie.

"I knew her husband, Albert, from the Knickerbocker Club. Nice man. Very old school."

"Stop it, Charlie." She poured herself a glass of water.

"Stop what?"

"I hate when you start with that 'old school' crap. You sound like a Republican asshole."

Charlie knew she would now pick a fight just for the sport of it. "I just don't want to have drinks with her."

"But you'd be happy to put her butt in your refrigerator."

"Honestly, you make me feel like some sort of cannibal." He picked up the phone and began to dial. "Darling, we have to call Judy Tremont and cancel or we'll be stuck with her at six o'clock. It's the right thing to do."

Samantha admired Charlie's innate decency. For all his recent polish, he wasn't hard like so many in their circle. He would always do "the right thing." Charlie was the kind of guy you raise a family with. In fact, for six years, Samantha and Charlie had tried every fertility doctor, in vitro procedure, and even a surrogate egg donor to no avail. Afterward, Charlie thought they should adopt, but Samantha had lost confidence in her ability to mother. Like everything else, it seemed too complicated, and not necessary. Besides, after years of hormone shots and biological procedures, Samantha preferred to avoid any prescribed intimacy, even with a baby. She longed for pure abandonment.

Sometimes Samantha thought she would be happier with a bolder man who had made a new fortune in the nineties that was even larger than her mother's. But most bolder men wouldn't have been so solicitous. Samantha married Charlie because he wanted her so much. And besides, everyone in New York adored him. After all, he made them all look good.

Samantha ran her hand over Charlie's chest, hung up the phone before he could place the call, and kissed him on the lips. "Oh fuck Judy Tremont! I love you, Charlie."

CHAPTER EIGHT

Charlie

"Det er med den største glede," Albert picked up his glass after the second round of martinis appeared. *"Å ønske alle tilstede, På nordisk mål—En heilnorsk skål, Så drikk hverandre til alle dere!"*

"What is that?" Charlie asked.

"Old Norse for 'It is with the greatest pleasure, I wish all of you present, in the Nordic way, an old Norse *skål,* let's drink together, all of you!' "

"I read *Beowulf* in Old English in college, but Old Norse is really something!" Charlie was honestly taken by Albert's eclectic scholarship.

"I feel we could all still learn a little something from the *Prose Edda.*" Albert sipped his drink.

"What?" Samantha asked.

"The Nordic *Beowulf* by Snorri Sturluson. I've read it twice." Albert caught himself and laughed. "And I'm sure everyone else here at The Breakers has, too."

"Here, here!" Charlie patted Albert on the back with friendly admiration while Samantha curled her lip into a wry smile.

Judy was so happy drinks were going well that she allowed herself another sip of champagne. "Yumbo!" she screeched as she downed half of a cocktail shrimp.

Samantha was relieved the cocktail hour took very little work. Albert was sweet and Judy mostly name-dropped people whom Samantha found completely pedestrian. To entertain herself as Judy chattered on, Samantha tried to imagine the Tremonts' sex life. She decided either they read in separate beds, him *The Song of Norway* in Old Norse and her *Palm Beach Life*, or she had a shocking pink rubber suit with a matching pink lasso and whipped him nightly.

"We flew down with the Rodmans." Judy was in high gear. "I have to say that with a family it doesn't make sense to go commercial anymore."

"Even without a family," Charlie added to keep things rolling.

"Well, dear, I can see where this is going." Albert nodded lovingly.

"Honey, I think we should just go for it." Judy took Albert's knee. She had been dying for Albert to buy a share in a private plane for years and she saw this as her opportunity to clinch the deal. "Next year maybe you guys will fly down with us someplace wonderful like St. Barths or Nevis."

Albert shook his head. "Absolutely. Next year we won't have to settle for Palm Beach or, for that matter, bother the Rodmans."

"What's Paul Rodman like? I've never met him," Samantha asked.

"You've never met Paul Rodman? I can't believe that!" Judy thought Samantha knew and did everything.

"I know he wanted to live in our building and offered to pay thirty for a twenty-million-dollar apartment, but the co-op board rejected him. Someone had it in for Adrienne."

"Really?" Judy was delighted to have this tidbit of information. "Well, now they live in that building on Fifth with the endangered bird's nest on top."

"You mean the red-tailed hawk?" Albert perked up. "Sometimes I take the girls to watch it from the park."

"I didn't know the hawk and the Rodmans moved into the same building." Samantha mused. "I sort of wish they did live in our building. I hear that their parties are memorable."

"No one throws better parties than you do, dear." Charlie took her hand.

"I'm sure that's true." Judy's sigh was an understatement. She was falling a little bit in love with Samantha. It was that kind of overwhelming whoosh when you can't believe the glorious person across from you could possibly do anything that wasn't touched by God.

"I heard that the reenactment of the *Odyssey* on Paul Rodman's yacht last year was the most obscenely extravagant evening ever." Samantha repeated what friends like Jil said about Rodman. "Wasn't it a two-million-dollar tab?"

"Two million two," Judy chirped. "But the thing is no matter how much money Adrienne Strong-Rodman spends, it can't come close to what you do because you have style in your fingertips. In my mind, Samantha, you're an artist."

"Oh, I really wouldn't say that I'm an artist." Samantha put her head down, almost embarrassed. "Did you see Alex Katz's small paintings exhibit at the Whitney last month? He's an artist."

"Oh, I love Alex Katz," Judy promptly piped in.

"He's the real thing. I just have a good eye."

"I think you're being totally unfair to yourself. I wouldn't know anything except for people like you who set the standards."

Against her better judgment, Samantha decided she didn't mind Judy's sycophancy because Judy didn't see the regrets in Samantha's life, and listening to her chatter on, Samantha could lose sight of those regrets also.

"I got invited to a conquistador party tomorrow night on Paul Rodman's yacht. Would you like to come with me? Albert hates these things." Judy turned to her husband. "Honey, wouldn't you be relieved to be out of it?"

Albert nodded his head. He couldn't care less if Ponce de León himself was at Paul Rodman's conquistador party.

Samantha finished her third martini. Between the heat, the reflex-ology, and the Plymouth gin, she was feeling a little woozy. She wouldn't mind going to see Paul Rodman's yacht. It sort of felt like a road trip she would have taken her freshman year at Vassar. Plus her mother would not be amused that she stood her up for someone as glitzy as Paul Rodman. The entire package had a definite prep-school bad-girl appeal. "I'd love to come," Samantha answered. "Charlie's kids are coming down so they could have a nice family reunion."

"You have kids?" Judy asked.

"Two girls from my first marriage. They live in Omaha with their mother."

"Omaha?" Judy rounded her *O* into an *Oh!*

Samantha looked at Charlie. "That's where he's from."

"What fun!" Judy chirped, careful not to add anything like she was originally from "Modest-oh."

"My kids are skiing with their mother in Telluride and then they're coming here to join me."

"Albert and I are building a house in Aspen. If it was up to me I'd go skiing every vacation." For a minute Judy imagined that by the time the house was finished Samantha and Charlie could be their guests. "There is nothing that makes me happier than setting tracks in fresh snow. I swear it's the only time I feel completely free and don't give a goddamn about the nanny."

When the waiter appeared offering a fourth round, Albert had run out of Old Norse toasts.

"I'd better get upstairs to the children. We're starting *The Last of the Mohicans* tonight." He sat back in his chair.

"Really! *The Last of the Mohicans!*" Charlie was impressed again.

"Albert reads to them every night, but I credit Spence. A first-tier school makes all the difference," Judy was quick to add.

"I hated that place." Samantha took out a cigarette.

"But . . ." Judy was stunned as Samantha continued.

"You think I can smoke in here or are they as boring as they are in New York?"

"Honey, the kids are waiting for us." Albert got up to leave. He didn't mind marijuana but too many cigarettes disturbed his equilibrium.

"Enjoy *The Last of the Mohicans*!" Charlie stood up appropriately. Albert shook Charlie's hand. "I hope I can keep them awake."

"Oh, Albert." Judy took her husband's arm. "The girls love your reading. They went absolutely nuts for *Bleak House*."

"Good for you! My girls would think *Bleak House* was a reality show on MTV." Charlie kissed both of Judy's cheeks. "Wonderful being with you."

Judy leaned in to kiss Samantha while the cigarette was still in her mouth. "So I'll tell Adrienne Rodman we're on for her party."

"Oh yes." Samantha took another puff. "Absolutely."

"Darling, careful with your hair." Albert touched his wife's shoulders before her blunt cut went up in smoke.

"Oh Albert, you really need to meditate!" She swatted his hand and they walked out toward the lobby.

"I liked him. He's a decent man. But she never stops." Charlie picked up a handful of nuts after the Tremonts left.

Samantha puffed her cigarette. "At least she's lively."

"Lively? She's a reason to live alone on a mountaintop in Tibet."

"I bet she becomes your patient." She blew her smoke teasingly toward him.

"Darling, you really shouldn't be smoking in here," Charlie immediately changed the subject.

"Why not?"

"Because if you don't take care of yourself the Judy Tremonts will take over your world."

"Stop it, Charlie, I sort of like her."

"What?" Charlie almost coughed out a cashew.

"She's amusing. She believes our lives have a purpose."

"She's ridiculous."

"Why? Because she said I'm an artist?"

"Honey, she just wants a dinner invitation."

"At least she wants something."

"Did you catch the nail polish?"

"You've become a terrible snob, Charlie." She began to take another drag.

The waiter approached them. "Madame, there's no smoking permitted anywhere in the building. Can I ask you to step outside?"

"No, you can't!" Samantha got up and began to walk out of the room. Charlie dutifully paid the bill and followed her.

"Darling." Samantha turned to him while the light reflected in her blue almond-shaped eyes. "I'm going to raid the newsstand. I feel like reading something a little lighter than *The Last of the Mohicans* tonight. Want to come?"

"No thanks." Charlie put his hand on her cheek. "I think I'll take a breath of fresh air and meet you upstairs."

Charlie watched her as she walked down the steps. She was wearing five-inch heels and tight white linen pants with her panty line invitingly peeking through. If she hadn't been his wife he would have spent his entire vacation trying to meet her.

When Samantha was finally out of sight, Charlie headed toward the oceanfront. Having been raised in the landlocked heartland, Charlie had had a long romance with the sea. Charlie had no idea how long he stayed on the veranda overlooking the ocean that night. As the whitecaps of the waves hit against the cement, he kept remembering the faces of the people he treated in the emergency room after 9/11. Charlie also had a secret. He resented that the Paul Rodmans of the world were not affected by 9/11. The captains of industry, the men with yachts and private planes, were mostly not in their offices at 8:57 when those planes hit. So it was the workers, the elevator men, the bond traders, the caterers, whose faces and hands Charlie tried to save. He never touched a man like Paul Rodman that day and Charlie couldn't forget it. But he would never tell his wife or his mother-in-law. It just was something he remembered as he watched the waves come in.

When Judy and Albert came back into the room she found her nanny watching *Punk'd* on MTV with the kids. She wanted to fire her on the spot, but she knew Albert wouldn't allow it. Discreetly Judy took the nanny into the hall.

"Why are you watching TV?"

"Charlotte threatened to poison me if I didn't let her," the nanny replied.

"That's no excuse. If I see this kind of behavior again, you're fired."

"I quit." The nanny stood up.

"You can't quit! We're on vacation!" Judy screamed.

"Yes I can. And you can't treat me this way. I could write a novel about you just like those other nannies, and don't think I wouldn't."

Judy took a deep breath. She couldn't afford to lose this girl right now. She had to go to that party on Adrienne's yacht and she wasn't leaving her kids with some Florida hotel babysitter. "Listen, tomorrow I'd like to buy you a pair of alligator sandals I saw in the shop downstairs. I think they'd be terrific on you." Judy forced herself to smile at the girl.

The nanny sat down while Judy continued.

"Oh yes, and there's a terrific little evening bag with the most darling gold clasp to match. Is that okay with you?"

By the time the nanny finally nodded her head yes, Judy was exhausted. She went back into her room to vent her frustration on Albert, but he had already taken the girls into their suite to hear James Fenimore Cooper. Judy sat down alone on the lemon yellow divan and started to weep. Her evening had gone so well and then that stupid selfish girl had to ruin it. Overwhelmed and emotionally spent, Judy picked up a blank piece of stationery on the coffee table and began to write. She decided she would try to do her version of that diary before her nanny ever got to it.

CHAPTER NINE

Frankie

Since her time as a resident, Frankie had offered to be on call Christmas Eve and Christmas Day. It wasn't that she was a practicing Jew, but she wasn't a practicing anything else either.

Christmas morning Frankie was at the hospital neonatal intensive care unit by 6 a.m. She planned to spend an hour there and then continue on her practice's rounds. When Frankie was still a resident, the six weeks she spent in the NICU had been her favorite rotation. In Frankie's eyes, the NICU was a cross section of humanity on the cusp of life; the premature triplets of two Scarsdale bankers were in incubators right beside the one-pound twelve-ounce offspring of a South Bronx crack addict. The survival of all the children, as Frankie saw it, was based on the perfect confluence of modern medicine and the inexplicable randomness of life. Frankie had toyed with specializing in neonatology but ultimately decided she preferred a practice where she could follow her patients' long-term development. But she remained fascinated by the evident human character in a one-inch heart.

On the morning of September 11, Frankie had been in the NICU examining Mrs. Caesar's "preemie" baby. Mrs. Caesar had developed pre-eclampsia at twenty-eight weeks and delivered her two-pound son, Clayton, in May. Over the summer Frankie had dropped by the NICU to visit the baby, and when Clayton reached four pounds Frankie took over from the neonatologist as the child's ongoing pediatrician.

When the news of the planes flying into the World Trade Center came into the NICU, Dr. Borstman, the unit's director, immediately activated the alternative generator. If the preemies were removed from their incubators or detached from their lung and heart monitors, they'd have been the youngest and tiniest casualties of terrorism.

Before Frankie left the NICU on Christmas Day she stopped by the nurses' station to drop off some Zabar's holiday cookies.

"Thank you, Dr. Weissman." Juan, the gay nurse wearing a Santa hat behind the desk, got up to kiss her. "Merry Christmas."

"You, too, Juan. Merry Christmas." He was, in fact, one of her favorites.

"Got any hot plans for today?" Juan asked.

"I've got a few patients to see here and then I might visit my dad. Guess that doesn't sound too hot, does it?"

"Well, if you're not doing anything later, I'm going clubbing with most of the babies here."

"Really!" Frankie recognized the NICU sense of humor and went along with it.

"Oh sure, we're hitting my favorite bar, Hell, and then I thought a place I know in the East Village called 'Cock.'"

Frankie laughed out loud. "Oh, the parents will like that."

"Yes, and I think Dr. Borstman in particular will like that."

Suddenly the heart-monitor bells on the Jiménez baby began beeping. Juan stood up and took Frankie's hand. "Dr. Weissman, you know I don't like to quote Judy Garland, but 'have yourself a merry little Christmas.'"

"Thank you, Juan, thank you. You, too." She squeezed his hand. The lights from all the incubator heart monitors were twinkling alongside the holiday ones. Frankie felt a tear welling in her eye. She hated when she became sentimental. She thought her professionally trained distance had cured her of that. But what the hell, it was Christmas.

As long as Frankie could remember, Christmas in New York was generally unseasonably mild with a misty autumn rain. As she walked down Madison Avenue from the hospital she tried to recall if the enormous red velvet bows draping the streetlights had been there when she was in high school. Of course she remembered the Christmas trees dotting Park Avenue, and, oddly enough, the garland winding around the staircase at the Colony Club where Samantha Acton's mother invited their entire ninth-grade class for a holiday party.

Before Frankie moved into Manhattan, she had hardly noticed Christmas. She certainly never had a tree in her childhood home in Queens, and her father took the family to Miami for the holidays. Passing by a Madison Avenue window display of white Christmas bikinis, Frankie flashed back to her father standing on Miami Beach at sunset on Christmas Eve, flapping his arms like a seagull so the birds would make a massive formation. Every holiday Frankie's mother would say, "Abraham, people are watching." And he would answer, "That's nice! Maybe they should join me."

Ever since her breakup with Jack, Frankie had taken herself to the movies after completing her hospital rounds on Christmas Day. Generally it was to an obscure foreign film so she couldn't be counted as part of a Hollywood holiday blockbuster trend. But today she didn't have any interest in finding one. Jil had mentioned that although Samantha had invited him to join her and Charlie in Palm Beach, he was staying in New York and having a little dinner with private clients at the Carlyle. He asked Frankie to come along. But the thought of those private clients with their pulled faces in holiday Oscar de la Renta with emerald wreath pins made her regretfully decline.

After walking a few feet past her father's apartment house, Frankie hailed a taxi and resolved to spend the rest of the day, barring an emergency, at home with her cat. But as soon as she got in the cab Frankie opened the door again and said, "I'm terribly sorry. I left something upstairs." She got out and turned back toward her childhood home.

"Merry Christmas, Frankie." Abraham's doorman called her by the nickname her father still used. "Here to see the folks?"

"Yes," she nodded. "Merry Christmas." Sometimes Frankie wished the doormen she had grown up with were still there. But then she would catch herself and think she was like those blue-haired dowagers who still lamented the loss of Rumpelmeyer's, Longchamps, and Schrafft's.

"I have an idea. Let's go to Florida for New Year's," Frankie energetically announced to her father and Helen in their living room. She had spontaneously come up with the idea in the elevator.

"I won't go to Miami." Helen sat on a divan with her pinkie up. "People like Puff Daddy go there now."

"His name is P. Diddy," Frankie corrected her.

"What?" Helen didn't like not having all the answers.

"Never mind. What about Palm Beach? We could find a nurse at The Breakers to take care of Dad. And Helen, you could have a real rest."

"I don't like nurses. They just watch *The Price Is Right*." Helen shook her head.

"We'll find one who doesn't watch *The Price Is Right*. We'll find one who watches *Wheel of Fortune*." Seeing her father's unanimated glare, Frankie was convinced she was doing the right thing. She had to liberate him from this overheated apartment. "C'mon, Helen, it'll be fun. My friend Samantha Acton will be there."

"You know Samantha Acton?" Helen was impressed. "I read about her all the time in Liz Smith."

"Yes, she's an old and good friend of mine." Frankie took her father's hand. She was banking on the Fashionable Mrs. to sway the vote.

"Is she a patient?" Helen asked.

"No, she doesn't have children."

"That's terrible such a beautiful girl doesn't have children. It's a crime."

"Yes, Helen. All women who don't have children should be arrested."

"I didn't say that." Helen was abrupt.

"All right. All *beautiful* women who don't have children should be arrested." Frankie smiled at her. She still relished her ability to trump Helen at her own game.

"Are you playing Ping-Pong with me?" Helen laughed. She often referred to their verbal spats as Ping-Pong.

"I just want to know if we're going to Florida."

"Is it cold at night in Palm Beach?" Helen asked. "Because I don't have any of those light knits. But I do have the pashmina shawl I got for nothing in Chinatown. They cost a fortune at Bendel's. I can wear that with my yellow mohair pantsuit."

"I have the same exact pink ostrich flats in my closet," Helen commented to Frankie while inspecting the Giorgio window in The Breakers lobby. "I got them at the Concord years ago when I was there for my niece's bat mitzvah. At the time it was a very exclusive hotel and that's where my sister became such good friends with Steve Lawrence and Eydie Gormé."

"Oh." Frankie nodded as if this were new information from the Helen canon. In fact, Helen mentioned her sister's friendship with the singers of "Cheek to Cheek" whenever possible.

Helen opened the lobby door into the shop. "I always said to Natalie, if you keep your things nicely they'll always come back in fashion, but if you throw them around like garbage they will become garbage."

Frankie was caught off guard by the mention of Natalie, Helen's daughter who hadn't spoken to her mother in over thirty years. She was ten years older than Frankie and already out of the house when Abraham and Helen married. Supposedly, she dropped out of Cornell to join a commune in Geneva, New York. Over the years it was rumored she had evolved into a New Age pig farmer.

"What's the matter?" Helen asked Frankie as she slipped on a size 6 Clementine display shoe.

"Nothing, I'm just having a nice time. I'm so glad we're here," Frankie answered truthfully. She had managed to convince Helen to let her hire a nurse for Abraham who was recommended by the hotel. A large and very sunny southern blonde woman called Miss Gee, short apparently for Gee Gee, had appeared at their suite an hour ago. Frankie was hoping that Miss Gee would be such a resounding success that she could persuade Helen to hire a regular nurse in New York, too.

"I don't think I really need anything." Helen looked up at the saleswoman after having tried on at least twenty pairs of flats. "Do you need anything, Frankie?"

"No thanks, I'm fine."

"Let's go upstairs and check on your father. I'm sure he's missing me," Helen confided to the tired saleswoman. "I can't even go to the bathroom anymore without him missing me."

When Helen opened the door to the suite Abraham was sitting on the couch watching the local Palm Beach news. Miss Gee had seen to it that he was bathed, shaven, and wearing the Breakers insignia terry cloth robe. Abraham was grinning while Miss Gee stroked his hair.

"I think they're having sex!" Helen whispered to Frankie.

"Helen, they're not having sex!" Frankie wasn't certain whether to take her seriously. What she did know, however, was that her father hadn't looked so good in months. He had the pampered glow of a patriarchal Rockefeller with his faithful nurse. He was radiant, though he didn't say a word.

Helen gave Frankie a little shove. "Do you think I should ask if they would like a three-way?"

At that moment Miss Gee smiled at Helen while still stroking Abraham's hair. "He's such a honey."

The next day Miss Gee was gone.

Abraham had begun forgetting whether he had already eaten or not. Around an hour after lunch he turned to Frankie at their cabana and insisted that he hadn't eaten all day.

"They're starving me!" he bellowed after a morning of complete silence.

"Who's starving you, Dad?" Frankie asked gently.

"You know. They are. The ones in charge." When Abraham mentioned "the ones in charge" he was usually referring to Helen, but at other times it could be his doctor or a hospital nurse.

"Dad, do you want to get some fruit?"

"Yes, fruit." Abraham seemed ecstatic. "Fruit. That's nice."

Frankie took her father's arm and helped him up from his chair. They began to walk to the snack shack on the beach. A week before Christmas Abraham had been diagnosed with Pick's disease, a form of Alzheimer's in the temporal and frontal lobes of the brain. A neurologist who specialized in memory-related dementia told Frankie there was no possible way to reverse her father's losing his ability to talk altogether. Medicine could only ease the anxiety of the situation. In other words, with the right prescription cocktail, Abraham could happily forget what he was forgetting.

"You live here?" Abraham asked her after they had ordered at a beachside table.

"No, Dad, I live in New York on West Eighty-first Street and Columbus Avenue."

"Don't let them take advantage of you. Those sons of bitches hike up the rents."

"I know that, Dad. Thank you."

The waiter arrived with a tropical fruit plate. Abraham devoured every pineapple, mango, and watermelon slice in sight. "Delicious! Delicious! Do you want one?" He offered a berry to Frankie.

"No, Dad. I'm fine." She looked up and noticed skywriting. "Dad, do you remember being on the beach when a plane scribbled in the clouds 'Nixon's the One' and you said, 'Don't believe everything you read'?"

Abraham stared at her blankly. "Who's Nixon?"

"Dr. Weissman? Dr. Weissman? I thought that was you!" Frankie bounced back from her childhood reverie to see Adrienne Strong-Rodman in a Miu Miu bikini and sarong charging toward her.

"She's very intelligent." Abraham was distracted from his remaining papaya. "Is she a movie star?"

Adrienne embraced Frankie. "I hope it's all right to kiss you, we're on holiday." Adrienne had the Teflon reflex of all Hollywood success stories. Whatever distasteful incidents happened a month or five minutes ago were all forgotten because you never knew when somebody might be exactly who you were looking for.

"Are you at this hotel?" Frankie asked.

"No, we're on Paul's yacht. I just came ashore to pick up a few things in town. The Hermès here has things they just don't carry in New York. Look at this bag." She modeled a canvas Birkin. "Isn't it fabulous?"

"I like it, I like it!" Abraham nodded his head.

"Adrienne, this is my father."

"Oh my God. He's adorable."

Abraham stood up. "Do you want to dance?"

"Dad, that's okay." Frankie put her hand on his arm to keep him seated.

But Abraham was suddenly humming "Pennies from Heaven." He grabbed Adrienne's hand and began twirling her.

"Dad, stop!" Frankie tried to cut it short but Adrienne wouldn't hear of it.

"Mr. Weissman, I can tell your daughter gets her bedside manner from you."

"Every time it rains, it rains / Pennies from heaven." Abraham began repeating the first line of the melody until Adrienne pulled away.

"Well, I've got a personal shopper waiting for me at Hermès, and you know how irritable the French are. But Frankie, if you're not doing anything tonight, we're having a few pals on the boat and it would be so fabulous if you came. We never get to spend enough time together. And also, Jessica has this rash that won't go away. Usually Paul and I never travel without our GP, but he's with the Chens this holiday, and I'm not sending my daughter to some Florida doctor I don't know."

"Thank you." Frankie was almost stunned by the circuitous nature of the invitation. "I'm probably busy with my dad."

"Oh honey, you don't have to worry about him. He's a real player! If you change your mind we've got a little puff-puff bringing our guests back and forth. Just go down to our dock. And you don't have to bring your medical equipment—we have everything you'll need.

Bye, handsome." Adrienne gave Abraham a big kiss on the lips and clomped away.

"Nice girl." Abraham watched as she left and then blurted, "Where the hell is the goddamn waiter? I'm starving!"

"Look, Dad, here comes Helen." Frankie tried to divert his attention from eating again.

"I was looking for you everywhere." Helen sat down at the table.

"How was your massage?" Frankie asked her.

"Not as good as my Korean girl in New York and twice as expensive!" Helen grabbed the remaining papaya slice out of Abraham's hand. "Frankie, he shouldn't be eating."

"He was hungry," Frankie replied.

"He doesn't know when he's hungry. You shouldn't listen to him." He turned to Helen. "Dear, I've had nothing to eat all day."

"Stop it, Abraham! Just stop it!" Helen suddenly shouted at him.

"Please don't yell at him," Frankie cut her off.

"You think this is easy? It's not easy." Helen's voice broke.

"Helen, I don't think it's easy. I just think you should have kept Miss Gee to help you."

"Oh please, I know these fat blonde women." Helen pulled herself together. "They're the kind who marry sick men with no prenuptial agreement."

"But Dad is married to you."

"Frankie, you went to Princeton and Harvard. Didn't they teach you anything? That fat nurse doesn't care who he's married to. She was moving in."

Anticipating another dinner with Abraham and Helen, Frankie decided to accept the invitation to Adrienne Strong-Rodman's yacht. As much as she knew that she had only been invited to examine Jessica's rash, she liked the idea of being separated for an evening from her life on shore by a substantial body of water.

CHAPTER TEN

Barry

"Christmas we usually sail from Tortola to Mustique. But this year Paul insisted we stay in the States. Personally, I like to be with the St. Barths crowd at New Year's, but Paul prefers Mustique. He'd rather be with a Brit aristo than anyone really interesting," Adrienne Strong-Rodman explained to her old friend Shelly Landon as her breasts heaved up and down in her skintight gold lamé Versace slip dress.

"Isn't Mustique where Princess Margaret lived?" Shelly asked as she looked back at the coastline of Palm Beach. Her husband, Mark, the former chairman of two movie studios, had just left her for his twenty-six-year-old acupuncturist. Shelly felt at ease for the first time in months on Adrienne's yacht.

"Yes, Princess Margaret and Mick Jagger have homes there." Adrienne wanted her friend to get the full picture. "The way Paul sees it, if you look at the Caribbean Islands as Manhattan, then Anguilla is the Upper East Side, Mustique is the new Time Warner Center, a superexpensive development, and St. Barths is Greenwich Village— it's just a little more downtown, a little more with it, and a little more 'caj.'" Adrienne was now in the process of trying to make her entire life more "caj," or casual, but she was having difficulty just letting go.

In fact, she was gearing herself up to do a little producing next summer. Adrienne saw herself as the red-hot center, and to stay in the red-hot center she didn't mind working now and then. Also she never liked the idea that other women were now having her career. Adrienne was raised to want it all.

A waiter in a lamé micro bikini and a matching gold conquistador helmet passed by with a three-tiered raw bar tray.

"No thank you," both women said simultaneously.

"I'd like something raw, but it isn't a clam." Adrienne ogled the waiter as he walked away.

"Where did you find these waiters? They don't even look this good at the Equinox gym in West Hollywood." Shelly lit a cigarette. She had cut caffeine, alcohol, carbohydrates, wheat, and dairy out of her life, but cigarettes were her one remaining treat.

"The waiters are mostly from the Miami Ballet." Adrienne smiled. "We pay them up the wazoo. Believe me, they don't make this kind of cash doing pirouettes."

"Adrienne! Adrienne!" Paul Rodman walked over to them. For a man who prided himself on his worldwide influence, he was surprisingly inconspicuous-looking. "Adrienne, my mother says there's nothing for her to eat here."

"Paul, your mother's insane!" Adrienne's voice changed completely. "There's half a million dollars' worth of raw food on this boat."

"She doesn't want raw. She wants it cooked."

"Then tell her to get in a rowboat and go to the Burger King in West Palm Beach." Adrienne blurted out the "Beach."

"I told you not to talk that way about my mother."

"I told you not to invite her."

"Shut up, Adrienne." Paul took her wrist while a helmeted waiter walked by with a tray of sushi spread out on gold doubloons.

"Tuna belly with horseradish sushi, Mr. Rodman?"

"Get that stuff away from me. It smells." The host turned around.

"Of course, Mr. Rodman." The waiter walked silently away, using his best Miami Ballet port de bras.

"Adrienne, why can't we have normal waiters? Why are they naked?"

"You said you wanted something festive. This is festive, Paul." Adrienne was now shouting as if her husband were a caterer who had refused to deliver.

Just then Paul noticed Samantha Acton arriving on the boat with Judy. "Adrienne, how did you get Samantha Acton to come to this party?" Paul asked admiringly.

"Is she here?" Adrienne turned around.

"You must have invited her, honey." He patted her on her rear.

"I don't even know her, but she probably heard about the waiters or that we're throwing your mother overboard."

Paul suddenly laughed uproariously. "C'mere, you."

"You're a pig." Adrienne snorted.

"Honey, I saw a bracelet in the window at Bulgari yesterday. I was thinking you should take a look at it." Paul took her hand.

"Let me just say it better take up a lot of space 'cause you've got a lot of making up to do. And tell your mother next holiday she can stay in the Bronx where she came from." She reached her hand toward his pants and grabbed him.

"Yes, dear." Paul was suddenly aroused.

"And by the way, when I stop in at Bulgari tomorrow there's also a ring I need from Buccellati." She continued to stroke him.

"Anything you want, honey."

Adrienne pulled her hand away. "C'mon, Shelly, I think Stevie Wonder is here."

"He is?" Shelly asked.

"Well, Sting wasn't available."

"My wife can do anything." Paul patted Adrienne on the rear again and walked away.

"How did you get Stevie Wonder?" Shelly asked. "I'm just curious."

"Beats me, babe."

"I thought you put this together."

"Are you kidding? I hired an events co-coordinator. I can't waste my time calling singers. I did that in my twenties. C'mon, let's go say hello to Samantha Acton."

"I'm dying to meet that handsome husband of hers. In fact, maybe if I had met him earlier Mark would have never left me."

"I can't believe Samantha's with Judy Tremont," Adrienne said.

"Who's Judy Tremont?"

"One of those women who just shops and exercises. We gave her a ride here. Shelly, I honestly thank God every day that I've got more in my life than just that." Adrienne waved and walked over to greet her guests. "Judy! So glad you could make it!"

Adrienne didn't know half the people on her yacht and she didn't particularly care. There were Paul's friends, investment bankers, CEOs, and familiar names in real estate like Rudin or Trump. But personally she preferred her old Hollywood pals—the ICM agents, the studio execs and television producers. Paul didn't mind the Hollywood people keeping Adrienne up to date. For example, it was fine with Paul if Adrienne wanted to have Barry Santorini on his boat as long as he didn't offer her a full-time position. But real society stars like Samantha Acton were not really among either of their acquaintance. As far as Paul was concerned, she lifted the party to another level.

"Judy!" Adrienne embraced Judy's size 2 ice blue Pucci shift. "You look absolutely gorgeous!"

And then came the moment Judy couldn't believe was happening in her own lifetime. She heard herself say, "Adrienne, do you know my friend Samantha Acton?"

Adrienne extended her hand, "I'm sure our paths have crossed. I'm so happy you're here. Are you in Palm Beach for the holidays?"

"Yes, we're at The Breakers," Judy rushed to answer.

Adrienne was stunned that they were spending the holidays together. Maybe she had underestimated Judy.

"This is my friend Shelly Landon."

"Yes, hello." Shelly smiled at Samantha. "I admire your husband."

Samantha was too discreet to ask if she admired Charlie personally or dermatologically.

"Is that Frankie Weissman over there talking to Tina Schultz?" Judy almost shrieked. "I certainly didn't expect to see her here."

"Oh, I love Tina. She has so much style," Adrienne answered quickly.

"I meant Dr. Weissman. You told me you were leaving her practice. You told me you hated going up to her office in East Harlem."

"Actually, I solved the Dr. Weissman problem. I got Paul to throw some serious money at her favorite public school health care center," Adrienne announced with pride. "And now she never keeps me waiting. I mean, what the hell is the money for? That's one of the first things you learn in Hollywood."

Samantha turned her head as Adrienne continued to talk. She found women like Adrienne Strong-Rodman insufferable. Under the Buccellati, the Bulgari, and the Botox, women like Adrienne were never particularly attractive or, for that matter, interesting. She was overkill, just like her three names. Samantha thought women like Adrienne used their sexuality with a manipulative cunning, similar to their husbands' dealmaking. In Samantha's eye, Adrienne Rodman symbolized the worst of new money. Unlike Judy Tremont, who had obvious naïve aspiration, Adrienne was merely hard and entitled.

"Pardon me, Adrienne. I think I'll go say hello to Frankie. I'm very fond of her." Samantha politely escaped her host.

"Oh yes, I'm very fond of her, too." Judy immediately tagged along behind her.

As soon as Frankie had arrived on the boat, Adrienne insisted that she find Jessica and treat that persistent rash. When Frankie located Jessica in the map room with her head in the lap of Shelly's fourteen-year-old son, she didn't mention that the cause of the rash could become chronic.

"Frankie, I'm so happy to see you." Samantha kissed both of her cheeks. "You know Judy Tremont."

"Yes, of course." Frankie shook Judy's hand and turned back to Samantha. "Jil told me you were in Palm Beach."

"Who? Who?" Judy didn't want Frankie to usurp the conversation. Samantha was her new best friend tonight and she would not permit this dreary interloper to come between them. She didn't care how smart Frankie Weissman was supposed to be. She was still wearing some black boxy Dana Buchman career skirt on a festive night in Florida. Black on a yacht was, as far as Judy was concerned, only appropriate for pirates.

"Jil Taillou is our art dealer," Samantha explained. "He used to work at Sotheby's."

"He's a lovely man." Frankie smiled.

"Oh, I love Jil." Judy beamed. Now she remembered she'd heard he was everyone's new favorite walker, the social euphemism for a delightful gentleman escort, who by and large was a little "light" in his Tod's loafers.

The strains of Stevie Wonder singing "My Cherie Amour" began wafting over the boat. Judy looked at the full moon reflected on the ocean and began to sway. "My cherie amour, pretty little one that I adore / You're the only girl my heart beats for / How I wish that you were mine." Standing beside Samantha with Stevie Wonder singing in the middle of the Atlantic, Judy felt an almost overwhelming rush of utter bliss. Samantha Acton would have to come to one of her dinner parties. After all, she had gotten her on Paul Rodman's yacht. Judy closed her eyes and imagined her seating chart. She had been told of such physical and mental harmony in her Ashtanga yoga class but she herself had never experienced it before.

At the moment of Judy's nirvana Barry Santorini first saw Samantha Acton.

"Who the fuck is that?" he asked Adrienne as soon as he walked on the ship.

"Which one?"

"The drop-dead gorgeous one. The classy one. The one who's hot as hell."

"Everyone on our boat is classy. Everyone on this boat is hot as hell. Are you talking about me, Barry?" Adrienne slipped her hand on his leg.

"Don't fuck around with me, Adrienne. Who is that?" he said, pointing directly to Samantha.

"That's Dr. Francesca Weissman, our pediatrician."

"Adrienne, I know who the hell Frankie Weissman is, she's my kids' doctor. You think she's hot as hell? No wonder you don't work in Hollywood anymore. I'm going over to say hello."

"I'll introduce you." Adrienne walked beside him.

"Don't do me any favors. I can do my own reconnaissance."

"Barry, where's Clarice and the kids?"

"What are you, my mother?"

"No, but Paul's mother is downstairs. Want to help me drown her?" Adrienne laughed.

"Clarice is back on our boat with the kids. She's got a stomachache tonight."

"I'm sorry." Adrienne acted suitably concerned.

"Me too. I like family vacations. It's great to be with her and the kids. There's nothing like family. Excuse me, Adrienne."

Barry walked right up to Frankie, Judy, and Samantha. He ignored the others, and looked Samantha directly in the eye.

"Hi. Barry Santorini. Want to dance?"

Samantha knew exactly who he was, and perhaps because of her husband immediately noticed his pockmarked skin.

"Do you know my friends Frankie Weissman and Judy Tremont?" she diverted him.

"Dr. Weissman. I'll tell Clarice you're here. She and Brooke have a stomach thing." He kept his eye on Samantha the entire time. "Maybe you should come over and see them."

"I'm afraid I'm not on call," Frankie answered.

Judy piped in. "I'm friends with Clarice, too. I'm sorry she's not feeling well. She's such a wonderful mother."

Barry didn't even respond. He wasn't going to waste his time listening to Frankie Weissman or Judy Whoever-she-was. He was a man who prided himself on trusting his instincts, and his instinct was you couldn't get any classier than this Samantha Acton. Looking at her in the moonlight, he decided to move on her with the same won't-take-no-for-an-answer mentality needed to sign an A-list movie star.

"C'mon, let's dance." He took Samantha's hand. "Anyone ever tell you you're Grace Kelly, Jackie Kennedy, and Catherine Deneuve all wrapped up in one?"

"No, anyone ever tell you that?" She rolled her lip.

"Hey, just dance with me and I'll die a happy man." He put his hand on her waist and pulled her toward him. Unlike Charlie, there was nothing gentlemanly about Barry. There was absolutely no way that he was ever rejected from the Ivy.

"*Så drikk hverandre,*" she whispered in his ear.

"What the fuck is that?"

"Old Norse for 'Let's drink together.'"

"Old what?"

"Norse. You know, Vikings."

"Right. Ingmar Bergman. He makes great movies. Let's dance."

Barry led her to the dance floor. Watching them, Judy whispered to Frankie, "I think he's revolting, but I would never have married Charlie either. He's bright but he comes from nothing."

As Stevie Wonder sang "You Are the Sunshine of My Life," Barry pulled Samantha toward him. She had no intention of not going home to Charlie that night. But as they danced, she felt a thaw from her face to her ankles. She had been so distant from herself for so long that the closer her body was to Barry, the closer she felt to her distant sensuality.

Samantha's and Barry's bodies remained one until they were alone on the dance floor. Long after Stevie Wonder had stopped singing, Barry held her face in his hands.

"My cherie amour, how I wish that you were mine."

CHAPTER ELEVEN

Judy

When Judy's book club read *The Age of Innocence* she became fascinated by the details of May Welland's dinner party. If Judy thought
she could get away with it, she would have silver candelabras adorn-
ing the center of her table just like May. She envied the formal place
settings of the previous century and the attention given to family
porcelains and finger bowls. Every year, just around the time of her
birthday, Judy would look through James Robinson, the famed antique silver shop, and have a serious treasure set aside for Albert to
present to her.

Theoretically, Judy knew that advances for women were a good
thing, but secretly, she thought she might have been happier in May
Welland's century. She wasn't particularly interested in late twentieth-
century social advances like sexual liberation, although she would
happily say that many of her favorite people were gay, simply because
they had the best taste. Judy had no doubt that she was in favor of
elitism because she was in favor of a beautifully ordered universe.
Her recent interest in contemporary art was a concerted attempt
to catapult herself into the twenty-first century. But in all honesty,
she'd admit to friends she'd rather have a family silversmith than a
washer/dryer.

Judy's personal assistant, Eileen, made most of her appointments and social calls unless they were a top priority.

"Anyone call?" Judy stuck her head into Eileen's office after her Pilates teacher left.

"Everything's under control." Eileen smiled from her swivel chair in the former nursery. Of all the personal assistants she'd had over the years, Judy preferred Eileen. She was married to a painter and had two teenage sons and needed the weekly paycheck. Every year, Eileen signed a confidentiality agreement, and every year, when she threatened to quit for one reason or another, Albert gave her an attractive bonus.

"Mrs. Tremont, do you want me to send out the invitations for the February dinner today?"

"Wait till tomorrow. I need to make a few calls first." Judy hunched over Eileen's desk. "I see you have Charlotte signed up for tap dancing there. I thought I told you to cancel tap dancing. Charlotte wants to play tennis instead. Also, Adrienne Strong-Rodman says there's this fabulous woman who will come to the house to teach the kids piano in Italian. But tell whoever it is I do not allow pizza or pasta in the house and I don't want them babbling about them either."

"Yes, Mrs. Tremont. Of course, Mrs. Tremont." Eileen nodded. Although she was the same age as Judy and a Smith College graduate, Eileen never addressed her by her first name. Eileen had read far more Edith Wharton than her employer, but she had the professional discretion never to mention it.

Judy left the room with a sense of determination. She had painstakingly waited two weeks after she left Palm Beach to call Samantha for dinner. She applied the same abstemious discipline she'd mastered in dieting in order not to place the call. Calling too soon would make her seem pushy or worse, a real climber. But today she gave herself permission to go for it.

"Hello, Samantha." Judy was almost shocked when Samantha and not her version of Eileen answered the phone.

"Yes?" Samantha did not remember her voice.

"This is Judy Tremont. How *are* you?" Judy had taken up emphasizing the "are's" so the question had more poignance than just a social pleasantry.

"I'm just fine," Samantha answered.

"My God, you actually answer your own phone!" Judy relayed her astonishment.

"My assistant is a grad student at NYU. She's at a seminar today."

"Oh, I love grad students." Judy couldn't believe her phone karma had worked out on the first try. "But they are completely unreliable. I mean, in the long run, I don't need someone who knows when *The Last Supper* was painted. I want someone who's happy to change my appointment at Frédéric Fekkai."

Samantha giggled.

"I am having a little dinner party on February 15th to get rid of the winter blahs. And I've invited Clarice and Barry Santorini and I was hoping you could come. They are so fun!"

"I don't know him very well, but she seems lovely." Samantha felt uncharacteristically anxious.

"So you'll come!" Judy's voice almost vibrated through the telephone.

"I'll have to ask Charlie about it. I'm assuming he's invited, too."

"Oh, oh Albert just adores Charlie. Adores him!"

"I will let you know. Nice talking to you." Samantha hung up and looked in her calendar. Charlie would say yes if she asked him, but it probably wasn't worth the effort. As for Barry Santorini, she didn't like how much she'd been thinking about him since the night on the yacht. At her last board meeting at the Whitney, while Grey Navez was talking about one thing or another, Samantha drifted off to remembering Barry's leg pressing against her thigh when they danced together. She had pretty much made up her mind to avoid him if possible.

As soon as Judy hung up with Samantha, she dialed Clarice.

"Santorini residence," the housekeeper answered the phone.

"Oh, hi there. This is Judy Tremont. May I speak with Mrs. Santorini?"

"Just a moment. I'll see if I can patch you through." The housekeeper put the phone on hold and reached Clarice on her cell phone.

"There's a Mrs. Judy Tremont on the phone for you."

Clarice was on the corner of Ninety-first and Madison on her way to a Spence board meeting. She assumed the call had something to do with Albert Tremont's attendance at the meeting.

"I'll take it, Gorgia. You can put her through." Clarice waited to hear a few beeps before speaking. "Hello, this is Clarice."

"Hello, how *are* you?" Judy was in business. "Albert and I are having a little dinner for Samantha Acton on February 15th and we would just adore for you to come."

"Thank you so much. I don't know Samantha very well, but I know Pippa Rose thinks the world of her." Clarice began to cross the street. "I'm actually on my way to school right now. I know Barry's shooting a picture in Shanghai in February so most likely he won't get there. But if my calendar is free I would love to. Thanks so much. Bye."

Judy scratched her chin. Judging from what had been happening under the stars on the Rodman yacht, Judy knew that Barry would fly in from Shanghai or from Neptune to get to her house to see Samantha again.

It was only 11 a.m. but Judy felt she had already done a full day's worth of work. She buzzed Eileen. "You can send out the dinner invitations now." Judy had already made the first-tier list for Eileen. She'd have Grey Navez and Tina Schultz, whom she was dying to get to her house. Adrienne and Paul and, of course, Dr. Arnie Berkowitz.

Dr. Arnie was a frequent guest on *Charlie Rose,* so perhaps he could persuade Charlie to come. And for sparkle Judy thought she'd sprinkle the table with a few artists. After all, Samantha was on the board of the Whitney, and Albert had just made a substantial donation to the Modern. Maybe even Brice Marden would come. Or at least it was worth a try. "And Eileen, I changed my mind about Francesca Weissman. You can include her, too."

Judy had debated having Dr. Weissman at the party. But the truth was, with that many glamour hard-hitters, you needed someone a little dowdy to take the edge off. Plus, Samantha seemed to genuinely like Frankie Weissman, and this was, after all, a dinner for her. Also, she had heard Frankie Weissman had become chummy with Jil Taillou, and having her there was one way to get him to accept.

There was a knock at the door, and Tina arrived in the room with a silver tray.

"Your snack, Mrs. Tremont."

"Thank you." Judy smiled as Tina put a silver tray in front of her.

Judy sat back and munched on her favorite midmorning pick-me-up—four soybeans, for protein, and a chocolate chip, for fun.

Although Judy had enormous energy, for a moment she felt truly drained. When she was an editor at *Mademoiselle* she dreamed of being one of the perfectly toned Upper East Side mothers picking up their children in chauffeured SUVs. But what she didn't realize then was that keeping it all together and doing it absolutely right took enormous concentration and discipline. Some days she even secretly envied women who worked. It might just be easier.

CHAPTER TWELVE

Charlie

Clarice found Charlie Acton's office surprisingly soothing. In fact, she was even a little ashamed of herself for having had so much anxiety before getting there in the first place. Both the walls and the furniture were a soothing pale white, and if Clarice hadn't known better, she'd have thought she was in the waiting room of one of the better ladies' spas. Although she immediately recognized both Adrienne Strong-Rodman and Grey Navez sitting across from her in saucer-sized Chanel sunglasses, she certainly felt no compunction in invading their space.

"Mrs. Santorini, Dr. Acton will see you now." A pleasant older nurse came into the room. As Clarice got up, she saw Adrienne and Grey simultaneously flick their glasses and then return to their magazines.

Charlie walked into the examining room wearing his office uniform—a white coat and suede-covered wooden clogs.

"Mrs. Santorini, Charlie Acton. What can I do for you today?" He shook her hand.

"I'm not exactly sure. I thought you could tell me." She smiled at him.

"Are you suffering from any skin irritation or have you noticed any new markings or moles?" Charlie always began his questioning as if his new patient had come to him with a genuine medical problem and not for elective reasons.

"Oh, I just wanted a second opinion. I've been getting Botox for the past five years from my internist for the lines on my forehead, but I'm wondering if it's time to face the music and go for the complete lift. I understand the earlier you start the better. At least my mother says that's why Barbara Walters looks so good." Clarice knew she was trying to sound in the know.

Charlie looked at the attractive forty-something-year-old woman with the gleaming dark hair in his chair. She certainly could get by as she was. Anywhere but New York or Los Angeles, she'd be considered a middle-aged homecoming queen. Though she wasn't particularly sexy, she had the affluent appeal of being very well-groomed and her features still reflected her Italian ancestry. These days, Charlie seldom came across a nose that betrayed any ethnicity, and he felt almost protective of his patients and their cartilage that did.

"Well, I'll tell you what, Mrs. Santorini." He leaned against the wall, taking a well-practiced chummy yet professional stance.

"You can call me Clarice."

"Okay, Clarice. I am not a plastic surgeon. Of course, if you like, I can recommend some people whom I trust. But I can tell you that we can certainly try something a little more natural than either surgery or Botox. I like to plump up the skin with your own fat cells. We remove it from places where you won't miss it and store it here in our refrigerator for whenever you need a touch-up."

"You really think I can get away with just that?" Clarice had no desire to turn herself into a plastic-surgery junkie like that famous

East Side woman who had so many catlike lifts she was nicknamed the Lion Queen. But she wanted to keep Barry and her kids happy. And in order to do that, Clarice believed she had to keep up with the refreshed appearance of all the other East Side mothers.

"Hey, I think you look great. Here's all I would propose we do." Charlie took out a red Magic Marker and began drawing on an outline of a female face as if it were from a children's coloring book.

"I would like to start with a face peel to take the gray hues from here, here, and here." Charlie drew arrows under her eyes, around the lips. "The peel will make you look like a corned beef for five days, but after that your age spots, freckles, and any dark material will disappear. And then we can discuss some maintenance options."

"When do I need to do this? My calendar is very full right now. My daughter Brooke is taking Suzuki violin." All the serenity of the waiting room had passed from Clarice's psyche.

"As I said before, honestly Clarice, you don't need to do anything. I'm just presenting you with some healthy options. Perhaps you want to talk this over with your husband."

"Oh no, my husband's very busy. I can't bother him with this. Do you know what I mean?"

"Yes, of course. I admire your husband's films. Thank heavens for him or there really would just be junk out there." Charlie repeated what he had frequently read.

"He doesn't even know I'm here," Clarice confided. "He thinks all my friends spend too much time on their appearance, but he really notices when anyone lets themselves go. He'd absolutely kill me if I looked like a corned beef for five days."

"What about a pastrami?" Charlie quipped. It was a quip he had mastered on at least a hundred patients. Personally, he didn't find it very funny, but it seemed to cut through the tension. "Tell you what. Why don't I call in my nurse and she can take your history and we can go from there. This way at least you can make a more responsible decision."

"I know this is silly." Clarice was embarrassed by the question that popped into her head but she had to ask it. "I recognized some people in your waiting room. Will they see my fat in your refrigerator? I know my husband wouldn't appreciate that."

"I promise you only my nurse and I know what's in there."

"I'm sorry. This is just so different from going to, say, the pediatrician." Clarice tried to cover her embarrassment. "At Dr. Weissman's, everybody shares information."

"Is Francesca Weissman your pediatrician?" Charlie seemed genuinely interested. "She's the best! Old friend of mine from Princeton. My wife really likes her, also."

"I only met your wife once but she seems like such a lovely person."

"Yes. I guess you and I share being very lucky with our spouses. Believe me, that's not the story you always hear in here." Charlie put his arm around Clarice as a signal for her to get out of the chair. "Let's take this one step at a time. Does that sound good to you?"

"That sounds great." Clarice began walking to the door with him. "Thank you so much, Dr. Acton. I really appreciate your seeing me."

Charlie pressed a call button on his wall phone. "Viola, would you please take Mrs. Santorini for a complete history, and I'll be there shortly."

The nurse appeared at the door momentarily. "This way, Mrs. Santorini. The first room down the hall." After Clarice left the room, the nurse turned back to Charlie. "Mrs. Rodman is waiting in room two."

"Thank you, Viola." Charlie nodded at her and headed back into his office. He knew he couldn't deal with another patient, particularly Mrs. Rodman, unless he took a break. Charlie put his headphones on and flipped through the playlist on his iPod, a large collection of modern masters like Satie, Cage, the Rolling Stones, the Grateful Dead, and the Band.

Charlie settled on the Rolling Stones' "You Can't Always Get What You Want," and started singing along. He knew Samantha said he should make an effort to listen to hip-hop or even U2, and he should also wear something a little less retro than clogs. But these were his ten minutes in the day, and goddammit, he was going to do and wear what made him feel good.

When strutting with Mick had replenished Charlie's energy, his mind drifted to how different his life was from his dad's in Omaha. Charlie's father had a reputation throughout Nebraska for being a very good doctor and a very generous man. He didn't bother charging those people he knew couldn't afford to pay—farmers down on their luck and disenfranchised Native Americans. When Charlie's father died of a heart attack at fifty-three during Charlie's sophomore year of college, he left a lot of goodwill and very little money. Subsequently, Charlie joined ROTC not out of patriotism but out of a real need to pay his college and medical school tuition.

Throughout his undergraduate years, Charlie was almost in awe of what he called "the polished people"—his classmates who had the time and the money to take six weeks to teach in a rural Mississippi school and then travel in Europe for the rest of the summer. They were the undergraduates who delighted in shopping at thrift shops because they knew there were two Armani suits hanging in their dorm room closets. Their privilege was not on the surface, but in their understated self-confidence. Charlie knew he was just as bright as any of them. But he feared in the light of day he was not only relatively unpolished, but a little dull.

When Charlie was a resident at a military hospital in Houston his marriage to his first wife, a high school girlfriend, failed. Subsequently, she remarried and moved with their children back to Nebraska. Charlie completed his military commitments and took a teaching job at New York-Presbyterian Hospital on the Upper East Side.

Although he casually dated a number of women, he mostly concentrated on his research. He was convinced that through a serious interdisciplinary study, including physics, literature, and philosophy, he could define the alchemy of aging. He met Samantha Acton when a friend brought her to hear him lecture at the Princeton Club. The topic was "The Dialectic of Time."

Charlie was wary of her at first. She was graceful, sexy, hard-edged, and nobody's fool. Then he recognized that she was wittier than most of the polished people he envied at Princeton and made an eighth of their insouciant effort. Charlie believed that Samantha really didn't need him, and therefore after one date decided that she would be his one true romantic act. What he didn't realize was that Samantha had decided very early on that the healthiest thing she could do would be to will herself to fall in love with Charlie.

When Charlie began seeing Samantha, his work evolved very quickly from aging research to age elimination. Women he sat next to at Samantha's dinner parties began sending their friends to him for consultations. Suddenly Charlie began appearing in women's magazines like *Vogue* and *Harper's Bazaar* as "the next must-see." He endorsed an antiaging skin care line that became the Upper East Side's best-kept secret, sold exclusively at Clyde's Madison Avenue pharmarcy.

"Mrs. Rodman said to tell you she has a dinner at Judy Tremont's tonight." The nurse poked her head into the room. "She also said the dinner's in honor of Samantha, and you obviously can't get there until you see her."

Charlie took off his earphones. "Tell her I'll be right there."

Charlie looked at the picture of Samantha on his desk. He didn't understand why in God's name she would want Judy Flibbertigibbet to give a dinner for her. It just sounded like so much work. But despite his passing irritation, Charlie not only knew they would go, but he actually enjoyed the fact that he and Samantha had become the number one couple in town to throw a dinner party for. And most important, Charlie knew that without Samantha, he would see his life and his work for what it really was.

Charlie picked up the phone to ring his nurse. "Viola, get Mrs. Rodman's butt the heck out of my refrigerator."

CHAPTER THIRTEEN

Frankie

Frankie asked one of her junior associates to cover for her while she accompanied Abraham to his second visit with Dr. Trenton.

"Mr. Weissman, can you tell me the names of some vegetables?" the Mount Sinai specialist in senior dementia asked him.

"Uh, let's see. Peppers, tomatoes, zucchinis, meatballs," Abraham answered.

"Very good." The doctor took a note and continued. "Now, can you repeat this story? The bad king told his wife he would not eat any porridge today."

Abraham stared at him blankly.

"Try to repeat this, Mr. Weissman." The specialist spoke slowly and deliberately. "The bad king told his wife he would not eat any porridge today."

Abraham turned to his daughter. "Why the hell should I repeat that? It's a boring story."

Frankie covered her mouth to hide her laughter. "All right, Mr. Weissman." The doctor made another note. "Let me ask you to raise your right hand."

Without hesitating, Abraham raised his right hand.

"That's perfect, Mr. Weissman! I am so proud of you. Good work today. Thank you."

"Am I through?" Abraham looked up at him.

"Yes, you're through. See you again in six weeks."

As Dr. Trenton walked Frankie and her father to the door, he whispered to Frankie, "If I were you, I would try to take his raising his hand as very good news. I didn't really think he'd be able to do it." The doctor patted Frankie on her wrist.

The days Frankie despised her profession most was when she witnessed reasonable men and women like Dr. Trenton toss off as positive what they knew were condescending diagnoses.

Frankie and her father left the doctor's office and walked together down Madison Avenue. Frankie had come to dread taking her father to lunch, but when they passed Three Guys restaurant on Ninety-sixth Street, Abraham asked to go in. She thought to herself, if Dr. Trenton only knew that Abraham recognized the coffee shop, perhaps he'd say he was practically cured.

Frankie ordered her father a tuna melt and got a Greek salad for herself.

"You were right, Dad," she said as she picked out the anchovies from her salad. "That was a very boring story."

"What?" Abraham bit into his sandwich.

"That story about the king was boring."

"Who?" he asked, while concentrating on the oozing tuna.

"The king."

"Who needs a king? I don't need any kings." Abraham finished his sandwich in two minutes.

"Dad, don't you think you should slow down a little bit? We have plenty of time." As soon as Frankie heard herself mention time, she knew she had pushed the wrong button.

"Who has time? I have to get to the office." Abraham began getting up.

"They'll understand, Dad." Frankie was now in the midst of it.

"No they won't. Goddamned bastards are holding on to five hundred pairs of nylons. They want to charge me two hundred dollars more for shipping."

"That's terrible," Frankie answered by rote.

"You're right. It is terrible. Where's our lunch? I need to eat so I can get down there." He began looking around for the waiters.

"Dad, you already had a sandwich."

"Who had a sandwich? You? So why did we come here?"

"I guess I was hungry." Frequently now, Frankie couldn't find her way out of their conversation except by going along with it. "Dad, would you like another sandwich?"

"No, I don't have time now." He got up from their booth. "Where's my coat? Goddamn bastards took my coat."

"It's right here, Dad." Frankie took his coat off the nearby rack. "Let me put it on you. It's cold outside. February in New York is always awful."

"Is it February?" His eyes sparkled with some recognition.

"Yes."

"That means it's Valentine's Day. Do you have anybody?" he asked Frankie while she buttoned his coat.

Frankie found these moments of lucidity almost more unbearable than the elliptical nonsense. Grasping at his mention of Valentine's Day would be just as desperate as celebrating his lifting his right hand.

"Yes, I do have someone," she heard herself tell her father. "His name is Jil."

"A man named Jill? Jill is a girl and Jack is a boy. Even I still know that." Abraham smiled broadly.

Frankie kissed her father's cheek. "Dad, you still know a lot."

Walking with Frankie down Madison Avenue back to his apartment, Abraham stopped at a garbage can on the corner of Ninety-second

Street, opened his fly, and started to pee. Frankie saw sixth-grade girls in their uniforms from Nightingale-Bamford pointing at him. Without hesitation, she stepped directly in front of Abraham as if they were having a casual conversation. All the while Frankie kept her eyes focused on the Madison Avenue street sign in order to give her father his privacy.

Frankie had arranged to meet Jil at his apartment for a drink prior to going on to Judy's for dinner. Sitting in his forest green double-height living room overlooking Tavern on the Green, Frankie tucked her feet up in his signed Mies van der Rohe chair that had launched a million replicas.

"You look very sweet over there, like a young girl all cuddled up in a ball." Jil affectionately patted her head as he passed her a vodka on the rocks.

"It's so calm here." Frankie sipped her drink.

"And you know, I did it all without feng shui." Jil pronounced the word with a knowing disdain. "You seem a little sad tonight. Is everything all right?"

"Just a hard day."

"I understand. Hippocratic oath and all that." Jil smiled at her. "Even Charlie Acton won't tell anyone who his patients are, although everyone knows they are the best-looking women in town. Well, I suppose that's what I get for dating a doctor."

Frankie quietly flinched whenever Jil mentioned that they were dating. It was fine for her to tell her father or even her girlfriends that she was seeing him. But Frankie still knew the difference between companionship and an affair. If they were really dating they'd have to be sleeping together, and as far as Frankie knew, they weren't.

"Doctors are a disaster," Frankie answered. "The last one I dated ran off with the sugar heiress."

"I hear they're miserable," Jil tossed off.

"You did?" Frankie hadn't heard about Jack and his sugar heiress since she saw pictures in *Architectural Digest* of their estate in Hawaii.

"No, I haven't heard anything." He came by the chair and kissed her on the lips. "Don't be so sad. You have no idea what a glorious woman you are."

"Thank you," Frankie answered softly. She was reticent to show Jil how deeply needy she could be. She had once heard a friend refer to a lover as having "the Grand Canyon of Need." Frankie's fear was that even the Grand Canyon could only contain a prelude to her need. "Really, Jil, thank you so much."

"That's it?" Jil looked at her. "I just laid my sword at your feet."

"I'm sorry, Jil." She took his hand. "I saw my father today."

"Is he worse?"

Frankie suddenly began to cry. "I am so sorry."

For the sake of her father's dignity, she wouldn't tell Jil about the incident at the garbage can that afternoon. "I don't know. Everything just seems so far from okay right now."

Jil kissed her hand. "Dr. Weissman, haven't you heard? It's a very hard and out-of-whack time. All we can do is try to be very kind to one another."

Frankie now began weeping uncontrollably. Her face and eyes were turning red and she was gasping for air. Maybe it was for the imminent loss of Abraham's unconditional love. Or it was for the very conditional affection that Jil, who was only ten years younger than her father, was offering her in his immaculate forest green double-height living room.

"You must think I'm some sort of high school girl on a bender . . ." Frankie finally stopped crying.

"Hey, things happen." He gave her a cocktail napkin to dry her face. "Although you might want to write yourself a good prescription. Everyone else in this city is on Zoloft now."

Frankie laughed. "Actually they're on Wellbutrin. Doesn't spoil your sex life like Zoloft."

"I'll remember that." Jil smiled and passed her another napkin.

She blotted her face again. "I guess we better get to Judy Tremont's dinner party."

"I could call and cancel," Jil immediately offered.

"Jil, I'm a doctor." Frankie smiled. "I don't want to be responsible for Judy Tremont having a heart attack. If we don't show up now, we really screw up her seating plan."

"I do adore you. Nothing passes that clinical and wry eye." Jil kissed Frankie's cheek and put her drink on the bar. "My daughter is always reminding me how lucky I am to have you in my life."

There were two things that Frankie consistently noticed about Jil. He never put a drink on a piece of furniture without using a coaster and he always managed to refer to his daughter. Jil spoke very little about his life prior to the one he had at Sotheby's. Frankie knew that he came to America at age ten from Budapest and did indeed grow up in Brooklyn. He referred to his high school as "Erasmus Hall," which to any other Brooklynite is better known as Erasmus, the alma mater of Barbra Streisand and the basketball star Jeremy Fine. Apparently, when Jil was thirty, he briefly married a book editor from Random House. And other than that, Jil revealed very little. Nevertheless, Frankie believed him to be, under the cultivated sophistication, the social gossip and endless opinions about art and décor, a genuinely kind and highly intelligent man.

"Please take the park drive," Jil asked the taxi driver as they entered a cab on Central Park West.

"You don't want me to go just crosstown!" the driver irritatedly answered.

"No, I said I wanted you to take the park drive." When Jil got angry, his elegant Middle European accent was replaced by the abruptness of a man capable of running a major auction house. "Make a left at Tavern on the Green and go around the park all the way to East Seventy-second Street."

"It's gonna cost you more." The taxi driver looked into the mirror.

"I've done it many times before, and no, it really shouldn't cost me more." Jil ended the conversation.

The driver made a left into Central Park and turned on 1010 WINS, the all-news radio station.

"Attorney General Ashcroft has advised the president to raise the national alert status to orange." The radio announcer spoke with the incessant beeps of breaking radio news behind him.

"You think they'll ever find bin Laden?" the driver spoke over the radio. "I mean come on, this is the U.S. Army and they can't find a guy living in a cave in Afghanistan?"

"Could you turn that off?" Jil asked the driver. "We'd like a little peace."

"Hey, mister, you can't keep your head in the sand. That's what the Jews did in Nazi Germany!"

"Just shut it off! Or we're getting out."

"You get out here and you got yourself a red alert, mister," the driver spoke quickly. "You won't even make it alive to the East Side."

"I said shut the radio the hell off right now!" Jil yelled into the front.

The driver complied and the taxi continued to wend its way past the Central Park carousel and Wollman ice-skating rink in silence. The park was covered with a soft dusting of snow and the lights of Central Park South shimmered in the clear winter sky.

After a few minutes, Jil reached for Frankie's hand. "This drive always reminds me of Fred Astaire and Cyd Charisse when they do 'Dancing in the Dark.'"

"Yes." Frankie looked at him blankly.

"You don't know what I mean, do you?" Jil smiled. "In the movie *The Band Wagon*, Fred and Cyd go for a late-night ride through Central Park and they stop to dance under the full moon at Bethesda Fountain."

"Sounds very romantic," Frankie spoke softly.

"It's more than romantic." Jil squeezed her hand. "It's exquisite!"

The taxi finally exited the park and made its way down Park Avenue. As Frankie felt Jil's hand still in hers, she thought that her life had never seemed so precarious. She didn't know if it was the American flags so proudly displayed on every Park Avenue building that made her feel so off-balance, or the now indelible memory of her father on Ninety-second and Madison. But for the first time in her life, Frankie believed there was absolutely nothing pinning her down.

Surprisingly, she found herself looking forward to the enforced formality of Judy Tremont's dinner party. The butler greeting her at the door, the standing cocktail hour, the seated dinner, the English plates, the silver centerpieces, the obligatory conversation to the gentleman on your right and the gentleman on your left, the after-dinner coffee and port, and the optional cigar in the library would all provide a grounding antidote.

CHAPTER FOURTEEN

Samantha

Samantha thought Judy Tremont's apartment was basically over-done. For whatever Judy had spent on decorators, architects, and contractors, which Samantha assumed could underwrite a season at the Met, Samantha begrudged the idea that Judy had been taken. To Samantha's well-trained eye, there was an apparent overabundance of everything, or, more simply, what her mother called "too much of a muchness." Even in the vestibule, there were brocade window treatments upon brocade window treatments and French Empire chaise longues with matching cashmere throws. Samantha thought to herself, If Robespierre saw this, he'd start another revolution.

"I must say, they have a lot of very good art," Charlie whispered to Samantha as they climbed the steps to the main living room. The walls were plastered with Degas, Pissarro, and, Charlie suspected, an early Picasso.

When Charlie and Samantha got to the top of the stairs, Judy rushed over to greet them.

"Hello. How *are* you?" She kissed Samantha on both cheeks. Judy was wearing Yves Saint Laurent red harem pants with a red velvet and gold-embroidered sleeveless vest. A Cartier diamond and a ruby cuff bracelet sparkled on her wrist.

"We're so happy to be here." Samantha took her hand. "I love what you're wearing."

"Oh, I'm so glad. That means so much coming from you." Judy's jewelry and her giddiness gave her an almost incandescent glow.

"I'm a sucker for anything Ottoman Empire," Samantha smiled.

"This is so great. That's actually what we're doing tonight."

"The Ottoman Empire?" Charlie asked.

"Well, I wanted to do something fun and fusion but I'm just so tired of everyone bringing in that chef from Nobu. And all that endless sashimi. I don't care how you slice it, it's still raw fish."

"Yes, indeed." Charlie had no idea how Judy had sailed so swiftly from Japan to the straits of the Bosphorus.

"So I decided, What the heck! Go for Turkusion!" She pronounced each syllable with pride.

"Beg your pardon?" Charlie was honestly not following.

"A little Turkish. A little English. A hint of Asian. Plus my own chef is topping it off with a good old-fashioned American dessert."

"Best part of the meal." Charlie decided to get Judy off the transworld menu. "This is a terrific apartment."

"Actually, we've hired Pippa Rose to simplify it. It's getting a little heavy for me. Plus, I told Albert it's unpatriotic now to sleep with the French these days." Judy laughed at her own racy joke.

"Well, we're delighted to be here," Charlie added. "Such a treat on a dreary winter night. Where's Albert?"

"You know Albert. He's reading the kids to sleep. I think it's *Silas Marner* tonight. That's Charlotte's favorite." Judy took both their arms. "You know some of the people here. There's Adrienne and Paul Rodman, Frankie Weissman, and your friend Jil Taillou. And that's our dear friend Dr. Arnie Berkowitz, and of course Clarice Santorini. Barry's coming a little later. And so is Charlie Rose."

"Sounds like a terrific group." Charlie was hoping she'd stop chattering so he could get himself a drink. "Okay kiddo, let's plunge in."

Charlie gave Samantha his signal for getting on with the proceeding and steered his wife toward the bar.

"You know Pippa Rose is going to cover this place with awful porcelain English pugs. Judy's better off sticking with French Empire, or going Ottoman all the way," Samantha whispered to Charlie as they walked into the living room. "I really should get Jil to suggest someone better than Pippa to her."

"Why? She seems perfectly happy." Charlie helped himself to a drink from a passing tray.

"I feel protective of her. She makes such an enormous effort."

A waiter in a black formal uniform offered a tray of foie gras on mint pita with pomegranate molasses.

"I just can't find any sympathy for a woman who has color-coordinated her furniture with her Degas." Charlie passed on the hors d'oeuvres.

"What's with you tonight, Charlie?" Samantha asked.

Jil waved at them from across the floor. Frankie followed beside him.

"What do you think of the Turkusion?" Jil asked Samantha. "Oh, if these Empire chaises could talk!"

"Nice to see you, Jil. Lovely to see you, Frankie." Samantha gave them both a double kiss.

"Hello, Francesca." Charlie took Frankie's hand.

"Traditional cured bonito with leeks and saffron pesto?" A waiter smiled at Jil.

"Wouldn't miss it." Jil took the small morsel. "Do you know Judy flew in the chef from Changa tonight. It must have cost a fortune."

"What's Changa?" Charlie asked.

"Best fusion restaurant in Istanbul. I stopped there last time on my way to visit the Erteguns."

Samantha took Jil's arm. "Oh Jil, you're so cosmopolitan. Frankie, how do you keep up with him? I know I couldn't."

"And you can't fault Miss Judy for her guest list," Jil continued. "It's a perfect blend. A little media, a little arts, a little social, a little décor, and even a little trash. And there's Dr. Arnie, everybody's favorite provider of antidepressants for three-year-olds."

"Actually, his specialty is adolescent male medicine," Charlie corrected him.

"Oh Charlie, don't protect him just because he's a doctor," Samantha chided him.

"Why did everyone come to this party, do you think?" Charlie asked.

"For the hummus?" Frankie whispered.

"Oh come on, Charlie." Jil rolled his eyes. "They came because they heard everyone else was coming. It even worked that way at Erasmus Hall—"

"I think you're all very mean," Samantha said. "Judy has spunk."

"She just wants to be you, dear."

"Jil, you're a terrible snob." Samantha gave him a playful shove.

"Of course I am, darling. I'm an arriviste." He smiled at her. "On the other hand, you're the last breath of the American elite, so you can afford to exhibit noblesse oblige."

"Jil, this is a ridiculous conversation. No one even thinks this way anymore except for you."

"All right, let's ask our medical staff." He looked at Frankie and Charlie. "Do you think most of the women in this room envy Samantha?"

"Do you mean, they all wish they were married to me?" Charlie smiled.

"No, do they all wish they could have the taste Samantha has in her pinkie." He continued, "When I was in high school, I compulsively used a book called *The Elements of Style* by Strunk and White so I could learn where to put a comma like an elegant American. After all, I was just an immigrant boy from Hungary. I bet these girls all wish Samantha would codify the do's and don't's of genuine style just so they could follow it, too."

"Why? So they could all become famous for having accomplished very little?" Samantha answered, and left the three of them alone while she walked into the dining room.

Judy had given a great deal of thought to whether to reconfigure her dining room into five tables of six or one long one seating thirty. There were valid arguments to be made for either scenario. The smaller tables afforded intimacy and conversation, but on the other hand, the seating plan was a nightmare. One table would get a media star like Charlie Rose, or an important producer like Barry Santorini. If Judy put her six biggest draws at one table, they would feel right at home but everyone else would feel cheated. After a week of sleepless nights, Judy opted for the one long table. The fact that she could get all of those people to one table really made, in her mind, the better statement.

If you asked Judy what her strong suit was, she would most definitely say not flowers. In fact, she sort of resented that some of the better hostesses in New York, like Pinky Graham and those Piel sisters, made a point of doing their own arrangements. On the other hand, Judy had been to enough dinners to know that traditional floral centerpieces were the kiss of death. She also knew that, ever since 9/11, austerity was in. This wasn't the time for floating gardenias and birds-of-paradise. But she couldn't live with herself if she just did spare orchids like a display table in the Takashimaya department store.

Aesthetically stumped, Judy phoned Adrienne Strong-Rodman for advice. Adrienne's personal assistant had just discovered Umit Afet, a party planner who began as a salesgirl in Bendel's napkin department and had recently worked for Lady de Rothschild, the Turkish ambassador, and several Hollywood bigwigs. Umit suggested a Turkish kilim running across the long dining room table and strategically placed Steuben glass bowls of red pomegranate and pistachios. For the center of the table, Umit provided a three-foot hookah pipe filled with white narcissus and purple anemones. Finally, for a splash of wit, multicolored evil-eye marbles and red snuff candles were dolloped everywhere.

"And I'd definitely do the eighteenth-century candelabras," Umit advised after she saw Judy's James Robinson collection. "That's what will keep it fusion and not dip into totally Turkey."

When Samantha walked into the dining room and saw the hookah flower arrangement, she promised herself to have a lunch with Judy and give her a list of who to avoid at all costs. Even at the Spence School kindergarten the girls learned to put away their marbles.

As a pianist in the adjoining room began to play "I Get a Kick Out of You," Albert approached Samantha and took her under his arm. "Guest of honor, let me escort you to your seat?"

"Hello, Albert." Samantha kissed him on both cheeks. "How did your girls like *Silas Marner*?"

"Not as much as *The Story of O*." Albert laughed. "I hope you'll honor us with a song after dinner," Albert said as he pulled out Samantha's chair.

Samantha had sung barefoot once after a dinner celebrating Grey Navez's divorce settlement. Now because of that damn magazine, she thought she'd never live it down.

"I'm really not much of a singer anymore."

"Nonsense. We'll do a duet. Do you know 'Honey Bun' from *South Pacific*?"

"'A hundred and one pounds of fun'?" Samantha looked up at him.

"'Get a load of honey bun tonight!' We've got a date in the living room after dessert!"

As Albert moved on to the next guest, Samantha thought he must love Judy deeply, otherwise why would such an intelligent man care whether or not she sang barefoot in his living room.

"I would be very disappointed if my girls worked." Judy turned to Grey Navez's current boyfriend, Lewis Franklin, the African-American head of Mergers and Acquisitions at Crédit Suisse First Boston. "I mean, why would they want to waste their life being lawyers when they'll have large enough trust funds to be genuine artists."

Samantha knew that Lewis had grown up in a Baltimore project and had been an ABC, "A Better Chance," student at Lawrenceville. She also knew he had the social grace to move the conversation.

"I'll tell you what I think," Lewis replied. "It's so hard to get into schools in New York. I just worry about my kids getting into kindergarten altogether."

"I have a relationship with every headmaster and headmistress in Manhattan," Dr. Arnie Berkowitz proclaimed with pride. "Where do you want your kid to go? I'll get them in."

"That doesn't sound very fair." Clarice looked up from her star-anise-and-ginger-infused smoked salmon.

"It's only because I've really treated most of the kids from the best families in this city." Arnie spoke while he swallowed a vine leaf mint oxtail ravioli accompanying the salmon. "My compliments to the chef." Arnie raised his fork.

In Samantha's mind, Dr. Berkowitz was the Tartuffe of the Upper East Side. He was a charlatan who manipulated titans of industry in their most vulnerable spots.

"We're pulling our kid out of Dalton." Paul Rodman leaned back. "You gotta be nuts to keep your kid in a New York City school when every other day there's an orange alert. Especially a school with a lot of celebrity Jews."

"There's no alternative to a school with celebrity Jews, if you're talking about the first tier," Dr. Arnie remarked without a hint of self-consciousness.

"Adrienne's starting her own school in the Hamptons."

"That's very impressive." Samantha's eyes surveyed Adrienne's breast implants. "Do you have a degree in education?"

"I have a Ph.D. in child development plus I know who to hire and that's all you need. I've got the ex-headmaster of Westminster to set the place up. We're paying him a fortune. We're going to have every kid making their own movie by age ten."

"Why would you want to do that?" Samantha asked.

Adrienne directly addressed her. "Do you think they should be wasting their time learning the multiplication tables? We have calculators for that. I want to take education into the twenty-first century."

Before Samantha could answer, Barry walked into the room. As opposed to all the men in shirts and ties, Barry arrived wearing his signature sweatshirt with an Armani jacket. "Sorry I'm late. We were shooting and we went over. Then I had Senator McCain on the phone. It's great to be here." Barry was led by the butler to his seat, between Samantha and Judy. "Thanks for having me. This is a fabulous apartment." He kissed Judy. Then he turned to Samantha with a perfunctory "Nice to see ya again."

"Nice to see you," Samantha answered, and was delighted that none of the heat from their dance in Palm Beach was still apparent.

Waiters, like clockwork, began revolving around the table with lamb arranged in silver trays like Busby Berkeley girls in a musical extravaganza.

"Istan-kebab," the waiter demonstrated. "Cubes of lamb in fennel seeds, braised lamb shank with marinated eggplant, cranberry-crusted rack of lamb with risotto stuffing, lamb loin with cabernet mint sauce, and lamb chops in champagne-chipotle."

Frankie whispered to Charlie, "Holy lamb!"

Behind the lamb was another rotation of chestnut and brussel sprout purée with horseradish cream, roasted Jerusalem artichokes, pomegranate soufflé, pistachio-infused tofu, and roasted potatoes in a balsamic reduction.

Barry helped himself to several chops. "I'm starving. And I'm on fuckin' Atkins."

"But you're so thin!" Judy looked at him. "You can have anything you want."

"Ask my wife." He called down the table where Clarice was seated between Charlie and Jil.

"Clarice, Judy wants to know what I can eat."

"Protein." Clarice smiled at him.

"That's enough about my eating. I spend too much time with actors and all they talk about is their diets. And meanwhile, the world's going to hell," Barry continued. "What kind of food is this? I'm so glad it's not raw fish."

"Thank you." Judy was thrilled with herself and Umit Afet. "It's Turkusion."

"It's a little this-a, a little that-a, and the emphasis on the latt-a." Jil smiled as he quoted Lola's opening number from *Damn Yankees*.

"You mean it's Turkish. It's delicious. But what the hell are the Turks doing?" Barry continued. "Are they on our side or not? Personally, right now I'm with the Kurds."

"I think it's complicated. You have to be there to really understand it." Paul Rodman put down his lamb shank. "Albert, this wine is fabulous! Bordeaux '85, am I right?"

"'82. Château Léoville Las Cases," Albert answered.

"Well, I'll tell you what I think. And I don't mind sticking my neck out even in this beautiful home." Barry took a sip of wine. "The entire Middle East is our fault, the Brits' fault, the Israelis' fault, and the Palestinians' fault. Sharon is a crazy person and Arafat is a son of a bitch."

"And you have the answer?" Adrienne Strong-Rodman asked Barry.

"Adrienne, you know me. I wouldn't presume to tell anyone what to do." Barry smiled. "But I know the Arabs and the Jews are all acting like studio presidents. They fuckin' lie and nobody's calling their bluff. Not even the Americans tell the truth."

Just as Barry proclaimed his lying theory of Middle East politics, he rubbed his leg against Samantha's. Her leg remained aligned with his.

"Well, I don't think Sharon is a crazy person and I still think there are good old-fashioned American values and telling the truth is one of them." Paul had another sip of wine.

"Hear, hear." Judy lifted up her glass. "To telling the truth!"

"Hear, hear." Arnie Berkowitz lifted his glass and gestured to the waiter to refill it.

"Have you read *The Corrections* by Jonathan Franzen? It's on the best seller list," Judy deliberately shifted the conversation away from the Middle East and onto literature.

Samantha looked over at Charlie, who seemed happily engaged in a conversation with Frankie. Barry's hand, when he wasn't gesticulating about Israelis or Palestinians, was now on her knee. She was grateful to Frankie for keeping Charlie's attention and perplexed by her own inability to move away from Barry's touch. Her eyes wandered to Clarice, who looked like a far kinder woman than Judy, and was, therefore, in some perverse way, far less interesting.

Since the book discussion didn't catch, Judy moved on to films. "Barry, tell us what films you liked this year." She cocked her head toward him.

"Every movie this year is shit." Barry pushed his leg up and down Samantha's while he leaned into Charlie Rose. "I'm the culture sheriff. If it weren't for me, there would be no integrity. Don't you think so, Samantha?" He squeezed her thigh under the table.

Samantha inhaled. "I thought it was the artist who had to have integrity."

"Artists suck! They can be bought and sold," Barry snorted.

"I completely disagree with you," Albert said forthrightly from the other end of the table.

"That's because you don't have to deal with them." Barry leaned back in his chair, finally letting go of Samantha's thigh. If this trust-fund baby wanted to talk about artists, he was ready for it. "Artists get a lot of credit for having fuzzy minds," he continued, "and not knowing shit about the real world or getting anything made."

"I don't think you can ignore the integrity of the individual voice." Albert began a long tirade about writing and sporadically cited passages from *The Song of Roland,* Balzac, and Proust. "You're talking about movie writers, and let's face it: even the great screenwriters are craftsmen and not true artists, since screenwriting is an expertise in which form dictates the content." Albert signaled the waiter to bring in another bottle of wine.

As Albert went on pedantically quoting Goethe in German and the *Aeneid* in Latin, Judy felt her heart racing. She didn't keep Ativan at the dinner table and the waiters were late with the desserts. In honor of Samantha, Judy had had her cook re-create old-fashioned flaming baked Alaska to be wheeled in on a silver trolley. She tried to catch the headwaiter's attention by bobbing her head and gently pointing.

"Personally, I think the more writing becomes about the opinions of producers and marketing M.B.A.s, the lower the quality of our culture will be," Albert concluded.

"Is that what you learned at Yale?" Barry asked him.

"I went to Amherst," Albert replied.

"Same thing." Albert was boring Barry, and Barry prided himself on never wasting his time. Even sitting next to Samantha wasn't easing his unrest. Barry abruptly got up from the table. "Let's go, Clarice. I have an early call tomorrow morning."

"But dessert is just coming," Judy said anxiously as the silver trolleys with flaming baked Alaska rolled in.

Barry kissed Judy. "This was great. Gotta do it again." Then he turned to Samantha. "Nice talking to you. Let's go, Clarice." He grabbed her arm and they left.

Samantha couldn't remember the last time she witnessed somebody behaving as rudely as Barry. She found it simultaneously repugnant and instructive. Until Barry got up, she suspected that she would be stuck singing barefoot at the end of the dinner, just to make her hostess happy. But Barry's departure, and the residual sensation of his leg pressed up against hers, gave her the courage to politely leave shortly after coffee in the living room.

"How could you do that to me?" Judy exploded at Albert after the final guest left.

"Do what?" Albert continued drinking his port.

"You forced Barry Santorini to leave."

"That man is a vulgarian." Albert lit a cigar.

"Barry Santorini produced fifteen Oscar-nominated movies, including *The Red and the Black* and *Costumes of the Country*, for which he got two Oscars, one for Isabelle Huppert and the other for Kirsten Dunst, who happens to be both your daughters' idol," Judy answered in one agitated breath.

"He's still a vulgarian." Albert puffed his cigar.

"Well, thanks to you, Samantha left right after one coffee and no one lingered for after-dinner drinks, except Pippa Rose and her husband and we fuckin' employ her!"

Judy slammed the door to the library and went upstairs to bed. She hated using foul language, because it sounded like all the nobodies in her high school class who hung out at Fat Taco and joined the army.

Judy sat down at her bedroom vanity and began taking off her jewelry. She was already planning her recovery from the evening. Samantha would call to thank her, and she would invite her to a lunch she was planning to throw for Narciso Rodriguez or some other hot designer. Judy didn't really know Narciso, but she would find out what charity he supported and could get Albert to give a large donation. Then she could throw a little luncheon.

The thought of this intimate gathering ordinarily would have cheered Judy immediately. But tonight it only underscored something she had been thinking about for a while and didn't dare mention to Albert. Ever since the planes went into the World Trade Center, Judy had begun thinking it might be nice to move back to Modesto. They could get the largest house in town, a historic landmark, and Judy could take classes at the local college. She liked reading Wharton and Jane Austen for her book group and wouldn't mind seriously studying either of them. In fact, she herself had enjoyed writing when she was at *Mademoiselle*. While she knew she was no Edith Wharton and had abruptly lost interest in the nanny diaries she had begun in Palm Beach, Judy was secretly sure she could write one of those Park Avenue princess novels. After all, she reassured herself, it takes one to know one. If she moved back, she wouldn't even be self-conscious about getting a master's in creative writing. There would be no insecurity or stress like tonight. In Modesto, Judy Tremont would be Brooke Astor, Samantha Acton, and a movie star all in one.

Judy slipped two Ativans under her tongue and took a deep breath. Gently stroking her face upward from her eye, Judy put on her La Mer antiaging moisturizer and, calmer now, prepared to go to bed.

CHAPTER FIFTEEN

Barry

"There's nothing I hate more than a puny, know-it-all kid from the Ivy League. Why the hell should I go listen to his reading?" Barry blurted at Yvonne, his assistant.

"Because you said you would," she answered. "It's on your schedule."

"Who the fuck put it there? You? I told you to check with me first."

Yvonne had worked for Barry longer than any other assistant. The others all had aspirations to become development girls or boys and move up to associate producer. Yvonne was mostly interested in staying put.

"This is the script you commissioned," she explained to him. "It's by the kid who won Sundance while he was still a Yale Drama student."

"Doesn't mean a fuckin' thing. I didn't get into Yale."

"His father is also the governor of Iowa."

"Why didn't you tell me that?" Barry suddenly got up from his seat. Ever since he was asked to bring his movies to the screening room at the Bush White House, Barry had had an interest in politics. He had no intention of running himself, but he was a man who liked to pull the strings behind the scenes. Plus, being a Republican and a moviemaker made him unique.

Barry walked into the reading an hour late. The actors had waited thirty minutes for him to show, and finally began to read the script because four of them had to get back to the city in time for a Broadway matinee.

The script was an updated version of the Comden and Green musical *On the Town*. The original had starred Gene Kelly and Frank Sinatra and was about three sailors on leave in New York. Barry commissioned the script because the pluses included a great Leonard Bernstein score. Barry knew that musicals were hot and boys were being shipped to fight wars overseas again. Plus a little escapism wasn't the worst idea either.

It usually took five minutes for Barry to make up his mind about anything. All those elementary school nuns who told him that he had a terrible attention span didn't end up winning twelve Oscars. Those nuns lived and died in South Philly and so did most of their A students.

Barry watched as the actors gave their best to the roles. In an almost gawking way, Barry was fascinated by theater. There was no real money to be made and most of the actors and playwrights negotiated for very little. When Nathan Lane and Matthew Broderick got $100,000 a week to appear in *The Producers*, it was a Broadway record-breaker. A Hollywood agent would hang up if a serious star got such a lousy offer for a television series.

There were maybe fifteen other people at the reading, mostly assistants, development girls, associate producers, and friends of the author. Barry could spot the writer right away: blue jeans, unpressed Oxford shirt over a T-shirt, sneakers. Barry thought it was one thing for him to wear a trademark sweatshirt and jeans because that's what you wore when you weren't in your goddamn Catholic school uniform in South Philly. But every fuckin' kid who wanted to grow up to be Spielberg, Soderbergh, or Lucas now dressed that way. Barry was secretly in awe of talent, but he also knew it was really rare.

After the reading, there was polite applause. The actors hugged and kissed. Barry got up to shake Swoosie Kurtz's hand. She was a classy stage actress and Barry never missed a chance to acknowledge class. He felt he didn't need to waste his time thanking the others, since it would only mislead them.

The screenwriter finally walked over to Barry. "I'm so honored that you made it," he said. "This has been a fabulous experience and I'm looking forward to working more on the script. I learned a whole lot today."

"I didn't know your father was the governor of Iowa." Barry put his arm around the young screenwriter. "Give him my best." Barry turned and walked away.

As soon as Barry sat back at his desk overlooking Manhattan from his office complex in Jersey City, Gretchen, a thirty-two-year-old development girl in a miniskirt and a tight tank top, walked into his office.

"So what did you think?" Gretchen crossed her legs.

"This is easy. Get rid of that goddamned writer and get someone who knows something about being funny," Barry said without looking up.

"But he's been working on this for two years and we've been giving him very good feedback." Gretchen spoke her mind.

"Well, we were wrong." Barry was getting hungry and popped open a Diet Dr Pepper, his signature drink.

"I think there's a lot of wonderful things in there."

"Gretchen, when someone says, 'There's a lot of wonderful things in there,' it means the fuckin' thing isn't working. We're making movies. This is not progressive school."

"But what am I going to tell him?" she asked.

"Fuck 'em."

"I understand." Gretchen walked out of his office.

The good thing about girls like Gretchen, Barry thought to himself, was at least they didn't cry. Barry fired the ones who cried right away. With girls like Gretchen, he could send them three dozen silver roses tonight and it would all blow over.

"Yvonne, get me a pizza! Extra cheese, sausage, and anchovy." He pressed the intercom. Barry couldn't get any comfort food at home, because his doctor told Clarice he should avoid fats and stick with protein and vegetables. Barry was never overweight, but everything ran in Barry's family—high blood pressure, angina, heart failure, prostate cancer, lung cancer, and colon cancer. So his doctors said he should try to be careful.

Barry was perfectly happy to have Clarice's chef feed him grilled whatever the hell she wanted at home. But at work, Barry, wasn't going to waste his time with string beans.

Half an hour later, Barry's new second assistant brought in the pie. "Here's your pizza. Smells fantastic. I also have last weekend's numbers. Do you need anything else?"

Barry opened another Dr Pepper. "I'm great."

"Do you want me to set the table?"

"Hell no. I hate pretentious pizza. Worse thing that happened to that food is fuckin' Spago."

When the second assistant left, Barry opened the box right on his desk and pulled out a slice. As he took his first bite, he thought nothing was as satisfying as eating and working at his desk. Barry hated formal dinner parties like the one at the Tremonts'. They were mostly a colossal waste because ninety-nine percent of the time Clarice was the best-looking woman and he was far and away the most interesting man.

Except, Barry chuckled to himself as he slurped down another slice, that Samantha Acton is one hell of a classy woman. You don't often come across someone who is that practically regal and hot. She has that thing like the great movie stars. Your eye just goes right to her and everyone else in the room drops dead.

A blob of oil fell on the sheet full of the weekend's numbers.

"Fuck." Barry slammed his hand on the table as he looked at the graphs. They weren't even up to snuff in their key markets, like Los Angeles, Chicago, and New York. Barry knew this was happening because the fucking critics were out to get him. He told Clarice the problem with critics is they are the kind of people who take the bus and fuckin' hate him for his limousine.

Barry bit into his third slice when a wad of cheese splattered on his chin.

"Goddammit—fuck!" He picked up the box and crushed it into a wad of sauce, anchovies, and cheese, then tossed it across the room.

Clarice had told Barry that he probably should start meditating to control his stress. But he knew he wasn't going to just fuckin' sit around repeating some goddamn Indian word. There were only two things that he knew would break his tension: food or sex. Barry had no interest in drugs or alcohol and had nothing but disdain for any-one, especially actors, who did. He considered them both a sign of weakness and stupidity.

In the old days, he would have ordered another pizza. For a mo-ment, it occurred to him to call Clarice, but she was probably with the kids at an Italian class, or Japanese math class, or at some Russian gold medalist skating rink. Barry made a point of appreciating how much Clarice did for the children. He wouldn't offhandedly disturb the family routine.

"Yvonne. Yvonne!" he screamed into the phone. Get me Saman-tha Acton on the phone."

"Who?" she called back.

"Call Judy Tremont's. Say you need the address and phone num-ber because I want to invite them both to a screening."

Barry leaned back in his chair. He remembered the smell of

Samantha's hair. It wasn't girlie like Clarice's ever-present Coco by Chanel. He Googled Samantha on his computer and was delighted to see that once again, his hunch was right. She was the real deal, an American thoroughbred.

"I have the number for you. I told the assistant you'd get back to her with a time and place." Yvonne was on the intercom. "Would you like me to dial it?"

"No."

Yvonne knew to ask no further questions.

Barry never dialed his office phone. On weekends, he used his cell phone to call Clarice or his weekend assistant. He watched his fingers as if he were a child mesmerized by the triumph of hitting the right numbers.

"Hello, this is Barry Santorini," he heard himself speaking when Samantha answered the phone. "I have to go to a set in Leonia, New Jersey. I'll send a car for you in an hour."

Barry hung up. One thing he had mastered from Hollywood agents was how not to take no for an answer.

When Samantha arrived on the set she couldn't find Barry anywhere. She walked past the armies of production assistants, cameramen, grips, and best boys. Her aunt had once dated the actor David Niven, and she had vague memories of visiting him as a child on a set in Los Angeles.

She approached a young woman with a clipboard. "I'm looking for Barry Santorini."

"I think he's in the trailer with Mr. Pacino," she answered.

"Can you tell me what movie you're making?"

"Here?" The young woman seemed nonplussed.

"Yes. I'm a friend of Mr. Santorini, but I'm afraid he hasn't mentioned it to me."

"This is a remake of *The Maltese Falcon,*" she replied, as if Samantha had just asked when was the War of 1812.

"The Humphrey Bogart movie?" Samantha asked.

"Yes. He's making it fresh for a new generation. Craft service is over there if you want to make yourself comfortable and get something to eat." The young woman strode away.

"Thanks." Samantha smiled. She noticed that the set was full of efficient young women in tank tops and blue jeans. She wondered what would happen to these girls when they began turning forty. No one, except the cameramen, seemed a day over thirty.

"Hey, you made it." Barry walked over to her and kissed her cheek.

If it was possible, Barry thought Samantha was even more beautiful today than the first day he saw her on the boat. Clarice's friends would always try so hard with their ultrathin bodies and winter white cashmere sweaters. Their obsessive grooming rendered them sexless. But Samantha wore an old lavender V-neck sweater and skintight lavender velvet jeans. She had an edge to her style which, like her perfume, had an underlying note of musk.

Barry had no time for Clarice's friends who thought they were hot shit because their husbands had made a fortune at Morgan Stanley or Goldman Sachs in the 1980s. But he was in awe of girls like Samantha, who could trace their family fortunes back to the Van Rensselaers and the Carnegies. He also knew that as much as he was in awe of Samantha, society girls like her couldn't get enough of real Hollywood players like him. And besides, Barry had seen her husband. He was a runt from Princeton. A dermatologist. That's practically like being a skin care girl at Bliss spa or Georgette Klinger.

"So you're doing a remake of *The Maltese Falcon.* That's a great idea." Samantha smiled at him. She really didn't have much of an opinion about it, but it was something to say. She noticed a large blotch on the middle of his sweatshirt. There was something about his out-and-out slovenliness that she found surprisingly appealing.

"Let's get the hell out of here." He took her hand.

"Barry, Barry," another efficient girl called as she ran over to him.

"You tell the director if I don't see the dailies of scene thirty-one tonight, I'll be back here tomorrow. To shoot the fuckin' thing myself."

"But . . ." she stammered.

"I don't believe in 'but.' "

He grabbed Samantha under the arm. "We're outta here."

"So what do you wanna do?" Barry asked Samantha as he walked her toward his car.

"I don't know. We could take a walk," she answered.

"In Leonia, New Jersey? I can tell you haven't spent much time here."

"How 'bout a drink?" she asked. "We passed an Olive Garden restaurant a few blocks back."

"You think I'd take a woman who has a reputation for setting the style standard in New York to the Olive Garden?"

"Actually, I'm a big fan of diners and coffee-shop food. Give me a tuna on rye anytime," she answered.

"I know just the place, then. Best tuna in New Jersey."

"Really?"

"A twelve-star salute in the fuckin' Zagats."

Barry seldom drove his own car. His driver Julian took him around the city and over the bridge to work every day. Barry spent most of his time in his car, talking on the phone, and Julian was well trained not to breathe a word of it. Like Yvonne and everyone else in Barry's organization, Julian signed a detailed confidentiality statement.

"Julian, the Lincoln Tunnel Motor Lodge," Barry offhandedly told his driver.

"You mean the place near the tunnel?" the driver asked.

"Well, it doesn't sound like it'd be near the bridge." Barry turned to Samantha. "Ever been there?" He smiled at her.

"Sure. My sister got married there." Samantha's lip curled up.

Barry smiled at her. "I'm glad I called you." He put his hand in her lap. "I've been thinking about you a lot."

Samantha looked at him. "Guess you haven't been very busy."

"Jesus, you're tough. Do you like music?"

"Sure. Why not?" Samantha decided not to give away any of her excitement.

"How 'bout Dion?" Barry asked.

"Who?"

"I forgot. You're a fancy girl. You probably want to listen to opera."

"I hate opera." Samantha said flat out.

"Dion DiMucci sang 'Runaround Sue' and 'The Wanderer.'" Barry smiled. "I'm thinking about making a movie about him. He was a kid from the Bronx."

"I'm a Beatles fan."

"You are so fuckin' white."

"Is Dion DiMucci black?" she asked.

"You are such a smart-ass."

Samantha took his hand. "I want to hear Dion."

Barry passed Julian a CD and put his arm around Samantha. Julian continued to drive on the New Jersey Turnpike while the Mercedes sedan blasted the sixties pop classic.

"I should have known it from the very start / This girl will leave me with a broken heart / Now listen people what I'm telling you." Barry sang the last line. "Keep away from Runaround Sue . . ."

Before entering a lane to the Lincoln Tunnel into Manhattan, Julian turned the car off the turnpike. He pulled the Mercedes into the parking lot of a six-story decrepit motor lodge that in its heyday might have been a condemned Holiday Inn. The curtains in the rooms were all drawn and in the parking lot were a small collection of diesel trucks and used cars.

Julian opened the door for Samantha.

"Thank you," she said as she got out of the car.

"Wait for us," Barry announced casually.

"Of course, Mr. Santorini." Julian watched them walk toward the entrance and then got back into the car.

"Should we go to the bar?" Barry opened the door to the motor lodge. The lobby was dark and dingy with a faded orange floral print on the wall.

"Do you really come here a lot?" Samantha asked him.

Barry knew there was nothing like slumming with a woman who can afford the Ritz. When he was dating Clarice, he'd take her to the toughest bars in South Philly and they'd have great sex in the back of his car. But that was a long time ago. That was when Barry still drove and Clarice didn't prefer grilled paillard at La Goulue.

"I gotta be honest with you. I've never been here before." Barry whispered to her. "I was waiting for someone who'd really appreciate it."

"I'd like to see a room." Samantha turned to him.

Barry truly thought they'd have a few drinks in the dark cocktail lounge, listen to a few Sinatra or Tony Bennett standards, and maybe he'd get to feel her leg a couple of times.

"I want to get a few redecorating tips." She curled her lip again. "I'm sick of postmodern. And who knows? Highway chic could be the next big thing."

Barry went to the desk and got a key. During his marriage to Clarice, he had gotten blow jobs from extras and P.A.s looking to better their careers. But he never endangered his marriage by taking anyone somewhere specific to do it. The back of a limo or a bathroom at a gala was fine. That way, it really didn't mean anything.

Barry opened the door to the room. There was a plywood bed with a mattress and matching dresser with an orange lamp. The bedspread was also orange and the room smelled of pine-scented Mr. Clean.

"I like it." Samantha smiled warmly and laughed.

"Good, 'cause I like you. I like you a whole lot." He pressed his face up to hers and kissed her lips. Then he ran his fingers up to the V-neck of her sweater.

"I like you, too," she whispered.

"You know, we can go somewhere else," he said.

"No. Not even Claridge's has a bed that looks as inviting as this." He put his hand on her breast and took off her bra.

Samantha held her head against his. "Barry," she laughed, "I'm calling *Manhattan* magazine to say this is my favorite hotel."

Barry looked up at her. "Wait till you try the room service."

Once, an interviewer asked Barry what was the key to his success and he answered, "I'm always fuckin' hungry." Later that afternoon, Barry stood with Samantha Acton at the window of their room at the Lincoln Tunnel Motor Lodge completely naked. Their bodies intertwined, they watched the rush-hour traffic crawling in and out of the tunnel.

For the first time in his life, Barry felt satiated.

CHAPTER SIXTEEN

Samantha

The night after the Lincoln Tunnel Motor Lodge, Barry sent Samantha a $40,000 bracelet from Bulgari with a note: "From all your fans in the Lincoln Tunnel."

Samantha kept replaying in her mind why she accepted Barry's invitation when he called. "I have to go to a set in Leonia, New Jersey. I'll send a car for you in an hour" was all he had said, and without hesitation, without a thought of any consequences to Charlie, to her marriage, or to herself, she had said yes.

"Have you ever seen Barry Santorini?" Samantha asked her therapist.

"What does he look like?" the therapist asked.

Samantha couldn't tell if her therapist genuinely didn't know or she was just being discreet.

"He's skinny, his face is pockmarked. He wears dirty sweatshirts and sneakers to dinner parties."

"How do you feel about that?"

"I think he's throwing himself in the face of the world and saying, 'Fuck you! Deal with me!'"

"And would you like to do that?" The therapist leaned forward.

"No. But I'm smart enough to know that people like Charlie and me, who still believe in social protocol, are slipping downward. But someone like Barry, unabashed, impolite, irreverent, is the future."

"Are you saying you admire him?"

"I admire his hunger. Barry wants to devour everything in sight."

"When will you see him again?"

"I'm not seeing him again. Barry Santorini was just a casual distraction. You can't think I'm taking this seriously."

"It's what you think that interests me."

"I think you'd never tell me if there was another of your patients who went to the Lincoln Tunnel Motor Lodge to give a blow job and got a forty-thousand-dollar bracelet the next day."

"No, I wouldn't." The therapist laughed. "What did you do with the bracelet?"

"I gave it to my cleaning lady. She likes emeralds."

"How did Charlie feel about that?"

"I think you need to work on your sense of irony. Not to change the subject, but have I told you Jil Taillou is helping me come up with a coffee-table book?"

"Really? About art?"

"The best New York private collections. And you know, when it's finished, maybe they could put my book on the coffee table at the Lincoln Tunnel Motor Lodge. I bet a lot of those truck drivers and prostitutes would be interested in Leon and Shelby Levy's personal treasures from ancient Greece and Rome."

"You don't need to work on your irony." The therapist's glasses fell down her nose.

"No, I'm good with irony. I'm a jaded socialite looking for a purpose." Samantha laughed.

"No you're not. Believe me, no jaded socialite would be willing to go on an adventure at the Lincoln Tunnel Motor Lodge."

"Oh, come on. You don't think Judy Tremont and Grey Navez drive out there for a smoothie after Pilates every day?"

"Unfortunately our session is over, but you do make me laugh."

"I'd rather get better."

"Who says you're not getting better?"

"Seeing Barry Santorini means I'm not getting better. I may not like me very much, but I do like my life. I'm not seeing him again."

"So what did you think of the bracelet?" Barry called Samantha at 6 a.m.

"Oh, hi." Samantha was half asleep. Charlie was at the hospital on early-morning rounds.

"I thought you were a well-brought-up girl. You didn't even write me a fuckin' thank-you note."

"I brought it back to Bulgari and told them to thank you." Samantha opened a box of cigarettes she kept hidden beside her night table.

"You know I don't listen to underlings. When a salesgirl at some jewelry store tells me a forty-thousand-dollar bracelet was returned, I tell them bullshit and hang up the phone."

"You shouldn't be calling here so early."

"Yes I should. I'm on my set and your husband's already on his hospital rounds. Don't forget I did that remake of *Dr. Kildare*."

"I thought you only do quality films."

"A man's got to eat. I made a killing on it. Dr. Kildare was gay and having an affair with Dr. Ben Casey. When can I see you again?"

"I'm very busy. The Central Park Conservancy benefit is coming up." She lit a cigarette.

"And what? They want you to set the table? I need to see you again."

"I don't think that I should." Samantha puffed on her cigarette.

"If you waste time thinking about what you should or shouldn't do, life'll amount to absolutely nothing. That I can promise you," he said definitively.

"Don't you ever have second thoughts?" she asked him.

"No."

The flat assuredness of Barry's answer gave Samantha the same kind of tingle up her leg as if he were still pressing against it.

"I'll send a car for you at noon. Let's have lunch at Chanterelle."

"What's wrong with the restaurant at the motor lodge?"

"I don't like their cheese plate as much as Chanterelle's. I'll see you later." Barry hung up.

Samantha pulled her feet under the Pratesi blanket Charlie had bought her last fall as an anniversary gift. When he brought it home he told her, "Darling, if the world blows up, we can always snuggle under our blanket." Charlie loved her, but he was also very predictable. He gave her a blanket every year.

The idea of a woman's life being defined by powerful men never really came into Samantha's perspective until Grey Navez explained to her that women ten years younger than them get the right job at the right Wall Street bank in order to marry the right money.

"Honey, the better nursery schools in New York are chock-full of mothers who graduated Columbia and Stanford Business, and even Yale Law School," Grey assured Samantha over coffee at Payard. "These girls can't wait to give up their work once they nab their security blanket, and then those nursery schools have the best-run bake sales in the country."

When Samantha was growing up in New York, she had no idea whose family did or didn't have real money. In fact, money was something her parents never talked about. Her first husband's family had a compound in Bar Harbor, Maine, where Samantha now believed he had sex for the first time with his Exeter roommate. But they drove a beat-up station wagon and his mother, Pussy (a nickname for Elizabeth), took pride in eating frozen fish sticks and peas on television trays. No one Samantha knew had a private plane, though in retrospect, they all probably could have afforded one.

But times were different now. No one was interested in rumpled old couples worth millions who collected supermarket coupons in their unheated twenty-room home in Bar Harbor. Paul and Adrienne Strong-Rodman were the new order. The only criterion was getting the best, which clearly meant the most expensive. In many ways, Samantha found that far more equitable than the silliness about family history that she grew up with.

When the phone rang again, Samantha toyed with not picking it up, but she certainly didn't want Barry to call all morning until the housekeeper answered the phone.

"You know there's also a fabulous cheese plate at the Days Inn in Ho-Ho-Kus," she whispered into the phone.

"Yumbo!" Judy chirped at the other line. "I love cheese."

"Who is this?" Samantha sat up.

"Samantha, it's me, Judy Tremont. Sorry to call so early today, but Bill is driving me to pick up a few things and I thought it'd be so fun if we did it together. I promised Narciso I'd see his new collection, and I'm dying to get to Carolina Herrera. Plus, I don't know if you need to give any children's gifts, but Monica Noel has the most darling cashmere twin sets and party dresses and she's showing today at the Carlyle. We can do it in two hours, I promise. Boom boom boom. Unless you're waiting for another call."

"No. No. I'm not waiting," Samantha answered immediately.

"Sorry you couldn't stay for a while after dinner the other night. It was so fun. I think Barry Santorini may be talented, but he's a pig. And in my book, the pig part really matters."

"Yes, he is a pig." Samantha caught her face in the mirror. "I hope you got my thank-you note. It was a lovely dinner."

"Oh yes. And you have to tell me who does your stationery. I'm so sick of boring old Tiffany's. Even Mrs. John L. Strong is too dreary."

Samantha grinned to herself. She couldn't tell Judy she bought stationery by the bulk at Barnes & Noble.

"I'll have Bill pick you up at ten and you'll be home by noon. It's the only way to get everything done."

Samantha and Charlie seldom used a driver. They never saw a need for it, except perhaps in a storm.

"I wouldn't mind stopping in at Carolina Herrera." Samantha lit another cigarette.

"Oh, oh! She's perfect for you. You have to." Judy was beside herself. "See you at ten."

When Judy hung up, Samantha had no idea why she couldn't muster the effort to stop Judy and Barry from sending cars and arranging her life. The phone rang again and Samantha got out of bed. She had no intention of talking to Barry again. If she wanted to do something self-indulgent, she'd tag along with Judy Tremont for two hours. Shopping would just have to satisfy her craving.

When Samantha got into the car, Judy had her agenda ready. "I thought we'd do Oscar, stop in at Monica Noel, then Carolina, and pop into Prada if we have time."

As the car began its way up Madison, Samantha thought of her mother in her sensible Belgian loafers and her couture Bill Blass suits. Her mother's style never varied. It was her uniform. Clothes, according to Samantha's mother, should be well made and flattering. This quick trip up Madison with the chauffeured SUV waiting was something her mother would disdainfully say was brought to New York by the Hollywood people.

When Judy walked into the suite at the Carlyle Hotel where Monica Noel was showing her children's line for private clients, the salesgirl practically sprang out of her seat.

"Bonjour, bonjour." The salesgirl and Judy kissed. Once the bonjours and kisses were done, Samantha watched Judy drop at least ten thousand dollars on hand-embroidered satin party dresses and twin sets.

"This is so fun," Judy said. "And my girls really need these. I can't stand when all these nine-year-olds dress like sluts. Jessica Rodman looks like she's the happy hooker."

Samantha laughed. The morning with Judy was surprisingly relaxing and it kept Samantha's mind off Barry's lunch invitation.

"We need to get you something. I mean, not here. But you haven't gotten a thing."

"I don't really need anything." Samantha looked at Judy.

"Who really needs anything? That's not the point of shopping," Judy answered, and turned to the salesgirls. "Just send it to me."

When they left the Carlyle, Bill was waiting downstairs.

"I think Carolina Herrera's next, Bill."

"Absolutely, Mrs. Tremont."

Judy started whispering to Samantha. "I like Carolina Herrera because at least it's a little sexy, a little zippy. I mean, women like Clarice Santorini dress like they're in Greenwich in 1952. She's got a great figure, but no flair. Don't you think so?"

"I don't really know her," Samantha mumbled.

"Oh, I don't really know her either." Judy touched Samantha's arm. "I'm just a terrible person."

"No you're not." Samantha looked at her.

"Hey, if the world's in such a lousy mess, we might as well have a good time, right?" Judy shrugged.

"Yes." Samantha smiled at Judy with affection. "I guess that's true."

When Judy entered Carolina Herrera's showroom, the routine was the same. The shopgirls came fluttering out with waves and kisses.

"This is my friend Samantha, and she is desperate for something a little sexy."

"I am so sorry Carolina isn't here. She will be so sorry she missed you. She's with a client," the salesgirl apologized.

"Well, call her and tell her Samantha Acton is here," Judy had no problem advising her.

"No, please don't disturb her. I'm fine. Really." Samantha examined a clutch bag. "You have lovely things."

Judy almost lunged at a low-cut pink cashmere wraparound dress.

"Oh my God! I think I'd have an orgasm if I saw you in that." Judy pawed the dress. "And believe me, I don't have orgasms all that often."

Samantha's mind skipped again to Judy in the pink wet suit and Albert in the harness.

"Would you like to try that on?" The saleswoman asked.

"Do it! Do it! Do it!" Judy began pushing Samantha into the dressing room. "I mean, only do it if you want to."

Samantha stared at herself in the dressing room mirror. She was slipping into a $6,000 dress that Judy Tremont had picked out for her and that Barry Santorini could possibly then unravel at lunch with the pull string. The entire scenario felt like she had taken the wrong turn into what her mother referred to as "Nouveau Hell."

"Oh my God," Judy squealed when Samantha walked out of the dressing room. "If you don't buy this, I'll kill myself." Judy stamped her foot and then turned to the salesgirl. "Wouldn't Mrs. Herrera want Samantha to wear this around town? I mean, I bet Nicole Kidman and all those movie stars never pay for their own clothes on the red carpet. Well, Samantha is better than a movie star. I mean, if there is New York society right now, you are looking at it."

The salesgirl nodded. "Is there an occasion you need the dress for?"

Samantha's interest was piqued. "I'm chairing the Friends of the Whitney luncheon."

"Plus you know she was featured in *Manhattan* magazine as a style icon."

"I think we could work something out," the salesgirl said.

"I knew it!" Nothing made Judy happier than a shopping coup. "Just one photograph and this will be the 'it' dress of the season. Oh," she added as she pointed to a satin blouse, "can you send that blouse to my house in whatever colors you have? It's adorable."

"Certainly. I think it comes in black, white, green, and blue. I'll send all of them."

Bill dropped Samantha at her house exactly two hours after the shopping spree began.

"God. I love feeling this accomplished." Judy gave Samantha a kiss as the doormen rushed out to the car. "Now I can deal with the rest of my day."

"I had a great time." Samantha turned to Judy. "I never do stuff like that."

"Oh, anytime you want to do something really expensive and superficial, just call me." Judy laughed wholeheartedly.

Samantha wasn't sure if Judy was being self-mocking or not. All she knew was the morning made her feel released from self-abnegation or any constraints of propriety.

Samantha met Barry at Chanterelle that afternoon wearing the hot pink cashmere wrap dress. Afterward, they went to the Mercer Hotel, where Barry unwrapped her like she was the Christmas present he'd always dreamed about.

Samantha began seeing Barry whenever she could. She knew that Charlie would always be there for her, but he couldn't really take care of her. And if buildings collapsed again, or a man with smallpox ran through the streets, Barry would lift her out in his private plane. Barry could make things happen. He could even breathe life into her.

"I think we should go into business together," he told her a month after they'd started sleeping together.

"You want me to star in your next movie? I heard girls go far by sleeping with the producer, but this is faster than I ever imagined."

Barry kissed her. "You're crazy."

"You brought it up."

"I have to do my annual spring rat-fuck for the independent film-makers. I shouldn't call it a rat-fuck. I do actually care about this. It's one of those benefits when you get rich people to eat in black tie so young artists can make movies. And I was thinking maybe you could chair it."

"There I was hoping you thought I had talent and what you really think is I'm just a society girl."

"Look, it's for a good cause. Plus it's a great excuse for me to call you when Charlie's home. And it's a no-brainer. We'll do it at Tavern on the Green or the Pierre."

"I'm bored already," she said as soon as she heard the standard locations.

"Okay. You want artsy? We'll go downtown to the Puck Building."

"Boring. Boring. Barry, we can do better."

"It's just a fuckin' benefit. Do it in the goddamn Rainbow Room."

"Who wants to stand around the Rainbow Room eating boring shrimp and looking out at that same New York skyline and then move into the main dining room for beef medallions." Samantha was adamant. "That's in the life's-too-short category."

Barry was a little surprised she took it all so seriously. "Honey, you're the producer. You do it wherever you want."

"Is anyone winning an award?" Samantha asked.

"Why, do you want to put it in the fuckin' Dorothy Chandler Pavilion?"

"I'm thinking. Who are these filmmakers?" she asked.

"I don't know. Young filmmakers. Some kid from USC. Some Russians, and I think some African-American kids Spike Lee recommended to me. All I know is I'm not giving anything to some kid with a trust fund from Vassar or Brown. Fuck them. Spoiled brats."

"Barry, I'm a kid with a trust fund." She hit him.

"No you're not. You're American royalty." He tousled her hair.

"No I'm not. Adrienne Rodman is American royalty now."

"She's a whore."

"I have an idea." Samantha perked up.

"We're not having this goddamn party on Adrienne Strong-Rodman's yacht. It'll cost me two million dollars and they'll reenact *Birth of a Nation*."

"No, I'd never do that." She kissed him. "What about someplace unexpected. Someplace that celebrates New York."

"The top of the Empire State Building?" Barry answered.

"I'm serious. Don't all these young artists and filmmakers live in Brooklyn now? We could have it in Williamsburg in an old school or factory."

"Sure. Or we could all go to Harlem."

Samantha lit a cigarette. This was getting interesting. "No, Harlem's already been done. Grey Navez had her daughter's sweet sixteen at Sylvia's Restaurant of Harlem. Columbia kids live in Harlem. It's the next Park Slope. What are the movies about?"

"You've lost me."

"The winners. What are their movies about?"

"I don't know. Coming out of the closet in Minsk, a serial killer in Houston, growing up in Bedford-Stuyvesant."

"That's it! That's where we're having it."

"We might as well have it at my father's old shoe repair shop in South Philly. It's safer."

"Barry, not only are we having it there, but we're raising additional money for other young filmmakers in the neighborhood." Samantha was getting excited.

"But who the hell is going to go there?"

"Trust me, Barry." She kissed him again. "Albert and Judy Tremont will go and they won't be walking."

CHAPTER SEVENTEEN

Frankie

"Pippa, I wanted to talk to you about Alex." Frankie leaned forward in her chair.

"He's doing much better at school." Pippa evoked her peace-treaty composure. "I think the Ritalin that Dr. Berkowitz prescribed has really calmed him down."

Frankie took a short breath. "I got the results back from the MRIs that we took last week and I've sent them to a number of experts. I'm afraid Alex has a tumor growing on the right side of his brain. We can't tell right now if it's malignant or benign, but I want you to go see Dr. Haim at Mount Sinai. He's one of the best pediatric brain surgeons in the world."

"You're making this up." Pippa's eyes penetrated Frankie's.

"I have sent the scans to two of the best radiologists I know, and they've come back with the same conclusion. If you like, I could show it to you."

Pippa's voice went soft. "I'm sorry, I'm just not taking this in."

Irina, the nurse, pushed open the door. "Dr. Weissman, I'm sorry to disturb you, but there's a problem in the waiting room."

"I'm busy right now. Can't you handle it, Irina?" Frankie asked.

But in the short time the door was open, Frankie could hear that this was no minor disturbance.

"It's Mrs. Tremont. She won't listen to me, and now she's screaming at the girls behind the desk." As Irina continued, she began swearing in Russian. "Сука! Глупая богатая корова! If you want those kind of people as your patients, then you can handle them, but I don't allow anyone to talk to me that way."

"You go ahead, Dr. Weissman," Pippa said. "I wouldn't mind a few minutes alone."

Frankie touched Pippa's shoulder. "I'll be right back. I promise you, we will get Alex the best care. And I'll be with you all the way."

Pippa grabbed Dr. Weissman's hand and squeezed it. "I know that."

Frankie looked at Irina and lowered her voice. "Okay, Irina. Let's go."

Frankie walked down the hallway and threw open the doors to her waiting room to find Judy Tremont screaming at the front-desk receptionist. "For all I know, there are communicable diseases in this waiting room. I might as well be in a bazaar in Baghdad."

"What seems to be the problem, Mrs. Tremont?" Frankie asked her formally.

"Dr. Weissman, I had to send my girls to wait with Bill in the car because I certainly wasn't going to have them sit here. This office is like Port Authority." Judy was so angry she felt her face turning red. "I know Adrienne Strong-Rodman doesn't have to waste time anymore in this waiting room and I don't see why I should have to either."

Frankie usually set aside Tuesday mornings for pro bono work with her uptown patients, except for special circumstances like Pippa Rose, or if a parent called with a sick child. Judy had called early that morning because Charlotte had a sore throat and Frankie squeezed her in. As she looked around the waiting room, it was very apparent that other than Pippa Rose, Judy and her daughter were the only other white patients.

"I want the same treatment as Adrienne Strong-Rodman. I'll pay you what she pays you." Judy took out her checkbook.

"Let me give you some figures first, Mrs. Tremont." Frankie felt her heart racing. "Do you know that forty-seven percent of East Harlem's children are living below the poverty line? In my office, I try to make these numbers irrelevant. In my office, all children are treated as equals."

"Looky here." Ever since she was a child Judy had said "looky here" when she was boiling mad. "I don't care how much of a donation I need to give to whatever clinic you tell me, I need to know when I come here that my children are your first priority."

Without hesitation Frankie turned to her nurse. "Irina, can you get me Mrs. Tremont's file?"

"It's right here." Irina handed Frankie a thick manila file.

"Mrs. Tremont, effective immediately, your family are no longer patients here." Frankie handed Judy her file. "I would give you a referral, but I honestly can't inflict you on one of my colleagues."

"I will sue you for malpractice."

"Good-bye, Mrs. Tremont. And if your daughters ask what happened, tell them you didn't want them to have to wait in a room you considered dangerous because people you wouldn't dream of inviting to dinner have the same ailments they do."

Frankie walked back into her office and found Pippa sitting silently where she had left her.

"Judy doesn't mean any harm," Pippa said quietly.

"I can't allow her to disturb my office like that." Frankie began clearing her desk.

"The thing is you don't even know what privilege really means until you get news like this."

"Nothing is conclusive yet." Frankie looked at Pippa.

"Do you think this is why Alex didn't get into Collegiate?" Pippa asked.

"Beg your pardon?" Frankie was taken aback.

"This tumor. Does this account for the hyperactivity and his crashing on the ERBs?" Pippa asked.

"I know a lot of brilliant kids who crashed on those tests." Frankie sloughed off the question. "I don't think it's related."

"But once we take care of this, do you think I could get Alex out of Trevor Day and into a first-tier school? I know he's as bright as my daughter, Jennifer. And she's at Brearley."

"Pippa." Frankie put her arm around her. "Let's take care of Alex first. I can make an appointment with Dr. Haim for you today."

Pippa got up. "Do you think it's because I let him eat Cheetos? I couldn't help it. He loves Cheetos."

"There's not many things I can promise in medicine, but I am willing to put my reputation on the line that it wasn't the Cheetos."

"Then life just sucks, doesn't it?" Pippa said uncharacteristically.

Frankie looked at Pippa, the pain in her eyes gave a humanity to her tightly pulled face and hair.

"Can you fix this?" Pippa's voice was now cracking.

"I know there's a good possibility we can." Frankie heard herself employing a practical distance.

"How good a possibility?" Pippa asked.

"My father used to say to me, 'Frankie, your problem is ninety-five percent solved.' And I'd ask him what about the other five percent and he'd tell me I'd have to have an 'in' with a much higher power than him."

"Was your father religious?" Pippa asked.

"No. He was just a very smart man."

"Did he pass away?"

"No. He's not very well."

"I'm sorry."

"You're right about privilege, Pippa. It's so easy to forget the privilege of having a parent or child that you love. I think we all get distracted by a pair of shoes."

"For me it's Staffordshire."

"My advice would be to call Dr. Haim and then go out and treat yourself to a couple of great Staffordshire pieces. Ones you've always wanted. Call me later. Here's my home and cell phone number." Frankie gave her a card.

"Thank you, Dr. Weissman." Pippa got up.

"Let's hear from the specialists before you talk to Alex."

"Should I talk to Arnie Berkowitz?"

"That's up to you." Frankie tried to answer nonchalantly.

"You don't like him."

"I'm not going to step on his toes."

Frankie handed Pippa her son's brain scans and called for her nurse.

"Irina, how behind am I?"

"I'd say forty-five minutes."

"All right. No lunch. Let me see the next patient."

If pediatrics was a seasonal practice, Frankie believed there were also days that seemed like nuclear winter. After Pippa Rose left, Frankie diagnosed and hospitalized a third of her East Harlem patients with asthma, which was consistent with her current figures that East Harlem had the city's highest pediatric asthma hospitalization rate at 23.3 percent. In addition, she sent a six-month-old baby to an emergency room with a collapsed lung, found lead poisoning in three eight-year-olds, got positive test results for an eleven-year-old Dalton student with lymphoma, and received a call that a former patient, a Harvard student and heir to an aluminum fortune, had died of a heroin overdose.

Frankie had promised to stop in to take a look at Abraham, but the lingering effects of Judy Tremont's tantrum and the day's prognoses made a walk down Fifth Avenue and perhaps a drink with Jil seem far more preferable. On the other hand, she didn't want to disappoint Abraham. She liked the idea that perhaps he would still notice that she came.

"Hi, Dad, it's me." She smiled at him when she entered the room and found him watching a CNN documentary featuring the president.

"Terrorist allies constitute an axis of evil, arming to threaten the peace of the world."

As the president continued, Frankie tried again to speak to her father. "Dad, how are you doing?" He shushed her.

"By seeking weapons of mass destruction, these regimes pose a grave and growing danger. In any of these cases, the price of indifference would be catastrophic."

"Do you know him?" Abraham asked Frankie.

"What, Dad?"

"Is he a friend of yours?"

"No, Dad, that's the president of the United States."

"This is a stupid war." He suddenly shut off the television.

"I think so, too, Dad."

Frankie was thrown by her father's lucidity.

"Can you please get the doctor for me?" Abraham turned his full attention to Frankie. "I haven't seen him yet today."

"Do you need to see a doctor?" Frankie asked her father.

"Of course I do. Otherwise I wouldn't be in the hospital," he snapped at her. "Would you like me to undress so that you can examine me?" Abraham began unbuttoning his pajamas.

"No, I know you're fine. Would you like some water?"

"Yes, water would be nice." Frankie held a glass of water up to Abraham's lips while he drank it.

"You're a very nice nurse. I wish you would come more often. Listen, would you mind turning the television back on? Because if we're going to war, I need to know. They told me, after the last war, that I wouldn't be drafted again. But you can't trust these sons of bitches."

Frankie kissed her father on the cheek. "You never know."

Abraham and Frankie sat in silence as the president concluded his speech from the Oval Office. By the time the documentary ended, Abraham had dropped his head forward and fallen asleep. As he continued to snore, Frankie turned off the television and began to sneak out of the room.

Frankie pulled out her cell phone when she left her father's apartment. "Jil, it's Frankie. I wondered if you'd like to meet me for a drink."

Whenever Frankie called Jil for a spur-of-the-moment movie or drink, he was never available. She assumed he was with clients or his daughter or had other social obligations. But tonight Frankie couldn't bear the thought of just going home.

"Can I get you a cab?" Abraham's doorman asked her.

"Yes, that sounds great."

The doorman hailed a cab and turned to Frankie. "Where to? Home?"

"The Carlyle Hotel," she answered quickly.

After Frankie and Jack had split up, she made a rule for herself never to drink alone at home. It wasn't that Frankie was particularly concerned about her alcohol intake, but the alone-at-home part of the equation felt like a self-fulfilling prophecy.

A hotel, however, had entirely different connotations. A drink at the Carlyle was like going to London and popping in for a glass of wine before the theater. And most important, according to Frankie, the Carlyle had the best oily and salty potato chips in town.

Bemelmans Bar was dark and half empty. In the corner table, a blonde English girl of around twenty-five was seriously necking with a sixty-year-old man Frankie recognized as a business partner of Paul Rodman's. At the center table were three women with thick Texas accents wearing what Helen would describe as skating-rink-sized diamonds. They were holding up shopping bags from Bergdorf, Valentino, and Barneys, like hunters displaying the day's game.

Frankie ordered a kir royale and began munching on the chips. She thought of calling Jil again or a girlfriend, but decided she preferred to sit alone and listen to the pianist's medley of Gershwin, Berlin, and Cole Porter. For a moment, her mind drifted to Pippa and her son, Alex. Frankie had convinced herself that she was incapable of loving anyone as much as a parent loved a child. She believed she had chosen the right profession because her gift was for analytical detachment.

The Texas ladies were toasting their second round of margaritas when the pianist began to play "There's a Small Hotel," a favorite song of her father's. Frankie began singing to herself.

"There's a small hotel / With a wishing well / I wish something something." Frankie felt a lump growing in her throat and waved to the waiter for a check. She would not allow herself to drift into some sentimental reverie about her father. She was determined to nip it in the bud.

Frankie waved again for the waiter.

"How did you know I'd be coming? I know you're intuitive, but it was really thoughtful of you to have already gotten us a table."

Frankie felt a hand on her shoulder, turned around, and saw Charlie Acton in a sheepskin coat.

"Charlie?"

"I assumed you were waving at me. Or are you here with someone else? Did I catch you in flagrante?"

"No, no. I was just getting the check." Frankie was completely flummoxed.

"Don't go. Stay and have a drink with me? Samantha is working late."

Frankie was reluctant to say that as far as she knew, Samantha didn't technically work, but she let it go. "Oh, sure. Please join me."

Charlie took off his jacket. He was wearing a surprisingly unformed old Shetland sweater and corduroy jeans. Oddly, it was the same sort of clothes he wore when Frankie first met him twenty years ago.

"I come for the chips." He smiled at her. "The greasier the better."

Frankie looked at his intelligent blue eyes. Without the chic setting of Alvar Aalto modern treasures and the sleek Samantha Acton on his arm, he had a warm innocence.

"What are you drinking? It looks like a Shirley Temple."

"Kir royale. Champagne and cassis."

"Girl drink." He stuck out his tongue. "I used to have a girlfriend from Skidmore who'd come down to Princeton and have those."

"She drank champagne at college?"

"Oh please. It was Asti Spumante." He laughed. "Who knows? Maybe that's why I didn't get into the Ivy." Charlie waved for the waiter. "I'll have a Grey Goose martini, up, olive, and my sister here will have one, too."

"But—"

"Oh ya gotta have a martini here. They come in little silver shakers in their own personal mini ice buckets. What did you get with what you've got? Just a skinny glass and some fizz."

"Two martinis?" the waiter asked.

Frankie looked at Charlie. "Absolutely."

Charlie stretched his feet out under the table. "Do you come here a lot?"

"Bad day. I'm a little bit on overload."

"I know what you mean. I hardly ever come here. Samantha says it isn't either edgy or chic enough. She and Jil prefer drinks at Milk and Honey, some speakeasy on the Lower East Side. But what can I say, I'm from Omaha, right?" He ate a chip and passed the bowl to her. "Funny what kind of place you think will be anonymous enough to make you feel at home."

The waiter brought over two martinis in their shakers.

First Charlie poured Frankie's drink and then his own. "Cheers. What good luck for me that you were here." Charlie clinked her glass.

"Yes, cheers." Frankie hadn't had a martini since she drank four her sophomore year after a Princeton-Harvard game and subsequently threw up all over her blind date.

"Perfect." Charlie put down his drink. "Samantha will be so disappointed that she missed you. She's getting all involved in planning a benefit in May for the independent film alliance in Bedford-Stuyvesant."

"She has?" Frankie didn't mean to sound quite so incredulous, but Bedford-Stuyvesant wouldn't have been her first assumption for Samantha's whereabouts.

"Do you know Barry Santorini? He asked her."

"I just met him at that dinner at Judy Tremont's."

"You mean the night he announced that there was no such thing as a truly original artist?" Charlie sipped his drink. "I thought he was a jerk. But maybe that's what it takes to make good movies."

"Maybe." Frankie wanted to get the conversation off Samantha and Barry Santorini. She'd rather talk to Charlie about whatever book he was reading.

"Anyway, Santorini hooked Samantha up with this independent film group and she thought it would be great for the city to do this benefit in Bed-Stuy. You know, she's very civic-minded."

Frankie sipped her drink. "Yes. She did so much for the park."

"Well, that's it really. She says after 9/11, it's very important to bring filmmaking back to the city. Plus it makes a lot of sense to bring the real money out to Bedford-Stuyvesant."

"I bet Adrienne Rodman can't wait to get there," Frankie blurted. "I'm sorry. I shouldn't have said that."

"Oh, I'm glad you did." Charlie laughed openly.

The pianist began playing "They Can't Take That Away from Me."

Charlie took a final sip of his drink. "I remember taking a girl here when I was a resident. She was a big fan of *Madeline* and told me all about the murals."

Frankie was beginning to feel the effects of the martini blending with the fizz of the kir royale. She began reciting what she remembered from the children's classic. "In an old house in Paris that was covered with vines lived twelve little girls in two straight lines . . ."

Charlie touched her hand. "I'm impressed."

"My dad used to read it to me. I have no idea why a Jewish girl growing up in Queens should have identified with Madeline in her convent. But I did."

"My father read me *Ivanhoe* in Omaha. I can assure you, there weren't a lot of Black Knights roaming around Nebraska." Charlie lifted his hand. "Will you have another drink?"

"I really shouldn't. I have to—"

Charlie cut her off. "Oh, come on. Pretend we're old friends who are meeting for a drink at Claridge's or the Connaught. We're not even in New York."

"What about Samantha?"

"I told you we're in London tonight. Samantha's planning benefits in New York."

The waiter came to the table. "We'll have another round. And many more chips."

The twenty-five-year-old English girl began straddling the sixty-year-old man in the corner. As they fell onto the banquette, Charlie put his arm around Frankie and whispered to her. "I have his wife's butt in my refrigerator."

Frankie began to spit out her potato chip.

"I have evolved into a repulsive person since you knew me." Charlie shrugged. "I have no scruples at all."

"That's not what I've heard," she tried to reassure him.

"What have you heard?"

"You've got a great reputation."

"And what am I doing with it?"

"I think we just do the best we can."

"You're a very nice woman, Francesca Weissman. You were when you were nineteen, and you still are now. And that's a much bigger accomplishment than being in *Manhattan* magazine."

"Thank you." Frankie felt a chill on her neck as the second round of drinks arrived.

They sat in silence until the pianist began a medley of Beatles songs: "Yesterday," "Michelle," and "Here, There and Everywhere." Frankie thought she saw Charlie beginning to cry during the last one, but decided not to say anything. Finally he broke the silence.

"How is your father, Frankie? Samantha told me he hasn't been very well."

"I just saw him tonight," she answered. "He was watching the president enumerate the axis of evil. My father said this will be a stupid war."

"Was your father in World War II?"

"Yes. A pilot in the South Pacific."

"My father was on the beach in Normandy."

"Really?"

"Was your father born here?" Charlie asked her.

"No, Austria. He came here at age twelve and landed on Ellis Island. He lived with his aunt on the Lower East Side. My father won a scholarship to Georgia Tech as an engineer. He was the only Jewish boy in his class. He began working in a textile mill in Alabama and invented a machine for manufacturing panty hose. But he came back to New York because he thought the segregation laws in the South were unconscionable. He opened a factory in Paterson, New Jersey, with a black foreman who had been a segregated factory worker in Georgia. My father thought this was a great country as long as the opportunities open to him were available to everyone. He was diagnosed with Pick's disease five months ago. When I saw my father tonight, he thought I was his nurse."

"In some ways"—Charlie looked directly at her—"maybe it's best that both our fathers don't know about this country right now. Maybe we can both take solace in that."

At that moment, Frankie felt closer to Charlie than she had to anyone since her relationship with Jack ended. She thought what it would be like to spend the night with his arm around her, listening to the Beatles, talking about their childhoods, as if they were still nineteen.

"Check, please." Charlie called for the waiter. *"Monsieur, l'addition, s'il vous plaît."*

As Charlie rattled off his French, Frankie felt the world of Pippa Rose and first-tier schools, Judy Tremont shrieking in her office, and the Fashionable Samantha Acton all fall back into focus.

CHAPTER EIGHTEEN

Clarice

Clarice asked both her thirteen-year-old daughter Venice and her personal assistant how she should dress for the indie film benefit in Bedford-Stuyvesant.

"Mom, you just can't go there in some preppie Ralph Lauren dress and pearls," her daughter told her. "You need a little bling."

"What?" Clarice asked.

"A little bling. You can't be so boring in Brooklyn."

"What does that mean?" Clarice sat down beside her daughter in the family room.

"I just mean they'll be really cool people there." Venice had exhibited a collection of her photography when she was twelve. It was about a day in the life of a cashier in one of her grandfather's supermarkets.

"Fine. I won't be boring. So what should I wear? Katherine, do you have any ideas?" She asked her assistant, a thirty-year-old former Mark Morris dancer. "You're cool."

"I'd try something ghetto fabulous. Like Lil' Kim," she answered.

"Who's Little Kim?" Clarice asked.

"Mother, you are so pathetic. I'm amazed Daddy stays married to you."

"I guess he just loves me." Clarice stood up. "I have to pick Brooke up from school. She has ballet today."

"Mrs. Santorini, would you like me to make a few calls and find something appropriate for you?" the assistant asked.

"That would be perfect, Katherine. And cancel my Pilates, please, because I forgot there's a birthday party after ballet."

"Yes, Mrs. Santorini." Katherine took notes.

"Mother"—her daughter slumped back on her couch—"when you were younger and you worked, did you make your own appointments?"

"Of course I did."

"So why don't you make them now?" she asked.

"Because I have two children, a husband, and four homes to run now and I couldn't get any of it done without Katherine here. Your father has a fit if his favorite orange juice isn't immediately available in all of his homes. Why are you asking me this?"

"We took a vote in our women's studies class. Half the class said they would prefer to stop working when they had their children. But they all said that raising a family in New York was impossible without wads of money, a nanny, a housekeeper, a cook, and a personal assistant." Venice leaned in toward her mother. "Mom, do you think that's true?"

Clarice wasn't sure how to answer. She hoped that her daughters would find work that would obsess them like their father's work obsessed him. Clarice loved her life but she knew ultimately that her real job was to make Barry's life work for him. If Barry called on the spur of the moment to say they were all going to Europe that night, Clarice would get the children organized and make it happen. And if Barry called the day of a long-planned vacation to cancel, Clarice called the staff back and dinner was on the table. It was difficult anticipating the moods and whims of someone as volatile as Barry. But after fifteen years of marriage, Clarice believed she had it down to a science. Clarice knew she wasn't a genius, but she knew Barry better than anyone else in the world. For Clarice, the fact that she was Mrs. Santorini wasn't just about love or money or even family obligation. It was her entire existence.

The First Annual Indie Film Benefit was held in May at an abandoned church on Jefferson Avenue in Bedford-Stuyvesant. The building had been partially burned down during a 1964 summer riot and never fully restored. Samantha had found the site while she was scouting the area with Barry's current favorite production designer. She chose not to hide the church's decay, but to light its Victorian details and wooden altar with blue and lavender Christmas lights. The lights were like tiny blue dots creating an air of mystery and sensual decay. The pews in the sanctuary were replaced with blue velvet leopard love seats and massive throw pillows. And for flowers, Samantha triumphed with the unheard of: she had stalks of red gladiolas at every table, the kind sold by the dozen for $6.99 at a Korean market. It was a style coup.

The chauffeured cars began pulling up at around seven o'clock. But children from neighboring housing projects began gathering outside as soon as a red carpet was placed on the street. By five o'clock, word got out on the news and the Internet that every African-American movie star from Denzel Washington to Will Smith to Spike Lee would be showing up along with the most recognized socialite faces from the Upper East Side—Samantha Acton, Grey Navez, and Adrienne Strong-Rodman. Among the anticipated guests were also the African-American CEO of Time Warner—the underwriting company for the event—the presidents of Disney, Sony Pictures, and Brown University, the Brooklyn borough president, the commissioner of cultural affairs, and the mayor. Awaiting their collective arrival were reporters from *Entertainment Tonight*, Black Entertainment Television, New York 1, and all the local stations.

As the guests walked down the red carpet, it became clear that the uptown socialites had taken the "Dress Ghetto Fabulous" salutation on the bottom of the invitation to heart. Adrienne Strong-Rodman arrived in gold lamé Dolce & Gabbana hot pants with a matching halter, while Judy and Albert Tremont dressed as Ike and Tina Turner. The African-American movie stars, on the other hand, were mostly in understated strappy gowns and fitted Armani suits.

"Samantha! Samantha!" At least fifty photographers began snapping pictures as she walked in sporting a vintage Halston gown worn by Diana Ross when she was still a Supreme. Samantha held on to Charlie's arm as photographers screamed, "Samantha, you look great! Over here, Samantha. Who's your husband dressed as?"

"He's my pimp!" Samantha laughed openly. She grabbed Charlie, who was wearing an open shirt and multiple gold chains.

"Are you gonna sing tonight, Samantha?" the gossip stringers from *Manhattan* magazine asked.

"We've got 50 Cent in there and much more talented people than me to do that." Samantha squeezed Charlie's arm and walked inside.

The police had formed a phalanx of cars to protect the powerful and the glamorous. When Barry and the mayor arrived someone in the crowd screamed, "How come the only time you come here is for a party with white people? Why isn't this kind of money going for education?"

The mayor took a microphone. "It is so great to be here tonight in Bedford-Stuyvesant to celebrate young African-American independent filmmakers. The arts are what make this city great. And I want to thank Barry Santorini for celebrating the incredible talent in this neighborhood and saying that the movie industry isn't turning its back on New York." Then the mayor put his arm around Barry.

The reporters began shouting, "Barry, over here! Barry, over here!"

Barry was wearing his traditional black sweatshirt and jeans. Clarice, on the other hand, was in oversized beaded homeboy pants, a backwards Yankee baseball cap, a matching beaded Oscar de la Renta twin set, and a Teflon vest.

"Barry!" The gossip reporter from New York 1 got his attention. "How did you choose this church?"

"It's all Samantha Acton," he answered. "She's a genius."

The reporter turned to Clarice. "And who are you dressed as tonight?"

"My daughter Venice said to say, 'I'm Super Mommy.'"

Barry looked at her and tried to cut her losses. "Let's go, Clarice."

"Back. Back." The police began pushing back a group of teenagers who were trying to get a look at Denzel Washington.

"Fuck you!" one kid screamed. The cop pulled him aside.

Barry grabbed Clarice. "I said let's get the hell inside!"

Inside the church, waiters circulated the pews with pinkie-sized ribs glazed with cassis, grits on endive with blue cheese, foie gras hamburgers on mini buns, shrimp curry on watermelon slices, bags of fried chicken fingers with french fries, endless flutes of Perrier Jouët champagne, and diet Dr Pepper.

While 50 Cent was rapping, "We're gonna party like it's ya birthday / We're gonna sip Bacardi like it's ya birthday," the A-list was getting down. Adrienne Strong-Rodman demonstrated her best moves from the Reebok Gym's aerobic hip-hop class.

Judy ran up to Samantha. "I swear, it's the best party I've ever been to. I'm going to have my daughters' next birthday here."

"I just hope our car doesn't get broken into." Albert winked at his wife.

"Oh Albert, stop it!" Judy gently pushed her husband. "And even if it does, this is such a magical night. I don't care." She turned back to Samantha. "Only you could pull this off. I mean it. This city has been dreary ever since September 11th. This is the only time it seems like fun again and you should really congratulate yourself."

A young African-American man in wire-rim glasses and leather jacket approached the podium underneath the crumbling altar.

"Hey, I'm Trevor Stokes and I just want to thank you all for coming tonight. We have raised one-point-five million dollars for the independent filmmakers' fund, and another anonymous donor has just pledged five hundred thousand dollars specifically for young African-American filmmakers from this neighborhood."

"I'll match it," Paul Rodman shouted from the balcony.

The room broke into whoops and applause.

"That is so dope!" Trevor clapped his hands in appreciation.

"Did he say dope?" Judy whispered to Grey Navez. "'Cause we're leaving if there's any dope. I have a very good relationship with the *New York Post*."

Trevor pounded his heart with his fist. "You guys are money! Thank you from the bottom of my heart. And now, the man of the hour, Barry Santorini."

Barry walked up to the stage.

"Wow! I don't think I can top that. First of all, I got to thank the mayor for being here tonight. I want to thank my pals Denzel, Spike, and Will for their generosity in showing up for the next generation of African-American filmmakers. And most of all, this night would not be possible without our benefit chair, the talented and truly beautiful Samantha Acton. Maybe if we're really lucky, she'll sing something for us. Not only does she have perfect taste, she has perfect pitch. Get up here, Samantha."

Samantha shook her head no. 50 Cent took the microphone. "Get up here, girl." He began applauding and the room followed.

Samantha approached the microphone and whispered to Barry, "What should I do?"

"Sing," Barry answered so the entire room could hear.

She looked around the room at the sea of white women dressed as rappers and beautiful black women in red-carpet glamour and felt herself losing her balance. She thought of running, but she saw enormous security guards at every exit. For a moment she had forgotten that the security for the evening would eat up a third of their profit.

"Sing," Barry whispered to her again.

"Uh, well, since I'm dressed like Diana Ross, I guess I'll sing Diana Ross."

She began to sing in a slow, husky blues voice. "You can't hurry love / No, you just have to wait / She said love don't come easy / It's a game of give and take."

Clarice sat on a plush velvet love seat while Samantha sang. Her eyes scanned the room for Charlie. He seemed like such a nice man. If she had to stay any longer at this, it would have been nice to talk to him.

When Samantha finished singing, Barry took the microphone. "Brava! Brava!" The room whooped again with delight. Barry quieted the crowd. "Hey, New York. We're still here! Let's dance!"

As the band broke into a Supremes medley, Barry began dancing with Samantha. While listening to all of "Back in My Arms Again," "Baby Love," and "The Happening," Clarice sat silently sipping a Perrier Jouët. She hadn't eaten anything all night. Her stomach was too queasy for short ribs or curry, and she would wait until she got home and have a peanut butter sandwich.

Judy came up to her. "Clarice, your husband is such a great dancer! Do you two dance a lot?"

"Only when we travel." Clarice kept her eye on Barry and Samantha, who had now joined the crowd to "get their freak on."

"Albert's worried there could be trouble when we leave. But I told him, it's not like we're on the Afghan-Pakistan border," Judy continued.

At that moment, Clarice saw Barry take Samantha's hand and leave the room.

"I'm sorry, what did you say?"

"Albert thinks we could get mugged or murdered. But I told him that's racist."

"Yes." Clarice had been trying not to take her eye off Samantha and Barry, but she had lost them.

"You know, there are a lot of African-American girls in Charlotte's class. Which I think is great. I'm a hundred percent behind diversity," Judy continued. "And some of them live on Park Avenue or Central Park West, and that's just a lot more convenient."

Clarice looked at Judy. "Have you seen Charlie Acton?"

"Beg your pardon?" Judy couldn't make the connection from the African-American elite to Charlie Acton.

"Dr. Acton. Have you seen him?"

"He must be here somewhere."

"Would you excuse me?" Clarice got up and followed the blue twinkling light to the exit. Her body was breaking into a cold sweat and she couldn't bear to be in the room for another minute.

The hallway was empty except for a couple of three-hundred-pound security guards.

"Can I help you, miss?"

"No, I'm fine." Clarice held on to the wall. "Where's the ladies' room? I'm not feeling very well." She took her baseball cap off, which left her hair damp and uncharacteristically matted.

"It's up the steps. You want me to take you?" the guard asked.

"No, I'm fine," she answered, still holding on to the wall.

"Watch out for those steps. This church was condemned until they decided to have this party here."

Clarice climbed the steps slowly. Her head was now spinning

from the continuous loud music, the lack of food, and only Perrier Jouët and Dr Pepper to drink. She thought she'd lie down on the floor in the ladies' room until Barry was finished schmoozing and rat-fucking or whatever the hell he needed to do at these kinds of events.

Clarice grabbed hold of the knob of the door and pulled it open. In front of her was Samantha on her knees in the backless Diana Ross gown and Barry with his pants down.

Charlie

Charlie lost sight of Samantha before she began dancing with Barry. Since the time they first started dating, Samantha had made it clear to Charlie she had absolutely no interest in having a man hang on her. She far preferred for them to part at any function and then, later in bed, deliver to one another the evening's choice anthropological findings.

"The only way to really enjoy a party," she once told Charlie, "is to treat it like a dig. If you explore it in the right way, it will give you some serious insight into how we live. And since it all is meaningless, at least that way it can be a little funny."

Charlie had begun talking to an African-American Princeton graduate who was planning to make an updated film of Genet's *The Blacks*.

"How are you going to finance this?" Charlie asked.

"My college roommate and I started an Internet company when we were sophomores. Basically, we never have to work again," the prospective filmmaker answered offhandedly.

When the filmmaker seized his opportunity to introduce himself to Spike and Denzel, Charlie wedged his way through the crowded room to find Samantha.

"Adrienne, have you seen Samantha?" he asked Adrienne Strong-Rodman while she was still in mid hip-hop.

"No, doll. But I would kill to have thrown this party. I'm so jealous. I could fuckin' kill her."

Charlie continued to look for Samantha.

Grey Navez waved at him. "Great party, Charlie."

"Only Samantha! Only Samantha!" Tina Schultz chimed in.

"Yes. She's incredible." Charlie smiled and went to get a drink.

"A Grey Goose on the rocks," he said to the bartender.

"Aren't you some famous doctor?" The bartender stared at him.

"I don't know about that. But I'm a doctor and I don't play one on TV," Charlie answered.

"Yes you do. I saw you being interviewed on E! Entertainment Network the other day. You were giving someone really famous a chemical peel."

"Oh, I'm not sure it was me."

"Man, it was you." The bartender tapped Charlie on his arm. "I'm an actor, so I bartend and watch E! You were giving one of those Piel sisters a chemical peel. How much does something like that cost?"

"I think you've got me confused with someone else." Charlie walked away.

Charlie looked down at his watch. It was getting close to 2 a.m. and the party was still going strong. Most weeknight events in New York ended soberly by ten-thirty so the captains of industry could get to work early the next morning. It was the rare evening when anyone over thirty stayed out past midnight.

"Have you seen my wife?" Charlie asked Jil, who was wearing a do-rag on his head.

"She's here somewhere."

"Where's Francesca tonight?" Charlie asked.

"She said she had to work late. Poor thing. She's such a good girl. But I suppose that's why we all love her."

"Yes, I suppose." Charlie continued to look around the room.

"If I see Samantha, I'll tell her you were looking for her."

"I'm sure we'll catch up."

There was something about the earnestness of Francesca Weissman working late that made Charlie want to leave before he said the wrong thing to one of those white women dressed up like Queen Latifah.

"Clarice! Clarice!" Charlie called as he saw Clarice Santorini moving very quickly toward the exit.

"Clarice, it's Charlie Acton!"

Clarice continued walking.

"I was just wondering where your husband is." Charlie stopped her. "I thought perhaps he's seen my wife."

"Who the hell cares," Clarice mumbled, and kept walking.

"Excuse me?" Charlie answered.

"I'm going home and I suggest you do, too." Clarice shoved her way out of the room.

"Clarice!" Charlie followed her into the street, but Clarice was on her cell phone until Julian pulled up directly in front of the abandoned church and whisked her away.

"Charlie! Charlie!" Judy Tremont began screaming from her car. Charlie turned around and Judy swung her car door open. "Hop in, Charlie. You're making me nervous standing out here alone."

"Have you seen Samantha?" he asked.

"She's inside with Barry. This party could go on till morning. Get in. You could get killed standing out here."

"Thank you, Judy. Good to see you." Charlie walked away.

Charlie knew he wasn't going back inside to that party and he wasn't taking the car and driver he and Samantha had arranged for the night either. Samantha could take that car home anytime she was ready to go. She didn't have to rely on the good graces of Barry Santorini. Even better, maybe she would wonder where he was. And he certainly had no intention of helping her figure it out by taking a ride with Judy Tremont. Samantha would just have to do a little work to find him.

Charlie pulled the gold chains off his neck and continued walking away from the party, and from all the cars stopping to roll down their windows with urgent pleas of "Get in, get in." He dismissed Clarice's hysteria. If she was envious of Samantha and the time she was spending with Barry, that was her problem. She clearly didn't understand the intricacies of a sophisticated marriage.

Charlie knew that Samantha would never let someone like Barry Santorini threaten her relationship with him. Barry was a powerful man, a rich man, a player, but he needed "a wife." And ultimately, Samantha was far too complicated and narcissistic to just be a wife. Samantha was a man's heart and soul. And Barry, from Charlie's point of view, had no need for either.

Charlie walked with his head down. The streets were dark and empty. He was too frightened to stand still and hail a taxi, and furthermore, there weren't any. Finally, he saw an entrance for the Utica Avenue subway stop. Charlie had not been on a subway, except during a major snowstorm, for over ten years. He ran down the steps while his eyes shifted from side to side.

Charlie bought a MetroCard from the machine and felt his heart racing. He imagined knife wounds and emergency rooms in Kings County Hospital and his photo on the cover of the *New York Post*: "Dr. Butt Takes Ride in Bed-Stuy." He only managed to calm down when he saw a cop standing at the end of the station. Charlie positioned himself directly in front of the police officer.

When the train pulled in, Charlie hesitatingly left his cop. Looking around the local for his potential assailants, Charlie was surprised to see a young couple necking and another avidly discussing a Tony Kushner play. From their conversation, Charlie gleaned that they all seemed to be returning from a dinner party. At the other end of the train were two young interns still in their hospital scrubs and an old man fast asleep, holding a bottle of Johnnie Walker.

There was something so reassuring about the passengers on that 3 a.m. train ride compared with Judy Tremont dressed as Tina Turner. After navigating a transfer to the 6 line, Charlie suddenly felt full of hope for New York, for his life, even for his marriage. As the train pulled into the safety of the Upper East Side Hunter College stop on Sixty-eighth and Lexington Avenue, Charlie felt a surge of strength. He was home and had made it. As Charlie walked out of the subway onto the Upper East Side, he had the self-assurance of an adolescent who had escaped a ridiculous prom.

Crossing East Sixty-sixth Street, past the gray Cosmopolitan Club that Samantha's grandmother had founded and onto the solidity of Park Avenue, Charlie decided his disappearance had probably tortured Samantha enough. Maybe they could have a late drink at the Pierre or the Plaza Athénée. Maybe they could take a room, like out-of-towners, and make love. As he took his cell phone out and began to call her, he felt a thrust in his back.

"Turn around and face the wall, motherfucker. I've got a gun."

Charlie felt a sharp jab in his back. He put his hands against the wall of 625 Park Avenue.

"Give me your wallet and cell phone, asshole."

Charlie passed both. He never saw his assailant's face and his hands were gloved. He thought he caught a glimpse of a white sliver of skin, but he couldn't really say.

"Take off your shoes, fuckhead. I said, take off your shoes or I'll shoot."

Charlie took off his shoes. He watched as they were hurled into oncoming traffic and the figure, who wore a hooded Harvard crew sweatshirt, ran off.

Charlie walked into Park Avenue to retrieve his shoes. When he went to pick them up, he saw they had been split in half by a hurtling truck. Returning to the sidewalk, Charlie stepped on the shards of a broken Colt 45 bottle. Limping while he held his bleeding foot, Charlie knocked on the door of the nearby apartment building, but the doorman wouldn't let him in.

Charlie shouted, "Goddammit, I'm hurt. Open up the goddamn door!" The more Charlie shouted and knocked on the door, the more the doorman of the stately building ignored him.

Finally, Charlie hopped to a pay phone to charge a call to Samantha. "Honey, are you there? It's me. I'm hurt." When she didn't answer he hung up and called the operator for Frankie's home number.

"Hello," Frankie picked up, expecting that it was some middle-of-the night crisis about her father.

"Francesca, it's me, Charlie Acton. I need help."

"What?" Frankie sat up.

"I, uh, just stepped on some glass and my foot is bleeding and I just got mugged on Park Avenue and I have no money."

"Charlie?"

"I'm not going to a fucking emergency room. You've got to help me."

"Charlie, get in a cab and I'll meet you in front of my office—1205 Fifth Avenue. A hundred and second and Fifth."

"You're a doll."

"Charlie, I'll be there in fifteen minutes."

At least three taxis sped by Charlie as soon as they noticed he was barefoot and bleeding. Charlie took his jacket and dangled it in front of him in order to conceal his injury. When a cab finally stopped, Charlie gave the address and said, "Someone will be waiting for me."

"I've heard that before." The taxi driver looked in the back mirror and spoke in a mixture of Brooklynese and Hindi.

"I promise you'll get your fare," Charlie answered.

Frankie was waiting in front of her office when Charlie got there, and she paid the taxi driver.

"Mister, you're lucky you've got such a nice wife. I wish I had someone who'd pick me up after I'd been out all night." The cabbie looked Frankie over.

"Good night." Frankie handed the driver the money and put her arm around Charlie. "Come on inside, Charlie."

"I owe you one for this, Francesca."

"Do you want me to call Samantha?"

"No. Just take care of this please. Fuckin' Park Avenue mugger made me take off my shoes."

"This is why I never spend money on shoes." Frankie smiled.

"He didn't want my shoes, honey. He just didn't want me to run after him." He grabbed his foot. "Oh Christ, this hurts."

"Come on. I'll take care of it."

Frankie brought Charlie into exam room five.

"Sit up here." Frankie washed her hands and came back to the examining table. "Now give me your foot."

Charlie put his foot in Frankie's hand and picked up *Go Away, Big Green Monster!* "Can I read this while you do it?"

"If you want. This is gonna hurt a little." Frankie took a few instruments from her drawer and sprayed Charlie's foot with an antiseptic.

Charlie began reading. "Go away, Big Green Monster, and don't come back until I say so—Christ, that hurts!"

"You got a big slice in there." Frankie sat down on the stool across from the examining table. "Maybe we should go to a hospital."

"I thought you were my friend. Why would you send me to a hospital?"

"I don't want you to get an infection."

"I'll get an infection at the hospital."

"Take a deep breath." Frankie put her hand on his shoulder.

Charlie held his breath while Frankie searched his instep with a scalpel.

"Charlie, you can breathe now."

"Aren't you going to give me an anesthetic?"

"If you're good, you get a lollipop." Frankie looked at him. "I just did this for Sea Bernstein after he fell from the helicopter pad in East Hampton."

"And I thought I had a pretentious practice!"

"Ready?"

"Ready."

Frankie put on rubber gloves and removed the glass while Charlie watched her.

"Most of my patients turn away."

"I'm around thirty years older than most of your patients." Charlie clenched his fist like a child.

"Charlie, where's Samantha?"

"I don't know."

"She was on television tonight with Spike Lee and Denzel Washington."

"You are so lucky you didn't come with Jil to that."

"Jil didn't invite me to that," she said nonchalantly.

"Oh, well, you didn't miss anything, except for Judy and Albert Tremont dressed up as Ike and Tina Turner."

"Oh God." Frankie laughed openly.

"What the hell time is it?"

"Around five a.m.," she answered.

"I have to be at the hospital at six." Charlie looked at her. "Do you mind if I take a little nap here? Maybe I could read the monster book again."

"Won't Samantha be worried about you?"

"Try to stop being such a good girl, Francesca!"

Charlie lay down on the examining table while Frankie stood in the corner.

"Sit down, Francesca. You're making me nervous."

Frankie sat back down on the stool.

"Sit up here." Charlie waved to her. "I was just mugged in my neighborhood. I might have nightmares with you all the way over there."

Frankie sat down on her examining table and Charlie put his head on her lap.

"There. That's much better." He snuggled into her.

Charlie began snoring immediately as Frankie sat looking at the everyday supplies in the room: rubber gloves, disposal, washcloths, and the drooping wire toy with wooden beads. It was then that Frankie realized she was falling in love with Charlie.

Charlie suddenly looked up at her. "Francesca, I left out the best part. My mugger was wearing a Harvard crew team sweatshirt."

Frankie laughed. "Do you think he was a cox or a stroke?"

"That's my girl." Charlie looked at her and closed his eyes.

CHAPTER TWENTY

Samantha

At 4 a.m., the morning after her triumph in Bedford-Stuyvesant, Samantha flew with Barry on his private plane to his house in Nantucket. Samantha didn't precisely say yes, but Barry would not take no for an answer.

On their way out to Teterboro Airport in New Jersey, Samantha took off her shoes and lit a cigarette.

"That was an unbelievable party." Barry began to massage her feet. "You raised two-point-five altogether for those filmmakers. Jesus fuckin' Christ. No one's ever done something like that for them before."

"They should make it an annual event." Samantha took a puff.

"No, you make it an annual event." He kissed her fingers.

"Barry, I'm sorry about—"

"You're sorry about what?"

"Well, what happened."

"Fuckin' door didn't lock. It's like an obvious movie with a basic plot point. I'd fire a writer who came up with shit like that."

"Maybe you should call her?" Samantha didn't know why she said that. She didn't particularly want Barry to call Clarice.

"Maybe you should call what's-his-name." Barry dropped her foot.

"Charlie."

"Fine, Charlie." Barry passed her his cell phone. "Call him. Tell him I called my pilot and we're flying to my house in Nantucket because I can't let you go."

"I don't want to call Charlie. He's probably asleep. He gets up early in the morning."

"So does Clarice. She takes Pilates."

"They all take Pilates!" Samantha puffed on her cigarette.

"Listen, there's no reason for me to call Clarice. What matters is my children and I will deal with that."

Barry had, early in his marriage, told his lawyers that if he ever got divorced, he would sue for the children to live with him. Clarice was, in Barry's opinion, too high-strung to be a single parent and much too polite. He didn't want his children growing up to be doormats.

When the driver pulled into the Signature Flight Support terminal, Barry looked up into the rearview mirror.

"Julian, I'll be back at around ten a.m." Barry instinctively knew that Julian had taken Clarice home and come immediately back to Brooklyn for him. "We're just going up to Nantucket for a little breakfast."

"Very good, Mr. Santorini." Julian opened the door for Samantha and Barry and the Teterboro security guard swung open the gate to the runway.

"Hello, Mr. Santorini. Great to see you." The pilot approached them. "Wonderful morning for a flight."

The fact that the pilot did not ask who is this woman, why did you wake me up to say you were flying to Nantucket at four-thirty in the morning, and where is your wife, gave Samantha a rush of well-being. It further confirmed her suspicion that true power and money insulated you from any logical reality. Climbing up the steps to Barry's Gulfstream jet, Samantha believed, given the precariousness of life, that Barry and men like him had devised the most bearable way to live.

"Didn't this house once belong to the Mellon family?" Samantha asked as they drove along a winding road to a classic shingle "cottage" perched on acres overlooking the ocean.

"How did you know that?" Barry asked.

"I used to come here with my mother when I was a kid."

"If I was lucky, I went to the boardwalk in Atlantic City when I was a kid."

"Have you lived here a long time?" she asked as they walked to the front door.

"Bought it last summer. I got sick of the Hamptons. Too many investment bankers and best-selling authors. And the Vineyard isn't any better. You get all the Hollywood people plus the fuckin' Clintons."

"I thought you liked the Clintons." Samantha looked at him.

"Hey, I like everybody. But I'm a Republican. Plus I want my privacy. I don't need to be going to parties every fifteen minutes. This house is just for me and my kids. And now it's for you, too."

There was a specific fragrance to the spring roses that grew on Nantucket fences that Samantha remembered from her childhood. The scent mixed in the air with the salty undertow of the sea. She remembered clambakes on this very beach and her mother dressed in baggy chinos and a pink Lacoste top and carrying one of those hand-woven Nantucket baskets with the ebony whale figure on top. At those clambakes, Samantha met boys and girls from the "good" families who came to Nantucket every summer. By the time the sun set and the grown-ups were distracted with their vodka tonics and conversation, the children of the "good" families would sneak into the dunes to get stoned.

There was no one like Barry at any of those clambakes, so it struck Samantha almost ironically that walking into Barry's house she felt that she was finally home. Maybe there was some dialectic of money, and it took someone like Barry, unpolished, abrupt, who had summered in South Philly, to bring her back.

"Wanna get some breakfast and take a walk on the beach?" Barry asked as they walked into the kitchen.

"Sure."

Barry's housekeeper had laid out a spread of bagels, smoked salmon, muffins, fruit, and yogurt that could have served fifteen.

"How did you do this?" she asked him.

"Oh come on. You're the Fashionable Samantha Acton. You call ahead."

"When did you know we were coming here?"

"Same time you did." He grinned.

"But how did they do it so quickly?"

"Honey, you sound like a girl from the burbs. I'm a producer. I make things happen. You wanna bagel?"

"No. A muffin is fine." Samantha took a large blueberry pastry.

"I love that you eat. None of those other East Side girls eat. What's her name, that one who threw the party for you?"

"You mean Judy Tremont?"

"That's not a body. That's a coat hanger. How does your husband deal with women like that? Each one wants to be skinnier than the next one. And they all want to look twelve years old. I swear, actresses are a day at the beach compared to these people. They're obsessed. But I guess that's what keeps your husband in business."

"I guess." She took a bite of muffin.

"I know Clarice went to see your husband for a consultation. Her personal assistant gives my assistant all her bills." Barry sprinkled salt on his cream cheese. "Why would any intelligent person want to waste their life poking at those women's skin? Or maybe I'm wrong. Maybe he isn't so intelligent."

"Charlie's very smart." She put down the muffin. "He went to Princeton."

"Fuck Princeton. I went to community college." Barry spread lox over his bagel. "I guess being a doctor is just a lousy job to begin with. In a way, you're a glorified nurse plus people can sue you right and left. And you're always satisfying your clients. I take it back about being a nurse. It's more like a glorified interior decorator. Am I being a son of a bitch?"

"A little." She shook her head. "You're forgetting about people like Jonas Salk."

"Has your husband invented a vaccine I didn't know about?" He smiled at her. "Should we finish our food and go take a walk on the beach and catch the sunrise so I shut up?"

"Yes, I'd like a walk."

"You can like me to shut up, too. Sometimes I'm better in small doses." Barry bit into his bagel.

Samantha took off her shoes as she climbed with Barry down to the dunes. Until Barry began speaking about doctors, she really hadn't thought about what she'd tell Charlie. In truth, she wasn't sorry she was missing his realization that she just wasn't coming home. She knew that Charlie could be both self-destructive and self-pitying and she wasn't very good at dealing with either. As she sank her feet into the sand, she decided that she loved Charlie but he deserved to find someone much more willing to focus on him.

As the sun rose, Samantha and Barry walked hand in hand along the beach.

"You know, we're meant for each other." He turned to her. "I know that sounds like a lousy line from a Julia Roberts movie, but it's true."

"I like Julia Roberts movies." Samantha nuzzled his shoulder.

He looked directly into her eyes. "Look, if we don't take advantage of finding each other, we're as stupid as everybody else, and we're not. I know we need to take this to the next step." He touched her face and laughed. "Sorry, now I sound like a fuckin' D girl."

"What's that?"

"A development girl."

Samantha pushed up against his thigh. "I meant, what's the next step?"

"Honey, we'll work that out." He kissed her hair. "It's just procedural."

"You make it sound so simple."

"I love you, Samantha." He pulled her closer. "I promise this won't get boring."

Samantha's lip curled. "Oh, I can promise you that, too."

He laughed and they walked in silence as the bright yellow and orange of the sun reflected on the crashing waves.

Barry pulled Samantha closer. "Everyone else is so frightened of what's going to happen next. But I'm excited. And now I've got you."

"I love you, Barry," Samantha whispered in his ear as the waves came in and gently tickled her toes.

When Frankie got Charlie up at five-thirty in the morning to go on his rounds, he had developed a fever which she believed was due to an infection in his foot.

"Charlie, I'm going to take you home. I'll call Samantha."

Charlie mumbled, "Call her. She must be worried about me by now. Do you have her numbers?"

"Yes. You rest." She lowered her voice. "I want you to see your doctor today."

"I saw my doctor. You took care of me," he mumbled.

"I'm telling Samantha to take you to a doctor. You rest and I'll be right back."

Frankie went into her office and dialed Samantha at home and her cell phone. Perhaps it was because Frankie was trained as a pediatrician, her instinct was to get in touch with Charlie's parent or guardian. Frankie thought of calling Pippa Rose to find out if there was some after-benefit party that Samantha might be at. But she didn't want to disturb the entire Rose family. Remembering that Judy Tremont got up every morning at five-thirty for Pilates, Frankie decided to bite the bullet and call her.

"Judy, it's Dr. Francesca Weissman. I hope I haven't disturbed you."

"I thought I wasn't your patient anymore." Judy's voice, even this early, was blunt. "I already have another doctor Arnie Berkowitz found for me. It's Lucinda Moore on East Seventy-fourth and I adore her." Judy was ready to hang up.

"She's a wonderful choice," Frankie answered quickly, and got to the point. "Judy, do you happen to know if there was another event after that benefit in Brooklyn last night? I need to know where Samantha Acton is."

"I'm afraid, Dr. Weissman, everyone in New York is talking about where Samantha Acton is. Clarice Santorini walked in on her and Barry with his pants down."

"What?" Judy, as always, was offering much more than Frankie bargained for.

"Well, Clarice went home from that awful place crying and told her daughter Venice. Venice e-mailed Jessica Rodman, and now every kid at Spence, Nightingale, and Hewitt knows all about it and so do all their mothers. They were doing it in the bathroom. I mean, how high school is that? And what about poor Charlie? I mean, I think he's not really the best dermatologist in New York anymore, but he does adore his wife. And you know that Samantha and I are extremely close now. And all I want is for her to be happy. I find Barry Santorini physically repulsive, but he's rich and very powerful. And even if you're *the* Samantha Acton, that kind of money and power are very intoxicating ingredients."

"Thank you, Judy. Good to talk to you." Frankie hung up before she had to endure a minute more.

Because Barry's children were her patients, she had his emergency numbers at his office and all his assistants' home numbers.

"Hello, this is Dr. Francesca Weissman. I need to reach Barry Santorini." She spoke efficiently to his half-asleep assistant.

"Is it an emergency?"

"Yes," Frankie said without hesitation. "It's a family matter."

"He's at his house in Nantucket. 508-529-3374. There's also his cell phone, 917-421-8087."

"Thank you." Frankie hung up and dialed. She wasn't quite clear if it was Charlie or really she who wanted to get in touch with Samantha so desperately.

"Hello, Barry. This is Dr. Francesca Weissman."

"You called my private cell phone!" he screamed at her.

"Your assistant gave it to me," Frankie snapped.

"Is something wrong with one of my kids?"

"As far as I know, your children are fine," Frankie answered. "Is Samantha Acton there?"

"Isn't it a little early for you to be making social calls?" He was still screaming.

"Barry, if she is there, I need to talk to her. It's urgent." Frankie said in a flat professional voice.

"But she doesn't have children."

"She has a husband and he's been hurt."

"So I'll tell her." Barry was furious at the intrusion.

"No, Mr. Santorini. I acted as his doctor tonight, and I will tell her the full details."

"You never struck me as a girl with these kinds of balls."

"May I speak to Samantha, please." She was cold and direct.

Barry called to Samantha. "Hey, babe, it's for you."

"Who is it?"

"My kids' doctor."

"Frankie Weissman?"

"I never knew she was such a pushy bitch. It's something about your husband."

Samantha took the phone. "Frankie?"

Frankie took a breath and tried to ground herself. "Hello, Samantha. Sorry to disturb you, but I thought I should tell you that Charlie was mugged last night and injured his foot."

"How was he mugged? Did the driver do it?"

"Apparently, he took the subway home and it happened somewhere on Park Avenue."

"On Park Avenue?" Samantha thought the call was surreal.

"That's what he said," Frankie answered.

"What was he doing on the subway in the middle of the night?"

"I really can't say. He called me when he needed help."

"Well, thank you for telling me." Samantha pursed her lips. "Charlie is so self-destructive. Does anyone know?"

"No, I took care of it," Frankie continued.

"Frankie, I think you should know that my circumstances have obviously changed. Of course I want to do what's right for Charlie."

Frankie sat back in her chair. "I see."

"Would you mind staying with him till I get there? I'll be home to tell him later this morning. It was very kind of you to make the effort and call me here. I really appreciate it. Good-bye."

"Good-bye." Frankie hung up and was momentarily unable to go back to Charlie in the examining room.

Frankie began to line up the empirical data. For some reason, she had remet Samantha Acton, and now she was bringing Charlie home so Samantha could tell him how their circumstances had changed. The one clear conclusion Frankie could draw was that for all her achievements, she had become an aide-de-camp to this court. But what was unclear to Frankie was why it meant so much to her to land this completely unenviable role.

Frankie asked her young associate to cover for her at the hospital, and brought Charlie home to Fifth Avenue.

"Where's Samantha?" he asked when they got to the apartment.

"She told me she wants you to sleep. She didn't want to disturb you."

"She's not much of a nurse. She must be out shopping. She likes to buy me things whenever I'm sick."

"That's probably it." Frankie walked Charlie into his bedroom. "Get some sleep. I'll be in the living room till she comes."

"Francesca, you don't have to do this for me."

"You're my patient."

Charlie looked up. "Do you always make house calls?"

Frankie smiled. "Only for Adrienne Strong-Rodman and people I truly admire."

"I love it when you're mean."

"Go to bed." She kissed his forehead and left the room.

Frankie sat in the living room and watched Central Park as the morning life of the city found its inimitable pace.

At 11 a.m. the door swung open and Samantha, still in her Supremes gown, walked in.

"Frankie, thank God you're here." She caught a glimpse of herself in a mirror. "I can't believe what I look like. I'm like a teenager who's sneaking back into the dorm after staying out all night. Where's Charlie?"

"He's inside sleeping. I think he will be fine."

Samantha embraced her. "Thank you, Frankie. Charlie and I are both so lucky to have found you again."

CHAPTER TWENTY-ONE

Clarice

Clarice's phone rang the minute she walked in the door from dropping Brooke off at school. Ordinarily she would have let the housekeeper or her assistant answer, but she hadn't heard from Barry since the benefit last night. When her daughters asked where he was she said he had left early in the morning to go to the set.

Clarice picked up, not knowing exactly what she would say if it was him. "Hello."

"Oh my God. I'm so excited it's you," a girlish voice chirped.

"Yes, it's me." Clarice had no idea who she was talking to except that it obviously wasn't Barry.

"Clarice, it's me. Judy Tremont."

"Oh, hi, Judy." Clarice had not been back to Judy Tremont's since the dinner in honor of Samantha Acton. "How are you?"

"I'm t – riffic." Judy was being decidedly upbeat at her faux-old-girl best. "I was hoping we could get together for lunch or coffee sometime. I really want to talk about some ideas for next year's school benefit and also about how permissive some of the other mothers have become. I would die before I'd let Charlotte wear couture under her uniform. In our house, Prada is only for the weekends."

Clarice wished she had never picked up the phone. "Oh," she mumbled.

"Anyway, anyway," Judy continued. "Albert hates when I'm catty, so it's so fun to get together with a girlfriend and say whatever the heck I want. It'd also be a nice chance for our girls to get to know each other. Maybe they could come back here from school together. Charlotte really admires Venice."

"But Venice is at least four years older than Charlotte."

"Charlotte is very mature. How 'bout next Monday at one and the girls can come here at around three?"

"Next Monday at one." Clarice hung up and poured herself a cup of tea to regain her composure.

Barry never mentioned to Clarice her opening the door on him and Samantha. He simply had Yvonne remove his clothes from the master bedroom closet later that afternoon. Yvonne informed Clarice's assistant that Barry would not be leaving the apartment but rather moving to the guest suite behind the kitchen. He planned to live at home until their separation was finalized because he would not give Clarice the option of ever suing him in court for abandoning the children. Yvonne told Clarice's assistant that Barry was certainly grateful to Clarice for the fine job she had done raising the children and Yvonne would inform her of his next move.

"She told you that?" Clarice stared at her assistant after returning from Brooke's class at Ballet Academy East. "I don't believe you."

"I promise you, Mrs. Santorini, that's what she said."

"What an asshole!" Clarice slammed her hand on the table, not noticing that her seven-year-old daughter had stumbled into the room.

"Mommy, you shouldn't talk that way," Brooke admonished her.

"I'm sorry, dear. I'm very angry."

"Mrs. Santorini, it's not my place to say this, but you shouldn't take this from him." Her assistant spoke with authority. "He's a real prick."

"What's a prick, Mommy?" Brooke asked.

"When you prick your finger with a needle."

"Like Sleeping Beauty." The child was intrigued.

"Yes, that's right," Clarice answered, pulling herself together in front of her child.

"So who's like Sleeping Beauty?" Brooke wouldn't let it go.

"Me. I'm like Sleeping Beauty, darling." Clarice patted her daughter's hair.

"I thought she said *he's* a prick."

"Katherine made a mistake. You're right, Brooke. She shouldn't have said that."

"I'm sorry, Mrs. Santorini," the devoted assistant apologized. "But you don't have to put up with this."

"Katherine, I'll deal with this when the dust settles." Clarice deliberately changed the subject. "Do you know Brookie was asked to demonstrate in ballet class today? And she did twelve piqué turns across the floor!"

After the Sleeping Beauty conversation Katherine never brought up the temporary living situation again. When Barry did sleep at home he would leave at 5 a.m. If he ran into Clarice in the kitchen between engagements he was always cordial. "Hello, howya doing. You look great." And he'd leave the room.

During the next week, Clarice took Brooke to riding class, ballet class, French class, and to every playdate. She went shopping with Venice, took her to a Broadway show, and even got up at 6 a.m. to play tennis with her. She coexisted with Barry in their fifteen-room apartment overlooking Gracie Mansion that her father had bought them as a wedding present.

.   .   .

"I've gotten my girls the most fabulous math tutor. He's gay, went to Brown, and he just makes it all so fun!" Judy confided to Clarice over an egg white truffle omelet with a splash of mesclun greens on the side.

"I'm teaching Venice Italian. I decided I could do it as well as any tutor," Clarice said proudly.

"Are you crazy? These boys from Brown are so fabulous! They're all smart as a whip and they all want to write screenplays and get into the movie business. They'd die to work for you and Barry. Unless you're teaching Venice yourself just to impress your husband?" Judy asked, hoping to move the conversation toward some information that would make Clarice really valuable as a lunch partner.

"I majored in Italian and I'm hoping Venice someday will live in Italy."

"Oh my girls love Italy and Paris. I've made traveling a real priority." Judy sipped her tea. "I hate these rich kids in New York whose lives are so limited. I mean come on, there's more to life than a Marc Jacobs purse. I'd rather spend a month at the Hôtel du Cap."

"Absolutely." Clarice knew it was in her interest to steer the conversation away from Barry's favorite hotel. "Isn't it great news about Pippa Rose's son? Thank heavens Alex's tumor was benign."

"Oh I love Pippa," Judy nodded. "I haven't spoken to her in a while because we fired her. It was just too much Staffordshire and chintzes. I have the most fabulous Swedish man now. I'm really into simple. All those tassels were driving me nuts. I hope she doesn't hate me."

"I'm sure she doesn't hate you. She's actually doing very well. Alex has recovered beautifully from his surgery and Jennifer has a big solo in a workshop at the School of American Ballet."

"I'd really love to see Pippa. Tell you what, why don't I throw a little fun lunch for you at Le Cirque and we could invite her, too," Judy gamely suggested.

"Oh, really, you don't have to." Clarice didn't want to go to another lunch. She was barely making it through this one.

"It'll be a little end-of-the-school-year get-together and a kickoff for the fall benefit. And we'll have Pippa and Grey Navez and Adrienne Strong-Rodman."

"Please, not her." Clarice involuntarily cringed.

"Fine with me!" Judy remembered that Samantha met Barry on Adrienne's yacht.

"I don't really care if you invite Adrienne or not." Clarice immediately covered her tracks. "If it's for the school benefit launch, then you might as well have her."

"Clarice"—Judy looked up at her with renewed respect—"I think you may be the best parent I've ever met."

Clarice dressed very carefully for her fun luncheon with the ladies. She went out early in the morning to John Barrett's salon to get her hair blown dry and her makeup professionally applied.

She had spent the evening before debating what to wear. A Chanel suit would look like she was trying too hard. But pants and a twin set were entirely too casual. She felt she needed armor to protect herself, but on the other hand she wanted it known that she was looking great. Finally, Clarice settled on a white linen Valentino pantsuit and four-inch Louboutin pumps.

At 11:45 Clarice examined herself in the mirror. For a forty-two-year-old woman she could pass for someone at least ten years younger. She was still a size 4, her auburn hair was gleaming, and her skin maintained a fresh and glowing quality. She looked no different from any of the other Upper East Side mothers, except she was now the one everyone else was talking about. Recently, she wondered if her life would have been happier if she had married a bright boy from Wharton who would have become a partner in her father's supermarket chain. She could have lived closer to her parents and spent the weekends with couples like herself at the country club. Her children would still have gone to private schools, Friends Seminary or Bryn Mawr Country Day, but the pressure to always be the best might have been less intense. Clarice never told Barry, but she wouldn't have minded if both girls had become cheerleaders.

This was not the first time Clarice played the what-if game with herself. Usually she would stop on the thought that if she lived in the suburbs she would never have been married to a man as exciting or important as Barry. But today on her way to the ladies' lunch she wished with all her heart that Barry had taken better care of her. She also wished that she could end her love for him.

Clarice had told no one about her current living conditions, and taking one last glance at her outfit before heading to the luncheon at Le Cirque, she promised herself she wouldn't say a thing about it today either.

"Every Tom, Dick, and Harry who can't get their kids into Spence or Trinity is starting their own school in Connecticut or the Hamptons now." Adrienne Strong-Rodman sipped a white wine spritzer and chatted breathlessly to Clarice, Pippa, and Judy. "At least I'm passionate about education. But the headmaster I hired was a total lush, plus he fell in love with Grey Navez's sister, who is richer than Croesus, so he doesn't need to run a school anymore. So my plan is temporarily on hold."

"Well, at least now you've got your summer back," Judy offered.

"Yes, I know. We were supposed to go to Saint-Tropez for June but Paul might not be able to leave the country."

"Why not?" Judy's nose for news was poised.

"He has some business here." Adrienne reached for a roll.

Pippa had heard rumors from her husband that Paul Rodman was about to be indicted for embezzling over $400 million.

"Oh it would be so sad to miss Saint-Tropez. I happen to love Cap-Ferrat," Judy offered as a revelation. "Of course, everyone says the place to rent a house is Marrakech."

"I've never been there." Clarice was surprised how much she was enjoying herself. The idle chatter about hotels, schools, and summer plans was surprisingly soothing. She wished Grey Navez had been able to be there but Grey had a tendency of canceling at the last minute.

"Pippa, it's so fabulous your son is doing so well. Clarice told me the good news." Judy bobbed her head.

"God, this has been the worst few years of my life," Pippa blurted. "The World Trade Center, Alex . . ."

. . . I fired you, Judy thought to herself.

"But for some reason things seem to be falling into place now. Jennifer's been cast as a Polichinelle next year in *The Nutcracker,* and it's looking like she'll be asked to be an apprentice in the New York City Ballet," Pippa said with great pride.

"How wonderful!" Judy smiled. "And tell me do you still see Frankie Weissman? Because Arnie Berkowitz has found me the most wonderful doctor. And she returns your calls in a flash and you never have to wait in her office with all those welfare kids hacking their faces off. I feel lucky my daughters avoided cholera in there."

The waiter appeared at the table. "Can I bring you ladies something else?"

"Yes. Will someone share a dessert with me?" Adrienne asked while chewing on a breadstick. "I'm on a roll and I'm not quitting."

"I shouldn't but I will." Pippa gave her a conciliatory nod.

"I'm sorry, Pippa, I know Frankie Weissman helped your son. But I could never bear her." Judy leaned in. "There are women I know who are single because, let's face it, all the good men are married or gay. But I think she's alone because she's so self-righteous. You know it would be a lot less pathetic if she was a dyke. But, honestly, I don't think she's got enough pizzazz to do it." Judy giggled. "How bitchy am I today?"

"Samantha says Frankie Weissman and her ex get on fabulously," Adrienne said offhandedly.

"Don't they have those delicious little cookies here?" Pippa was quick to deflect the conversation from Samantha. "That's my favorite part of the meal. Waiter! *Garçon!*" She lifted her hand. "We want those scrummy cookies."

"And crème brûlée!" Adrienne quickly added.

But Judy was not going to be sideswiped by a pot of burnt cream or petits fours. Finally, this meal with far too many carbs and oily salad dressing was going somewhere.

"Did Samantha really say that? I'm sorry but that is so gross, as my daughter Charlotte would say."

"I really shouldn't have told you that. I'm sorry, Clarice," Adrienne apologized. "Paul's been under a lot of pressure recently and I think it's making me a little nutso."

"I'm fine." Clarice picked up her spoon and broke the sugar crust of the brûlée as soon as it arrived.

"Clarice, we just want you to know that we are with you." Judy lifted her water glass to toast her and the other women followed.

"I have to say, I always liked Barry," Adrienne added when they lowered their glasses. "He's so brilliant and can be a lot of fun."

"Well it's clearly entirely Samantha's fault," Judy said pointedly. "I mean if she came on to Albert, I'm sure he'd get distracted, too."

"Albert is devoted to you." Clarice appreciated Judy's camaraderie.

"You never know," Judy confided. "This is a strange world with no values. Honestly, some days the only thing that I think I can rely on is my love for my children. That's my number-one priority." She paused. "I know that sounds like I read it in some Dr. Brazelton book or something, but honestly I know I can go over the top and they always bring me back to earth."

"Me, too." Clarice smiled, feeling even more of a bond with Judy.

Pippa looked down at her watch. After years of working in a service industry, Pippa kept her public opinions to window treatments and swatches. But frankly, she was always happy when the ladies' lunches, especially with clients who had fired her, were over.

"I have to go and he never brought us our cookies." Pippa began getting up.

"Wait a minute. I'll get them. I love telling waiters they fucked up." Adrienne had another sip of spritzer.

"That's all right, I can live without them." Pippa got up.

"I'll get the check." Judy raised her hand.

"No, my treat. Really." Clarice raised her hand.

"Clarice, I'm really sorry—" Adrienne began to apologize again, but Clarice cut her off.

"Judy, I'm going up to school to pick up Brooke after lunch. Can I give you a lift?"

"My daughter would shoot me if I picked her up." Adrienne looked at Clarice. Clarice knew from Pippa Rose that Jessica Rodman was already giving blow jobs on the bus ride home from Riverdale Country Day School soccer matches.

"I've got to go." Pippa stood up and air-kissed all three women.

"Guess Jessica's extracurricular activities scared her away." Adrienne laughed.

"Pippa's just a little prissy. That's why I fired her," Judy chimed in.

"But you have to hand it to her, that daughter is supposed to be a great dancer," Adrienne added.

"Oh she's a beautiful dancer." Clarice signed the check just as the plate of petits fours and cookies arrived.

"But you know what"—Judy picked at a cookie—"unless that

daughter marries the president of a network or a major banker, her life is going to be shit. It's all over for a dancer by forty. I'm sorry, but it's just us girls."

Clarice smiled. Judy swearing reminded her of Barry and his rat-fucks. She looked forward to sharing a ride with her uptown.

"Where's your car?" Judy asked as they left the restaurant.

"Barry has the car. I thought we'd share a cab."

"Don't be ridiculous! You don't know who the hell is driving cabs these days. They're all on the phone to their Al Qaeda cell in Buffalo. I told Bill to pick me up at Saks in an hour but I'll just get him to come now." Judy took out her BlackBerry.

"Mom! Mom!" Brooke bounded out of the school. "Mom, look what I made!" Brooke presented her mother with a wire and papier-mâché sculpture.

"Honey, that's fabulous." Clarice kissed her. "You remember Mrs. Tremont."

"Mom! Mom!" Brooke said, pulling on her sleeve.

"Brookie, aren't you going to shake Mrs. Tremont's hand? Where are your manners?"

"Mom, look! Dad's car is across the street."

"What?" Judy turned immediately.

Clarice immediately turned her head to look as Julian opened the door for Barry and Samantha.

"Brooke, stay here with Judy. I mean Mrs. Tremont."

"But I want to go with you," the child whined.

"You stay here with Judy," Clarice whispered.

Barry crossed the street before Clarice had a chance to reach him.

"What are you doing here, Clarice?" he asked abruptly.

"I called the school and told them I was picking Brookie up this week."

"You should have called me." He avoided acknowledging Judy or his child.

"Who talks to you?" Clarice felt her heart pounding. "Brooke, take a walk with Mrs. Tremont."

"Mommy, I want to stay with you." The child held on to her mother's white jacket.

"Clarice, if you have any questions just call Yvonne and she'll give you my schedule." His voice was devoid of emotion.

"Barry, why is that woman here?" Clarice felt her hands shaking.

"What woman?" Barry remained businesslike and spoke softly.

"I don't want that woman near my child." The more controlled Barry was, the more Clarice could not contain her anger.

"That's not up to you, Clarice," Barry said softly.

"Mom, who is she?" Brooke asked.

"Honey, shhhh," Judy hushed the child. She couldn't believe her luck. She was in the middle of the best story in town.

"Barry, I want you to move out tonight!" Clarice's neck had turned red.

"You mean you're throwing me out. That won't look very good in court."

Clarice grabbed Barry by the arm. "Barry—"

"Let go of me, Clarice," He took her hand off his jacket.

"Let go of Daddy, Mom." The child was now crying.

"I want you the hell out of my house tonight!" Clarice shrieked.

Although Judy was the first one to say she enjoyed a good gossip, she actually wasn't interested if it came at the expense of a child. She put her arm around the child to comfort her. She never liked scenes, and she was so grateful that she and Albert seldom had them. On the other hand, Judy couldn't help thinking that with access to this kind of story she could get anybody to one of her dinner parties now.

CHAPTER TWENTY-TWO

Samantha

"I thought she knew I was coming." Samantha took Barry's hand during dinner at Da Silvano, a Greenwich Village restaurant where Barry seemed to be best friends with Silvano and everyone else.

"She knew you were coming. Yvonne told her." Barry began waving to a young girl Samantha thought was either a famous model or a movie star.

"Is that Gwyneth Paltrow?"

"Jesus Christ, honey, Gwynnie is at least ten years older than that girl."

"Sorry."

"Don't be sorry. I love that you're not a celebrity whore." Barry looked up for the owner. "Silvano, where's our meal? I'm getting old sitting here." He dialed his cell phone. "Tell them we're going with Plan B. But let them think we're going with Plan A until we get it the fuck away from them." He put the cell phone on the table. "Sorry, baby. Have I told you how beautiful you are?" He pushed his leg against her as two plates of penne arrabbiata arrived.

"Barry, I know this may sound self-serving but I don't want to hurt your children any more than I probably already have."

Barry put down his fork. "What the hell are you talking about?"

"I just don't want to get off on the wrong foot. I never had children and I'd like to try to have a decent relationship with yours."

"Samantha, you're talking like you're on *Oprah*." He swallowed two bites hurriedly and lifted his hand. "Silvano, we need water here!" He moved in closer. "Listen to me. Clarice knew you were coming today. This is all some betrayed-wife scenario that her lawyers cooked up. And as far as my kids are concerned, they'll listen to me. Plus, what girl wouldn't want to grow up to be you?"

"Barry, I haven't done very much." She kissed his hand.

"For Christ sake, stop with the I-haven't-done-anything." He swallowed a mound of penne. "I'll tell you what we're gonna do. You wanna be a household name, we'll make you a household name. You can be an A-plus Martha Stewart. You wanna go on the *Today* show and talk about flowers and entertaining, we'll do it. You wanna design plates and champagne glasses and sell them on QVC, we'll do that. I'll do whatever you want." He kissed her on the mouth. Then his cell phone rang.

"Yvonne—you tell Clarice that she has no business calling you after office hours."

Samantha picked at her piece of bread and had a sip of wine while Barry continued talking. "Yvonne, unless it's about one of my children, you tell Clarice she can only call during office hours. And be sure both of my kids have my new cell phone number, and tell them they can call anytime." He put the phone in his pocket. "Let's go. I'm not hungry anymore."

He got up from the table. "Silvano!" He waved his hand, giving his standard just-put-it-on-my-bill good-bye.

"Of course, Mr. Santorini," Silvano nodded.

Julian rushed to open the door for Samantha and Barry. As they got into the car at least five photographers were waiting outside.

"Samantha, over here! Barry, over here! Samantha, how's the doctor?"

"Fuckin' assholes." Barry slammed the car door shut.

"Julian, let's take Ms. Acton home please."

"Miss Bagley." She smiled at him.

"Who the fuck is that?"

"That's my single name. I mean, the name I was born with. I'm going back to it."

"I like it." Barry kissed her neck.

"I'm glad. I like it, too." She leaned into him as the car drove up Sixth Avenue.

"Hey, Julian, can we have a little music?" Barry asked.

"Of course, Mr. Santorini," the driver replied. "Anything in particular?"

"Nothing that makes me feel old."

"Barry, that's not very helpful." Samantha laughed.

"Oh, he'll know. Am I right, Julian?"

"Absolutely, Mr. Santorini." Julian put in a CD of Frank Sinatra singing "Witchcraft."

Barry took Samantha's hand and sang along as the car drove uptown. "It's such an ancient pitch / But one I wouldn't switch."

Samantha looked at him and he grabbed her face. " 'Cause there's no nicer witch than you . . ." He turned her chin toward him. "This is sort of fun, isn't it?"

She sat up. "I hope it's better than sort of fun."

"I mean, usually those photographers are traipsing after twenty-two-year-old good-looking assholes. I'm a middle-aged guy with bad skin from South Philly. You know how much I've paid ridiculous PR people to put me in the papers, and all I have to do is kiss you hello and suddenly I'm Tom Cruise."

Samantha swatted him with her purse. "Stop it, Barry."

Barry took her purse away. "I am so nuts about you."

The car pulled up to The Sherry-Netherland, where Samantha had rented a temporary one-bedroom apartment.

As Julian opened the door for Samantha, Barry turned to him. "Julian, I'm just going to go around the corner to The Lowell to get a few things."

"Barry, this is crazy," Samantha whispered. Barry had taken a room at The Lowell after the school confrontation with Clarice. "You should just leave your things with me."

"Not until the lawyers start talking. I'm not giving Clarice that kind of ammunition."

"But—" She thought it was ridiculous to make the rules of their life together about his future divorce.

He kissed her. "I'll be right back."

When Samantha got out at the Sherry, she didn't stop to watch Barry's car pull away. She knew she had him as long as she never seemed to really need him. She also knew that by the end of the summer she'd make their moving in together seem like his idea.

Samantha smiled broadly at her new doorman. "Good evening."

Being with Barry had made her feel she was no longer going around in circles. She had been a perfectly crafted set piece. But now she was a player.

"It's crazy. I think the world is falling apart, and for some reason I am finally getting it together," Samantha spoke rapidly to her therapist.

"Then I assume things are going well." The therapist leaned forward.

"I think so. I mean, everything's temporarily up in the air and we've got to deal with his kids and his wife and do all that stuff right. But I know I made the right choice, even if Charlie does call me crying all the time."

"How do you feel about that?"

"Charlie is a very decent man. But that's not love, that's, I don't know—I guess doing the right thing, being like my mother, afraid to feel any passion or something. I mean, in some way I blame Charlie for my never really accomplishing anything."

"You feel he got in the way?"

"Charlie's just too accommodating. He was so eager to please me that I forgot I needed to please myself."

"And Barry is different?"

"Oh, Barry, yes! Want to hear something funny?"

"Sure."

"Barry is a Republican."

"What's so funny about that?"

"No one in the movie business is a Republican."

"Well, Ronald Reagan."

"Yes, and Arnold Schwarzenegger and Rupert Murdoch. I mean Barry's pro-choice and pro-gay, but he also says only an asshole would wait for the United Nations' permission before we bomb a country that's against us."

"And Charlie wouldn't say that?"

"Oh my God no! Charlie, in his heart, believes in love thy neighbor, just like my mother. In fact, if Charlie had been born rich and a woman, he would be my mother." Samantha took a sip of coffee. "All I know is I was drowning. Now I know what I want."

"And what is it that you want?"

"I want to get on with my life with Barry. I want us to move in together, and I hope to get married. I even thought the other day maybe we would adopt some kids from Rwanda or China. Now I sound like my mother."

"You've wanted a child for a long time."

"And I was thinking maybe I'd begin a new project instead of that coffee-table book. Maybe it would have to do with that church in Bedford-Stuyvesant. Really create a community center there, bring in some great artists. I'm sure I could get Julian Schnabel and Eric

Fischl involved. Also I'd like to redecorate Barry's studios in New Jersey. I just . . ." Her voice trailed off.

"What is it?'

"Remember Judy Tremont?"

"Of course," the therapist said quickly.

"Yumbo, right?" Samantha laughed. "Well, she once said that the Upper East Side is like a happy village. And I think everyone in that village is so happy getting to the next stop, the next apartment, the next school, the next benefit, the next purse that I feel sort of disoriented because for once in my life I don't want to get anywhere. I think I might be the only person who feels contented with the status quo. And that's I guess the thing that drives me so crazy about Charlie. I feel like he just wants to pull me back down into this world of tired dinner parties and being on an endless treadmill to the next get."

"What's a get?"

"Oh. That's what Barry calls the next thing you gotta get." She smiled at the recollection. "I wish I didn't have to see Charlie."

"Do you?" the therapist asked.

Samantha hadn't realized that almost a year had gone by since September 11 when she agreed to meet Charlie for lunch at Three Guys restaurant on Seventy-fifth and Madison. During their marriage, Charlie would go to Three Guys every Sunday for blueberry pancakes and sausage and afterward bring Samantha an egg white omelet with mozzarella and bacon "to go." She always joked that the mozzarella and bacon made up for her desperately missing the yolk.

"You look good." Charlie smiled as he cut into his pancakes while Samantha sat with a cup of coffee.

"You sure I can't get you an omelet?"

"No, no. Coffee's fine."

"Thanks for meeting me." He nodded awkwardly.

"How are things?"

"How are things? How are things?" Charlie muttered twice. "Well, there was a flurry of activity about Serena Curtis, who died from a reaction to a chemical peel at Alice Ringer's office."

"Yes, I heard about that."

"But that seems to have died down. And there's a new laser peel that claims to offer the benefits of a mini face-lift."

"Maybe I should try it."

"You don't need it." Charlie looked at her. "What else can I tell you? I'm teaching again this fall."

"That's good, you like that."

"And I've seen Jil." His mouth was going dry.

"I heard he's in love." Samantha poured cream into her still-untouched coffee.

"Really? He didn't tell me. Is it with Francesca Weissman?" Charlie asked.

"Charlie, please. He has some exotic male dancer in New Jersey that he won't introduce to any of us. At least that's what I hear."

"Why not? This is New York." Charlie felt easier talking about Jil than himself.

"Maybe this guy's a stripper on cable TV."

Charlie spit out his coffee. "What?"

"Who knows. That's what Judy Tremont told me. She also said the poor fellow has AIDS."

"Who, Jil?" Charlie was caught off guard.

"No, the dancer."

"I don't think you can believe Judy Tremont. She'd say anything just to get your attention."

"She amuses me."

"I hear she's very palsy with Clarice Santorini."

"Why do you say that?" Samantha put her coffee down.

"I think Clarice mentioned it."

"Since when are you very palsy with Clarice Santorini?"

"We're hardly what I'd call palsy. We have a professional relationship."

"Oh come on, Charlie. Don't pull this patient-doctor crap on me." Samantha was getting even more irritated by his bringing up Clarice than she intended to. "You mentioned her deliberately."

"No I didn't. She's a nice woman, but I don't really know her."

"She's not such a nice woman. She's got that nice-woman, I'm-such-a-good-mother bullshit thing down. She's completely manipulative."

"Samantha, I don't want to talk about Clarice Santorini."

"Why? Because she appeals to your fuckin' sense of honor and sanctity?"

"You don't even sound like yourself anymore. I have to say, Samantha, that man's language doesn't work coming out of you."

"Charlie, did you ask me to breakfast to give me an elocution lesson?"

"No. I want to talk about us," Charlie leaned in toward her.

"Charlie, there is no us," she answered flatly.

"Honey, I understand." Charlie cleared his throat. "Maybe you needed to shake things up. So now you've done it. You've changed our dynamic. Just come home."

"Charlie, I'm not coming home." She was furious at him for assuming it was all so easy to erase, as if nothing of consequence had happened.

Charlie took both of her hands. "Please, please, please, Samantha." He started to cry. "This is a cold and very mean town. Just come home."

Samantha stood up. "Charlie, don't do this to yourself. Someday I'm sure we'll be great friends. But right now, please don't call me anymore."

When she left the coffee shop she walked about five feet and into the Carolina Herrera showroom where she knew Charlie would never have the nerve to follow her. He had the butts of too many of her clients in his refrigerator.

"Hello, Mrs. Acton," the salesgirl chimed immediately.

"Miss Bagley," Samantha corrected her.

CHAPTER TWENTY-THREE

Charlie

Charlie came to the conclusion that everything in his life would have been different if he and Samantha had moved downtown. He decided that if he and Samantha had lived downtown, they'd have had more interesting friends: artists, writers, playwrights, a different kind of wealth. If they lived downtown he wouldn't be just an Upper East Side dermatologist but someone who was on the edge and an integral part of fashion. If he and Samantha had lived downtown she would have seen that Barry Santorini wasn't a real artist. He was basically a parasite who preyed on artists.

"Maybe Samantha and I should get a loft in Tribeca," Charlie mentioned to Jil as they walked around the Sonnabend Gallery in Chelsea. They had made a date for Saturday morning gallery-hopping followed by lunch.

"You could get a loft for a song now. Everybody's moving out since the Trade Center." Jil had had this conversation with Charlie at least eight times since Samantha moved out but he went along with it anyway.

"Or we could get a nice town house in the West Village. Or one of those glass Richard Meier apartments on the West Side Highway."

"Too open. Too much light." Jil stopped in front of a sculpture of bicycles that were smashed by the Trade Center. "I don't know if I can quite accept that as a valid piece of art yet."

"I can't believe it was over a year ago."

Charlie looked at the smashed spokes on the wheel. "I hate how much everything's changed."

"Charlie, are you talking to anyone?" Jil asked him.

Charlie began to cry. He cried every time Jil saw him since Samantha moved out. "You mean a shrink?"

"I mean, a shrink or a friend. For instance, do you see Frankie Weissman much?"

"She's terrific. But no, I haven't. I'm not good company these days."

"Tell me about it." Jil put his arm around him and laughed.

"You're one of the few people I still find it comfortable to be with," Charlie confided.

"Maybe you should call Frankie. She can be very soothing and I find her quite witty as well." They passed a Chris Ofili piece adorned with elephant dung and Jil immediately turned away. "I have to say if I never see another Ofili I'll die a happy man. This may be the most overrated crap I've ever seen in my life, except for anything by Damien Hirst. Let's get something to eat. This is making me famished."

Charlie and Jil walked down Tenth Avenue to Bottino. When they walked in, the hostess, a five-foot-ten blonde in a black tube dress, lit up. "Mr. Taillou, how nice to see you."

"Nice to see you, Natalia." Jil gave her two kisses. "This is my friend Charlie Acton. I told him you'd take care of him next time he comes."

As they sat down in the garden, at least five tables waved, winked, or blew kisses at Jil.

"You're very popular here." Charlie smiled.

"None of them like me very much. They're all art dealers." Jil nodded at the room.

"Sorry I got so sloppy before," Charlie apologized.

"Charlie, I don't know why the hell Samantha's doing this. You two had the best life in New York."

"Maybe it just wasn't good enough. You know, compared to everyone we know, maybe we weren't powerful enough, rich enough, something enough."

"Who the fuck cares, Charlie." Jil looked at him. "It can all be gone tomorrow."

"Do you think I should call her?" Charlie asked as he did every time they spoke.

"Charlie, my gift in life is repression." Jil knew the answer Charlie wanted and wasn't going to give it to him. "I know everyone in this country says be open, spill your guts, tell us all your secrets. What I know is I got out of Hungary by never revealing my religion and I've gotten to this position by keeping my personal life personal. My advice is spend some pleasant and painless time with our friend Frankie Weissman or even the lovely hostess here. Leave Samantha alone and she'll come home wagging her tail behind her."

"What's that, Little Bo Peep?" Charlie laughed.

"For all I know it's Little Miss Muffet. Let's eat." Jil waved his hand, "Waitress, we're starving here."

While Jil was waving at the staff, Adrienne Strong-Rodman, who had been gallery-hopping with Grey Navez, caught his eye. Adrienne waved brightly and began walking over to their table.

"Sorry, dear," Jil whispered to Charlie. "Instead of a waitress I've gotten you Adrienne Strong-Rodman and she's all in leather," Jil whispered. "You see, even if you go downtown they follow you. Nothing is safe." As Adrienne approached the table Jil immediately stood up.

Adrienne kissed Jil on the cheek. "Hello, Jil darling."

"Adrienne, if I didn't know better I'd say you were a Harley chick who just rode into town." Jil smiled at her as he patted her leather. "Of course you know Dr. Acton."

Now Charlie was standing up as well.

"Hello, Charlie! Why do you look younger every time I see you?"

"Great to see you, Adrienne. How's Paul?" Charlie asked, knowing that Paul was now devoting himself full-time to his legal problems.

"He's terrific. And guess what? I've been thinking of going back to work. I have some very exciting prospects. Especially now that I don't have to devote my time to the school."

"Well, good luck with that and give Paul my best." Charlie smiled.

"Charlie." Adrienne put her arm around him. "You know that I adore you. For God's sake, I slather your cream on my face every night! That stupid item in the *New York Post.* I never said that."

"What item in the *New York Post?*" Charlie was confused.

"It's really nothing. You know, they make things up. Plus nobody's going to read it 'cause it's Saturday."

"Today? It's in today's?" Charlie looked at her.

"Honey, I would never have seen it but my daughter found it. She was out all night with an ex-boyfriend of Paris Hilton and ended up in there last week. She loves being in the *Post.* Well, I better get back to Grey. Who would have ever thought we'd all run into each other on Tenth and Twenty-fourth? Don't you just love New York?" She kissed Charlie again and walked away.

Jil pushed his chair back. "I'm completely exhausted from her. I don't need lunch. I need a beer."

"I don't think I can stay here." Charlie suddenly got up.

"Oh come on, Charlie. She's a forty-year-old woman in head-to-toe leather talking about a gossip item in the *New York Post.* They once published that the local weatherman was my secret boyfriend." Jil laughed. "I should only be so lucky. I'd love to have that warm front coming in."

"Thank you for a wonderful day, Jil. Let's do it again." Charlie began to walk out of the restaurant.

"Is anything wrong?" the hostess asked.

"Nothing. Nothing at all. I just need some air. Thank you for all your kindnesses." Charlie reached into his wallet and gave her sixty dollars.

While Charlie hailed a cab on Tenth Avenue, Jil ran out of the restaurant. "Charlie, you left your catalogue of the complete career of Chris Ofili."

"I'm sorry to have ruined your day." Charlie embraced Jil.

"Careful, darling, or now you'll end up in the columns for breaking up my affair with the weatherman."

Charlie thought very carefully about which newsstand to buy the paper from. He had a favorite place on Seventieth and Lexington where from time to time he bought lotto tickets and gave them to his nurses. But there was a chance he could run into a client rushing out for the latest issue of *W* or the same issue of the *Post*.

He decided to ask the cabbie to drop him at the Hilton hotel on Fifty-fourth and Sixth. Chances were he wouldn't know a single conventioneer, businessman, or tourist there.

Charlie walked to the newsstand and bought a copy of the *Post* and sat down at the anonymous bar. He methodically ordered a martini, put his cell phone on the table, and ate a bowl of cashews before opening the paper to a large photo of Samantha and Barry under a banner headline, "So Happy Together."

Charlie took a sip of his drink, put the paper down, and looked around the room. For a moment, he thought perhaps he should try to sleep with one of the young waitresses. Maybe the brunette was an aspiring actress from Omaha. Maybe the blonde was an ex-Rockette and would be happy to hook up with a Fifth Avenue doctor. Maybe within two years she'd be planning benefits with Grey Navez. But the fantasy of the young waitress wasn't working. In fact, it only depressed him. He continued to read the item.

"Who says romance isn't in the air? 'Barry and Samantha are absolutely made for each other,' says gal pal Adrienne Strong-Rodman."

Charlie swallowed another sip of his martini and continued reading.

"But we hear not everyone is so upbeat about the hot couple—especially Mrs. Clarice Santorini and society doc Charlie Acton. In fact, Clarice Santorini, who is suddenly very popular in the social set, is quietly gathering forces. Clarice is too tasteful to talk, but trust me, her friends have plenty to say. As for Dr. Acton, we hear his refrigerator is so full he hardly has time to come out from the cold."

Charlie put his drink down and dialed his phone.

The machine picked up. "Hi, this is Samantha Bagley. You've reached me at my new number. Leave a message."

Charlie breathed and said nothing. He hadn't heard the message that eliminated both his name and their marriage. He dialed the phone again.

"Dr. Weissman, this is Dr. Acton," he spoke quickly. "I haven't gotten mugged again, but I'd still like to see you. I'll call you back if I'm ever sober."

Charlie had ordered another drink when his cell phone rang.

"Dr. Weissman," Charlie answered.

"How did you know it was me?" Frankie had called from the hospital where she was covering for a young associate.

"Because you're the kind of earnest do-gooder who would call me right back."

"Where are you?" she asked.

"I'm at the New York Hilton. There's a sign up here saying 'Welcome Pharmaceutical Supply Conference.'"

"Maybe you should see if there's any leftover Vioxx," Frankie immediately replied.

Charlie laughed, not so much at the joke as at the warmth of her voice. "Francesca, I'm sorry I haven't seen you since the night you rescued me." He took a sip of his martini.

"Are you all right? Do you want me to meet you?" Frankie asked.

"No. I just wanted to say I'm sorry I haven't seen you since the night you rescued me," he said again and took another sip of his martini.

"Hey, no problem. I've been worried about you, that's all."

"I'm worried about me, too, Francesca. I would really like to see you."

"We can see each other, sure. Anytime," Frankie said.

"Don't say anytime, Francesca." Charlie laughed again. "You have to learn to be a little difficult. Maybe we could teach each other that. I'll call you, darling. Thanks."

Charlie put down the phone and asked the bartender for a spare cigarette. He would just get through this. He'd see his friends like Frankie and Jil, the people he knew were still genuine. And once this uncertain period was over maybe he'd change his life completely. Maybe he'd move downtown.

CHAPTER TWENTY-FOUR

Frankie

Frankie had begun planning the health initiative at Intermediate School 104 in East Harlem around three years ago. The strategy Frankie developed was twofold: a class taught at the school by community physicians and nurses and a weekly open clinic. In the year that the initiative was up and running, student awareness about nutrition, smoking, asthma, and even flu shots had made a marked difference in the health profile of both the children and the parents at I.S. 104.

When Frankie asked Charlie Acton to meet her at the school she was deeply suspicious of her own motives. A man calls her and says, "You have to learn to be a little more difficult," and her response is to phone him a week later and invite him to an intermediate school health fair in Harlem. In her mind it was the same kind of twisted thinking that led her to identify with the movie *The Nun's Story* when she was nine. In the film, Audrey Hepburn played a Belgian nun who went to a leper colony in the Congo and fell in love with a good-hearted doctor. The only problem with this scenario was Frankie was a Jewish girl from Queens, and she was not Audrey Hepburn. Moreover, she would have been scared to death of a Congo leper colony.

"I'm so glad you called me." Charlie kissed Frankie hello on the steps of the school. "I'm really excited to see this!"

Charlie took Frankie's arm as she led him into the building. I.S. 104 was only ten blocks away from many of the first-tier New York City private schools, but as opposed to the first tier, for around ten years the school had been ranked as one of the worst in the city, with one of the highest drug abuse and dropout rates.

"How often do you come here?" Charlie asked as they walked through the halls decorated with paper pumpkins and pilgrims.

"Maybe once a week. And I see patients from here most Thursday mornings."

"Must be very rewarding." Charlie watched as one of the students passed by and waved. "Hey, Dr. Weissman."

"Some days it's the best thing I do," Frankie answered him as they climbed the stairs. "Other days it makes me crazy, just like anything else. You meet some exceptional kids who are singled out for all those 'Prep for Prep' programs that will lift them out of here to places like Groton or St. Paul's. But for others the deck is just stacked against them."

Frankie took Charlie to see the classroom she had set up as a clinic and science center. There were anatomy charts on the walls and students' drawings about AIDS, smoking, and drug addiction.

"Francesca, I'm so proud of you for this," Charlie said genuinely.

"It's really the principal here who got me to do this," Frankie explained.

"You can take some credit. I'm sure the principal doesn't drag all her doctor friends up here and make them feel silly about their insular lives."

"I'm sorry, did I do that?" Frankie suspected the *Nun's Story* scenario was backfiring.

"Can I ask you a personal question?" Charlie sat up on a desk.

"Sure." Frankie tried not to seem apprehensive.

"Why didn't you ever try to have a child? You'd be such a good mother."

"Did you ever read *The New Viruses*?" Frankie asked.

"You mean Jack Stanley? I know him. He's married to some friend of Samantha's. I didn't think much of the book. Mostly scare tactics."

"Well, we were together for ten years before he married Samantha's friend, and I suppose I thought I'd have a child with him."

"Promise you won't tell anyone what I'm going to tell you." Charlie put her hand on her heart. "You have to promise."

"I promise."

"She's not really a friend of Samantha's. She's a patient of mine and she's a complete nightmare. She's been getting chemical peels and Botox since she was eighteen. By now her skin is made of AstroTurf."

Frankie laughed openly. "Tell me something. Does she also have a beard?"

"I love when you're as mean as the rest of us." Charlie laughed.

"Oh, I promise you, I'm disgusting." Frankie put her feet up on a desk.

"But why didn't you have one alone? Isn't that what a lot of women in your situation do now?"

"I thought about it. Then my dad got sick. And, I don't know, I'm not that good at being close to people. I mean I might be better with the kids here than with one of my own. I need a little distance," she explained while fidgeting with a nearby eraser.

"You don't seem that way to me. You are such a caring person." He smiled.

Frankie hunched over. "I guess a person can care too much, and that's not good for anybody either."

"Yes, I understand that." Charlie dangled his feet. "Samantha tried to have a kid for a long time; in vitro, G.I.F.T., surrogate eggs, the whole shebang. Maybe I didn't realize the toll it took on her. Maybe I'm the one who isn't very good at being close to anyone."

"Dr. Weissman?" Venette Caesar came bounding into the room with five sixth-grade friends. "My mother found out you were speaking here today so she sent me here with a neighbor. This is Sandra. She goes to school here."

"Hi, Sandra." Frankie smiled. "And this is my friend Dr. Acton."

"Hey, wait a minute!" Sandra interrupted them. "Didn't I see you on VH1? This guy's famous! He knows Janet Jackson! He's her doctor or something."

"Actually, they were just asking me my opinion about her doctor and what he does to her face."

"That's not her real face, is it?" Venette asked.

"I heard she wears a mask," another girl interrupted.

"All right. I'll tell you what I know." Charlie got up and went to the blackboard. "There are a number of procedures Janet Jackson may or may not have had done. I can't say she had any of these for certain. But I'll explain to you how each one works so you can form your own opinion."

Charlie proceeded for the next hour to explain in depth to a classroom of sixth graders and eight-year-old Venette Caesar the procedures of microdermabrasion, laser resurfacing, electrocautery, Thermage, and radiance. With each procedure Charlie named a pop star or celebrity he thought either used it to enhance their appearance or would benefit from it. As he spoke in detail about the makeup of the epidermis, its textures, colors, and functions, Frankie witnessed a connection between him and the students she would have never predicted.

"The thing you've got to understand is so many of the judgments we make in life are about what's on the surface." Charlie leaned against the desk. "How we look, how old we appear, the color of our skin. What I want you to understand is not only are we all the same beneath the surface, but the surface can be altered in so many ways that what gives us real character is using your mind and never forgetting about your heart." Charlie looked over at Frankie. "That's something I'm only just beginning to learn. Dr. Weissman here has mastered it. And just like you guys, she's my teacher."

Simultaneously embarrassed and touched, Frankie looked away.

"Okay. I've embarrassed her. Any questions?" Charlie asked the room.

For another hour, the students asked Charlie about every possible skin problem a sixth grader could have. When Frankie and Charlie finally walked out of I.S. 104 that afternoon, he kissed her and said, "Thank you. That was the happiest I've been in months."

"Charlie, you should come again. They loved you." Frankie took Charlie's arm, but he suddenly pulled away to hail a cab.

"I hope none of them knows Janet Jackson. She could sue the hell out of me." Charlie waved his arm for a cab. "I'm going swimming at Asphalt Green. Can I drop you?"

"Sure." Frankie was hoping they'd have a drink together and talk a little more.

When the cab stopped Charlie held the door for Frankie to get in. "Are you going home?" he asked her.

"Uh, no." Frankie didn't want him to know that she had absolutely no plans that night. "Actually I thought I'd stop in and visit my dad."

"How's he doing?" he asked.

"Not great."

"He's lucky to have you." Charlie put his hand on her knee. "We're all lucky to have you."

"Charlie, I'm sorry. We haven't really talked about you. Are you doing okay?" She couldn't believe she'd said something so inane. For a minute she thought she didn't know fuck all about men and what to say because she had gone to that goddamn girls' school. But then she remembered that Samantha had gone to the same girls' school and seemed to know exactly what to do.

"I'm doing okay. I read that I'm moving to Los Angeles and I'm dating a twenty-three-year-old for revenge. The truth is all I'm doing is swimming. You should see my butterfly."

The taxi stopped at a red light at Eighty-ninth and Madison.

"I get off here." Frankie picked up her purse.

"Is this where you grew up?" Charlie asked her.

"This is where I lived when I went to high school."

"This is only two blocks from where Samantha grew up."

"Yes, that's right. She was at 1175 Fifth."

"You remember."

"She loomed large even then."

"I gotta say I must have a thing for girls from this neighborhood." He kissed Frankie on the lips this time. "I'll call ya. Thanks for a great day."

Frankie walked into her father's building remembering the night a Collegiate boy kissed her on the lips after their first date seeing *Jules and Jim* at the Regency. She remembered distinctly the romantic anticipation surrounding "I'll call ya" followed by a kiss on the lips.

Frankie rang the doorbell to Abraham's apartment at least twenty times before she opened the door with her key. The doorman had told her that they were home and she should go right up.

"Helen? Helen? Are you here?" Frankie called, walking into the living room. "Helen?"

She walked from the kitchen into the library with visions of that late-night commercial of an old woman passed out on the floor and a voice-over saying "If only she could have contacted you."

"Dad! Helen!" She went into her father's bedroom and found no one. She pushed open the door to the bathroom frightened she'd find them both headfirst in the bathtub.

Now racing through the apartment, she opened the door to the terrace and found Abraham nude on the porch.

"Dad! Dad!" She took him under the arm.

"Mommy. Mommy." He looked at her.

"Dad, it's me, Frankie. Where's Helen?"

"Mommy, it's cold."

Frankie brought her father inside and wrapped a blanket around him.

"Mommy. That hurts!"

"What hurts?" Frankie asked him.

"It hurts."

Frankie touched his arm. "Tell me what hurts. Does this hurt?" Frankie ran her hands up and down his ribs.

"Mommy, it hurts."

"How about this?" Frankie touched his leg.

"Stop!" he screamed at her.

"What are you doing to him?" Helen walked into the room.

"He says he's in pain," Frankie snapped at her, not mentioning that she suspected a possible recurrence of prostate cancer that was operated on ten years ago.

"He doesn't know if he's in pain or not." Helen stared at her with terrified eyes.

"Helen, he's in pain. Where were you?"

"I went downstairs to get the laundry. Our machine is broken and I can't get anyone here to fix it on the weekend."

"You shouldn't leave him alone." Frankie lowered her voice with a professional chill. "That's completely irresponsible. He was out naked on the goddamn porch. Helen, I'm getting you help."

"I don't want you coming here and telling us what to do!" Helen slammed the porch door shut.

"Mommy! Mommy!" Abraham looked at Helen and she took his hand.

"Yes, baby. Mommy's here. Everything's going to be fine." Helen kissed his forehead like a baby. "Why did you go out of the house? Mommy told you not to go outside."

"Mommy." Abraham put his head on her shoulder. "It hurts."

"C'mon, honey. Mommy will get you dressed."

Helen sat Abraham down and began to slowly put on his pajamas like he was four years old. She pulled each pant leg up slowly and whispered, "Pull your tushy up, honey, so Mommy can get the rest up. That's right." Helen turned to Frankie. "I don't want to lose him. He's my life."

Helen began to cry as she gently pulled his pant leg over his thigh. "I know if you take him to a doctor they'll start shooting him up with God knows what. He doesn't deserve to be in pain."

Frankie watched as Helen buttoned his top.

"Don't take this personally, Frankie, but I really hate doctors. Even the supposedly good ones like you."

When Helen finished dressing Abraham she sat him down in front of the television between Frankie and herself.

"Abe likes to watch either old movies or the news and that's it. Sometimes I think he now confuses the president with a World War II movie."

"It's wishful thinking." Frankie tried to lighten the conversation. "I prefer Henry Fonda in *Mister Roberts* to watching the president."

"Oh, I had such a crush on Henry Fonda." Helen began to feed Abraham chocolate pudding that was on the side table. "'We're the people!' Right! Isn't that what the mother told him in *The Grapes of Wrath?*"

Frankie sat still as Helen wiped her father's chin with one hand and switched the channel with the remote in her other. She clicked past a rerun of the president predicting "gathering danger in Iraq."

"They'll never find those weapons. But if it's good for Israel, it's good for me. Right, Abraham?" Helen squeezed his hand.

"Mommy, that hurts." He looked at her.

Helen kissed his head. "I know, sweetie, I know." She stopped clicking the remote when she came to *Bringing Up Baby* on Turner Classic Movies.

"You're gonna like this one, Abe. It's got Cary Grant. He reminds me a little of you." She touched his face lovingly.

Abraham smiled and stretched his arm around Helen.

Frankie stared at her father's skin. She examined the properties of color, protective covering, and identifying characteristics, just as Charlie had asked the students to do at I.S. 104. Looking at her father's hand, she concluded that the age spots on his knuckles and the lifeline on his palm belonged to a previous century.

CHAPTER TWENTY-FIVE

Clarice

Clarice made a list of her abilities for her new nutritionist homeo-
pathic adviser.

1. Manage household staff in four homes—New York,
Nantucket, Malibu, Aspen.
2. Make certain that Barry's favorite English muffins and
orange juice were made available by the household staff
in each home if he happened to drop in at a moment's
notice. Assure availability of Barry's favorite potato chips,
pizza, Diet Dr Pepper, Newman's Own pretzels, Russ &
Daughters whitefish salad, no-fat soy gouda, and all
medications.
3. Access to the best doctors in New York, Los Angeles,
Denver (for Aspen), and Boston (for Nantucket), and
remaining current on them. In-depth knowledge of all
Barry's ailments: high blood pressure, gallstones, lower
back pain, and frozen elbow. Have access at all times to
Dr. Frank Petito (professor of neurology at NewYork
Weill Cornell Medical Center) and his cell number.

4. Keeping the children happy, healthy, and succeeding
at school.

5. Knowing she was very lucky.

From her years of throwing birthday parties and attending movie events with her husband, Clarice knew that the secret to any success was getting the right people to do it. She used to be in awe of women like Samantha Acton because they had such an innate sense of style and organization. But when Barry moved out Clarice decided she would teach herself what every other successful Upper East Side woman seemed to instantly know—the best people to hire, from closet organizers and calligraphers to events coordinators.

When Judy Tremont took Clarice to tea at the Colony Club and asked her to be on the benefit committee of the Museum of Modern Art spring gala, she was at first hesitant.

"I'm not sure what I could do." Clarice smiled. She had never even listed herself on an invitation as Clarice Santorini. She was always "Mrs. Barry Santorini."

"You can do as much or as little as you want. You can just write a check and buy a few tables or you can get more involved in planning this event."

"I see." Clarice was noncommittal.

"Look, as your friend I gotta tell you something," Judy whispered. "You're really hot now because your husband left you for one of the most famous women in New York. Everyone's sympathy is with you and you're crazy if you don't make the most of it."

"I appreciate your candor." Clarice had a habit of escaping embarrassing conversations by lapsing into formality. It was a defense she had mastered when she worked in sales at Armani. "If we do it, can we get Umit Afet to help us with the look of the evening? I remember that Turkish-English dinner party was so inventive."

"Are you kidding? She's suing Albert because I refused to let him pay her last bill. Umit says everything is about balance and meanwhile flowers are half dead and who knows where that filthy hookah has been."

"I'll do some research about other event coordinators." Clarice took a tea sandwich and offered one to Judy.

"But the museum has development people for that."

"I'd enjoy it. It will give me something to sink my teeth into."

"That means you're saying yes." Judy passed Clarice back the untouched plate.

"I think so. Yes," Clarice spilled.

"Oh, by the way." Judy flipped her hand in a there's-just-a-little-item-more gesture. "We can definitely take Adrienne Strong-Rodman off the benefit committee. It looks like Paul's definitely going to trial and probably jail. Plus her daughter Jessica was caught selling marijuana to a Nightingale-Bamford sixth grader at a Colony Club dance."

"Right here? That's terrible." Clarice knew about the Rodmans' financial picture, but the news of the daughter hadn't reached her yet.

"Plus Arnie Berkowitz says the daughter will definitely get tossed out of Spence and it's not so clear that even any third-tier school is going to have her now. She could end up at the Valley Forge Military Academy."

"I like Jessica," Clarice said honestly.

"Oh come on, Clarice. You'd kill yourself if one of your daughters became a slut like her. As far as I'm concerned, Albert can read my daughters to sleep until their wedding night. Maybe even on their wedding night."

"Carumbo!" Judy suddenly exclaimed while looking at her watch. "I've got to get home. Don't tell anyone, but I'm taking my twin boys for a little bit of lipo. Arnie Berkowitz says boys are as narcissistic as girls these days."

"But do your kids really want to do this?" Clarice was genuinely surprised.

"It really isn't up to them. You're too nice a person, Clarice. But then again that's why everybody loves you. Everyone just puts up with me because I make Albert throw gobs of money at them." Judy laughed.

Clarice shook her head. "That's not true."

"Yes it is. How do you think I managed to become a benefit cochair?" Judy kissed Clarice on the cheek. "Bye, dear. I'm so excited about our little project."

When Judy left, Clarice began making lists. She would find out from Pippa Rose who to meet for the flowers, the food, the lights, the party favors, the entertainment, even the invites. She knew that the development office at the museum had talented people in charge of all those things, but she decided she wanted to keep her hand in it. Judy was right: this was her opportunity to take her place in New York without Barry.

Even in college Clarice was never particularly attracted to feminism or the idea of a woman's need to define herself outside her family. But thinking about this event, Clarice had a new sense of importance. For the first time, she understood that style was not just a cashmere uniform but a powerful skill.

"Mom, want to hear what happened to Jessica Rodman?" Venice bounded into the apartment after school.

"She sold drugs to a Nightingale sixth grader at the Colony Club." Clarice looked up. "How stupid is that?"

"Mom. Who told you that?"

"Nobody." Clarice answered.

"Was it Pippa Rose?"

"No."

"Jennifer says her mother gossips."

"No, it wasn't Pippa Rose," Clarice answered.

"Well, whoever it was got it wrong. Jessica was smoking marijuana in the bathroom of the Colony Club during one of those stupid Knickerbocker dances. And this girl from Nightingale asked for a puff and Jessica wouldn't give her any, so she went and got the security guard."

"That's a terrible story! How do you know this?" Clarice asked.

"Everybody in New York knows this, Mom."

"Honey, do you think we should just leave and move to Philadelphia?" Clarice asked her daughter.

"Mom, there's drugs and stupid dances in Philadelphia, too." Venice looked at her mother as if she had Styrofoam in her brain.

"I know. But stories like this . . ." Clarice took a sip of cold tea.

"Want to hear some good news?"

"Yes. That would be nice."

"I'm going to be in the School of American Ballet workshop of a Christopher Wheeldon ballet. Jennifer Rose is in it, too."

Clarice embraced her daughter. "Honey, that's wonderful news!"

"So we can't move to Philadelphia."

"No, honey." Clarice held on to Venice. "We're staying here. We deserve a very good year."

"Mom?"

"Yes, dear." She pushed her daughter's hair out of her eye.

"Would you tell Daddy to stop calling me."

"I thought Yvonne calls you."

"No. He calls every half hour. He says, 'What's new?' He was easier to deal with when he lived here. Then he never bothered me."

"He just loves you, honey." Clarice didn't know exactly what to say.

"Mother." Venice pulled away from her.

"What?"

"Stop being such a simp." Venice walked out of the room.

"I'm planning on that, dear!" Clarice smiled.

CHAPTER TWENTY-SIX

Barry

Barry had Julian drop him off in front of the playground on East Sixty-seventh between Third and Second.

"Are you sure this is it?" Julian asked him as he opened the door.

"Yeah. I'm meeting one of my kids here," Barry answered quickly. "And you don't have to wait. Go get a cup of coffee."

"Mr. Santorini, I don't mind. I'll wait."

"Julian, I said come back in two hours," Barry yelled at him in a way he mostly reserved for assistants and development girls.

"Yes, Mr. Santorini."

When the car pulled away Barry walked down the street to the Memorial Sloan-Kettering Cancer Center Department of Urology. Barry knew that Julian was discreet but his fuckin' prostate was his own business. He wasn't risking his balls for anybody.

Barry went to his doctor for his annual checkup feeling absolutely fine. In fact, things were going great. He was deeply in love with Samantha, the remake of *The Maltese Falcon* was up for six Golden Globes and was the dark-horse choice for the Oscars, his kids seemed to be taking his leaving in stride and were being cast in ballets, and Clarice wasn't particularly getting in his way—in fact, her kicking him out would definitely work to his legal advantage.

When his doctor called him a week after his annual physical to say he had tested positive for prostate cancer, Barry thought he must have been making it up. Of course he knew that people got sick. Steve Ross, the chairman of Warner Brothers, died of prostate cancer for Christ sake, but that was ten years ago. And besides, Barry was only forty-five and at the top of his game. Barry suspected that the lab fucked up or some nurse was part of a Christian conspiracy and knew he was about to produce a gay marriage movie even though he was a Republican.

Walking into the cool glass building marked "Sidney Kimmel Center for Prostate and Urologic Cancers," Barry strode up to the receptionist and spoke in a low, decidedly calm voice.

"Barry Santorini for Dr. Vartan."

"Hi there, Mr. Santorini." The receptionist smiled warmly. "If you don't mind filling out these forms, then I can send you upstairs to the second floor."

"Andre Karl, the chairman of the board here, made this appointment for me. I don't need to fill out these papers." He handed them back to her.

"Everyone needs to fill out these papers, Mr. Santorini. We need your medical history." She smiled again and returned them to him.

"I'm sure you didn't make King Hussein or Robert De Niro sit here and fill out these papers when they came to see Dr. Vartan. I'm going to the second floor." Barry walked toward the elevator.

"I can't let you do that, Mr. Santorini." The receptionist stood up.

"You call the chairman of the board and tell him that. Here's his number."

Barry pulled out a card from his wallet, handed it to the receptionist, and walked into the elevator.

When he got off at the second floor, Barry was depressed to see a waiting room of mostly older men accompanied by their devoted spouses. Immediately he assumed they must have a VIP waiting room for guys like Rudolph Giuliani that the bitch downstairs wasn't telling him about. Dr. Victor Vartan was the most famous prostate cancer doctor in the world. These regular people couldn't be his only patients.

He went up to the second-floor receptionist. "Barry Santorini for Dr. Vartan."

"Can I have your papers?" The young woman didn't look up.

"I don't need papers. Is there a VIP room here?"

"Excuse me?" the receptionist asked.

Barry couldn't believe he was wasting his time with all this civilian bullshit. It was worse than flying fuckin' commercial.

"Where do your big donors wait?"

"Right here." The receptionist pointed without looking up again.

Barry made a note to himself to throw Sloan-Kettering a premiere. Andre Karl was obviously holding out for something.

"If you'll have a seat, Mr. Santorini, I'll tell Dr. Vartan's nurse you're here and that you have no papers." The receptionist rattled off instructions.

As Barry sat down he thought he saw his daughters' doctor sitting with an old man who was obviously in pain.

"Mr. Weissman, Dr. Campbell will see you now," Barry heard the nurse call, and knew he was absolutely right—it was Dr. Frankie Weissman. He watched as the pediatrician gently got the old man up. He seemed to be completely out of it, but gave her a kiss on the cheek when she managed to get him standing. Barry was glad that at least the Weissmans weren't seeing Dr. Vartan. He knew that kids' doctor had a very good reputation, but she certainly wasn't a world-famous celebrity like Dr. Vartan.

The kids' pediatrician nodded at Barry as she and the old man passed him, but Barry ignored her. If that fuckin' cunt violated the Hippocratic oath or whatever the fuck vow it was of privacy, he would sue her ass so fast she'd have trouble getting a job as a nurse in a kindergarten.

"Mr. Santorini, Dr. Vartan will see you," the receptionist called out.

Barry got up. The good news was, happily—since the pediatrician left plus he was sitting in the bleachers—no one important recognized his name. And at least he didn't have to go through the shit with the blood and the nurse. Obviously they'd made a mistake and he wasn't really that sick. Maybe this was all about getting them a fuckin' premiere.

"I loved *The Maltese Falcon*," Dr. Vartan told Barry while he walked his fingers up and down his leg. "Have you been having any pains in your legs?"

"No. I don't have any pains." Barry was expecting a distinguished Indian doctor in a white coat and instead he got a guy in Gucci loafers who looked like he sold real estate in Short Hills, New Jersey. Barry hadn't seen a man in diamond cuff links and a Gucci belt since he used to spend time with his father-in-law, the supermarket king.

"How 'bout your ribs?" The doctor felt up Barry's side. Barry couldn't help noticing that Dr. Vartan also had a manicure. He wasn't even like the supermarket king. He was more like his old friends from South Philly who went into "the Family Business."

"I told you, I feel fine," Barry said as the doctor took off his gloves and washed his hands.

"Mr. Santorini, I need you to go with my nurse to let her take some blood."

"This is crazy! If you need a donation or something, call my office." Barry was ready to go. "Don't jerk me around here."

"According to your doctor's blood test, you have tested positive for prostate cancer." Dr. Vartan sat down on a stool. "Hopefully it hasn't spread. But I can't give you a full prognosis unless you cooperate."

"Let me be candid with you, doctor," Barry spoke softly. "It's pre-Oscar season and I don't really have time for this."

"I need your blood sample and a number of X-rays, Mr. Santorini, and then we can make some decisions."

"But it's the early stages, right?" Barry asked. "I'm thirty years younger than the old men out there."

"I need your cooperation, Mr. Santorini." He extended his hand to Barry. "It was great meeting you."

As the world-famous Dr. Vartan walked out of the examining room, Barry looked at his relatively small Gucci loafers.

Fuckin' nouveau riche Harvard boy, Barry thought to himself. Must have a small dick.

Barry walked down East Sixty-seventh street and pulled out his cell phone.

"Yup. What's up?" He dialed his office.

"Terry Franks from the *Times* called again and Jack Koppelberg from Warner's—says it's urgent. Also Kevin Huvane wants to know if you've read that script, and Samantha called a few times. She said you weren't picking up your cell."

"That's it?" he said distractedly.

"Do you want me to call anyone back?" Yvonne asked.

"No, not particularly." Barry put his phone in his pocket and continued to walk as Julian pulled the car up beside him.

"I'm right here, Mr. Santorini."

"Just a minute, Julian." Barry pulled out his phone and walked a few steps away.

"Clarice?" he said as soon as she picked up.

It took Clarice a moment to respond. "Barry?"

"Clarice, have you forgotten my voice already?"

"What's wrong? Why isn't Yvonne calling? Did something happen to one of the kids?" She began to panic.

"No, the kids are fine. Clarice, I need to see you."

"Is it something I can help you with on the phone?"

"How 'bout dinner tonight?" He didn't want to pussyfoot around.

"I already have a date with Pippa Rose."

Barry could hear Clarice flattening out her voice.

"Okay. How 'bout tomorrow night?"

Clarice began to lose her composure. "Tomorrow night?"

"I'll see you at Vico at eight-thirty." Barry clicked his phone and his cell immediately rang.

"What, Yvonne?"

"Honey, it's me," Samantha whispered. "Are you all right? I haven't been able to reach you."

"I'm fine. Fuckin' Hollywood agents are takin' up all my time. I'll see you later, baby. I love you." He put his phone in his pocket.

Barry got into his waiting car. "Back to New Jersey, Julian." He slammed the door. As the car got onto the West Side Highway, Barry looked into the rearview mirror.

"Hey, Julian."

"Yes sir," the driver answered.

"You still got those Al Green CDs?"

"Yes sir, Mr. Santorini."

"Let's hear one. And if anyone calls looking for me, I'm playing golf in fuckin' Scotland."

Barry leaned back in the car. Al Green began singing "For the Good Times" and Barry shut his eyes and remembered an Asian woman he met on a shoot in Toronto. She came back to his room and spanked him in his suite at the Four Seasons while an Al Green CD was playing. Barry saw her every night for the rest of the shoot.

As Julian drove over the George Washington Bridge to New Jersey, Barry closed his eyes and smiled.

"You look good, Clarice." Barry sipped a glass of Pellegrino. He had chosen Vico because it was an uptown family restaurant. Barry didn't want to get distracted by agents and media hangers-on like you get at Da Silvano. He didn't need chic. He just needed to get this done. "I like your scarf," he complimented her.

"It's the Christmas one you gave me. You got it at Hermès in Paris." She sat straight-backed in her chair.

"So what's new, Clarice?" He decided to get the bullshit out of the way.

"Brooke's teacher says she's participating more in class. She seems to be very interested in the Greek myths they're studying."

Barry looked at her well-scrubbed face. She could talk all night about the teachers and the Greek myths. She had that ability to take whatever regular stuff that went on during the day and make it seem earth-shatteringly important.

"Clarice, I need you in my life," Barry said firmly when she had finished describing the daily trials and accomplishments of each child.

"You mean you're not seeing Samantha anymore?" She certainly wasn't anticipating this.

"That's not what I'm saying." He reached for her hand. "I don't understand why I can't have you and Samantha. Both."

"What?" Clarice couldn't contain her emotions the way her nutritionist was training her to.

"You are both very different, and I need you both in my life. You are my anchor, what we call in the movies my through-line. The thing that connects all the dots. The mother of my children. She's my heartbeat, my flesh."

"Barry, thank you so much for not having Yvonne call to tell me this." Clarice couldn't believe that came out of her mouth.

"That's a bitchy thing to say." He pushed his plate away from him.

"Sorry." She looked at the pasta still sitting on his plate. "Barry, you didn't eat anything. Are you not feeling well?"

"I'm fine, Clarice," he said defensively. "But your thinking is very narrow and very selfish. I need you right now."

"I'm working very hard at getting better, Barry. Please don't confuse me."

Barry didn't like this new coolness that Clarice seemed to be showing. If this is how she was getting because of the nutritionist or the hypnotist or the acupuncturist, he was going to stop paying for them.

"Just don't listen to your friends or your stupid lawyers or psychiatrists. They don't know anything. And they certainly don't know what's best for you. Those are little minds. Don't think small, Clarice." Barry had told her not to think small since he first told her he had no intention of ever running her father's supermarket chain.

"Barry, you destroyed our marriage." Clarice was careful to take calm breaths from her diaphragm.

"I destroyed what was getting stale. Now we can reinvent it."

"With her?"

"She doesn't concern you. I need to know I have full access to you and my children. I love you, Clarice. I need to know you're still here for me."

"I'll think about it, Barry," she whispered.

"Good. That's all I need to know." Barry pushed his chair back and kissed her on the lips. "Waiter, check."

"Barry, you haven't eaten and I'd like coffee."

"Coffee will kill you. And don't let my kids drink coffee either." Barry got up to get their coats.

As Clarice stood up, Jil Taillou, who was sitting with Grey Navez and her boyfriend, waved from across the room.

"Who the fuck is that?" Barry asked.

"Art dealer. Friend of Judy Tremont. You met him at her dinner a while ago."

"It's amazing how many leeches there are in the world, Clarice," Barry whispered to her. "Doctors, art dealers, decorators, all they want is to suck our fuckin' blood dry." His voice began to crack. "At least you and I aren't looking to take ten percent of each other."

"Barry, I gave you two hundred percent."

"That's love, babe. You always have to give two hundred percent. Who are the other people with him?"

"Grey Navez and her boyfriend Lewis Franklin. He's the new president of Morgan Stanley."

Barry now waved back to them. Then he took Clarice's hand and walked out of the restaurant.

When they got out on Madison Avenue, Julian and the car were conveniently waiting.

"Let Julian take you home, Clarice." He quickly opened the door.

"I can walk," she answered.

"Get in the car, Clarice. I'll call you tomorrow." He kissed her cheek.

"Thank you for dinner, Barry." She used her formal voice again.

"Don't thank me, Clarice. Just don't make a stupid decision."

As he shut the door and waved good-bye, he noticed a photographer outside the restaurant.

"Fuck you, twerp!" The paparazzo ran away.

Barry began walking down Madison Avenue. As he passed his daughter's school, Barry thought that he wasn't afraid of dying. He just had no desire to spend any time in hospitals or at the mercy of insufferable nurses and big-shot doctors like Victor Vartan. If he was sick, he'd get Clarice to set up a room for him at their apartment, and Yvonne and his daughters and even in time beautiful Samantha would be there for him. He was not going to be another body on a bed. Clarice was good at mothering, and he'd let her do that for him.

If Samantha was the love of his life, she'd understand and go with the flow.

Jil called Samantha to say he saw Barry out with Clarice before Barry got to her apartment that night.

"She was looking very Jackie O," Jil said. "Very Upper East Side old guard, the red and green holiday Hermès scarf, the Chanel boots, *le tout ensemble*."

"Did it seem like they were having a good time?" Samantha asked.

"Girls like that never have a good time. They're too busy being martyrs in cashmere. But I have to say they did seem fairly chummy."

"What do you mean chummy?" Samantha couldn't help probing.

"Darlin', isn't this a little high school? I mean, ho-hum. On the other hand, I'd kill for a piece of Grey Navez's chocolate candy. Do you think it's too late for me to go work at Morgan Stanley?"

"Jil, how chummy?" Samantha was adamant.

"I'm sorry I told you."

"Well you did, so now it's too late."

"Grey says they were holding hands but I didn't see it." Jil truly wished he had never mentioned it.

"Thanks, Jil. You're a pal." She had had enough.

"Maybe they were discussing his divorce."

"Good night, Jil."

Samantha poured herself a vodka and sat on a couch watching the Food Network until the doorman said Barry was on his way up.

"Hi. I couldn't reach you all day." Samantha kissed him.

"Long day. Fuckin' agents had me on the phone till ten."

"Poor darling." She kissed him again. "Want a drink?" She began to get up.

"No, I'm tired. Let's go to bed."

She put her arm around him. "I'm sorry it's been so rough."

"You have no idea, babe." He began to kiss her neck.

"Maybe I do. Jil called to say he saw you having dinner with Clarice."

"The fuckin' art dealer?" He was definitely not in the mood for recriminations.

"He's one of my best friends."

"Well he's a gossip and a drama queen. I took the mother of my children to dinner. Big fuckin' deal." Barry poured himself a Diet Dr Pepper.

"Barry, have you told her we're moving in together?" Samantha asked him for what Barry thought must have been the thirtieth time.

"She doesn't need to know that." Barry always avoided the question, and it usually went away in five minutes.

"But we are moving in together," she repeated it.

"Of course we are. Can we go to bed? I've had an awful couple of days." He began to walk toward the bedroom.

Samantha sat down. "Barry, I need to know we are moving forward."

"Jesus fuckin' Christ." He pushed over her coffee-table books. "Some fruit calls to say I had dinner with my wife, and suddenly you need to know every goddamn thing I'm doing. Give me a break." He put on his jacket.

"Where are you going?"

"Back to my hotel to get a night's sleep."

"Barry, try to think about it from my perspective."

"You know what?" As he looked at her he thought she was truly beautiful and was behaving like a privileged cunt. "I don't have the energy to think about your perspective right now. Right now I need to be a little selfish. And if you can't deal with that, fuck you." He could hardly breathe.

"Barry, where is this coming from?" Samantha followed him.

"I don't owe you any explanations." He walked out of her apartment and slammed the door.

Barry kissing Clarice on the cheek in front of Vico was on the cover of the *New York Post* the morning after their dinner.

"Aren't we going to war with Iraq or something?" Barry asked Yvonne while he held the paper. "Who the hell cares about me and Clarice?"

"Oh, she called here when you were downstairs at the screening," his assistant said efficiently. "She said she thought about your offer, and her answer is that it would be impossible."

"Get her on the phone for me," Barry screamed.

"Clarice told me if you have anything to say to her you can do it through me. Also, Dr. Vartan's office called and they're setting you up for tests." Yvonne made no vocal differentiation between his ex-wife and the doctor.

"Get me a pizza!" Barry yelled.

CHAPTER TWENTY-SEVEN

Judy

Judy's arms were driving her crazy. But the couture Chanel she had bought in Paris for the Museum of Modern Art spring gala was cutting her in a way that made her arms look thin but not sculpted. Judy did not want this kind of anxiety on the day of her potentially greatest triumph. Although she'd had Botox six weeks ago and a facial peel two weeks ago, just knowing the imperfection of her arms could make her entire face look puffy and not relaxed.

Since MoMA was being renovated and was temporarily located in Queens, Clarice mentioned to Judy the idea of holding the gala downtown to give the party a little more zip. The development office ran with the downtown plan and so did the rest of the benefit cochairs. Samantha Acton's indie film event in Bedford-Stuyvesant set the precedent for benefits finding new urban venues to celebrate the rebounding city.

Having looked at the Puck Building, the Singer Building, Trinity Church, and the Stock Exchange, and even at placing a tent on the Brooklyn Bridge, the events coordinator settled on an old nylon factory where the first Lycra panty hose in Manhattan had been manufactured.

Eyeing the vast open space of the hosiery factory for the first time, the museum development director got increasingly excited. "We can get Melissa Meyer in here to do a mural we'll auction off, and there's even space for an Ann Armstrong installation during the benefit." He smiled while looking at the high ceiling.

"I like it. It's so New York!" Clarice, who had asked to come along, got very excited. Judy put her arm around Clarice. "I told you, this is going to be so fun."

The benefit became a symbol of the city and the arts community pulling together. At least twenty artists, from Frank Stella, Elizabeth Peyton, and Susan Rothenberg to Santiago Cucullu donated new works to be auctioned off for families of artists who had suffered from 9/11. Among the scheduled entertainment was the chorus of *42nd Street*, Bernadette Peters, Renée Fleming, and the entire cast of *Sex and the City*. The evening itself would be hosted by Wynton Marsalis, and David Rockefeller would pay tribute to Mayor Rudolph Giuliani.

In the week leading up to the gala, Judy was mentioned in columns in the *New York Post*, the *Daily News*, the *New York Observer*, and *W*. She hired a publicist, and the "peppy" Mrs. Tremont was seen absolutely everywhere.

"Do you know if Clarice is still seeing Barry?" Samantha asked Judy at lunch at La Goulue after they had gone shopping for Judy's gala shoes. Judy had noticed a few dark circles under her great friend's eyes.

"Why? Did he say he was still seeing her?" Judy asked. "Everyone saw that picture in the paper months ago, but you know that means nothing."

"I wonder how that picture got in there?"

"I think all our handbags are wiretapped. I swear I think my Birkin is connected directly to PageSix."

Judy didn't mention that when Grey Navez saw Barry and Clarice she called Judy shortly after. Coincidentally, Judy just happened to be having a few friends over, including a *Post* columnist.

"You know Clarice is seeing Barry again. They're having dinner tonight at Vico," Judy whispered to the columnist.

"You really are the red-hot center, aren't you," he said teasingly.

"You know I love Clarice and Samantha. They're both my best friends, so I try to keep out of it." She cocked her head demurely.

"Oh, you're good, Judy." The columnist winked at her, "You're really good."

Judy Tremont was quickly emerging as the girl next in line to rule the roost.

Judy began the day of the gala with her traditional sunrise Pilates class. Then Albert brought the girls to school while Judy took a quick run around the reservoir with her aerobics trainer.

When she came home she arranged for her facialist to come to her house for a lavender herbal rejuvenation treatment. She followed that with a deep-root massage on her scalp and a quickie highlight perk-up. Early this fall, she had stopped running to Frédéric Fekkai for appointments. It was just much more efficient to have them all come to the apartment.

At noon she told the cook that she was much too excited and nervous to eat lunch. Instead she had the cook prepare half a Slim-Fast bar, steamed broccoli rabe, and iced green tea.

Judy believed she had never been happier. She was becoming a style icon in the most stylish city in the world. Any yearnings she had about moving back to the largest house in Modesto were gone. She had a fantastic life and she had created it all herself. Albert had real money but he was clueless about how to spend it. Judy had stuck to her vision, and in the hours before the gala she felt she had accomplished as much as any editor, doctor, account executive, or any other kind of working mother. The names of successful women lawyers, bankers, and even big-deal doctors like Francesca Weissman are soon forgotten. But icons like C. Z. Guest, Slim Keith, or Bunny Mellon would endure. And let's face it, Judy thought to herself as she nibbled her Slim-Fast bar, what remains indelible is a woman's style.

"Mrs. Tremont, the gentleman from VBH is here," the house-keeper interrupted her snack.

"You can send him up." Judy rang the bell for the cook to collect her used plates.

Judy still hadn't settled on an evening clutch. She had her Judith Leiber $10,000 egg-shaped one that Albert bought her last year for Christmas. But she felt it was a little Palm Beach dowager for the Museum of Modern Art. She knew if she went with her Prada, Chanel, or Herrera, there was a very good chance that someone else would also have it tucked under their arm. Judy wanted to inject her style with a hipper grace note, a little bit of rock 'n' roll. So she arranged for VBH, the new exclusive handbag, jewelry, and home accessories store on Madison, to send over a few little items.

"I love this one," the very chic pencil-thin salesman with a cashmere sweater tied over his black jacket cooed as Judy lifted a lavender alligator box.

She put it under her arm and looked in the mirror. "Do you have anything in python? Alligator may still be a little staid."

"Well, I adore this envelope one and the handle on the chain is to die for." He showed her a purple and orange python flat purse. "But it may be a little too Madonna for you."

Judy pulled the clutch toward her. "Do I dare?"

"I think you can pull it off because you're not really going for it, you know what I mean?"

"How much is it?" Judy asked, although the price wasn't going to stop her.

"Just three thousand. Half the alligator," he said offhandedly.

Judy pulled it closer. "I think I'm falling in love, although it may wreak havoc with my shoes."

Just then the housekeeper came into the room.

"Mrs. Tremont, I need to speak with you."

"Later." Judy waved her away.

"Ma'am, it's an emergency."

"Are the children all right?" Judy dropped the clutch.

"Why don't I leave these and a couple other favorites of mine with you and let you decide." The accommodating salesman got up, leaving the purses behind for her to salivate over. "I'll send someone over later for the ones you don't want."

"Oh, that should be perfect. Who knows, maybe I'll keep them all." Judy giggled. "I mean I shouldn't, but they're hard to resist."

"I know what you mean." He extended his hand. "It's been a pleasure."

When the salesman left, leaving an array of $20,000 worth of evening bags, Judy turned irritatedly to the housekeeper.

"Okay. Let's have it. You realize you interrupted a very important meeting."

"I'm sorry, Mrs. Tremont. But I think you should know that Emily quit."

"What? Emily the nanny?"

"She left an hour ago. She found out her mother's sick, so she went home to Baton Rouge."

"She can't just do that. My gala is tonight." Judy was furious. "Call her."

"She left a note, Mrs. Tremont. Here it is." The housekeeper took it out of her pocket.

"I'll take that." Judy grabbed the note and read: "Dear Mrs. Tremont, Decided to leave today. Have an emergency at home. Love to the girls."

"This is the most ungrateful, crude behavior I have ever heard of." Judy began pacing the room and hyperventilating. "I bet she took my jewelry. I bet she's pregnant, too. I wonder if she figured out our PIN number." Judy suddenly began screaming. "Goddammit! This is the last time I'm hiring white trash from the Sutton Agency. No one who isn't Irish and directly from Ireland is setting foot in this house."

"But I thought Emily was a Skidmore graduate from Connecticut. She isn't white trash, ma'am," the housekeeper noted.

"I want you to assemble all the staff in the kitchen in ten minutes." Judy began to walk out of the room. "I'm just going to go upstairs to check on my jewelry. Also I want you to stay here tonight so the girls won't be alone or with someone they don't already know. I can't believe this is happening to me."

Judy raced to her room, opened her jewelry box, and was relieved to see that her day-to-day things she kept in the house were still there. She took a quick spin through her closet, but evaluating the damage there would take far more time. Finally, she went into the bathroom, threw cold water on her face, took half an Ativan, inhaled a sustaining Ashtanga breath, and then marched into the kitchen.

The help was dutifully assembled: housekeeper, cook, cleaning lady, laundress, personal assistant, kids' personal assistant, calligrapher, and after-school coach.

"Looky here." Judy stood up while they all sat. "You all have the privilege of working for one of the best families in New York. And I expect each and every one of you to behave accordingly. My children are the children who set the standards in this city and deserve to be treated with the same respect and professionalism that Mr. Tremont and I are." She took a breath and continued.

"You all make a hell of a good salary and Mr. Tremont is much more generous than he should be. But if any one of you gets any ideas like Emily, I want you to know that not only will you be replaced in a shot, I will track you down wherever you go and make certain that you never work again." Judy saw the cook catch the housekeeper's eye and made a note to herself that they were potential troublemakers.

"Finally, maybe some of you have an idea of what it meant to be working for an Astor, a du Pont, or a Vanderbilt. Well let me tell you something, that's exactly where you are right now. This is a very important home and very important people come here. I want each and every one of you to know how lucky you are or I will fire you all."

Judy walked out of the kitchen, went to her room, and got into bed. Of all the truly irritating things to happen on what was meant to be the best day of her life! She knew she had to snap out of it and shouldn't take another Ativan, so she picked up the phone.

"Hello, this is Mrs. Tremont. I'd like to talk to the salesman who just brought those yumbo evening bags to my house. Yes, I'll hold."

Judy took another deep and relaxing long breath.

"Hello, how are you. Yes, I've thought about it. These bags are just so delicious I'm going to take all of them." Judy felt a wave of relaxation from her hand on the telephone down to her toes.

"I think that's wise. They're one of a kind," the salesman spoke serenely on the other end of the line.

"Oh. I can't tell you how much happier they're making me already. Thanks so much. I'm sure I'll see you again."

Judy hit the intercom buzzer for the housekeeper.

"Would you bring my new bags to my room, and a cup of chamomile tea."

Judy shut her eyes. She was going through her catalogue of potential shoes for tonight and matching them with her new purse. It was simultaneously soothing and exhilarating.

"Judy! Judy!" The flashbulbs were popping on the red carpet outside the old factory building. "Who made your dress?"

"Chanel Couture." She smiled and held on to Albert. It was as if she were Cinderella without the downside of a glass slipper.

"Over here, Judy!" The lights from the cameras continued to pop.

"And my bag is VBH," Judy squealed, knowing that if she got those magic letters into *W* or *Vogue,* next time they wouldn't send over just a few clutches. Next time she could get them made to order.

As Judy walked into the former factory, she stopped to take her photo with David Rockefeller and the governor's wife. The space had been transformed into a postmodern fantasyland, with hundreds of crystal chandeliers and lavender glitter falling constantly from the ceiling onto a lavender Nycra (a combination of nylon and Lycra) floor covering.

"You look so beautiful," Judy squealed when she saw Clarice's Yves Saint Laurent. "I love this!" She brushed Clarice's bare shoulder, which made her especially happy, since Clarice's arms were in no way better toned than her own.

"Hey, Clarice." Barry walked by them wearing his signature black sweatshirt underneath a tuxedo.

"Hey, Barry." Clarice air-kissed his cheek. She hadn't spoken with him since their dinner at Vico. "You know Judy Tremont?"

"Hey, Judy. Great party." Barry moved on.

"He's a pig!" Judy commented as he walked away. "How could he wear a sweatshirt to this kind of party?"

"Oh, that's just Barry." Clarice shrugged.

"I wonder where Samantha is." Judy was secretly delighted she had the spotlight to herself. "Maybe something really is going on," Judy conjectured.

"I wouldn't know." Clarice cut short the Barry conversation and waved to Pippa Rose.

"Pippa. Have you seen Jil? He's my escort tonight."

"He's in the corner chatting with Frankie Weissman and Charlie Acton." Pippa motioned toward them. "Frankie just told me the most interesting thing. Apparently, this building was her father's old nylon factory."

"How fascinating!" Clarice was honestly intrigued. "I didn't know that."

"Frankie didn't realize it either until she walked in," Pippa continued. "Her father invented some sort of stretch material and apparently they manufactured it right here. Now that's a real New York story! From factory to chichi catering hall."

"There's Grey Navez and Lewis. She always looks great." Judy had no interest in discussing the history of hosiery manufacturing in Manhattan. "And I must say, I adore her boyfriend."

The chimes for dinner began to ring. "Ladies and gentlemen, please take your seats."

"I better go find Jil." Clarice gave Judy another kiss. "Thank you so much for inviting me to be part of this with you. It really came at the right time for me."

As Clarice walked away, Judy turned to Pippa. "I hope she's not getting overly dependent on Jil. He's such a climber! He just attaches himself to every important lonely woman who comes on the market. And you know he's dating a stripper."

"I think they want us to sit down." Pippa smiled.

The chimes rang again.

"I have no idea where Albert is. He's lost at these things without me." Judy kissed Pippa on both cheeks. "I'm so happy to see you."

When the eight hundred guests were finally seated, the chairman of the museum's board of directors and the museum's director approached the microphone.

"I want to welcome everyone here tonight to our annual gala. The success of this evening is a tribute to the dedication of New Yorkers to their city and to the city's great art institutions. We are here tonight because our beloved museum is being renovated. In two years, we will return to our permanent home." The house broke into applause. Before I introduce David Rockefeller and our guest of honor, former mayor Giuliani, I want to ask our benefit cochairs to stand." He began to read a list of eight names in alphabetical order.

While the others each rose from their chairs to polite applause, Judy felt a rush of heat from her toe to her crotch all the way to her hand clasping her python clutch. She knew she would be next. Judy had even prepared short remarks about New York and the arts. Even when she was in college and had orgasms, it felt nothing like this. This was like being on top of Mount Everest.

The director continued, "Judy Tremont." Judy got up, looked around the room, and saw the best possible gathering of people; the stylemakers, the world she fantasized about when she was ten years old. She forgot her speech altogether.

As the applause ended, she remained standing and started to cry.

"Sit down, honey," Albert whispered to her as he tried to nonchalantly pull her down.

Judy wept. "But Albert, it's just so fun!"

CHAPTER TWENTY-EIGHT

Samantha

"I have an offer to do some sort of cable TV show on style," Samantha casually mentioned to her therapist.

"Sounds interesting." The therapist tried not to engage Samantha's dismissive tone.

"Well, it would be entertaining, fashion, and decorating, so it may be superficial but at least it's not limited. It has diverse superficiality. And I could tie it in with another coffee-table book since I never wrote the last one." Samantha scratched her palm. "It's for Plum TV. Ever hear of that?"

"No, but that doesn't mean anything."

"It's the cable station in the Hamptons. It was my friend Adrienne Strong-Rodman's idea. She has a house there and she thought we could do it together. Her husband Paul is the one who just got indicted."

The therapist leaned back in her chair. "Yes, I know who Paul Rodman is. He makes the Enron people look like philanthropists. You didn't used to like Adrienne Strong-Rodman."

"Oh, who the hell knows who I like or dislike. I thought her sexuality was crass and manipulative." Samantha ran her hand through her hair. "But who am I to make comments about anyone else's sexuality. I'm the Whore of Babylon!"

"You're certainly down on yourself today."

"Sorry." Samantha nodded.

"You don't have to apologize."

"Sorry." Samantha smiled. "Anyway, turns out Adrienne just makes a lousy first impression. But she's actually very impressive and very smart. She really does have all these degrees—she went to UCLA night school and took adult extension courses in child psychology while she was still a Hollywood publicist. I think because she's actually worked she knows what's real. We've gone out for drinks a few times and she's very loyal when it comes to gossip and all that crap."

"She sounds like a good friend for you."

"I'm not really sure what she gets out of it. I think I'm boring as hell."

"Did something happen?" the therapist asked.

"Well, I'm telling you that I'm seriously considering becoming a cable TV host who has serious discussions about napkin rings. That sort of gives it away, doesn't it. I do have an M.A. in art history. I have, in fact, been a real influence at the Whitney."

"So don't do it," the therapist said quickly.

"And what do you propose I do instead? Sit around at the Sherry Netherland and wait for Barry to call?" Samantha was getting increasingly agitated. "Or read about benefits I refused to go to because I didn't want to watch my boyfriend kiss the hem of his sainted wife, Clarice. She used to be another skinny mother with blown-straight hair on the Upper East Side and now she's the Martyr of Madison Avenue. Look, I have nothing against the woman but she's dull as dishwater. She's a shopper and a professional playdate scheduler." Samantha stopped her train of thought. "I've turned into such a fuckin' bitch."

"You really don't give yourself a lot of credit, do you? You accomplished a lot in your life before you ever met Barry."

"Did I tell you Charlie's seeing someone?" Samantha took a sip of coffee. "At least I think he is."

"Really?"

"Frankie Weissman. A doctor he knew from Princeton."

"You told me about her. You wanted him to date her."

"Well, I don't really know that they're dating. I don't even know that they're sleeping together. She might not be glitzy enough for Charlie. I just heard they were dancing together at the Modern gala and have been seen together at the opera and the ballet."

"And that bothers you?" the therapist asked.

"Not at all." She looked down at her hands. "This is terrible, but I hardly ever think about Charlie."

"Why is that terrible?"

"Well, I mean, what kind of person am I? He was my husband."

"I told you, stop beating yourself up."

"I'm sorry, bad habit." Samantha put down her coffee. "I have a good title for our cable show—*That's Entertaining!*—Jil Taillou suggested it to me. By the way, here's a New York tidbit. Jil's now escorting Clarice."

"Does that bother you?" The therapist would not let her skirt the issue.

"I just don't understand why that woman is suddenly all over my life. She's dating my gay best friend, she's out to dinner with my lover, she's throwing benefits with Judy Tremont. I don't mean her any harm. I just want her gone from my life. And gone from Barry's life, too."

"So this is really about Barry." The therapist crossed her legs with a we've-finally-gotten-to-the-point assurance.

"Of course it's about Barry," Samantha snapped at her. "I want to marry Barry. I don't want to be his debutante wet dream. He's the one who said let's take this to the next step."

"And if Barry doesn't marry you?" the therapist asked.

"Oh I'll just kill myself," Samantha replied quickly.

"Don't make jokes like that."

Samantha smiled. "I was just getting your attention. And I'm not worried. Barry's a negotiator. He wouldn't dream of not closing this deal. I just have to make it impossible for him to say no."

"You sound like you've adopted his strategy."

"That's very insightful of you." Samantha looked at her doctor directly. "Do you think my strategy will work?"

"Do you have a specific plan?" the therapist asked.

"I can put together this cable show and hide in the Hamptons. I mean if I refuse to see him until he shows up with a ring, won't that get him to heel?"

"Certainly some people have been successful by doing that."

"You mean you don't have an opinion?" Samantha egged her on.

"I'm afraid our time is over." The therapist stood up and Samantha began pulling her cashmere poncho over her head.

Samantha managed to keep herself from calling Barry for almost six months. She never mentioned to Adrienne or even her therapist that she checked her messages four times a day to see if he had called and half expected a Bulgari bracelet waiting for her when she came home.

Most of that summer and fall Samantha stayed in Adrienne's house in Bridgehampton. She had very little interest in going to the city for her board meetings or attending any benefits. She walked on the beach every day, taped her show once a week, and read all the books she had postponed in order to go out to dinner parties: Trollope, Dickens, Tolstoy. At night, Adrienne's housekeeper would prepare a small salad with grilled fish, or Samantha would send her home and make herself a peanut butter and bacon sandwich.

By October, the lead-up to Paul Rodman's trial became so overwhelming that Adrienne would more often than not phone Samantha on the morning of a taping and say, "I can't make it. You do it."

It wasn't that Samantha couldn't do the show alone, but she missed Adrienne's crass yet energetic spirit. Adrienne knew exactly who all their guests had slept with and how much was in their bank accounts. When Samantha's mind drifted to what her therapist called "beating herself up," Adrienne would move right on to whose husband had done worse things than Paul and never been caught. She was happy to name names of every embezzler or crook with a Gulfstream jet.

Bridgehampton is relatively quiet in the late autumn. The damp ocean winds and falling leaves create a golden blanket on the well-trimmed lawns. Samantha wore sweatpants and a V-neck cashmere sweater every day. When she got to the small television studio she'd let them put on makeup and fashions from the chic shops in Southampton. But as soon as she left she decided she couldn't care less. In her mind she was taking a sabbatical from her life until things were resolved with Barry.

Adrienne called her on a bright December morning. "You have to come into the city and see me. You can't sit out there like a nun."

"I like being a nun." Samantha laughed. "Every morning I take a walk on the beach and sing the score of *The Sound of Music*. I'm particularly good at 'Maria's not an asset to the abbey.'"

"I'm going to shut my house down if you don't come in. I swear I am calling Con Edison," Adrienne jokingly threatened.

Samantha sat up in the wicker chaise longue overlooking the ocean. "Adrienne, New York means people. I don't like people. Except if they want to talk to me about how to throw a dinner for six.

Why don't you come out here? I'll make you peanut butter and bacon."

"I need a friend, Samantha." Adrienne burst into tears. "Things here are really shitty. And I can't leave Paul. I'll send a car for you. I just can't handle this anymore."

"Adrienne, what happened?" Samantha had never heard her like this.

Adrienne was now hysterical, heaving for breath. "It's nothing. It's just my whole fucking life is falling apart and I don't know if I can handle it. And I'm tough, honey. I'm really tough. But I just goddamn hate everything." She continued to cry and heave for air.

"Adrienne, take it easy," Samantha spoke softly.

"They're gonna subpoena me too. I could be disbarred. And I know this is all because we're fuckin' Democrats."

"What?" Samantha didn't follow.

"It's 'cause the Justice Department hates us for my throwing all those fund-raisers for the Democrats. Plus there's the fucking fifty-pound bird!"

"Who?" Samantha asked, but Adrienne was on a tear.

"The fuckin' bird that built like a three-hundred-pound nest on our building and was tossing pigeon and rat carcasses on the street. So Paul takes the nest away one night because I don't want my children to get West Nile disease because we live in an apartment we paid thirty million fuckin' dollars for. And the next day the Audubon Society and the entire world is picketing and the goddamn bird makes the cover of the *Financial Times*. So I tell Paul we have to pay someone to rebuild the nest but the goddamn thing has moved to the Carlyle, so even the bird is trying to screw me. And the crazy thing is we're sending boys to an immoral war to die and all anyone cares about is my husband's bank account and the rights of a bird who should be in a forest to live in a Fifth Avenue co-op." Adrienne was now alternating between shrieks of laughter and sobs.

"Adrienne, take it easy. Of course I'll come in," Samantha said reassuringly.

"Oh, by the way. I left one thing out. Jessica met a girl in her new school's gymnastics class and says she's now a lesbian."

"What's wrong with that?" Samantha didn't want Adrienne to go hysterical again.

"It's the goddamn teacher! She's twenty-five."

"Oh." Samantha didn't know what to say.

"Hey, there's a silver lining." Adrienne finally stopped crying. "She's convinced her to eat organic and stop drinking. My daughter's an ex-alcoholic and a bisexual and she's only eleven."

Samantha and Adrienne met for dinner on the West Side.

"Let's stick to anywhere west of Central Park. I have no desire to run into Grey Navez or Judy Tremont," Adrienne told Samantha. "I'm just not equipped for it."

"How about a Japanese restaurant on Columbus, the kind with a four-course meal for fifteen dollars?" Samantha asked. "Judy Tremont definitely won't be there."

"You want me to meet you at Teriyaki Boy?" Adrienne laughed.

"All right, let's go to McDonald's," Samantha suggested.

"No, fifteen-dollar sushi on Columbus it is," Adrienne agreed.

During their entire meal the two friends never mentioned a word about Barry or Paul. Adrienne had all the latest news on Judy Tremont's last dinner party, to which she supposedly had the parents from all the "best families" at Spence over to her house. The school found out about it and demanded that Judy write an apology to every uninvited parent. Samantha and Adrienne drank four sakes and split a green tea ice cream. As they walked out of the restaurant Adrienne took Samantha's arm.

"Thank you for coming, honey. This is the best time I've had in forever. Walk with me to the crosstown bus."

"Did you just say the word 'bus'?" Samantha stopped.

"I'm doing a little experiment. It's just in case I end up selling makeup at Lord & Taylor and taking the bus there every morning," Adrienne quickly answered.

"That won't happen," Samantha assured her.

"If it does it won't be the worst thing. I'll still have my nose. They can't take that away from me. Dr. Diamond did too good a job."

As the two women walked up Columbus Avenue, crowds of people began pouring into the streets.

"They must be filming a late-night *Who Wants to Be a Millionaire* at ABC on Sixty-seventh Street," Adrienne said. "At least our lives aren't so pathetic that we'd want to go to that."

Ambulances and fire trucks began roaring down the street as a black smoke filled the air.

"Oh God!" Adrienne grabbed Samantha's hand. "Do you think it's happening again?"

"Don't jump to conclusions, Adrienne!" Samantha tried to cover her own fear.

Fire engines were clanging down the street. Police cars with sirens followed with loudspeakers announcing "Clear the street. Clear the street."

"Dammit! Of course this is what happens when I decide to take the bus! Well, the good news is maybe Paul will never go to jail 'cause we're all gonna blow up." Adrienne began pushing her way through the crowd.

Samantha pulled Adrienne over to a newsman with a camera crew.

"What's happened here?" Samantha asked.

"The Starbucks on Sixty-seventh and Columbus blew up. It's not clear if it's a suicide bomb or a water main break."

Samantha and Adrienne fell in line with the flow of people walking away from the broken glass and the still-flying shreds of paper cups and jewelry and Christmas-blend coffee. She took Adrienne's arm and they walked uptown in silence.

When the women reached Eighty-sixth Street they began to walk home through the park.

"Maybe I could sell makeup in some nice place like Bangor, Maine," Adrienne finally broke the silence. "Say something, honey. We're walking through the park at midnight and it's too scary to be quiet. Just say anything."

Samantha looked at her and the skyline still gleaming over the park.

"I miss Barry. I really miss Barry," she said, and silently kept moving.

CHAPTER TWENTY-NINE

Frankie

Frankie had worked late the night of the explosion. There had been an outbreak of thrush at All Souls nursery school, plus five girls at Brearley were diagnosed with mononucleosis. From Frankie's perspective, every sophomore at Trinity, Sacred Heart, Horace Mann, or Brearley who wanted to avoid school suddenly came down with mono and was rushed by a caregiver to her office.

When Frankie came home she poured herself a glass of wine, reached for her phone to check on Abraham, then decided she'd do it all in the morning and watch an old movie on Channel Thirteen or American Movie Classics instead. Recently she had found any film produced after 1970 decidedly unsettling.

While surfing the networks, Frankie absentmindedly heard a woman say, "Bill, it's still not clear if the Starbucks incident was a water main break or the first New York suicide bombing."

Frankie dropped her cat and sat up in her chair. She changed the channel so she could hear the news from someone who wouldn't be quickly moving on to a canceled celebrity marriage.

"An explosion rocked New York's Upper West Side," an anchorwoman reported with a furrowed brow. "The Starbucks at Sixty-seventh and Columbus exploded at 10:36 p.m. So far the death count is thirty and may grow larger. The mayor has urged New Yorkers to stay in their homes and not to jump to any conclusions."

Frankie immediately picked up her phone. "Charlie! Charlie! There was an explosion at the Lincoln Center Starbucks. Thirty people were killed."

Charlie got to Frankie's house in fifteen minutes. The streets were eerily quiet and most of the taxis were already off duty. Charlie managed to get a ride from Judy Tremont's limo driver, Bill. Apparently as soon as Judy heard about the explosion she had Bill drive her and the children to the heliport on Thirty-fourth Street to fly to Southampton. Bill had just dropped them off and was on his way home to the Bronx.

"I'm here if you want to come down," Charlie spoke on the intercom in Frankie's building. "I'm gonna go see if I can help them."

"I'll be right there." Frankie grabbed her coat.

Frankie's doorman now recognized Charlie from the repeated times he dropped Frankie off and kissed her a friendly good-bye. "You know, Dr. Acton," the doorman said in an Irish accent, "this explosion is not about a suicide bomber or Con Edison. It's those blankety-blank politicians who are trying to scare us half to death. I know, I come from Ireland."

As Frankie stepped out of the elevator the doorman continued, "Dr. Weissman, there's no one on the street tonight. Why don't you stay in."

"We were thinking we could do some good, George." Charlie turned to the doorman and took Frankie's arm.

"You take good care of her, Dr. Acton," George called to him as they left the building. "I don't want nothing happening to her. When I tell people I know Dr. Frankie Weissman, they tell me I'm a lucky man."

Frankie and Charlie walked out onto Columbus Avenue. Traffic had been stopped and the stillness was reminiscent of a winter night when a blizzard halts the life of the city and the only pedestrians are children cross-country skiing.

Frankie broke the silence. "I remembered you went to the World Trade Center after 9/11."

"Yes. I'm very glad you called me." He squeezed her hand.

"Do you think it was a suicide bomber?" Frankie asked. "That's terrifying."

"I don't know, Frankie." He turned to her. "I don't believe what anybody tells me except for you."

By the time they got to Seventy-second Street the smell of the city was thick with fire, burning flesh, and hot coffee.

"You can't go past here." A policeman stopped them at the barricades.

"I'm Dr. Charles Acton, I'm with the burn unit at NewYork Hospital." Charlie pulled out his ID card and the note he had used from the mayor's office during 9/11. "I was at the World Trade Center. And this is Dr. Francesca Weissman. She's a pediatrician from Mount Sinai."

"Go ahead." The cop let them through the blockade.

As they approached the former gathering spot the scene began to look more and more like a newsreel from Jerusalem. There were remains of coffee cups and body parts randomly tossed out toward the Reebok Sports Club. A mother was screeching while holding on to a dead infant. Glass was scattered on the street like an American Kristallnacht, except the shards were splattered with nonfat Frappuccinos.

"I'm Dr. Acton with the NewYork Hospital burn unit. And this is Dr. Francesca Weissman with Sinai Pediatrics. What can we do for you?" Charlie approached an emergency worker while the ABC News team was shooting footage.

The emergency medic quickly dismissed him. "Just go home. We've got enough people here."

"I was at the World Trade Center," Charlie added.

"Listen, if you need to get your thrills, watch *CSI* or some TV show. I've got work to do here."

"Here's my card if you need me." Charlie gave him a card and took Frankie's hand. They walked past three girls who must have been ballet dancers. Their toe shoes were dangling in one piece out of their dance bag. Their faces had been blown wide open.

As they walked back home Frankie said nothing until Charlie finally spoke.

"Do you remember at medical school when you got your first cadaver?" he asked her.

Frankie's mind had just drifted to walking hand in hand with her parents to the Radio City Christmas show and believing there was nowhere in the world she'd rather live than New York. A year later her mother was dead.

"Yes, I remember," Frankie answered him. "I called mine Harriet and made up an entire life for her. I believed she was both a Torah scholar and a hula dancer."

"I couldn't look at mine for the first week, and every night I'd go home and throw up," Charlie spoke softly. "I preferred learning about life in textbooks or inspecting a cell under a microscope. I like the deconstruction of life: the smallest elements, like a hair follicle on skin. But I found the whole picture overwhelmingly disconcerting because any moral center to it all seemed completely up for grabs."

"You're a good man, Charlie. I never got further than what an interesting skeletal system. I wondered if Harriet the cadaver had good posture," she said honestly.

"Well, if she was a hula dancer she must have been flexible." Charlie smiled slightly. "How old was Harriet?"

"I'd say around thirty-five," Frankie answered.

"How did she die?"

"Ovarian cancer," Frankie answered immediately.

"Mine had a heart attack at fifty-six."

"Not a bad life," Frankie said almost too quickly.

"I'll be fifty-six in ten years. I suppose you're right. It's not a bad life."

"Charlie, you're not going anywhere."

"How do you know that? I could go in for a cup of coffee at Starbucks one night." He began to recite as they approached her house: "Things fall apart; the centre cannot hold; / Mere anarchy is loosed upon the world, / The blood-dimmed tide is loosed, and everywhere / The ceremony of innocence is drowned; / The best lack all conviction, while the worst / Are full of passionate intensity."

Frankie whispered, "Surely some revelation is at hand; / Surely the Second Coming is at hand."

"Of course you know the Yeats." Charlie touched her face. As they arrived in front of her building, he said, "You know everything."

"No I don't, Charlie," Frankie answered quickly. "Charlie, please come upstairs. I don't think I can bear to be alone just yet."

Charlie held on to Frankie's hand as they walked inside.

"Good night, Dr. Acton. Good night, Dr. Weissman. Let's hope we're all here tomorrow." The doorman pushed the elevator button.

"Good night, George," Charlie answered for both of them.

On all the nights that year Charlie had escorted Frankie to the opera or a play, he never came upstairs. Charlie always made excuses about running late or having to get up early for morning rounds.

"I thought you'd have a lot of books," he said, examining the book-lined living room while she hung up their coats. "Samantha never let me put my books in the living room. She told me only Hollywood decorators did that."

"Really?" It was a concept that had never occurred to Frankie.

"Yes, they buy up used books by the caseload to warm up the living rooms of ex-television stars' homes."

"So you mean my books make me like an ex-star of *The Partridge Family*?" Frankie asked.

"No, your books make you exactly who I hoped you would be," he answered, and immediately took down a volume of Edwin Arlington Robinson poetry.

"Would you like a drink?" Frankie asked.

"No, no. If I have one drink I'll want thirty-six, and you can't possibly have enough for that. I'd like a cup of tea and some very junkie cookies. Chips Ahoy! or some other thing full of BHT and riboflavin. If this isn't a night for additives, then I don't have any other answers."

Frankie went into her kitchen to make a pot of tea and took a look at her face. She was ashamed of herself for being vain on a night when she had seen body bags on Columbus Avenue. But on the other hand, she knew that nothing affirms life like random death.

Charlie had sat down on the living room couch with the cat. He was still reading the Robinson when Frankie came back into the room.

"It's nice, Frankie. It's very warm," Charlie said. "I'll be happy thinking about you living here."

"Thank you. I really should do more with it, or move," she mumbled. "Sorry, the only cookies I've got are Fig Newtons. They might be too healthy." She handed the bag to him.

"Darn tootin'. I love Fig Newtons." Charlie closed his book and popped a cookie in his mouth. "Okay, I'm ready. Should we turn on the television and find out if the rest of us are blowing up tonight?"

"Maybe we should just avoid it and go out eating Fig Newtons. That would be all right with me." Frankie grabbed two cookies. "I'm double-fistin'."

"C'mere, honey." Charlie outstretched his arm around her. "We're gonna do this together. You, me, and Edward Arlington Robinson."

"You left out my cat. Gilda's coming with us, too."

As Frankie cuddled into Charlie and signaled for her cat to jump on her lap, Charlie put on the television.

"We're getting a better count of the damage at Starbucks, Dave." A young reporter was on the scene. "The dead count is now forty with around seventy wounded. Among those believed to be dead are at least three Juilliard students, a number of New York City Ballet apprentices, and the Upper East Side art dealer and socialite Jil Taillou."

"What?" Frankie looked up at the television.

"Apparently, Mr. Taillou was at the opera tonight and left after the first act."

Frankie stood up. "I'm going to Jil's house."

"Frankie, sit down." Charlie put his hand on her leg.

"I should go over there. I should see his daughter."

"Frankie, you're not going anywhere tonight. They could be blowing up Starbucks all over Manhattan."

"I don't care."

"Well I do."

"Charlie, you know as well as I do that it was some water main break and homeland security—or fatherland security for all I know—is turning it into a bombing so we can invade the entire goddamn Middle East." Frankie stood up and began to walk to the door.

"Frankie, take it easy. You'll make yourself sick."

"Charlie, what the hell did Jil do to deserve this? He was a nice man who sold art and went to parties."

"Isn't the point, Frankie, that none of them deserve this? And it could have been you and me who walked out of the opera tonight."

Frankie sat down beside Charlie again.

Charlie put his arm around her. "It's my fault for putting on the stupid television."

"No, no," Frankie muttered.

"Tell you what. I have a proposition." He turned off the TV and put his hand on her face. "Since the world is so lousy, do you mind if I spend the night here? We can eat Fig Newtons and tell each other our nightmares."

Frankie looked at him. A few years ago she would have said, "Sure, you can stay on the couch," assuming they were really only friends.

"Yes." She took his hand. "I'd really like that."

"Good. And I think Jil would have liked it, too. He always told me I should get to really know you."

Charlie pulled her toward him and ran his hand along her breast and neck. He wiped away her tears and kissed her.

"Don't cry, honey. I'm here now and I'm going to take care of you."

"Charlie, how can you sound so hopeful?" she answered between her soft gasps for air.

"I promise you." He put his arm around her waist and unfastened her skirt. "This is the most positive thing we can do."

Charlie pulled her up from the couch.

"You're very strong, Charlie," she whispered as he led her to the bedroom.

"No, you're strong, Francesca Weissman. I am surprisingly weak."

While sirens and ambulances whirred down Columbus Avenue Frankie and Charlie made love.

"Darling, do you mind if I smoke?" Charlie asked when they were through. "Because if the world is blowing up tonight, I figure what the hell." He took a cigarette out of his pants pocket and lit it.

"No, fine with me." She snuggled into him.

"Want one?"

"No," she answered.

"Such a good girl." He stroked her hair. "I know I wouldn't want to be anywhere else right now but here with you."

After Charlie fell asleep, Frankie remained awake looking at his face and listening to the ambulances. He had lovely hair, still curly, and gray at the temples.

When the phone rang at 4 a.m. Frankie was still awake. She immediately assumed it was some news about her father.

"Yes, this is Dr. Weissman," she answered.

"Hello, Dr. Weissman, this is the answering service."

Frankie sat up. "What's happened?"

"Pippa Rose asked me to call you. Your patient Jennifer Rose was at Starbucks tonight after a rehearsal for *The Nutcracker*. Apparently, her foot was blown off in the explosion."

"Where is she?"

"St. Luke's-Roosevelt. Mrs. Rose said she'd phone in the morning."

Frankie got out of bed and went to find Pippa Rose's phone number. When Frankie's mother died, she had dismissed the possibility of a loving God. But she always believed in the healing property of art. On the day after 9/11, Pippa Rose took Frankie to watch Jennifer's ballet barre class. There was something about those young ballerinas in their black leotards and pink tights concentrating on making their pliés deeper and their extensions longer that made Frankie have faith that the best of civilization will always survive.

Frankie sat at her desk while Charlie slept. Involuntarily she began to mutter, *"Yisgadal v'yiskadash."* She stopped the ancient kaddish mid-sentence, gathered herself, and dialed St. Luke's Hospital.

CHAPTER THIRTY

Barry

As soon as Barry heard about the Starbucks incident he knew it was time to leave New York. He had no intention of taking a let's-wait-and-see attitude. Barry knew that anyone halfway important would get in their planes and get the hell out.

Barry was still living at The Lowell, though he kept a suite at the Mercer in SoHo as well. The downtown place was a good spot for taking young directors to dinner or an occasional threesome with aspiring NYU drama students. The uptown place was more about family.

Barry's oldest daughter, Venice, was close friends with that young ballerina whose foot was blown off in the blast. He wanted to be with his kids to help them get through this, but Clarice took them away to Palm Beach. Barry didn't want his children staying in New York either, but he resented Clarice for not taking him into consideration. Technically the kids were hers this week, but given the emergency circumstances he made a note to bring this up in court.

Clarice had told some gossip columnist that she was thinking of opening a shop on Worth Avenue in Palm Beach. It was going to be some sort of Sicilian ceramics thing that could never break even but would keep her occupied. Clarice had become one of those good-looking New York women who gave quotes to style reporters like "Don't call me a socialite. I'm opening a store."

Fine, you're not a socialite, Barry thought to himself when he saw her picture in *Manhattan* magazine or *Town & Country*—you're James Watson and you've just unraveled fuckin' DNA! And Samantha on her entertaining talk show was fuckin' David Letterman! He wasn't going to let either one of them manipulate him. Fuckin' rich women were ridiculous!

Barry grabbed his leg. Recently he'd been having shooting pains in his arms and legs. He took around ten Tylenol a day and had refused to call his doctor for painkillers. As far as Barry was concerned, painkillers were for stupid actors who thought it was fun to cruise Sunset Boulevard high on OxyContin. But the truth was, the pain had gotten worse, and he had recently gone to see Dr. Vartan for X-rays and blood tests after blowing him off for months.

Barry called Yvonne at home. It was now 1 a.m. and it made no sense that she wasn't answering. She must have a boyfriend or something, he thought. But her job was to always be available to him. It crossed his mind that she could have been at that Starbucks except he knew she lived in Jersey City.

Biting into a minibar bag of Smartfood popcorn, Barry pulled out his BlackBerry. If all these women were disappearing on him, he'd take matters into his own hands and get the fuck out.

"Hello, Jack." He continued eating his popcorn when he reached his pilot. "I wanna leave tomorrow morning at ten."

"Where are you flying, sir?"

"I don't know yet," Barry answered. "Maybe London, except there are a lot of crazies there, maybe Nantucket. But it might be too close, and what am I gonna do if they can't get enough food on that island. Maybe Aspen. They got survivalist crazies out there in Colorado, too. But I can introduce them to movie stars."

"Yes sir! See you at Teterboro at ten."

"If they blow us up again before that, I'll call you." Barry closed his phone.

Barry thought of putting on the television but he just didn't want to know who was responsible. If artists were nutso, these people with bombs were bona fide crazies. Plus they were evil. And Barry had no time for evil. He had no time for sissies who thought courage was blowing up innocent people like that young ballerina. Barry firmly believed that those people should rot for eternity with the vermin in hell.

Another spasm of pain ran up Barry's thigh. Instead of calling Dr. Vartan after he'd had the new set of X-rays last month, Barry continued to meet his masseuse at the Lincoln Tunnel Motor Lodge. He called her Yuki even though when she said her name it was something closer to Yushiro. He started seeing her when Samantha moved to the Hamptons. She always wore patent leather boots, a mini Burberry skirt that showed her navel, and a cashmere twin set. They were the kind of classy suburban clothes Clarice wore, but on Yuki they were a completely different story.

He thought Yuki could really put him to sleep tonight, but it was much too nuts out there to drive to the Lincoln Tunnel. And he certainly wasn't having her come up to The Lowell. Barry picked up his phone again.

"Yuki, it's me. I can't sleep," he said when she answered. "I need you to calm me down."

"Do you want me to come over?" she asked.

"No. Please just put me to sleep on the phone. Put your hands on my legs, nice and firm, and put me to sleep."

"Poor Barry. No one knows how much you need to relax. No one knows what it takes to be a man like you. Do you feel my hand on your thigh? Answer me." Her voice became hard.

"Yes, Yuki."

"Yes, Miss Yuki," she snapped at him.

"Yes, Miss Yuki. Please accept my apology, Miss Yuki," he whispered.

"Now do you feel my hand rubbing up and down your thigh and my fingers deep inside the inside of your leg. Deeper. Deeper. Deeper down your leg, Barry."

"Yes, Miss Yuki."

"Say I can do anything I want to you, Barry."

"You can do anything you want to me, Yuki," he moaned with his eyes now shut.

"I own you, Barry," she repeated.

"You own me, Miss Yuki," he repeated again. "You own me."

Barry was sound asleep three minutes later.

When the phone rang at 8 a.m. the next morning Barry assumed it was Yvonne with a good story about why she disappeared last night, or Clarice and the kids wanting to make sure he was safe.

"Hi, Barry, this is Dr. Vartan." The unexpected voice was upbeat.

"Yes." Barry wished he had looked at the goddamn caller ID and not picked up.

"We got your X-rays back and we're seeing tumors in your ribs and brain areas. I'd like to talk to you about your options."

"I'm listening."

"Can you come in and talk about it?"

"I'm busy right now."

"I would advise radiation, chemotherapy, and possibly surgery."

"I'm feeling fine."

"I would advise we schedule something for next week," the doctor continued.

"It's Christmas. I've got two movies opening next week," Barry answered abruptly.

"It's up to you. But I would suggest no later than New Year's."

"I'll think about it. And I suggest you not mention this to anybody."

"I'll have my office call your secretary to make an appointment."

"You guys never stop, do you?" Barry sat up. "The world might have blown up last night and you guys are still hawking your show. It's a real racket you've got."

"Barry." Dr. Vartan lowered his voice. "You are not well and I want to help you."

"Do you think it was a suicide bomber or a water main break, doc? Tell me what the medical community thinks."

"I think I need to see you regardless." The doctor was not going to be deterred.

"Tell you what. I'll get you invited to a few screenings whether you see me this week or not," Barry said quickly. "You like Nicolas Cage? 'Cause I'm throwing a dinner for Nic Cage. Great guy."

"Barry. Come in as soon as possible. We need to deal with this. Are you in pain now?"

"No. I'm good," Barry said quickly.

"Glad to hear it. Hopefully we'll see you before the end of the week. And by the way, I think it was a water main break. It's the only way I can get my kids to sleep at night. Call me if you need me." The doctor hung up.

Barry began dialing Clarice. When he got her voice mail he put the phone down. He wasn't going to leave a stupid message. He didn't need to beg Clarice to be a decent human being. If she were ill he'd help her. He wouldn't run off to Palm Beach to open a shop. He was sick and tired of other people's selfishness.

Barry began to dress to get to the airport. He decided he would definitely fly to Aspen. The altitude, the snow, even the dry cold would do him good. And he wasn't going to be thrown by that doctor's call. He had legally worked out his own mortality. He wouldn't allow anyone to pull the plug, and under no circumstances would he be put in a hospital. Rather, he'd stay at The Lowell, or Claridge's in London, or the Little Nell in Aspen with round-the-clock care and room service. He had seen the $10,000-a-day hospital suites at Sloan-Kettering and Mount Sinai. They were bullshit places designed to get money from people like the Aga Khan. Bottom line, they were still hospitals. And anyway, nowadays anyone with serious ambitions wouldn't become a doctor because they made far too little money. Even if Dr. Vartan was the personal physician to the entire House of Saud, he was in truth just a glorified personal assistant.

Barry's phone rang as he was about to leave. He looked at the number this time and didn't recognize it. Fuckin' asshole doctor. He was going to tell him to only call the office or he'd sue him for malpractice. But then Barry felt a shooting pain down his leg.

"Yep," he answered.

"Barry, it's me, Samantha, I was just checking that you're all right." Her voice was breathless.

"I'm going to Aspen in half an hour," he answered bluntly without any sense of surprise.

"Aspen?" She didn't quite know what else to say.

"I won't let those motherfuckers ruin my holiday. Are you coming?"

"Barry, we haven't spoken in almost a year. Would you like to know how I am?"

"Goddammit, Samantha!" he shouted. "Are you coming or are you going to wait for some other motherfucking lunatic to blow us up."

"I can be there in an hour," she heard herself say before she had even thought about it.

"Ten minutes. Julian will pick you up." Then Barry hung up on her.

He felt another shooting pain, this time near his rib. Goddamn doctors. They have no real power, so they hold on to every sadistic morsel they can get their hands on. It's like that pathetic wimp who was married to Samantha. He spent his life flattering ridiculous rich women like Judy Tremont and poking botulism in their faces. It's just like blowing up innocent people at Starbucks. No balls.

CHAPTER THIRTY-ONE

Samantha

Samantha threw three sweaters and two pairs of jeans into her overnight bag. She grabbed her Susan Ciminelli moisturizer and Hermès pill bag—she had been having trouble sleeping recently and just in case kept a supply of Ambien and Sonata, plus the Wellbutrin her therapist had recently recommended.

Although Samantha grew up loving to ski at places like Saint-Moritz and Gstaad, she never really liked American ski resorts. And it didn't matter to her if it was Aspen, Telluride, Jackson Hole, or Sun Valley. In every one of them she thought there were too many New York money managers and Hollywood producers wearing Indian belts and cowboy boots. She personally had never developed a taste for turquoise jewelry and associated it with divorced women from Scarsdale who moved to Santa Fe to follow their muse.

Samantha's father had been on the ski team at Williams, and since childhood she always had a graceful ease on the slopes. But Charlie worked so hard at skiing that Samantha started resenting the sport altogether. For years Samantha lied to Charlie, saying she had never liked skiing and had done it only for her father. But the truth was skiing made Charlie seem pathetic in her eyes. With Barry, however, Samantha believed it would be completely different. He wouldn't even attempt to ski. He had a house in Aspen because everyone else had a house in Aspen.

The doorman buzzed her. "Mr. Santorini is here."

Until that moment, Samantha had no hesitation about seeing Barry. When she called him it just seemed like the right thing to do. He was her friend and she was just checking in. The fact that she didn't check in with Charlie seemed completely appropriate. Charlie would take it as a sign of a reconciliation, which would be completely misleading.

Samantha took a last look in the mirror. The time she had spent in East Hampton had given her a kind of weather-beaten beauty she didn't have before. She liked the new lines in her face. She was surprised that they gave her character.

When Samantha saw Julian holding the door she smiled at him.

"Hello, Mrs. Acton," he said as if he'd seen her yesterday.

"Miss Bagley," she corrected him. "It's good to see you, Julian."

Samantha was surprised to see Barry already in the car and on the phone with Yvonne.

"Listen, you tell them unless every Frappuccino in this country blows up I want them back on the set tomorrow. And please take good care of yourself, Yvonne. And your family." He then spoke uncharacteristically slowly. "We all need to be there for each other."

Barry stuck out his hand and put it on Samantha's knee. "How ya doin', babe?"

"I'm fine." She smiled at him. He looked thinner than she remembered, and if it was possible his skin seemed worse.

"Is Yvonne all right?"

"She's fine, thanks." He smiled. "I just wanted her to know I'm here for her. I've changed a lot since you last saw me. I've been taking anger management classes. I'm trying to show the people I rely on how much I really do care about them."

"That's nice." She nodded. She had heard from Adrienne about the anger management.

"You look good. Really good." He squeezed her knee.

"Thanks," she answered. "You, too."

"Me? No." He laughed. "I look like shit. My life sucks."

"It's nice about your Golden Globe nominations." She tried to change the subject.

"Foreign press. You can buy them with a television."

"I didn't see your remake of *Rear Window*." She tried to keep the conversation light.

"It sucked. I would have been better off giving the money to world peace." Barry looked outside the window. "There's no traffic today. Do you think everybody knows it's the end of the world?"

"I couldn't watch the news last night." She put her hand over his. "I guess I know too much about television now."

"I saw you on your TV show once," he said. "I was in the Hamptons with the Spielbergs. You were pretty good. I'm surprised no one picked you up for network."

"It's not what I want." She looked at him.

"What do you want?"

"I still want to be with you." She kissed him firmly. "I don't care if I ever go back to that stupid show. It's utterly meaningless. I don't care about anything right now except being with you. I haven't felt safe until I walked into this car."

Barry voice trembled. "You know what's funny, Samantha? You think your life is falling apart and then poof! a woman gets in your car and it all makes sense again. Thank you for your vote of confidence."

"Barry, this isn't a vote of confidence. I love you."

Barry pulled her toward him. "Baby, you are safe with me. I promise. Daddy's here now. Everything's going to be fine."

Teterboro Airport was jammed that morning. Samantha saw Grey Navez, Lewis Franklin, and Tina Schultz with her entire family. Real Chen was at the Signature Flight Support desk demanding "What's happened to my daddy's plane?"

Samantha remembered Barry saying to her that until he met her he always preferred flying alone. He enjoyed reading a newspaper in the sky or catching up on script coverage. He had once mentioned that Clarice had tried too hard to make conversation when they flew together, and he resented it. This was his only time to really unwind, and he didn't want to waste it on inane pleasantries.

As they walked to the plane Samantha noticed that he was limping slightly and once or twice stopped to wince in pain.

"Are you okay, Barry?" she asked him. "I get leg cramps now whenever I play tennis."

"I'm fine. I get leg cramps when I don't play tennis."

Barry let Samantha walk onto the plane first. She saw that he was holding on to both sides of the small banister but didn't want to say anything. Once inside, Barry spoke quickly to their stewardess.

"She'll be watching a movie. Bring her whatever you've got. And an Absolut on the rocks. And I'll have my papers and a Diet Dr Pepper."

"Thank you, Mr. Santorini." The stewardess took her orders graciously.

"No, thank *you*." He smiled at her and then looked at Samantha for approval. "See what a nice guy I've become."

Samantha took his hand. "I've missed you, Barry."

Barry stroked her fingers. "I missed you, too, babe. I didn't even know how much. I was an idiot not to knock your door down. I just thought you were playing fucking games with me."

"Oh, who knows what I was doing. It made no sense." She shook her head.

"No, it made a lot of sense." He turned her face toward him. "I was a total asshole. But next time promise we'll talk about things before you disappear, like grown-ups. Promise?"

"I promise," she said as Barry kissed her fingers.

"You are the love of my life." He looked directly at her. "Forgive me."

Barry's house in Aspen was stocked with exactly the same food that Samantha remembered in Nantucket. For Samantha's taste, the house was a little too aggressively western. There were a few too many quilts, moose heads, wood-beamed ceilings, and Native American rugs.

"It's a lovely house." She smiled when she walked into the living room. "So cozy."

"Clarice did it," he answered. "You gotta hand it to her. She does have terrific taste."

As soon as Samantha heard it was Clarice's taste she dismissed the entire décor as suburban ski resort from the Ralph Lauren western home collection.

"How is Clarice?" she asked.

"Who the fuck knows," he blurted. "She wants to open a shop in Palm Beach. All these fuckin' rich women now want to pretend they've got something to do. They should all go collect tolls on the George Washington Bridge for a day. Then they would shut up about work giving meaning to their lives."

Samantha was sorry she had brought up Clarice at all. "How are your daughters?"

"Clarice tells them lies about me. And Venice's friend had her foot blown off the other night."

"What?" Samantha sat down.

"You know, that woman decorator who had a daughter who was a promising dancer."

"Pippa Rose?"

"Yes. That's her. The daughter was at Starbucks."

"That's so awful!" Samantha hadn't heard this before. "Barry, why has the world become so terrible?"

"You were just protected, baby. The world has always been terrible," he said, reaching for a bagel.

"Not like this. Not Pippa Rose's beautiful daughter at the Starbucks near Lincoln Center."

"What. You think the crazies care if Pippa Rose's daughter did pirouettes or went to Spence? Don't be such a fuckin' elitist."

Samantha poured herself a vodka. "I'm not an elitist."

"C'mon. You can't say you haven't had an easy life. You're beautiful, you're smart, men dig you, and your parents had a shitload of money. What the hell else did you want?"

Samantha thought perhaps Barry's anger management was wearing off. "I wanted to be happy."

"Only rich girls can afford to want to be happy. Most of us think we'll be happy once we make enough money."

"And are you?" she asked. By now the two vodkas on the plane plus this new one were sinking in.

"I know most men don't have what I've got," he replied.

"You didn't answer me." Samantha put her hand on his thigh.

"Fuck you." He tickled her and playfully pushed her against the wall. Then suddenly he stopped. "Let's go to bed."

"What's the matter, Barry?" She ran her fingers through his hair while he winced as if he was in pain.

"I'm tired, I'm going to bed." He began slowly walking up the steps that looked like log-cabin Tinkertoys.

"Are you okay, babe?" she asked, following him.

Barry didn't answer. He continued walking slowly up the stairs, grabbing both banisters with his hands.

. . .

When Samantha woke up Barry was already downstairs and on the phone. He waved at her. "I have crazy actors who won't shoot in New York. Go shopping. This is going to take me all morning."

"Okay." Samantha shook her head.

"Have I told you I'm really glad you're here?" he whispered in her ear and went back on the phone while opening his wallet. "Here, use my credit card. Get something that drives the antifur people crazy." Then he went back to the phone and closed the door.

Samantha had no intention of spending Barry's money. Except she thought some kind of extravagance might lift her spirits. She had been up most of the night thinking about shattered glass and paper cups. The darkness in Barry's log-cabin mansion scared her.

Samantha hiked to town from Barry's house. The air was clear and brisk, and the snow on the mountains pristine and invigorating. New York, Judy Tremont's dinner parties, her ridiculous cable television show, and the unfinished coffee-table books all began to fade into a distant world. A red Hummer passed by and Samantha stopped to look who was inside. Years ago she would have disdained some movie star who felt the need to drive a $100,000 army vehicle. Now she thought maybe she and Barry should get one. They have armor.

Once she was in the middle of town, Samantha had no interest in poking her head into Tiffany, Cartier, or the western-gear Dolce & Gabbana. But when she walked past Gorsuch she stopped to look at a mink-lined parka in the window. Samantha laughed to herself. It was the sort of thing she used to love to wear largely because her mother dismissed it as "Alpine vulgarian." In the opposite window was a bright yellow one-piece Postcard ski suit with a fur-trimmed hood. Samantha knew she could still pull it off and went in and within five minutes bought it.

A few blocks later she passed the library and decided she'd get a couple of books in case Barry fell asleep again tonight. She had just finished Trollope's *The Way We Live Now* and thought she'd read another by him. The good thing about Trollope was there seemed to be an endless supply.

"Well, hello!" A tall figure in a puffy pale pink Bogner ski jacket tapped her on the shoulder at the door. "How *are* you?"

"Judy!" Samantha kissed her on both cheeks. "Honest to God I was just thinking about you."

"We just finished building the most fabulous house here, and thank God it was ready just in time. I mean, who would stay in New York this week? We went to Southampton for a night, and even that wasn't far away enough. Oh my God, it's so creepy!" Judy forensically examined Samantha. She looked weather-beaten but somehow even more riveting. "What are you doing here?" Judy was talking at a hundred miles an hour.

"Oh, I thought I'd get some books from the library."

"Me, too." She was in super-best-friend mode and was working overtime to remember everything Samantha uttered so she could immediately call Clarice. "I thought I'd get Albert all of Proust so he'd read and just let me ski." She pointed to Samantha's shopping bag. "Have you been shopping? Show and tell!"

"Oh, it's just a ski thing." Samantha was evasive.

"I wanna see! I wanna see!" Judy pulled at the shopping bag as if they were schoolgirls.

Samantha stuck her hand in the bag and showed her a small corner of her yellow purchase.

"Oh I love it!" Judy squealed. "It was in the window at Gorsuch. I would have bought it but I'm just too tall. But I bet you look fantastic in it."

"Thank you." Samantha didn't know what to say. "Actually, I'm so happy when I'm skiing I don't really care what I'm wearing."

"Me, too. It's my absolute favorite thing in the world to do. The one time I feel completely free."

Samantha remembered the night in Palm Beach when Judy had said something about wanting to set tracks on fresh snow.

"That's right. You're a wonderful skier," Samantha said.

"I used to ski as a kid at places near Modesto. Dodge Ridge or Mount Shasta. My dad took me."

This was the first time Judy had ever openly mentioned Modesto to her.

"My dad was a cop and we used to go to the mountains with these forest rangers he knew. It was the only time I remember being happy in my childhood."

Samantha hadn't seen Judy since she read about her social alliance with Clarice. But here in front of the Aspen library there was something very grounded about her.

"I guess you heard about Pippa Rose's daughter." Judy was chattering again. "She was unbelievably talented. But it's ridiculous to let a child get so involved in ballet. What's the poor thing going to do now? And I hear she's no academic genius either."

Judy's moment of human revelation had passed. Samantha watched as Judy's lips kept moving, and didn't listen to any of it. "Can you join us for dinner tonight?" Judy snapped back into focus.

"No," Samantha answered. "I'm having dinner with Barry Santorini. We're here together."

Samantha turned without even glancing at Judy and walked into the silent library.

CHAPTER THIRTY-TWO

Frankie

Frankie generally got up at 5:30 a.m. But as soon as Charlie began spending the night she awoke even earlier. When she and Jack had lived together she always brought him morning coffee. Lying in bed with Charlie, she realized how much she missed that early-morning ritual with a lover before the outside world intruded.

On Saturday morning Charlie made Frankie promise they'd sleep late. When she finally got up to bring him coffee the phone rang.

"Yes, this is Frankie Weissman," she answered.

"Francesca," Charlie whispered, still half asleep.

"My name is Morgan Crown," the low voice continued. "I was Jil Taillou's estate lawyer. Sorry to call so early on a Saturday."

"Jil was a wonderful man. His death still hasn't registered for me." She turned away from Charlie.

"I am calling because Jil left explicit instructions in his will that he did not want his friends to gather for a shiva or any religious function in his apartment."

"Jil never really talked much about being Jewish. He spoke about being an immigrant from Budapest." Frankie poked her hair out of her eye.

"Was Jil Jewish?" Charlie snuggled back toward her.

"What he did stipulate was that in the event of his death he would like certain close friends to come to his house and select something meaningful to them from his collection of art, paintings, and personal possessions."

"And you'll let me know when this would be?" she asked.

"He was emphatic that this collection take place the weekend after his death and that the invitation be made the day of, so there is no opportunity for either religion or sentimentality. Only shopping. Those are his words."

"So it's at Jil's house tonight?"

"Yes, tonight at around seven," he confirmed.

"I will see you there."

"I look forward to it. Jil spoke so fondly of you." He hung up the phone.

Charlie sat up. "What's at Jil's home tonight?"

"He left instructions for his friends to come by his apartment and take home a memento. I'm sure you'll have a message on your service."

"I'm sure not," Charlie answered her quickly. "And for that matter, I'm sure Samantha won't have a message either."

"But you were his close friends. I knew him because of you." Frankie was not following.

"Samantha and I aren't Jewish."

"But for all intents and purposes neither was Jil."

"Jil was a man who lived a life of subterfuge," Charlie explained. "He never completely told the truth about his sexuality, his early life, or his religion. He was a highly cultivated, deeply suspicious man. But of all of us, he trusted you."

"Charlie, this makes no sense. He was escorting Clarice Santorini when he died. I hardly ever saw him."

"He was in love with a stripper from New Jersey when he died. But who he felt safe with was you. He was in awe of Samantha, and even me by marriage, but somewhere he had total disdain for us, too."

Frankie pushed Charlie's hair out of his eyes. She had forgotten that he had as much distance from the world Jil aspired to as she did. Charlie seemed so genuine to her that she had forgotten he knew what it was to invent yourself, too.

As Frankie got dressed that morning Charlie watched her. "I wish you weren't watching me." Frankie pulled a turtleneck over her arms. "I'm like the ideal 'before' ad for dermabrasion."

Charlie began to tickle her arms. "No, I'd say you'd be perfect with a little lipo here, a tummy tuck there, butt lift here, and I would suggest a breast reduction and a neck inflation. Inflated necks are very big this year."

"Stop it, Charlie." She chuckled.

"I'm not through yet. Then I'd sandpaper the face, and seal it with my own signature Dr. Charlie's shellac. Finally I think a few 'CA' Charlie Acton gold logos on the chin would give you that perfect final touch."

Frankie fell down on her bed laughing.

"Will my insurance cover all of this, doctor?" she asked between gasps for air.

"Just let me see you tonight, Francesca," he asked. "I still don't think I can face my apartment alone. When I'm with you I think there's some semblance of sanity."

Frankie remembered that she once saw Adrienne Strong-Rodman advising on Samantha's TV show, "Go slow when starting a relationship. Don't let him make any assumptions too quickly." But as much as Charlie wanted a quickie semblance of sanity, Frankie believed she was beginning to fill that Grand Canyon of Need.

"I would love to see you tonight." She kissed him.

"Perfect. I'll meet you here after you run off with Jil Taillou's art. If you can't get me the Matisse sketch I'd settle for the William Merritt Chase in the library."

When Frankie and Charlie left her apartment it was the first time her doorman had seen her holding hands with a man in the morning.

"Have a nice day, Dr. Weissman." He tried not to show his interest in her new personal life.

Charlie and Frankie continued to walk together on the crisp late December day. The cars were now running down Columbus Avenue and children were getting back on the crosstown buses on their way to holiday playdates.

Charlie hailed a taxi. "Will you drop me off first?" he asked Frankie.

"Sure." She smiled.

As he opened the taxi door Frankie felt a very unfamiliar ease as if she had joined a club she had forgotten existed. Life was clearly tenuous, even horrifying, but she was, for the first time in years, not merely examining it.

Walking into Jil's apartment that night, Frankie half expected to find him in the forest green living room. She hadn't been to the apartment for so long, but it seemed very much the same—with the exception of a brown velvet deco couch replacing the brocade in the living room and a large art deco mirror over the fireplace. Jil had predicted that Judy Tremont would be slashing her brocade and replacing her elaborate Chinese mirror with sleeker ones resembling the deco Radio City powder room. Obviously he had practiced what he predicted.

Frankie didn't recognize many of the people milling about the apartment inspecting Jil's trophies of decades of exquisite taste and a cultivated eye. She expected to see Clarice or Grey Navez but they were decidedly not present.

There were one or two women with helmet hair, the kind that, Jil had explained to her, bubbles around the head and stays put until the next visit to Kenneth. But mostly the small gathering of around thirty of Jil's closest friends were men in suits and older relatives.

A young man in his thirties approached Frankie. "You must be Dr. Weissman. Jil talked about you all the time."

Frankie sized him up. If this was the stripper in Hoboken, he seemed perfectly comfortable with his clothes on.

"Oh I loved Jil. He was such a lovely man." She didn't want to ask who he was until the young stranger offered it.

"I'm Dennis Shaloub. I was Jil's partner for the past ten years."

His partner? Frankie thought to herself. Jil supposedly had just met him.

"Of course." She smiled at him. "Jil mentioned you work in New Jersey." Frankie assumed he would cover up the stripping by admitting he was in show business.

"Actually I live here in New York on 101st and West End, but I commute to Newark. I'm an architect with the downtown redevelopment plan there."

"You're an architect?" Frankie blurted. So either Jil or Judy Tremont or someone else had come up with the go-go boy. "Isn't Jil's daughter an architect, too?" she asked, trying to hide her confusion.

"Jil didn't have a daughter."

"Did you go to Harvard to architecture school?" she asked.

"Yes."

"I'm sorry. I must have it confused. Of course he mentioned you."

"Jil very much wanted you to have something. He thought of you as family."

Frankie kissed his cheek. "I'm so sorry for your loss."

As Frankie walked through the apartment a waiter offered her a blinchiki with caviar. Because of her friendship with Jil she immediately noted that the waiters were wearing formfitting black T-shirts and Helmut Lang jeans. Clearly, Jil had been his own special events coordinator.

When Frankie entered the library she was alone. She picked up a silver cigarette box and rubbed her finger on the initials. She noticed that the ten white lit candles in the room were a deliberate mix of Jo Malone citrus, Diptyque gardenia, and Annick Goutal spice. The flowers were two-foot-long white French tulips each in a separate antique Steuben vase. Jil must have left detailed instructions.

Frankie ran her eye past Jil's books, Heinrich Wölfflin's *Principles of Art History*, a 1913 edition of *Swann's Way*, a signed volume of Josef Albers' *Homage to the Square*, and a copy of Zsa Zsa Gabor's *One Lifetime Is Not Enough* with the inscription "For my darling Jil—if only you were richer we could have been so happy together."

Frankie laughed and continued to look over his collection until she stopped on the bottom shelf. She found a group of paperbacks he must have saved from school—*The Scarlet Letter, Modern History: Europe Since 1600*, an underlined copy of *A Midsummer Night's Dream*, and a paperback edition of Strunk and White's *The Elements of Style*.

She opened the book and found in the corner, in a precise version of Jil's handwriting, "Julius Taittenbaum, Sophomore Class Erasmus Hall High School, 1955, 625 Ocean Avenue, Apt. 6G, Brooklyn, New York. Cloverdale 8-4847."

Frankie looked out at the park. She realized, holding Jil's or Julius' book, that for him style created content. Frankie wasn't angry at Jil for camouflaging his life. She just wished he'd known it was all so unnecessary.

Frankie put the paperback in her purse.

· · ·

"You know my father was a student of William Strunk, who wrote that book," Charlie said to Frankie later that night in the quiet time after they had made love.

"Really?" Frankie stroked his chest.

"Yes. He was a student of his at Cornell. But I still really wish you had snatched at least the William Merritt Chase."

Frankie laughed. "I hope he left it all to his partner."

Charlie lit a cigarette. After the Starbucks incident he really saw no reason to quit. "Why would a gay man like Jil who was an art dealer hide his life?"

"Who knows. It's all in the Taittenbaum, I suppose," Frankie answered.

"So you see I was right. He trusted you because you're Jewish."

"Charlie, you sound like my father's wife, Helen." She pushed him away.

Charlie took another puff. "From what you've told me about Helen, I don't think I want to sound like her."

Frankie ran her hand down his back. "I'm sorry, honey."

Charlie pulled Frankie on her side. "No, I'm the one who's sorry, darling. I am so sorry about Jil."

"Charlie, you know what's crazy?" She looked at his kind eyes. "I can't help but think if my father hadn't lost his mind none of this would have happened."

Charlie held her face. "That's very sweet, honey."

"No, really." She felt herself about to weep as Charlie ran his fingers on her lips. "Somewhere I believe that like a five-year-old child."

"I know." He jostled her fingers.

"It's sort of ridiculous." She looked away from him.

"No, I promise it's sweet." He turned her back to him.

"Don't you think sweetness seems a bit out of context these days?" She put her leg on his.

Charlie smiled. "No, but that's why ever since the time I was snubbed by the Ivy I've been quietly in love with you." He curled up to go to sleep.

Frankie couldn't help herself from grabbing onto his declaration as if it were a prelude to living happily ever after. And the more insane it seemed to hold on to that notion, the less she could let it go.

CHAPTER THIRTY-THREE

Judy

"You'll never guess who I ran into here." Judy was almost giddy on the phone when she finally reached Clarice.

"Who?" Clarice was distracted from reviewing the sketches for her new shop on Worth Avenue.

"Samantha Acton."

After Clarice heard about Starbucks and Pippa Rose's daughter, she made arrangements to transfer her girls from Spence to Palm Beach Day School. She decided she'd rather cope with natural disasters like hurricanes.

"That's nice," Clarice said, cutting Judy off. Her daughters had told her that Samantha and Barry weren't seeing each other anymore.

"I think she's here with Barry. Poor thing. She must be really desperate." Judy took a sip of water.

Clarice had no intention of being drawn into this. She had recently met a seventy-year-old widower in Palm Beach who was a golf buddy of Samantha's father. He was a Republican and owned, as far as Clarice could make out, half of St. Louis. Clarice was not attracted to him the way she was to Barry, which was why she decided she would probably marry him.

"I see Samantha's parents down here. They're a terrific couple," Clarice casually answered.

Judy knew she was getting nowhere. "Did you hear about Jil Taillou?" she said, moving on. "He left everything to the stripper from Hoboken."

"Yes, poor Jil." Clarice decided it was time to end the conversation. "I'm so sorry, Judy, but my daughters just walked in. I've got to go. Lots of love and Happy New Year." Clarice hung up.

For a moment Judy felt abandoned. She was certain she would run into Samantha at dinner one night since Barry and Albert were both members of Caribou, the best private restaurant in Aspen. She was looking forward to reporting every detail to Clarice after supper. Now there would be no one really satisfying to share her news with.

Judy thought that she and Clarice had gotten close during their work on the museum gala. And frankly, she resented her polite chilliness because she really needed a friend right now. Albert had gone into some sort of depression after the Starbucks incident. He was horrified that a man as cultivated as Jil could be erased in such an ignominious way. Albert hadn't even wanted to leave Southampton for Aspen. He just sat in the library looking out at the ocean listening to Mahler.

"Hi, honey." Judy walked into the living room of their new western home. "What's doing?"

"Nothing much," he answered quietly.

"I was thinking we could go out to dinner tonight." She put her hand on his shoulder.

"I'm perfectly happy to stay here," he said flatly. "The cook is here. There's no reason for us to go out."

Judy couldn't contain her irritation. "Albert, you've got to stop this! Yes, something terrible happened. But we can't stop our lives because of it."

"When are we going back to New York?" He suddenly got up.

"Are you insane? I'm not returning until this whole thing is cleared up."

"I called the plane and said we'd go back tomorrow," he said firmly.

"Albert, I don't know what the hell is wrong with you." She had raised her voice.

Albert walked toward the window without looking at her. "I miss my books."

Judy felt her neck tightening. If she had known they would be having this conversation she would have prepared by booking a massage for afterward.

"Looky here," she said. "We're having a dinner party tomorrow night and the kids are skiing during the day. We're not flying back so you can sit in your room and read Old Norwegian."

"Cancel the dinner party."

"Albert, do you know how long I've wanted to get the Landons to our house? That Hollywood circle is very tight, and believe me, when I realized Laila Landon was in my yoga class here I was like a dog with a rat in its mouth. You know she was Mark's acupuncturist when he was still married to Shelly and was the chairman of Warner Brothers. The Landons are going to make our lives here so much more fun. They know everybody."

Albert began to walk out of the room.

"Albert, where the hell are you going?" she called after him.

"To watch television." He kept walking.

"But we're having a conversation."

"Judy, we never have a conversation!"

"Don't say that, Albert." Judy stopped him. "We talk about everything."

"I'm watching television, and then I'll read to the girls."

"What about dinner at Caribou tonight?"

"You can arrange for us to do whatever the heck you want." He left the room.

Judy looked at her watch and was reassured to see it was exactly four o'clock. Ever since the museum gala Judy took a nap every day at this time. It wasn't that she was tired; it was more a temporary melancholy that even shopping or time with her children couldn't relieve. She had no desire to speak to a therapist or get a new prescription. She knew she had a damn good life and a very happy marriage. She began to walk up the stairs to her bedroom. She just needed a little escape every day.

Harley, the doyenne of Caribou, gave Albert and Judy a prime table at dinner. Judy was beside herself. In the room were pop stars, Hollywood names, and a veritable who's who of American moguls worth over ten figures.

Waiting for the gravlax to arrive, Judy gossiped to Albert about everyone in the room. So-and-so is having an affair with so-and-so, so-and-so and so-and-so have lost all their money and are just putting up a front, so-and-so must have just had her face done because she looks so youthful, so-and-so had to sell his house in Paris.

She was even excited about the faces she didn't recognize. "Albert." She touched his shoulder. "I have to say, there's something so liberating about being out west."

Albert nodded and silently ate his first course, followed by the entrée.

"I thought we'd see Samantha Acton and Barry Santorini tonight. I ran into her in town the other day."

For the first time during the meal Albert responded. "That's the girl we had drinks with in Palm Beach? We had a dinner for her."

"Yes, exactly. She's here with Barry Santorini."

Albert put his fork down. "I thought she was married to a doctor. That nice guy from Princeton."

Judy couldn't believe what she was hearing. "Honey, that was like two years ago. Don't you ever listen to me?"

"I thought she was very bright." He placed his silverware on his plate to signal that he was finished.

"You can't have thought she was very bright!" Judy was agitated. What if things didn't work out with Samantha and Barry. What if next Samantha went after Albert. She knew she had joked about it, but the truth was Albert would be a logical target. He was rich, decent, and unbelievably malleable.

"Albert, she's a terrible person and a complete phony."

"What can I say." He put his napkin on the table. "I thought she was quite attractive and very bright. I liked her a lot."

Judy reached for the bread. "Albert, why do you want to hurt me like this?" she asked as she had her first bite of bread in ten years.

"I don't want to hurt you," he answered matter-of-factly. "You said you wanted me to talk more so I'm making an effort and talking."

Just then, Judy saw Laila Landon walk into the room and began madly waving to her.

"Who's that?" Albert asked.

"That's Laila Landon. Remember, she's coming to dinner tomorrow night."

"Well, she's not as attractive as Samantha Acton." Albert smiled for the first time in weeks.

"Albert, stop it right now!" She felt her face turning red. "I want to go home."

"Absolutely. Excellent decision." Albert got up and waved to Harley for the check. He pulled out Judy's chair.

As they walked to the door Judy stopped to give Laila Landon two kisses. "How are you? We are so excited you are coming to dinner tomorrow. And this is my husband, Albert."

Albert shook her hand. "Yes, my wife's anticipating your immi-nent arrival." Judy stopped herself from admonishing Albert for the "imminent arrival" remark when, to her utter delight, Samantha and Barry walked in.

"Hello, how are you?" Judy kissed Samantha.

"How are you, Judy? Nice to see you again, Albert."

Judy watched as Samantha gave Albert two well-positioned pecks. Immediately she imagined Samantha redecorating their apartment. Since Samantha never had children Judy thought her twins and the boys at Deerfield would clinch the deal with Albert.

"It's nice to see you." Albert kissed Samantha's hand.

"You remember Barry Santorini," Samantha said casually.

"Hi. How ya doin'." Barry grinned. "Let's go, Samantha." He put his hand on her back and moved her toward the dining room.

"I'll call you," Judy chirped.

As Judy and Albert drove up the mountain to their house she couldn't help but comment on Barry's dissolute appearance.

"Barry Santorini is a pig," Judy blurted out as soon as they got into the car.

Albert nodded his head. "I suppose you're right. She could do better."

Judy looked over at Albert. He had decidedly large lips and very small hands. She was in her flat feet an inch taller than he, and cer-tainly no one would have described him as a flashy physical speci-men. But he had, in fact, saved her life, and she never considered getting old without him.

"Albert, if you want to change something in our life, please let me know. This family is the most important thing in the world to me. If you want me to stop having silly dinner parties, I'll do it. If you want me to go back to school so I can read Sanskrit with you, I'll do it.

Only please, please, don't pull the rug out from under me. I love this family!" Judy's hands were shaking.

Albert stopped the car. "Honey. I don't want to change anything." He took her hand. "I love our life. I can't even believe I'm having our life. I just want to go home because I'm so happy there and that's where we belong." He kissed her on the cheek.

"That's fine, honey." Judy looked at his hand. "I'll just go skiing tomorrow to clear my head, and then we'll go home tomorrow night."

This time Albert kissed her lips. "Thank you, dear. I really appreciate that."

Albert didn't stay up late reading that night. He went to sleep at ten beside Judy. "Good night, dear," he said as he turned off the light. "I cherish the life you've given me."

Judy couldn't sleep and at midnight went out on the porch to meditate. She looked up at a distant mountain as the snow began to fall. She had begun to loathe the side of her that was so full of empty gossip. Judy knew her behavior was all based on some lingering insecurity that was irrelevant now. She wanted to change because she knew the more she chattered, the more isolated she was becoming.

Judy took a number of deep breaths. Tomorrow morning she would get up early and ski in the fresh snow. That would cleanse all the impurities from her heart. And then there was her dinner party with the studio chairman to be happy about. Albert wouldn't mind if they just stayed two more days.

CHAPTER THIRTY-FOUR

Barry

When Barry saw Samantha kissing Judy Tremont hello he knew it was time to cut the bullshit. If he didn't like a project, he dropped it, and this one was a well-intentioned mistake. He had no time for sentimentality, especially now that he was a sick man. He had pains in his ribs, in his legs, and the fuckin' cold air in Aspen wasn't making it any better. He needed a caregiver right now. And this woman wanted too much. She wanted sex, she wanted attention, she wanted to know what the fuck was going on in his life, and she wanted him to really love her. Yes, he had been very attracted to her. But the world had changed since then. Now coffee shops were blowing up, and he was just as fragile as anyone else.

Ever since Barry found out his illness was spreading he had begun working very hard at being philosophical. He knew that he could be off-putting, but what no one realized was that his manner was gruff because his feelings were so deep. Other people like Judy Tremont or even Samantha wasted their lives being cordial and lying half the time. On some level Barry decided they were all immoral because he always told the truth.

He didn't regret taking Samantha on the trip. And he wasn't going to worry about a woman who was born on Fifth Avenue and was probably worth two hundred million dollars. Maybe more. You never knew with old money; they belonged to secret clubs with secret bank accounts. He didn't regret breaking up his marriage—it was the right thing to do at the time. But with distance he realized that he and Clarice were still fundamentally a shoemaker's son and a vegetable peddler's daughter from South Philadelphia. They were real people and they knew that, bottom line, family really mattered. This other woman was from Planet Privilege.

"Listen, I think you should know I'm going back to Clarice permanently," he said as soon as the waiter took the drinks order.

"Excuse me?" She looked at him as if she hadn't heard him.

That's exactly the fuckin' problem with her, Barry thought to himself. Goddamn limousine liberal. She should have spat in my face and instead she is giving me that condescending elitist crap. It's the way Ivy League liberals speak to their hired help.

"I changed my mind about this. It's just not working for me. You can stay or go. I'll tell the housekeeper to send your bag over to the Little Nell. Don't worry, I'll have Yvonne call the hotel with my credit card." He was speaking as if he were firming up a deal with a talent agent. "Feel free to stay as long as you like and call for the plane to take you home. It's the least I can do to repay you for your time."

"Fuck you." She startled him by swearing and almost breaking her glass on the table. Barry prided himself on being strong on dialogue, but this truly took him by surprise.

"I've ruined my life for you," Samantha blurted.

Barry knew from years of negotiations that the best way to walk away from a deal is to remain devoid of emotion. "I can't really analyze other people's lives. Only movies. I'm sorry you feel that way."

"You bastard!" She dug her fingers into his arm.

Barry got up from the table. "I don't like women who use foul language."

He walked to the door of the restaurant and got into the waiting car.

"To the airport," he told the driver, and took out his cell phone. "Yvonne, where the hell are you? It's me. Call the plane and tell them I'm flying to New York in half an hour. Get the housekeeper and tell her to send my things. Call Dr. Vartan—tell him I want to see him at nine a.m. tomorrow. If they say he's busy, call the chairman of the board of the fuckin' hospital and tell him to tell Vartan that he's seeing me at nine a.m. tomorrow. And call Clarice—you know what Yvonne, call Bulgari or Cartier—whatever the fuck—and send Clarice a bracelet. Better yet, call Fred Leighton—get something antique—that's more personal. Spend around forty thousand dollars. Oh and one other thing, send something to that friend of Venice's who got her foot blown off. Maybe three hundred dollars' worth of flowers. That's a terrible story. Jesus fuckin' Christ, Yvonne, where are you? You're supposed to be on call when the office is closed. I'm in the car. Call me."

Barry sat back. He took out the magazines from the car-door pocket. The Starbucks incident, now called "the Latte Blast," was on every cover. He glanced at the Hollywood trades' Golden Globe edition. According to their predictions, it looked like if he rat-fucked the foreign press he'd do okay again this year.

Barry felt a surge of pain in his leg. Who knew a disease of the balls could make you feel like you had a clamp pushing down on your ankle. This doctor better fix this, Barry thought to himself, or I am taking all of Sloan-Kettering down with me. No one has had more movie premieres to benefit breast cancer, AIDs-related cancer, throat cancer, or skin cancer than me. They better show they're fuckin' grateful or there will be hell to pay.

Barry picked up *Variety* again and then put it down. The truth was, ever since he found out he was sick he couldn't concentrate on business. He knew how to make money. He knew how to win

Oscars. What he wanted now was to express how much love he felt. He knew he had a lot to share and had kept it hidden. Now that time could be limited, he wanted Clarice, his children, even that poor ballerina, to know how much he cared.

Barry rolled down the window and looked at the snowcapped mountain. He closed his eyes to rest and instead saw that young ballerina twirling without her foot at the top of the mountain as if she were in a snow-globe music box.

Another jolt of pain ran up his leg and Barry began to cry. He didn't mind that he cried every day now. He liked being in touch with his emotions. But what he wasn't used to was being so scared. He pulled his leg toward him and continued weeping. People are so goddamned petty, he thought to himself. No one understands the big picture. That's why there's so little kindness in the world. Barry decided he would give a million dollars to the ballet in the name of that kid. At least he still had a commitment to the future and humanity. At least he still had a heart.

CHAPTER THIRTY-FIVE

Samantha

Samantha took a taxi to her room at the Little Nell. Adrienne had told her once about a business trip when she ate and drank her way through the entire minibar. As she walked into the hotel, it seemed clear to Samantha that she was in no state to make any decisions or plans except to pillage the minibar.

"Mrs. Acton, should we use the credit card we have on file for your room charges?"

Samantha thought, I don't want that bastard paying for me.

"Yes, absolutely," she said. "Use the card you have on file."

"Do you have any additional luggage, or just the bag that was sent here?"

"Just the one that was sent here," she mumbled, impressed at the speed and finality of Barry's commandos.

As Samantha walked to the elevator, she noticed in the lobby several pretty twenty-something-year-old girls in exotic fur ponchos holding the arms of men who looked their fathers' age. There was also a family of five blonde children sitting by the fireplace with a forty-year-old athletic-looking mother in a headband and cashmere après-ski sweatsuit. Finally, she saw in the corner a sixty-year-old woman with fabulous skin laughing hysterically with two young, well-tanned buff men.

Samantha had developed the habit of summing up other women's lives and debating if she regretted that any of them weren't her own. She clearly wouldn't be twenty or even thirty again, and even when she was she hadn't auctioned herself off to the highest bidder. She had too much integrity and personal wealth for that. She would never be the mother of five, herding the brood off on a family holiday, and she had no intention of being a stylish older woman surrounded by amusing young escorts.

When Samantha opened the door to the hotel room she turned on the light and headed straight to the pint-sized refrigerator. She began pouring miniature vodkas one after another and gathered cans of Pringles, pretzels, cashews, honey-roasted peanuts, M&M's, gummy bears, and Toblerone bars to take into bed. She got under the covers, shut off the light, and focused on consuming her entire stash.

"Son of a bitch. It isn't working fast enough," she decided after the fourth miniature vodka, and got up to get the Percocet she had taken for a root canal out of her Hermès makeup bag.

After Barry left the table Samantha felt as if she were sitting naked in the middle of Park Avenue. It was worse than humiliating. She hated herself with a venom that had yet to dissipate. She took two Percocet, gulped down a Diet Coke, and ripped open a bag of Famous Amos cookies.

Finally, Samantha began to feel the effects of the drugs, the alcohol, and the chocolate swirling together in her body. Secretly, Samantha always envied women like Adrienne Strong-Rodman, whose switches were always on. For them, there was always something to strive for—a richer husband, a more impressive job, another degree, more power, more notoriety. Samantha had never been ambitious in that way. She knew most of her life that other people envied her and she found their jealousies enviable. At least they knew they wished they were her. She, on the other hand, had no idea what she really wanted.

Samantha took the remote control from the side of the bed. She mostly never watched television, since she and Charlie went out at night and in the past few years she preferred to read. She clicked on a beautiful woman eating worms on a survival show in Africa. When the woman finished swallowing, she said, "I don't believe Sharon really ate hers. I think she keeps chocolate kisses in her pockets."

"Bitch," Samantha snapped at her, and changed the channel. She clicked past familiar faces laughing on an episode of *Friends*, a tour of a forty-million-dollar home owned by Jennifer Lopez, the details of a local fire in Denver, and a rerun of *Jeopardy!* and finally settled on Jil Taillou's mother being interviewed by Jane Pauley in a gated assisted-living community somewhere in Arizona.

"It's a terrible thing that this should happen in this country," Jil's mother said, crying, with a thick Hungarian accent. "My son Julius loved this country. He loved the people and the art. Who would do such a thing?"

"Mrs. Taittenbaum, that's what we all want to know." Jane touched her shoulder.

Samantha sat at the edge of the bed. "Poor Jil. Poor sweet Jil."

Jane was back seated behind her reporter's desk. "As of today, the responsibility for the suicide bombing that took Jil Taillou's life has been claimed by a solo avenger from an upstate New York militia and the Newark cell of Holy Hezbollah. But in either case, all our hearts are with Mrs. Taittenbaum in Phoenix, Arizona."

Samantha clicked off the TV and opened another vodka mini. "God bless you, Jil, and God bless your mother in Arizona," she toasted as she slugged it down and lay back on the bed.

For a minute Samantha thought of swallowing all the Percocet like another bag of M&M's. But even that was pointless. She had already been featured in *Manhattan* magazine. She didn't need to be next week's disastrous life story of the rich and famous. Judy and Clarice would just chuckle about it. And Barry would make it into a movie with Nicole Kidman as her and Nicolas Cage playing the sensitive and sexy him. Samantha began to feel the room swaying as if she were nine years old and with her parents sailing on the *Queen Elizabeth* to Europe. Samantha loved that trip because every night she'd leave her parents dancing and sneak up to the deck to look at the stars. Samantha learned all the constellations that crossing. She began to recite them slowly: Andromeda, Aquila, Canis Major and Minor, Cassiopeia, Corona Borealis, Orion, Pegasus, Perseus, Ursa Major and Minor.

A chill ran up Samantha's body. She pulled the extra mohair afghan at the foot of the bed over her just as she had done on those deck chairs under the stars. She tucked her legs up and breathed the fresh winter air. If she took too many Percocet, it would seem almost spoiled. And Samantha knew she was privileged, but she wasn't spoiled. She had gotten past realizing she'd never be known for being a singer, a curator, a mother, or frankly anything else but a well-educated ornament. And to survive all that plus Barry Santorini meant she wasn't spoiled. She was, in fact, deceptively strong.

Cozy and warm now, Samantha clicked the remote back on. She sat up and grinned when she saw that *I Love Lucy* was on. There was something very restorative about Lucy and Ethel singing "Babalu" at Ricky's nightclub. Samantha began giggling. She wished she could work at the Tropicana club with Ethel and Lucy. She'd be happy to be a hatcheck girl if they'd let her sing "Misty" in a black slip dress on Monday nights.

Samantha laughed heartily out loud until she felt her eyes beginning to water. She went to the window to draw the curtains and see the stars. Instead she saw a heavy snowstorm, a blizzard covering the town with maybe a foot of fresh powder. She decided that if it kept snowing tomorrow she would go skiing. Set new tracks. She was old enough to know that men like Barry don't get punished. Barry would win more Oscars, take over more studios, find another younger, more accomplished woman, or perfect Clarice would take him back. But she was independent. She had backbone from her mother, and just like Lucy and Ethel, she had joie de vivre.

When her wake-up call rang at 6 a.m., Samantha ran to the window as if it were Christmas. She wanted to be sure it was still snowing. She wanted to be certain that she would be the first one on that mountain. The Toblerone bars, the vodka minis, and Percocet of only four hours ago now sat comfortably in the middle of her fore-head like a cozy fox hat. The giddy anticipation of being out in the fresh powder transformed the heaviness in her body into a childlike comfort of being swaddled in a snowsuit by a nanny in Gstaad or Saint-Moritz.

Samantha caught a glimpse of herself in her sinewy yellow ski suit as she walked out the door of the hotel. She remembered that her mother referred to some of her friends as having "the hoofprint of life" stamped on their face. Making her way to the Silver Queen Gondola at the foot of Aspen Mountain, Samantha felt the possibil-ity of finally abandoning those embedded imprints.

While she waited for the first lift up, she stopped at a bronze-plated espresso cart for a cappuccino with a double shot of grappa to warm herself up.

"Must be about two feet of fresh snow up there," she overheard the girl behind the cart say. Samantha decided not to wipe the snow from her goggles. She would allow the chill to coat her vision and let the warmth of her drink envelop her.

As Samantha rode the Silver Queen Gondola lift, the snow continued to fall. When she reached the top, the entire mountain was a blurry white universe. Samantha took a deep breath and felt that she had never been so close to happiness.

She reached into her pocket for her remaining few Percocet and Wellbutrin. She wasn't really sure which was which and she really didn't care. She deserved a glorious ride.

Samantha took off, heading down through the pure, untracked snow, picking up speed. She was finally free of everything: the men, the dinner parties, the face peels, the regrets about children, the confusion about ambition. Nothing mattered anymore except this rush of life. All Samantha could hear was the sound of her own breathing.

Samantha increased her speed. She could barely see through the falling snow sticking to her goggles. She sped down the slope effortlessly.

Midway down the mountain, another trail merged with hers. She saw a pink blur approaching. She assumed the pink was a reflection from the snow. Through the muffled silence she could hear scattered words, "Samantha! Something something Barry! Something something yellow!" Samantha pointed her skis straight down the narrow trail, skiing even faster. She was convinced speed would erase from her consciousness these fragments of her ridiculous past. Barry was over. Being "the Fashionable Mrs. Whoever-she-was" was over. She would not let this pink dot of self-recrimination obstruct her path.

But the dot suddenly emerged through the snow as a full pink figure heading straight for her. As they collided, Samantha slammed the body away. She watched as the pink figure veered off sharply, disappearing into the all-encompassing white.

Samantha continued down the slope and felt she had regained her path. She smiled with renewed confidence. "I just saved my life."

.   .   .

Samantha walked back into the Little Nell late in the afternoon and took off her goggles for the first time that day.

"How'd it go today?" the doorman asked her.

"Fantastic." She smiled.

As she approached the elevators, Samantha noticed a flurry of activity in the lobby.

"Did you hear about Judy Tremont?" The athletic mother with the brood of five children was talking to a friend. "Skied right into a tree."

"It was an accident of course," the friend immediately reassured the children.

The memory of that pink figure brushing up against her and the insurmountable joy of heaving it away began pounding in Samantha's head.

Samantha closed her eyes and saw the tiny pink dot transform into a pink-lipsticked face splattered in the snow. The pink Bogner jacket was frosted flat like a cartoon or a dream.

CHAPTER THIRTY-SIX

Charlie

When Charlie started dating Samantha he trained himself to always order first for his dinner companion and wait before mentioning his preference. In fact, the first time Charlie met Samantha's father for dinner at La Grenouille he made a mental note that the old man not only ordered first for his wife and his daughter before getting to himself, but was never truly engaged and therefore everybody always thought they had a great time with him.

"What's your pleasure, Francesca?" Charlie asked Frankie as they looked over the menus in a booth at Shun Lee West. They had just been to see an evening performance of *The Nutcracker* at the City Ballet. The performance was dedicated to Jennifer Rose.

"I don't know. What do you want?" Frankie smiled at him.

"I want pig's feet, Francesca." He took her hand. "But only if they're raw. How 'bout you?"

She laughed. "Raw feet is good. But I like them a little salty."

Charlie squeezed her fingers. He enjoyed his evenings with Frankie. There was something about her earnestness that was very grounding for him. Nothing crazy would happen with Frankie.

"I'm going to force you to choose something. Anything."

"Egg drop soup," she answered.

"The answer is no," he replied without a moment's hesitation. "The next thing I know you'll want chow mein."

Charlie took some pride in knowing his way around sophisticated menus. He wasn't a "foodie" but he certainly was conversant with the right do's and don'ts in food and wine. Sure, he would have a grilled cheese at two in the morning and watch a rerun of a hockey game. But when he was at a good New York restaurant Charlie knew exactly what to order.

"Okay. I'll have the dumplings and the ribs to start," Frankie said emphatically.

"If you're insisting on Cantonese, get the shrimp balls. Trust me."

"You're right. Let's get the shrimp balls."

Since Charlie and Samantha had separated he had been fixed up by friends with what seemed like an unending stream of you've-got-to-meet and you're-gonna-love women. They ranged from thirty-year-old high-powered Wall Street lawyers, to twenty-something models, to well-to-do forty-something Park Avenue divorcées. He would see them for dinner once or twice. Within two weeks there were inevitable little chats about future dinner parties, trips to Barbados, and his feelings about commitment. Charlie thought all these women were much more interested in fulfilling their own expectations than actually getting to know him. At least he felt that he and Frankie had a real bond. They were old friends and he felt that he had very carefully made certain there were no other agendas.

"We'll have the shrimp balls, the thousand-year-old egg, the black cod that's not on the menu—tell the chef to do it with ginger and bok choy—the ants climbing a tree, and steam for us some light crunchy green vegetables, no MSG," Charlie rattled off to the waiter.

"Yes sir." The waiter walked off.

"Ants climbing on trees?" Frankie asked.

"Uh-huh. Fried ants on slices of birch." Charlie took a sip of his martini. "Then they cook it all in Mr. Clean."

Frankie smiled. "Sounds refreshing."

Charlie thought Frankie had sad eyes. He didn't know if it was because, for all her accomplishments and even humor, she lacked access to her own sensuality. He enjoyed sleeping with her because it was comforting but never exciting. He looked forward to the cuddling afterward more than the penetration. As Charlie looked at her tonight he decided the sadness came from her own sense of duty. It wasn't that Frankie couldn't be entertaining, but she could never allow herself the ease or narcissism of Samantha's fizz.

"I was glad they dedicated the performance tonight to Jennifer Rose," Frankie said, breaking the silence. "Her mother's devastated. I can't imagine anything worse."

"Jil. That's worse," he said.

"Too much loss, Charlie. Too much loss." Frankie felt a lump in her throat. "I hate the times we're living in."

"Honey, there's always too much loss. You and I are in the too-much-loss business." He looked up at the waiter hoping the appetizers were on their way. He had no intention of having the evening take a turn for the maudlin. "Did I tell you there's going to be an Alvar Aalto exhibit at Cooper-Hewitt? And they've asked for a number of my pieces."

"Really." Frankie admired Charlie's ability to move a conversation along from loss to an upcoming exhibit.

"Absolutely. I was at the forefront of the Aalto renaissance. Jil would have been very proud of me." Charlie lifted his hand. He was becoming unusually anxious about his appetizers. Before the Starbucks incident, before his marriage broke up, he could go to any black-tie dinner party in New York, sit next to anybody, and start jabbering about the ballet or Alvar Aalto. But tonight, sitting with Francesca Weissman under a Chinese paper dragon, he was aware that his conversation was deliberately empty.

"The shrimp balls, the thousand-year-old egg, spareribs, and the chef sent over the crispy wontons. Should I split it?" the waiter asked.

"Yes, we're sharing. We're good children," Charlie answered.

The waiter divided the portions in half while Charlie pointed to various small pots with sauces. "Francesca, this is for the shrimp balls, this is for the spareribs, this is for the ancient egg. If you mix them up you get sent to the basement to peel snow peas. Am I right?" He smiled at the waiter.

"Yes sir." The waiter laughed.

"And I'd like another martini. And my friend would like another glass of wine."

"I'm okay." Frankie put her hand over the glass.

"She'd like another." Charlie knew Frankie didn't really like to have more than one drink, but he also knew she would ultimately always match him. In the past few weeks Charlie needed more than two martinis every night.

Frankie didn't know if Charlie's increased drinking was the aftermath of the Starbucks incident or because of the gossip that Samantha and Barry Santorini were in Aspen together. Pippa Rose had shown her an item about them and said, "Isn't it reassuring that even at the most hideous times life goes on?"

Recently, after two martinis, Charlie would talk to Frankie about taking a trip to hike across Bhutan and how it would be good to start a reading group about New York architecture with Jil's ex-lover. He'd prattle on about moving to one of Richard Meier's new buildings on the West Side Highway or his thoughts on the Gehry drawings for the Guggenheim downtown. But tonight he was uncharacteristically quiet.

"I've been reading Jil's copy of *The Elements of Style,*" she commented, breaking the unaccustomed silence again.

"I remember that as a perfect book. No more, no less." Charlie started looking around the rooms. "Just perfect."

"It's funny," she continued. "One of the rules is omit any unnecessary words. I was thinking Jil took that too much to heart. He omitted mostly everything."

Charlie continued to watch the waiter bringing drinks to other tables.

"Charlie, are you okay?" she asked, and leaned toward him.

"I'm fine. Tell me, how was your day?" he asked distractedly.

"My day? I advised Mrs. Martinez not to have heart surgery on her four-pound baby."

"Were you right?"

"Yes. The radiologists misread the X-ray."

"Brava, Francesca."

The waiter arrived with the drinks. Charlie took a sip. "I'm sorry I'm such bad company. I've been tired all day."

"You're not bad company."

"You mean, I'm no different than any other night."

"I mean, I dragged you to that ballet." Frankie tried to be reassuring.

"To tell you the truth, dear, I never liked *The Nutcracker*. Samantha used to harangue me into going, too. The only good part is that Christmas tree on steroids."

Frankie remembered that Charlie wasn't with Samantha when she re-met her at the *Nutcracker* family benefit. She also remembered she met her at Clarice Santorini's table.

Charlie took a large gulp of his fresh martini. "Francesca Weissman, I hope you know that you've saved my life these past few weeks. In fact you've saved my life all year." He lifted his glass. "Here's to you."

Charlie clinked her glass and that's when his phone rang.

"Excuse me for a second. It's probably my insane service. They're the only one with this number." He had another sip. "Hello, Dr. Acton here."

Charlie suddenly moved. "Oh. Hi."

Frankie knew immediately it was Samantha.

"So come home." Charlie turned his head for privacy. "Come home immediately." He paused, his face turning grave. "Did anyone see you?" He paused again. "That's good. Yes. I'll be there. Don't mention it." He put the phone back in his pocket and looked up at Frankie. "It's Samantha. She's out of town and not feeling well, so I told her to come home tonight."

Frankie usually had a don't-ask, don't-tell policy about Samantha. But now she was palpably at their table.

"Do you want her back, Charlie?" Frankie asked him.

Charlie didn't see the question as a recrimination or even as self-protective.

"Other than you, she's the one person who I feel genuinely connected to."

"I see." Frankie nodded.

"You must know I think you're a fabulous woman and a great doctor." Charlie kissed her hand.

"I don't know about that. But thank you." She felt her voice catching and decided to stop the conversation.

"You have to understand that Samantha doesn't have what you do. You've made this entire life for yourself. Samantha just has a very good eye." He laughed slightly. "Not for men exactly. Just for things."

Charlie had no doubt that Frankie knew him well enough to see that Samantha defined him. He assumed Frankie knew he cared for her deeply. They had become, in fact, very close. But he was ultimately drawn to Samantha because she was so self-centered. And only that impeccable self-centeredness could absorb his weakness.

"I want to help her," Charlie explained. "You of all people should understand that."

The waiter brought over an array of plates. "Black cod, ants climbing on tree, crispy vegetables. Shall I split?"

"It looks fantastic and we're famished," Charlie said with renewed excitement. "It's true what they say about Chinese food. One minute you're full and then you're hungry as a bear. Please just split it in half for me and my gal, here."

Frankie looked at the ants climbing on tree. They were cellophane noodles with tiny specks of beef over broccoli. It looked like a science experiment she had done in fifth grade before she knew anything about men who effortlessly ordered exotic main courses or got cell phone calls from their ex-wives in Aspen during dinner with their lover. It was from before the city she grew up in seemed as vulnerable as she was and even the most privileged were scurrying to ensure their survival like ants climbing a tree.

"There's nothing like sitting down to a good meal with a person you really adore." Charlie took a sip of his martini and finished his drink. His words were beginning to slur. "I'll always treasure our friendship, Francesca Weissman. I hope you know that."

"Excuse me." Frankie got up from the table.

"Are you okay?" he asked with polite concern.

"An ant went down the wrong tree."

Charlie laughed. "We can get chow mein if you prefer."

Frankie headed to the ladies' room and never came back.

Charlie called Frankie twice that night and left a note with her doorman. He had no regrets about Frankie Weissman. He had never misled her. If Charlie had accomplished anything since the day he was rejected from the Ivy, it was that he had become a gentleman.

CHAPTER THIRTY-SEVEN

Samantha

Samantha asked Charlie if she could meet him under the canopy at the Carlyle. She couldn't bear to walk past her old doorman or be inside their old apartment. Standing in the cold, Samantha felt the heat from the hotel canopy's electric red grille on her hair and the brisk cold on her face. It was the same sensation she had thirty years ago when she would wait with Grey Navez, who lived at the hotel, for her father's chauffeur to give them a ride up to a school dance.

"Samantha! Samantha!" she heard a voice call from behind her. She hadn't seen Charlie for over a year but she was certain she would recognize his voice. When she called him she'd had half a moment's hesitation. She knew it was possible that Charlie would be solicitous but have already moved on.

"Samantha, it's me, Pearson." She turned around and saw her first husband, still with his Exeter roommate.

"Oh my God! Pearson, what are you doing here?" She kissed him.

"Our daughter wanted to come in to see *The Nutcracker* and Radio City." He smiled. He was still boyishly handsome with a water polo medalist physique.

"Your daughter?" she asked.

"Yes. Rick and I adopted Cecilia eight years ago. She goes to the

Windsor School in Boston where we live. Honey, you remember Samantha?" He put his arm around his partner, who was at least five inches shorter.

Rick shook her hand. "Of course. You look wonderful."

"Well, so do both of you," she answered, thinking Pearson looked unbelievably well and Rick had succumbed to middle age.

"Crazy time to take a vacation in New York, huh?" Pearson flashed a huge grin.

"Yes." She had just gotten off the plane two hours before.

"But we love it. What do you say, Rick. There's nothing like it."

"Nothing like it." Rick kept his arm around him in that possessive way partners do when they run into their spouse's exes.

"We're staying right here if you want to call us. We'd love you to meet Cecilia."

"Oh yes! That would be great!" Samantha was now wanting to wrap it up.

"It's great to see you, honey." Pearson kissed her. He had never called her honey during their marriage. She thought Cecilia must have made him warmer, more accessible.

"Great to see you." She embraced Rick. "Good to see you, Rick. Congratulations on everything."

As she watched them walk into the hotel, Samantha took out a pack of Marlboros that she'd bought at the Denver airport. When Pearson first told her he was gay she thought it was because he knew she wanted a child as part of their marriage and he clearly didn't. Samantha watched in a haze as the nighttime traffic on Madison Avenue trickled by. Nothing ended the way she would have called it. She would never have predicted Pearson being the one with a child, or her being anxious as to whether Charlie would actually show up. And she would never ever have dreamed that Judy Tremont wouldn't be chattering away somewhere tonight planning her New Year's Eve dinner party.

The cigarette smoke and the fact that Samantha hadn't eaten since she left the Little Nell made her almost speedy. She wanted to think logically and all she could come up with was that she deserved someone to make everything all right. And if she deserved it simply because she had always had it, then that was all right, too.

Samantha began to feel the sidewalk swaying from side to side when she felt an arm around her.

"Miss, do you have another cigarette?" the voice asked her.

"Charlie!" She threw her arms around his. "Charlie, I'm so scared!"

"Shhhh, honey, shhhh."

"Charlie." She wouldn't let go of him.

"It's all right. I promise." For the first time since she left he felt like himself again.

"Do you really want one of these?" She offered him a cigarette.

"If it'll make you feel better, I do." He smiled at her.

Samantha was relieved that any doubts about his coming back were unfounded.

"I'm so hungry, Charlie, I haven't eaten all day." She took his hand.

"Do you want to go in here?" He pointed toward the hotel.

"It's too complicated. Let's go to Swifty's and get chicken pot pie with creamed spinach and peas."

"Yes. Comfort food." Charlie nodded. "Nothing better."

"Our comfort food," Samantha whispered.

Charlie and Samantha walked down Park Avenue to East Seventy-third Street. The Christmas trees on Park Avenue were twinkling and the sky was clear with a perfect crescent moon. As they waited for the light on Park Avenue to change, Charlie looked at Samantha.

"I look awful. I'm so sorry." She put her hand over her face.

He pulled her hand away. "I was just thinking how ironic it is that this is a perfect New York night, and you've never looked more beautiful."

"Charlie, I'm a spoiled, selfish coward."

"Darling. We're all spoiled, selfish cowards." He kissed her again. "The more the merrier."

"Charlie Acton, you used to be so sweet. You've become a cynic."

"I'm an intelligent man, darling."

"I'm cold." She pushed her body toward him.

"Put your hand in my glove and let's go."

Samantha slipped her hand inside his glove and felt his warm fingers wrap around hers. The realization that she had created Charlie and therefore possessed him made her feel suddenly powerful.

When Samantha and Charlie walked into Swifty's the headwaiter rushed over to see them as if one of the Romanovs had just returned from exile.

"It's so nice to see you two here together again." The headwaiter kissed Samantha and hugged Charlie. "At least there's some real style left in New York."

"We're glad to be here." Charlie beamed.

"Let me take you to a nice table in the back. Follow me."

They followed him through a half-empty restaurant.

"Most of our regulars are away during the holidays. But your friend Mrs. Strong-Rodman is coming in tonight. Is the corner table all right?"

"Perfect." Charlie smiled.

Charlie and Samantha sat down. She put her hand across the table and Charlie immediately took it.

"Thank you, Charlie." She smiled at him.

"For what?" he asked.

"For making it all so easy."

"Let's talk about something else." He was delighted to be back at their favorite table. "Would you like a drink?"

"Yes. Yes."

"Waiter!" Charlie raised his hand. "We'd like two martinis up."

Just as Samantha was easing into her chair she saw Adrienne

Strong-Rodman looking tighter and even thinner coming toward their table.

"I wish I had known you guys were in town. Thanks for calling me." She kissed Samantha.

Samantha didn't dare ask where Paul was. She had read that it was inevitable now that he would be going to jail.

"Did you hear about Judy Tremont in Aspen?" Adrienne leaned over their table. "Poor Albert. And those kids. I heard she died on the ski slopes. Ran into a tree or something."

"It's an awful story," Samantha replied.

"It's been so tense here. It's hard to remember about human accidents," Charlie replied, and put his hand on Samantha's knee. "I asked Samantha to come home yesterday because I've been so anxious here alone."

"That's right. I heard you were out there," Adrienne said.

Samantha knew Adrienne was well aware that she was in Aspen with Barry. She had impulsively canceled her show to go there with him. And she also knew Adrienne was enough of a real friend not to ask any more questions. Just like Samantha wasn't asking anything more about Paul. Women like Adrienne didn't dwell on the facts of other people's mistakes. They were on to the next.

"I think we all have had enough of Samantha being away." Charlie managed to smile with the heart of Omaha on his sleeve. "We need her right here. Isn't that true, Adrienne?"

"Absolutely. Well, great seeing you both." Adrienne touched both their shoulders.

"Give our love to Paul," Charlie added.

"I'll tell him. He'll be so happy to hear you were here together." Adrienne walked back to her table.

Samantha tried to see who Adrienne was with but didn't recognize them.

"I don't think we know who she's with." Charlie read her mind and had comfortably reverted to using the mutual "we." "All the regulars really are out of town. Even my business is slow. Adrienne must be with her B-team. I've never seen them before."

The waiter arrived with their martinis.

"Shall we have a toast?"

"There isn't very much to toast to."

"To us. Long may we wave." He lifted his glass.

"Yes, to us." She clinked his glass and they took a sip.

"Do you remember that crazy Old Norse toast Albert Tremont gave? I'll never forget that." Charlie leaned back. "I'll bet it was the first and last time that Old Norse was spoken in the Breakers lobby."

"Poor Albert." Samantha took another sip.

"Darling, I promise you Albert will get snatched up in a week. And maybe even by someone who doesn't chatter quite as much as Judy."

"Charlie, you really have become hard." Samantha was surprised by the cold glibness of his remark. It was a social-gossip style she didn't admire. "I hope I didn't do that to you."

Charlie took another sip. "Please give me a little credit here. I may be shallow, but I happen to know my clientele. Trust me, Albert will not be lacking for company. If Paul Rodman goes to jail, maybe even Adrienne will bag him."

Charlie finished his drink and lifted his hand for another round. Samantha began to feel the alcohol easing her anxiety. Sitting here next to Charlie at Swifty's, she believed she should never have moved outside her own circle. But then maybe that's what brings people back together. After all, when she went off with Barry, Charlie was seeing Frankie Weissman. Both were sort of taking a junior year abroad. Her mother had once told her, "Travel and experience. That's how the upper classes refresh their order."

"I never liked Paul Rodman." Charlie was halfway through his second martini. "Much too voracious. He's like that predator bird that lives on his building. He should go to jail."

"And me?" she asked him quietly.

Charlie put down his drink and looked at her.

"You? I love you," he said.

"But . . ." she barely spoke, "Charlie, I pushed her."

"No you didn't." Charlie held her hand. "You never saw her that day."

"Charlie, she was a friend of mine."

"Did you see her hit that tree?"

"No." Her voice began to crack.

"Samantha, it was an accident."

"She could have knocked me over." She began to cry.

"Samantha, shhhh. Enough. You never saw her that day."

"I'll write Albert a note." She nodded her head, gathering herself together.

"Definitely write Albert a note. And we should go see Albert. I thoroughly enjoy his company."

Charlie understood now he would never lose her again. If he wanted to say Paul Rodman was voracious, it was fine. If he wanted to smoke cigars at the end of dinner to prove what a close personal friend he was of the maître d', it was fine. If he wanted to cast aspersions on all of his patients who would chase Albert Tremont, that was fine, too.

Samantha and he were bonded together now. They could reinvent their lives. Make plans to move to the Richard Meier building downtown, or a loft in the Flatiron District. They could change their circle of friends. Charlie preferred magazine editors, successful actors, and hip young entrepreneurs to aging socialites and bankers. He could even start collecting again. The art would be healing.

"We're together. That's all that matters." He pulled his chair toward her when he saw more tears in her eyes.

"Thank you, Charlie." She kissed him hard on the lips. "Thank you." She knew she had no choice but to be grateful to him.

CHAPTER THIRTY-EIGHT

Frankie

After Frankie left Charlie at Shun Lee West she walked home up Broadway and drifted into the Lincoln Square Barnes & Noble, Tower Records, and Fairway market, and finally landed in Zabar's housewares department. Wandering absentmindedly through rows of German coffee bean grinders, Italian espresso makers, French food processors, and retro American toasters, Frankie's mind kept reverting to Charlie asking Samantha, "Did anyone see you?" She couldn't stop herself from enumerating the possible meanings.

Did anyone see Samantha wearing last year's ski parka? Did anyone see her calling Charlie while he was toasting a sedentary pediatrician? Did anyone see that Charlie and she were embedded in their own Grand Canyon of Need?

Frankie managed to stay in the store until it closed. Avoiding going home, she moved on from appliances to olives and smoked fish, then circled a special on Spanish Gorgonzola. Finally, she bought a tin of caviar for New Year's Eve. Charlie had suggested that he come to her apartment and make dinner that night.

"Let's do something low-key," he had said. "Drink too much red wine, rent *North by Northwest* or some other great old flick, and if we're really lucky we can be happily curled up together and asleep by ten o'clock."

When Frankie finally got home her doorman nodded his head. "Dr. Weissman, you're out late tonight."

"How are you?" Frankie wasn't in the mood for a chat.

"Where's Dr. Charlie?" he asked. "He's such a nice guy, Dr. Weissman, and my girlfriend says he's famous, too."

"Your girlfriend knows Dr. Acton?" she asked, drawn in despite herself.

"Oh, she loves those ugly-duckling-into-beautiful-swan reality makeover stories. Anyway, I was at her house, and I see Dr. Charlie on one of her TV shows, and I says I know him! He's Dr. Weissman's friend." The doorman was now beaming. "And I gotta tell you, I got points with my girlfriend. Dr. Weissman, you deserve the best."

"Thank you. Good night, George." She began to walk toward the elevator.

"Happy New Year, Dr. Weissman." He followed her.

"Happy New Year." She walked into the elevator.

Frankie brought her Zabar's bag into the kitchen, opened the tin of caviar, and put it in the cat bowl.

"I'm sorry, kiddo. It's just Osetra. Not Beluga. But you'll just have to deal."

She watched as the cat leapt at the tin. If New Year's Eve dinner was not going to be deliberately low-key tomorrow, then Gilda might as well celebrate tonight with a bang. "Don't gulp it down in one lick, kiddo." Frankie patted the cat on her head and went into her bedroom.

She turned off the lights and was prepared to cry for her foolishness and disappointment. But instead she quietly watched the reflection of car lights on her ceiling until 4 a.m. when she inadvertently fell asleep.

Frankie had arranged to take the morning off for a New Year's visit with Abraham. She got up at eight and clicked on the television. A reporter was standing in a red coat underneath the Christmas tree in Rockefeller Center.

"Paula," the reporter said as the wind swept through her hair, "this is usually the scene of holiday crowds, but because the terror alert was once again raised to orange this morning, the skating rink at Rockefeller Center is virtually empty."

Frankie turned off the television and dressed hurriedly. If every Starbucks in New York was about to blow up or someone wanted to convince her that they were about to blow up, she wanted to be out walking in the city. Only walking the city streets made her feel that nothing had changed.

On her way up to her father's apartment, Frankie bought Abraham all the morning newspapers. She knew there was no possibility of his actually reading them, but sometimes he still liked to hold the paper as if it was a distant memory, like playing with blocks. In the past month, Abraham's disease had rapidly accelerated. Not only had he forgotten how to speak or when to pee, he had also forgotten how to eat. Now he stared at food as if he didn't know if it was a yo-yo or a turtle.

As recently as October, Abraham took all the pictures from Helen's wall and smashed them on the living room floor. Later that month he tried to eat the plants in the apartment lobby. Exasperated, Helen took Abraham for an interview at the Carnegie Hill Home for the Aged. But they rejected him.

"I've heard of people being rejected from Harvard or a Park Avenue co-op," she commented to Frankie, "but who the hell gets rejected from an old-age home!"

Recently Abraham had become eerily easy to manage. When he

stopped eating, he also stopped breaking plates and standing naked on his porch. He spent his days sitting in his room, unless the nurse Helen recently hired took him in a wheelchair to Central Park. On the morning of New Year's Eve, Frankie found him silently staring at a dark television.

"Mr. Abraham. Mr. Abraham, look who's here, darling." The Filipino nurse touched his cheek.

"He's very thin." Frankie examined his emaciated arms and legs. He seemed to have lost at least ten pounds since she had seen him last week.

"He don't eat. I try to feed him but he don't." The nurse attempted to turn his head. "Abraham, look, it's your daughter!"

"That's all right. I'll just sit with him." Frankie thanked her.

"We got the Marilyn Monroe movie. He likes that one. Should I put it on?" the nurse asked.

"Sure. That would be great," Frankie answered her.

The nurse put on *Gentlemen Prefer Blondes* and began to leave the room. "Mrs. Helen is at Bloomingdale's and I'll be right next door."

"Dad, I brought you the papers." Frankie began to give him the morning papers while Marilyn Monroe and Jane Russell were singing "Two Little Girls from Little Rock." Abraham didn't move. He just stared straight ahead.

"Can I sit next to you, Dad, and read?" Frankie asked him.

While Marilyn and Jane continued to sing in their suits and hats, Frankie opened the *Times*. She flipped past an ad for a Chanel fur-trimmed quilted purse and an announcement for the January Burberry sale, and finished the front-page piece on the recent intelligence from a prisoner in Guantánamo Bay that led to the change in the terror alert color code.

Abraham began to nod his head. "Dad, can I get you anything?" Frankie asked him. "How 'bout some water?" She picked up a glass and brought it to his lips. She tried to open his mouth, but he had forgotten how to sip. He lifted his finger slightly for her to stop, and Frankie sat down.

She distractedly picked up the *Post*. Half watching her father, half listening to Marilyn and Jane, Frankie turned the pages until she came across a photo of Judy Tremont in her museum gala couture under a headline reading "Socialite Dead at 43." Frankie lifted the paper as if she could say to Abraham, "Look, Dad. I know this woman. Her daughters were my patients."

Marilyn and Jane were now dancing in red satin evening gowns. Frankie continued to read. "Judy Tremont, a prominent socialite who cochaired the Museum of Modern Art gala this spring, died in a skiing accident in Aspen, Colorado, on Tuesday. The cause, according to her husband, Albert, was complications after she skied into a tree."

Frankie looked again at Judy's face. There was something so willing about it. She was desperate to do everything right. Not morally or ethically right. But the perfect Turkusion dinner party with the perfect seating chart. She would not have liked being relegated to the bottom corner of a paper devoted mostly to terrorist rumors. And she would definitely not have appreciated the references to Modesto and Fresno City College. On the other hand, she would have been delighted with the final sentence calling her "a leading member of the new breed of socialites."

It seemed odd to Frankie that Judy's very codified sense of social order couldn't have protected her from a random accident. Judy's world had far more rigid rules than even Jil's old grammar manual. But ironically, the random accident that took Judy's life may have somehow been caused by a scion of the social order Judy so admired. Frankie had no way of methodically proving her theory. She just based it on what she overheard sitting under a paper dragon in a Chinese restaurant.

Marilyn was now singing "Diamonds Are a Girl's Best Friend."

Frankie put down the paper and stood beside her father. Marilyn was sliding diamond bracelets up and down her wrist and imploring, "Speak to me, Harry Winston, speak to me."

"Me, too," Abraham suddenly answered.

"Dad, can I get something for you?"

Abraham turned his head toward his daughter and smiled broadly with pride as if she had just walked for the first time or told him she got into Harvard Medical School. He squeezed her hand, but his fingers were so thin and his hands so weak it felt as if he had only brushed it.

"I love you, Dad." She kissed him on the forehead.

But the smile was gone. Abraham put his head back. He was immediately asleep.

Frankie knew that this would be the last time she'd see him smile or even respond. In a short time, he would forget how to touch, how to swallow, and how to breathe.

When Frankie left Abraham's apartment she walked down Madison Avenue, passed the empty Whitney Museum, Carolina Herrera, Givenchy, and the Ralph Lauren shop in the former Rhinelander Mansion. She passed Judy's street and thought of stopping in to see Albert but kept walking. She was no longer part of that world. She no longer had a lingering belief, like Jil, that they knew how to live better than anyone else. Or that by being in their light she'd become imbued with their glow.

She strode past the sleek and strangely quiet Armani, Valentino, and Krizia flagships. In some ways Frankie was now grateful for Samantha's call at that Chinese restaurant. It made it clear to her that Charlie, like Samantha, was infatuated with his own self-image. She had been infatuated with it, too, but she hadn't understood that the image was all that was left.

Samantha and Charlie were not unintelligent. They weren't even aspirational like Judy or obfuscating like Jil. Looking at the window displays, Frankie realized that they were polished people, and ultimately destructive because they would maintain the entrenched ease of their lives at any cost. Ironically, unlike Judy or Jil, Samantha and Charlie had very small imaginations.

Frankie looked at the Tiffany clock on Fifty-seventh Street. For no reason, she had wandered at least forty blocks. Every day now she walked more and more as if to hold on to her father and her city before everything changed.

She found a gypsy cab to take her back to Mount Sinai.

"They say the terror alert was a joke," the driver said to her. "April Fools' on New Year's Eve."

"That's good," Frankie said.

"They thought they found something in the food supply at Citarella, but they got it wrong. You going to the hospital?" he asked.

"Yes. I'm a doctor," she answered.

"You look young to be a doctor." He laughed.

Frankie took the elevator up to the fourth floor in the children's pavilion at Mount Sinai and walked into the NICU. She would check on her patient, Emanuel Martinez. The little boy, who was now four pounds two ounces, was scheduled to go home today.

Frankie opened the isolette and held the child in her arms. She carefully adjusted the wires connected to the heart and lung monitors. She looked at his face, no bigger than an apple. He had struggled to survive and passed the turning point. She stroked his finger, the size of a thimble.

"Can he still go home today?" The child's mother approached her.

"That's the plan. He's ready to roll. His heartbeat is steady and his breathing is normal." Frankie smiled.

"Did you bring a car seat and a snowsuit?" the nurse asked.

"Yes." The mother started to cry. "I'm sorry. I just can't believe he's coming home. He's been here for two months. Will he be all right?"

"He's doing remarkably well so far," Frankie answered. "Get him dressed and I'll walk you downstairs with his nurse."

Frankie went over to the reception desk to get the child's release form.

"Dr. Weissman." Juan, the nurse, was on call. "Will I see you dancing at Avalon later?"

"Honey, I can't." Frankie smiled at him. "I'm going on tonight as Lorelei Lee."

"Really?" He laughed. "Where?"

"Four a.m. The Burger King at Sixth Avenue and Eighth Street."

Juan kissed her. "Happy New Year, Dr. W. It's great news about the Martinez baby going home."

Frankie smiled at him. "Sometimes you just get it right."

Frankie escorted the child with his parents and the NICU nurse to the hospital door. It had begun to snow outside and Frankie pulled up the baby's hood.

"Here, let me sign you out." She signed the baby's outpatient papers and handed a copy to his mother. "Hold on to this."

The father extended his hand. "Thank you, Dr. Weissman. Happy New Year."

"Just a minute, I forgot something. He still has our jewelry on." Frankie turned to the hospital guard. "Can I borrow a scissor?"

Frankie cut the regulation identification bracelet the child had worn since birth. "Now he's officially free."

Frankie watched as the couple brought the child to a waiting car. She couldn't help but see hope in a life beginning. Frankie pushed open the hospital door and walked out to the snowy street.

Permissions Acknowledgments